Consumption has ravaged Louise Pinecroft's family,
leaving her and her father alone and heartbroken.
But Dr Pinecroft has plans for a revolutionary experiment:
convinced that sea air will prove to be the cure his wife
and children needed, he arranges to house a group of
prisoners suffering from the disease in the cliffs beneath
his new Cornish home. While he devotes himself to
his controversial medical trials, Louise finds herself
increasingly discomfited by the strange tales her new
maid tells of the fairies that hunt the land, searching
for those they can steal away to their realm.

Forty years later, Hester Why arrives at Morvoren
House to take up a position as nurse to the now partially
paralysed and almost entirely mute Miss Pinecroft.
Hester has fled to Cornwall to try and escape her past,
but surrounded by superstitious staff enacting bizarre
rituals, she soon discovers that her new home may be
just as dangerous as her last...

BONE CHINA

ALSO BY LAURA PURCELL

The Silent Companions
The Corset

BONE CHINA

Laura Purcell

R A V E N 🐦 B O O K S

LONDON · OXFORD · NEW YORK · NEW DELHI · SYDNEY

RAVEN BOOKS
Bloomsbury Publishing Plc
50 Bedford Square, London, WC1B 3DP, UK

BLOOMSBURY, RAVEN BOOKS and the Raven Books logo are trademarks of
Bloomsbury Publishing Plc

First published in Great Britain 2019

Copyright © Laura Purcell, 2019

A catalogue record for this book is available from the British Library

ISBN: HB: 978-1-5266-0253-4; TPB: 978-1-5266-0252-7; EBOOK: 978-1-5266-0251-0

2 4 6 8 10 9 7 5 3 1

Typeset by Integra Software Services Pvt. Ltd.
Printed and bound in Great Britain by CPI Group (UK) Ltd, Croydon CR0 4YY

MIX
Paper from
responsible sources
FSC® C020471

To find out more about our authors and books visit www.bloomsbury.com
and sign up for our newsletters

No voice divine the storm allay'd,
　　No light propitious shone;
When, snatch'd from all effectual aid,
　　We perish'd, each alone:
But I beneath a rougher sea,
And whelm'd in deeper gulfs than he.

From 'The Castaway'
by William Cowper, 1799

Cast of Characters

MORVOREN HOUSE

Esther Stevens/Hester Why – A lady's maid working
  under an assumed name
Mrs Quinn – Housekeeper
Merryn – Scullery maid
Lowena – Housemaid
Mrs Bawden – Cook
Gerren Tyack – Coachman and groom
Creeda Tyack – Longest serving member of staff

Miss Louise Pinecroft – Mistress of the house
Miss Rosewyn Pinecroft – Her ward

Mr Trengrouse – Curate of the parish church
Dr Bligh – Vicar of the same

MORVOREN HOUSE – FORTY YEARS AGO

Dr Ernest Pinecroft – Physician
Miss Louise Pinecroft – His eldest daughter
Mrs Louisa 'Mopsy' Pinecroft – His deceased wife
Miss Kitty Pinecroft – His deceased daughter

Master Francis Pinecroft – His deceased son
Pompey – The family dog

Creeda Nancarrow – Maid and former porcelain worker
Gerren Tyack – Stable boy

Seth
Michael
Harry
Tim
Chao

} Consumptives from Bodmin gaol

HANOVER SQUARE

Sir Arthur Windrop – Master of the house
Lady Rose Windrop – His wife
Mrs Windrop – His widowed mother

Esther Stevens – Maid to Lady Rose
Mrs Glover – Housekeeper
Burns – Maid to Mrs Windrop
Mrs Friar – Nurse and *accouchuer*'s assistant

PART ONE

Hester Why

Chapter 1

Love is fragile, my mother once said. It can break.

Maybe that is true, for some people. Not for me. My love is a grasping thing. A vine I cannot extricate myself from, pulling me down, down.

It is dragging me all the way to Cornwall, a county I have never set foot in before. Had I felt this chilling mist, perhaps I would have thought twice about answering the advertisement for a nurse and personal maid. But what choice do I truly have? I can never return to London. I must take the Mail coach somewhere, and it seems appropriate to flee to the end of the country, a place teetering on the edge of the map.

This is the bitterest winter I can recall. Too cold, even for snow. A world washed innocent and white might bring me some comfort, but no – this is the season of sleet and gunmetal skies. Everything is grey and cold. It is like purgatory, like my heart.

Frosted branches scrape their fingers across the roof as we dash along, our wheels skating on the road. Not even the sour breath and body odour of my fellow passengers serve to warm the air inside the coach. An elderly woman who smells of chamber pots squashes in close to me; on the other side, a brute beast of a man is spreading his legs. Officially, the Mail coach boasts room for but four interior passengers; however, this driver has squeezed in six of us. My arms are pinioned to my sides, numb. And we are the fortunate ones, riding inside instead of on the roof.

The windows rattle in their frames without intermission; the sleet persists in its sullen patter. Shadows creep over the faces of the passengers opposite me, spreading like a stain. Only their eyes remain bright, gleaming now and then with a rodent cunning.

It seems an age since we last baited the poor horses. My dry lips begin to twitch. All day I have been travelling with scarcely any relief.

Dressed as I am in her discarded clothes, my appearance is one of respectability. It would not do to produce my hip flask now and draw attention to myself. It would be indecorous. Reckless. And yet ...

My lips are very dry.

I might risk it.

I *must* risk it.

Struggling against my companions, I manoeuvre my reticule from where it hangs on my wrist to the lap of my gown. The pewter flask inside bangs against my thigh. With practised hands I line the neck up with the drawstring opening of my reticule and pull the stopper. The other passengers will see me raise the bag to my mouth, but not what it contains.

Only a sip – swift and fleeting as the touch of a lover's lips. It is sufficient. Medicinal.

I lower the reticule, refasten the stopper. Not one person marks it.

Even without their scrutiny, I experience a flush of shame. Some inner consciousness that I have come to rely rather too heavily upon spirits of late. But alcohol cleanses a wound, does it not?

Water races across the windows. Drear mist creeps through the cracks in the doors, an uninvited guest. Just now it seems to me that this must be hell: not a fiery pit after all but leaching cold, and a yearning for rest never to be granted. Dead flesh, the marble statues overlooking graves: both of these are cold.

Finally, there is a shout from the roof. 'New London Inn, Exeter!'

Our destination, yet there is no check to our wild pace. Instead, there is an awful high-pitched shriek.

All at once, the carriage spins. We are hurled against one another. The old woman beside me screams. For the first time, I am glad to be wedged between her and the large man. Their mass holds me in my seat.

Others are not so fortunate.

As we jerk to a halt, I hear a crack, feel it tingle in my back teeth. The silence that follows is deafening.

The man next to me clears his throat. 'Most likely a sack of mail,' he says unconvincingly.

I know it is not that.

Shouts outside. The other five passengers stare at one another. I alone lean forward and listen to the guard cursing up on the box.

His words ring like a summons, stirring something I presumed long dead.

The old feeling of purpose.

'Let me out,' I cry. 'Move. For heaven's sake, move!'

The hulking man barely shifts; I am obliged to climb over his legs and tug the door open. Cold air rushes in, burning my cheeks with its touch. I leap from the coach.

I land heavily on my knees, grazing them, narrowly avoiding a pile of dung. The tight knot of my reticule rubs against my wrist. Although it is only late afternoon, the yard is fearfully dark. Everything is flavoured with smoke and straw.

Our carriage is turned almost completely the wrong way, facing back towards the entrance of the yard. Thick black lines on the frosted cobbles show the pattern the wheels took as they hit the ice too fast. It is the guard's fault – he did not apply the chains in time. The carriage lamps illuminate wisps of steam rising from the horses and beyond, inky spots of blood on the cobbles.

'A surgeon!' someone calls.

As I suspected, a passenger has toppled from the roof.

He retains consciousness; his eyelids flick and his lips splutter their pain. Yet no one approaches. A few ostlers stand in a semicircle, regarding him as if he is contagious.

I should mimic them. Leave it be until a surgeon arrives to assist the injured man. But I have already broken my resolution to stay inconspicuous by jumping out of the coach.

He releases a heartbreaking moan, and I know I cannot delay any longer.

Pushing past the ostlers, I drop to my knees beside the patient. The aspect is not a pretty one. His head is cracked at the hairline and hints of a meaty coral-coloured substance frill the wound. If I do not intervene, he will die for certain. Clamping a gloved hand either side of the break, I push it shut, speaking the words of comfort I have learnt by rote. Coppery blood hums beneath the stench of horses and woodsmoke.

'Hush, now. I will help you.'

He groans.

Nothing but a break can explain the angle of his right leg. I pray it is not an open one, for then he will lose the limb altogether. If, indeed, he survives the amputation.

Glancing up, I see that the guard and the coachman have dismounted. Three of the interior passengers have also ventured out to gape, but those travelling on the roof sit petrified. I cannot blame them. If I had seen this man tumble, I should be terrified of falling myself and sharing his fate.

I recognise the portly man who took up so much space next to me in the coach.

'You there!' My voice booms out full of authority. 'Come here. Lend me your cane.'

He stumbles forward, drops his amber-headed walking stick and makes to retreat but I – impelled perhaps, by an unworthy sentiment of revenge – bark, 'Now, the ties from the luggage. String, cord, anything strong. Bring it to me. Make haste!'

The other two passengers hurry to assist him, their shapes moving back and forth against the shadowy hulk of the coach. Despite everything, I experience a thrill of elation. I have not felt this alive for many weeks.

The muscles in my hands are not so sanguine; they begin to complain. The patient's blood pulses beneath my fingers, in time with my own heartbeat.

I turn to the guard beside me. 'Sir, please place your hands here, where mine are.'

He stares at me as if I have lost my mind. 'Put them …?'

'Either side of the wound and press, hard. You possess the strength, do you not?' It is a needless question: I have seen dray horses with less muscle about them.

His face puckers. 'Really, miss, that's not what I'm paid for.'

'Good God! What manner of man are you?' I cry. 'A pretty tale this will make in the coaching inns: how you bungled the chains and then left a woman screaming for aid, because you hadn't the stomach for blood!'

This touches home. He obeys, although not without resentment, eyeing me as a dog that has turned on him. I expect that before now he mistook me for a lady. It is an illusion I can no longer support.

Retrieving the hip flask from my reticule, I slosh gin into the patient's gaping mouth. There is no chance of my companions mistaking it for water this time; the perfume rises like a blush to condemn me. Eyebrows are raised, but I cannot regret my actions. With this poor man's injuries, I am only sorry that I do not have something stronger to administer.

He stirs. All vestige of colour has fled his face. His eyes stare but they are glassy and I doubt they discern me, or anything except the pain.

Tentatively, I touch his leg. His breeches and woollen stockings are torn, revealing brutal grazes, but my prayer has been answered: there are no punctures, no sickening flashes of bone poking through the skin. The break is clean.

I gulp at the gin myself, gaining courage for what I must do next. It is like drinking splinters of ice. A few sharp mouthfuls give a spur to my senses, and clarity to my vision.

I place my hands on the leg, will strength to my fingers. Pull.

There is a terrible wet pop.

My patient roars. The horses rear in their harness. Even the guard looks as if he might swoon.

'You will thank me, in time,' I shout above the commotion. The injured man does not hear; he has fainted away.

Laying the cane along the length of his shin, I tie it in place with the pilfered string. A poor excuse for a splint, but it is better than nothing. I have seen the result of breaks that reset at the wrong angle: it is a lifetime of malformation and pain.

But this man's leg looks good – straight.

How long it has been since I felt this gentle triumph, the warm tingle that spreads to the very tips of my fingers. Even gin cannot recreate such a sensation. I have fixed what is broken. Perhaps, *perhaps*, if I can continue in this path ...

A heavy hand falls upon my shoulder.

The shape of a man, dressed all in black, is articulated against the lamplight. He wears a powdered wig and a haughty expression. In his free hand he holds a portmanteau – made of ox leather, unlike the battered one belonging to Father, but it is smaller, and I doubt it contains much of use inside.

I know a quack when I see one.

'That will do, madam. I shall direct matters from here. Which of you fellows will carry this man to the inn?'

There is a great flurry of movement. Hooves clang; another coach approaches the yard. The onlookers who were so reluctant to follow my instructions bustle to help this stranger.

'But I – please wait, I have not—'

My words are useless, I am invisible. They snatch up the patient who brought me purpose and bear him away.

'I am sure you have assisted to the best of your ability,' the quack sneers. 'You must allow a genuine physician to attend him now.'

'Could I not help you?' I plead.

'I have no need of it.' He waves his hand airily, stalking away. As if I am of so little consequence that he need not look at me.

I am left alone.

Breath pants from my mouth, turns to mist.

Good God, what have I done?

They will remember me now. There is no doubt about it. No one taking the Mail from Salisbury to Exeter will be able to forget my face, my manner as I assisted the injured man. They will recall both if they are asked.

How cold it is. Colder than I had realised when about my tasks: a punishing, pinching wind. I wish I'd had time to pack my cloak before I ran away.

I stamp my feet, try to bring feeling to my legs. Dear God, dear God. Why did I help that man? It achieved nothing. Under the care of that supercilious quack, he will probably perish anyhow.

But the memory of my actions will remain.

This is my weakness. I act on impulse, without heed. I have not learnt. After all the terrible consequences of my folly, still I have not learnt.

My frozen hands prick, as though stuck with pins. I rub them together. Gasp.

Blood soaks my kidskin gloves. There are splashes on my travelling dress too, along with wisps of straw and a stain I fear is horse muck. But the worst is the gloves.

Blood, on my hands.

I yearn to rip them from me and trample them underfoot, but I resist, knowing the stain will be there on my skin, ground into the cracks on my palms.

A pair of ostlers leads out fresh horses. The animals skitter and roll their eyes at me as if I am a threat. The windows of the inn are populated with faces. Staring. Wondering who and what I am.

How could I have been such a fool?

My small, battered trunk sits in a puddle of frosted mud, where the large man must have thrown it in for searching for string. I rescue it and hug it to me. When all is said and done, this is the only home I have left. Everything I treasure can be contained within this trunk, and now I worry that it has been handled roughly; something may be broken.

I am tempted to check, but there is no time. The Old Exeter Mail waits for no man, and it has already stopped its appointed ten minutes. Our new horses champ at the bit while the coachman resumes his seat, the many capes of his greatcoat flapping.

Another arduous journey lies ahead and I am already fit to expire. In the small amount of time between stages, I had planned to relieve my bladder, at the very least. But every moment of my leisure was devoted to the injured man. Now I must put my trunk in the basket and climb back inside the coach, next to the smelly old woman.

She does not squash close against me this time.

The passengers all keep their distance.

Chapter 2

I did not expect to start this position without recalling the beginning of my employment in Hanover Square. Much as I try to forget, that day is etched upon my memory. I was bound to make comparisons. But I was not prepared for a contrast this stark.

It is nearly four o'clock in the morning. The Falmouth coaching inn reeks of stale beer and tooth rot. Its grizzled landlady will not allow me the use of a chamber unless I pay for the entire night, so instead I crouch behind the cover of a nearby bush and attempt to change my costume in the poor light.

I have sunk low indeed. It pains me to recall how happy I was when I secured the position of Lady Rose's maid. My fond hopes that this time I would have some luck. Mother and I sewed a new dress and I donned it carefully, standing stiff to prevent the material from creasing.

'Don't ruin it,' Mother said.

She was not talking just about the dress.

Now I am scrunching a bloodied gown and gloves into a ball and pushing them as far beneath my other belongings as they will go. Most of the gore has dried, even that clinging to the palms of my hands. I spit on them and rub them together before pulling on fresh gloves.

The linen bundle at the top of my trunk is still wrapped tight. Gingerly, I shake it. There is no sickening jangle of broken porcelain. Relief pushes tears into my eyes. I thought I could not grow more desolate, but now I realise that if I were to lose this …

My lips are very dry.

I close the trunk and lock it. Struggling out from the bush, I dust myself down and find a place to stand beside the inn, where I have arranged to meet my new employer. The night remains like pitch and I am thankful for its secrecy. I cannot be altogether sure that I have fastened my gown straight, or that there are not twigs poking from my hair.

What a miserable beginning! The wind salts my lips. Gulls wake and call from the harbour, but it is not the pleasant sound I expected: their voices are shrill, hostile.

I had hoped … But those were the thoughts of a green girl. I keep thinking I can blot out the past.

I do not deserve to be happy here.

Only one thing can aid me. I put the cold rim of the hip flask to my lips and suck.

It is empty.

How can it possibly all be gone?

Of course – the man who fell from the roof. Once again I see his gaping mouth, his face torn with pain. And wicked as it is, I begrudge him every drop. He is like to die, anyhow. My liquor will have done him no good. I should have kept it for myself.

All at once I am aware of the fear, clenched in my chest, and the noxious smells carried on the wind: tar, old rope, dead fish.

Without gin, memories will swim up to the surface.

I must not panic. Am I not at an inn? Whole casks and bottles of spirits wait inside. I must dash to the taproom, ask the landlord to refill my hip flask.

I start forwards but as I do so a harness jingles to my right. A pony-trap edges out of the darkness, driven by an old man.

'Miss Why?'

Dismay pounds me so flat that I forget to respond to my assumed name.

'Hester Why?' he repeats.

'Yes.' Too loud, too quick.

'I'm come to fetch ee to Morvoren House.'

He is bent nearly double over the reins. As for the pony, it is a poor-blooded thing, indifferently bred. It throws up its head and snorts, as if it does not think much of me either.

'I have a trunk.'

The old man does not dismount to help me. His face is weathered and hard, like the heel of a foot. Two eyes peep out from narrow slits below his forehead. Perhaps he is purblind.

It does not recommend him as a driver, but at least he cannot see the slatternly way in which I am dressed.

My tired arms just manage to hoist up my trunk. I follow it without a modicum of elegance. A change from Hanover Square, indeed. There, a carriage with yellow brocade squabs, matching curtains and liveried footmen ferried me and Lady Rose such short distances. I am fortunate that the wind is so fierce; I need no excuse for the watering of my eyes.

'And what is *your* name?' I enquire.

'Gerren.'

The pony raises his tail and releases a clump of steaming dung.

Gerren clicks his tongue. He steers the trap away from the yard and my last chance of precious gin, out into the world beyond.

We soon leave the lights and bustle of the Falmouth coaching inn far behind. To my eyes, the darkness seems absolute. Our lamps are woefully feeble, illuminating only the rump of our pony as it jogs along. Each hoof beat resonates through my hips. It is almost enough to make me miss the springs of the Mail coach.

Mile follows mile. Cobbles give way to a rutted dirt track. Our trap is exposed to the four winds, buffeted this way and that. Sleet strikes my cheeks, each drop a cold pinprick. I draw my knees close together, fold my arms and try to imagine myself far away.

Hours seem to pass.

Finally, the wheel bumps on a pothole and jerks me from my doze. Is that the sea I hear, mumbling to itself? Such a strange sound: fretful and louder than I expected. I lean forwards, eager for my first glimpse. But what I see makes me shudder.

A sheer drop yawns to my left, perhaps twenty feet, terminating in a flash of sand and black water. Lost in dreams, I had not observed that our rickety pony-trap was scaling the side of a cliff.

My stomach churns along with the waters below. One of the few consolations I had cherished before this night was that I should behold the ocean at last. I had imagined it blue, serene. What seethes beneath me is dark, frighteningly powerful: a cauldron of demons.

Stones slip beneath the pony's shoes. I grip on for dear life, longing for just one dram of gin to steady my nerves. It feels as if I have been travelling forever, and I cannot see an end to it.

At length, dawn grazes the horizon. The clouds are too heavy for much of a display; only the faintest ribbons of peach and lemon unfurl. Nonetheless, there is the hope of light, and colour steadily returns to the landscape. To my left, the sea softens to shingle grey. Gulls materialise, their white bellies wheeling above us. They sing a dirge at the coming of the sun, mournful and foreboding, telling me to turn back.

'We be on Morvoren land now,' Gerren croaks. It startles me to hear his voice.

'I did not notice us pass through any gates,' I observe.

Most landowners zealously guard their game against poachers, but I see there is little cause for that up here. The land is not arable but scrubby, with clumps of thrift and heather. No hares brave the exposed position. The only birds are dull of feather.

'There. See it?'

After the nightmare journey and wizened driver, I half expect to behold a gloomy castle straight from the pages of Mrs Radcliffe's novels. But Morvoren House stands sentinel on the crest of the cliff, braving the elements with stern indifference. It is wide and squat, two stories high, finished in grey mortar with an assortment of small stones protruding from the walls – roughcast, I believe it is called. Chimneys crown the grey slate roof. One of them is steaming.

There is no courtyard. No fountains play; no wooded groves lurk at the rear of the house. A stable block and a thin scattering of ash trees prove the only additions to the landscape.

There is no danger it will remind me of Hanover square. I close my eyes for a moment, relieved and disappointed in equal measures.

Why would someone choose to make their home up here instead of in the valleys? I have heard that fishermen keep cottages set into the cliffs, but there is no sign of them. In fact, there is little hint of society at all save for this one, incongruous gentleman's abode stood close to the precipice.

Our pony stumbles to a halt beside the front door. Something crunches beneath our wheels. Perhaps it was once a gravel drive. It is merely stony grass now.

All of the window shutters remain closed. The house appears blind but untroubled. Yes, that is the prevailing impression Morvoren makes upon me: one of stoic calm. As if it has always been here, and will always remain, despite the frenzy of the sea beneath.

I struggle down from the trap and retrieve my trunk. My limbs are stiffer and far less willing than when I climbed up. Giddiness overpowers me. I am obliged to place a hand on the pony's rump and wait for the spinning to stop. Should I fall, I do not suppose Gerren would come to my aid.

At least the ride in the trap is an excuse for my blowzy hair and dishevelled gown. By grey morning light, my lacing appears only slightly skewed; rather a miracle considering that it was done in the dark.

At any rate, I am not covered in blood.

The front door is an old wooden thing; it does not appear terribly thick. Light pulses around the cracks at the edges – a candle, moving behind. A bolt slides.

I swallow, hard.

This is the moment, the climax of my journey. The vague, shadowy future I have imagined for myself is to become a reality.

Without my hip flask, I feel unfit to face it.

The door clunks open.

A girl of sixteen years of age, or thereabouts, appears, a woollen shawl wrapped around her throat and shoulders. She holds a candle but the wind snuffs the flame out in a matter of seconds.

'Get thee inside!' she bawls to me above the wind.

She shuffles back, as far inside as she can manage while propping the door open with her foot. I scent dough, and something like cinnamon.

My legs cannot convey me and my trunk fast enough.

The girl slams the door behind us with a sound of relief. She does not mention Gerren, still outside, and I am not minded to recall him to her memory.

With her free hand, she begins to rub at my shoulder, as if she would chafe warmth into me.

'Look at thee, poor thing! Soaked through and wisht as the moon. I'm Merryn,' she adds with a smile. She has a winsome way and a personable face, despite a large birthmark that mottles one cheek. 'Always up afore the rest of un.'

'Miss Why,' I introduce myself. I have remembered, this time.

'Oh, don't I know it! Naught but "Miss Why this" and "Miss Why that" all week. Follow on. We'll soon get thee warm.'

Of all the welcomes I imagined, I had least expected this. Back in London, a scullery maid would be afraid to address an upper servant, let alone a woman more than ten years her senior.

'Don't mind thy boots on the floor. I'll be scrubbin' un later, anyhow.'

Her words rouse me to observe my surroundings.

We are standing in a grand entrance hall, incongruous with the outside of the house. All is stucco and classical without a trace of colour. Grapevines are moulded into the ceiling; Greek gods stare down from a pediment above the fireplace. It puts me in mind of the displays in confectioners' windows: shapes made entirely of meringue.

It is not at all like the dazzle of crystal and sienna marble in Hanover Square.

Merryn leads me through a baize door that conceals the servants' quarters. Coffee-toasted air elicits a growl from my stomach. We enter a long, narrow kitchen where a fire crackles merrily, its orange light dancing in the copper saucepans that hang upon the wall.

The only occupant here is a stout woman of middle age, round-faced and smiling, as she unwraps a loaf from its linen folds.

'Miss Why! Here already. You must be exhausted. Sit you down – Merryn, take her shawl and hang it to dry. Come closer to the fire. That's right. I'll cut you a slice of this bread and Merryn can fix us some tea.'

Sensation returns to my skin, painful at first. My clothes steam in the heat. It requires all of my composure not to lunge for the victuals laid out before me and wolf them down. I must make a good impression.

'Goodness, how thy hands do shake!' Merryn cries as she pours my tea. 'Take care thee don't catch a chill.'

Yes. Let her think it is the cold.

'We usually break our fast in the servants' hall,' the older woman informs me. 'But that's not for another hour or so yet. I thought you'd rather take refreshment here, and then I'll show you about the house. There's time enough to meet the others later.'

'Thank you. Mrs …?'

'Quinn.' She offers another smile. One of her front teeth is missing. 'You only know me by post.'

'Mrs Quinn!' I cry. 'So it was with *you* that I corresponded! Forgive me, I had no idea.'

This woman, then, is the housekeeper! I had expected someone more austere. She does not carry a bearing of authority or dress finer than Merryn; both wear a woven striped-cotton gown and linen apron. The only distinction is in her cap, which sports a pink ribbon; Merryn's does not.

'We're a small staff with plenty of work to go around. I'm not above helping in the kitchen.' She speaks with a quiet pride. 'Just imagine how pleased I was to find a lady's maid with your nursing skills! You're rare, you are.'

I chew on a piece of bread so that I am not obliged to reply at once. Merryn watches me with a girlish, admiring grin.

'It is not so very remarkable. My father was an army sawbones, my mother a midwife. I could not help but learn from them.'

'All the same, we're lucky to have you.' Though her voice is kind, she regards me quizzically, and I focus on the food to hide my blush. I know what she is thinking, for I hear it myself: the accent I have gleaned from Hanover Square. My diction does not correlate with the upbringing I have described. 'Your letters of character were handsome.'

Forgeries always are.

Merryn produces a saucepan and begins to grate a cake of drinking chocolate. I expect that shall be my task, once I am settled in. She pours some milk, cuts sugar from the loaf and adds a handful of spices. Cinnamon – I smelt that from the doorway – cloves and nutmeg.

Not cardamom. That was what Lady Rose liked.

To the right of Merryn, occupying the corner, is a square brick structure. Steam pushes up the edges of a round wooden lid on top. There is a stove built into the bottom. Presumably, they can use this to boil large quantities of water. That will come in handy.

Mrs Quinn tends to the main fire. It is an unruly beast, hissing and flaring as the weather creeps down the chimney. There is a rattle in the flue.

Merryn pauses, listening. 'Be it knockers again, Mrs Quinn?' she laughs. 'Bringin' the house down about we?'

The housekeeper makes a hushing sound but mischief sparkles in her eyes. 'Don't let Creeda hear you!' She catches my bewildered glance and wipes her hands upon her apron. 'Forgive us, Miss Why, 'tis a little amusement of the maids. There's an elderly servant here. One of the family, she's been at Morvoren so long. 'Twould be cruel to contradict or upset her, but she's a mite ... she can be ...'

'Cakey,' Merryn supplies. This must be a local word, I have no comprehension what it means, but from the way Mrs Quinn's cheeks are colouring, I expect the translation is impolite.

'Fanciful,' Mrs Quinn amends. 'Folk hereabouts have customs that might appear strange to you, Miss Why. Our families have always taught us to respect the little people—'

'Little people?' I echo, bemused.

'Fairies.' She tries, but does not altogether manage, to hold my eye. 'Now, I can't say as I do or don't believe in them, either way. It don't seem likely they exist, but strange things have happened to people I know, and I can't explain it. Most of us show willing, leave a jar of cream out or the like. But Creeda … Creeda is strong in her beliefs.'

'Creeda be more superstitious than me own father,' Merryn chirps as she whisks the chocolate with a molinet. 'And he's a fisherman!'

What answer can I possibly give? I stare at my plate, now empty and sprinkled with crumbs. Perhaps it is fortunate that all the laughter has been knocked out of me.

'The maids have a little joke about it, now and then,' Mrs Quinn adds hurriedly. 'In private. But of course they'd never speak out to her. And I shouldn't allow any silly talk to reach the mistress.'

Ah, that is her concern.

'I can safely promise she will hear no such thing from me, Mrs Quinn.'

'Good. Now, have you eaten enough? Will you rest while the others break their fast?'

I should like to rest forever. The refreshment has only increased my lethargy. My temples throb, whether from lack of sleep or lack of gin I cannot tell.

'If not inconvenient.' I dust off my hands, make to stand. 'There are a few clothes I should like to unpack in my room.'

'You'll be sharing with Merryn.'

The chair leg squeaks on the floor. Impossible to conceal my dismay, but I try nonetheless. 'Oh.'

''Tisn't a large house,' Mrs Quinn explains. She is watching me closely. 'No spare beds. You'll see that when I show you about.'

I simply nod.

A lady's maid, an upper servant, sharing a bed! That is an insult in itself, but to be paired up with a lowly scullery maid … In Hanover Square I enjoyed a room of my very own, while maids like Merryn would bed down with straw in the kitchens.

I pick up my trunk and cast a glance over my shoulder at Merryn as we leave. She is smiling, merry as a grig. I do not dislike her. She seems an amiable girl. But surely even Cornish servants can comprehend how unusual this is? What an affront it must be to my pride?

A headache tightens its claws around the top of my scalp. Vision softens at the edges. I follow Mrs Quinn with little regard for that around me. She has promised a tour later – I will pay heed to the house then. For now I have simply to conquer these stairs, which seem like miniature cliffs in their own right. The iron banister lends some support, but it is charged with cold and burns my palm.

'You've been travelling a good while,' Mrs Quinn says. ''Tis three and twenty hours from Salisbury to Falmouth.'

'Thereabouts. Thank you for booking me a seat inside. The expense ...'

She clucks to stop my expressions of gratitude. 'A body would freeze solid on the roof! Still, you do look pale.'

'A little rest is all I require.'

'Maybe I'll heat some wine when I fetch you after breakfast. Bring the colour back to your cheeks.'

If she does not, I believe I shall weep.

We come to a corridor with windows on one side, the other interspersed with wooden doors. The white paint has chipped upon them, so I do not think they are used by the family. Mrs Quinn turns the brass door-knob of the second and says brightly, 'Here we are.'

Pale green paper hangs upon the walls. That is a comfort I did not expect. There are few others besides.

Wooden slats on the floor. No fireplace. The bedstead appears to be made of oak and has seen better days; from the tidemarks on it, I would say it has been doused for bugs more than once. There is a window above with rough, unmatched curtains. It shows a view of the sea. The presence of the ocean still unnerves me, as it did when our trap scaled the cliff. It is so much bigger and more powerful than I imagined. Looking at it does not inspire me as I had hoped. It makes me feel cold.

To the left of the bed is a press for our clothes, to the right a washstand and ewer. One of each. I had more space when I shared a room with my sister Meg.

'Thank you,' I say. 'I am sure I shall be most comfortable.'

But of course I shall not. Every movement I make will collide with Merryn. Her bright, sharp eyes will dig into all my secrets.

I place my trunk by the press, remove my bonnet and sit it on top. Already I feel hemmed in.

Mrs Quinn waits by the door. 'You'd like some hot water, Miss Why?'

I would like her to go away.

'Not for now, thank you.' A yawn escapes me and I make the most of it, stretching theatrically. 'I believe I will just close my eyes.'

'That's a sensible notion.' But she is not moving. Worry folds her plump forehead. 'Truly, you do look unwell. Rest up. I'll return for you by and by.' At last she withdraws. I have never seen someone leave a room so slowly. She shuts the door with such softness that I am not sure it is fully closed.

I pause for a moment, listening. Mrs Quinn does the same. It seems my patience is the greater, for presently, I hear the floorboards outside creak and her heavy steps fading away.

I take a breath, push the door to make sure it really is fastened. Then the tears come.

Once I made a noise when I wept. I remember racking sobs against Mother's breast, snuffles on Meg's shoulder. Not now. Teardrops flow down my face like moisture on the neck of a bottle. There are no ragged breaths, no bursts of passion. Weeping appears to be my habitual state.

Dropping onto the bed, I instinctively roll to the right. But that is not necessarily my place here. Which of these pillows is Merryn's I cannot tell; both are equally flat and laced with the scent of dough.

Now both are also wet.

I am wasting precious time. Who knows when I shall next snatch a moment alone? Although it makes my aching head shriek, I force myself up and wipe my eyes with the heels of my hands.

I must check my trunk.

My fingers shake as I work the key into the lock and push the lid back on its hinges. The precious package falls into my hands, as if it has been waiting.

I unwrap the linen, layer by layer. A glimpse of rose-petal pink. Gold, flashing. Cold to the touch but warming, quickly, with the heat of my flesh.

Finally, the snuffbox sits in the palm of my hand.

Porcelain, tooled gold and the lingering ghost of Violet Strasbourg; these are my only relics of a former life. And it will cost my life, if I am caught with this box.

Sir Arthur, my previous master, is not a forgiving man. He possesses so much. He ought to spare me this one trinket. But I saw his advertisement in the newspaper. Ripped it out and stuffed it in my trunk, so that no one else might read the damning words.

Whereas Esther Stevens, maid to the advertiser, absconded Hanover Square in London on 17th December last, carrying off with her sundry items of her employer's personal property including a pink porcelain snuffbox worked with gold. She is about five foot three inches tall, full of face though slender in person with light brown hair, and was wearing a grey stuff gown and black shawl. She is believed to have travelled West. Whoever apprehends this criminal will be thankfully requited. Whoever harbours her shall be prosecuted as the law directs.

Chapter 3

'Miss Why? May I enter?'

Although the hand taps gently against wood, its sound reverberates in the base of my skull.

A door creaks. My eyes are gummed together. Rubbing them hurriedly, I gain a watery sort of vision. A large lady approaches me. She makes the air heavy, luxurious with a scent I cannot yet place.

'Good to see you've slept. You'll feel brighter now.'

Sleep crusts over my thoughts. On instinct, I raise myself to a sitting position and hold out my hands to receive the vessel she passes to me.

I recognise the aroma now: wine. It calls me back to myself.

'Mrs Quinn. Forgive me, my wits are still gathering wool.'

She nods. ''Tis to be expected. You won't have got much rest in the coach.'

This is true, but I did not expect a housekeeper's sympathy for that. Mrs Glover in Hanover Square wouldn't pity an underling unless their arm had fallen off, and even then she would do it grudgingly.

'It was good of you to remember the wine.'

'You need something to drive out that chill. I sent Lowena – that's my other maid – out to collect the eggs. Poor girl came back stiff as a ramrod! She said there's frost all over the rocks. Won't be surprised if we have snow before long, and 'twill be a trial. You can imagine how difficult 'tis, Miss Why, perched up here when the roads are impassable.'

Greedily, I slop wine into my mouth. It has been warmed and spiced. Mrs Quinn does not make a remark about the rapidity with which I drink; she seems content chattering away.

'I know you left London backalong, but have you seen the London papers? Dr Bligh – that's our vicar – he gets them now and then. Told me that the River Thames has frozen solid! Can you credit that?'

Her words form ice crystals inside me. Resolutely, I swallow the last sip of wine. 'It makes me feel cold simply to imagine such a thing.'

Mrs Quinn believes I only quitted the capital to attend on my dying mother. In fact, Salisbury was simply the furthest destination I could reach with the money given to me by my sister. My actual parents, still alive, will be shivering along with the rest of the Londoners. Nursing their shame, wondering what has become of me.

Mrs Quinn offers me a gap-toothed smile. 'Ready to be shown about? Thought I'd take you to meet the mistress first. That's the most important.'

Running a hand over my head, I realise my hair has not been improved by lying upon a pillow. 'Certainly. Let me first put on a cap and then I shall be ready.'

I hand Mrs Quinn my cup, hoping against hope she will decide to take it downstairs while I am tidying myself. She does no such thing.

She will be in the room when I open my trunk; there is no avoiding it. I think of the bloodstained clothing, the snuffbox.

'Tell me about Miss Pinecroft.' It is the brightest tone I have used all day and it rings false. Rising from the bed, I kneel down beside my trunk and put the key in the lock. 'I believe you wrote that she has lived threescore years?'

'I did. But she'll appear much older to you, I daresay. 'Twas about a decade ago she had the last apoplectic fit and she hasn't been the same since.'

Winching the lid of my trunk open a crack, I slip my hand inside and grope for a plain cap.

'Miss Pinecroft can talk but she don't choose to, much. We've tried all we can to perk her up. She don't seem to want it. She prefers to ...' Mrs Quinn makes a vague gesture in the air, '... sit. I used to fancy she was going over all her fond memories, but they don't seem to cheer her.'

Thank heaven, I have it. Pulling the cap out quickly, I slam the lid of my trunk back down. Mrs Quinn starts at the sound.

Her eyes linger on my luggage and I begin to feel that she is rifling through me, like the pages of a book.

'I believe the muscles can be affected,' I say quickly, jamming the cap over my hair. 'You mentioned one side of her mouth was palsied, did you not? It may simply be that her face can no longer express her mood.'

I stand before her, smile, a little too widely.

'Yes,' she replies with a touch of wariness. 'Happen you're right. Let's go down, and you can tell me what you think.'

It is a relief to leave that cramped room. Haggard daylight struggles through the windows in the corridor, casting patterns on the stone flags. At least the white paint gives an impression of space. Wind creeps along the walls outside. It sounds like a woman, pouring hushed secrets into her lover's ear.

My ability to focus appears to have returned, and not a moment too soon. I must learn the layout of this house by heart in case I find myself less competent at another time. There is a strong likelihood that I shall. With the inn so far away and my hip flask dry ... I must not dwell upon that. I shall contrive something, I always do.

Mrs Quinn leads me to the head of the staircase that descends into the stucco hall. Now my mind is clearer,

I can appreciate the artistry. It really is a masterpiece; the engravings are pure as fresh fallen snow. I wonder how Merryn and Lowena manage to keep it clean.

Mrs Quinn pauses with a chink of her housekeeping keys. 'No. I'll show you the mistress's bedchamber before taking you down.'

She continues to walk along the corridor, away from the room where I slept. I see now that the landing and staircase serve as a divide between the wings: the east belonging to the servants and the west to the family.

The west wing is decorated in the style that I am used to. Rich mahogany panels the floors. The walls are papered in china blue, interset here and there with brass sconces for candles. Rosemary leavens the air with sharp lemony notes. My new mistress must have a great many gowns in storage.

Sound is intensified on this side of the house, which sits closer to the cliff edge. The wind scolds and is answered by a defensive mutter from the sea.

Yet that is not all I can hear. There is something low, resonating beneath.

I tilt my head. Yes, there.

For all its depth, it is sweet. There is a music to it. Something bewitching, humming right through me.

But Mrs Quinn jangles her keys, and the effect is shattered.

'This one here. You'll have your own copy of the key, remind me to give you that later.'

The lock on this door is peculiar. Brass, attached to the wood in the old way instead of a mortice mechanism. An engraved pointer dog extends its paw in the direction of a dial. As Mrs Quinn turns her key, it moves, and the dog's paw indicates the number sixty-six.

A lock to detect the number of times a room is entered. Who would have purpose for such a thing? It implies distrust.

The door opens without a sound. I catch a breath, struck by what I glimpse behind it.

'Yes,' says Mrs Quinn, ''tis very handsome.'

Toile-de-Jouy dominates the room. A repeating pattern of blue pastoral figures against a white background. Not simply the paper and bed hangings but the dressing screen, the easy chair and the tiles around the fireplace. The result is overwhelming. Wherever my eyes turn, they meet objects picked out in blue: mostly shepherds and their sweethearts, but there are horses and trees besides.

'I wonder Miss Pinecroft can sleep in such a chamber,' I observe. 'I should feel as though I were being watched!'

Little people. Was that not the term Merryn and Mrs Quinn used? They are here now, with their crooks and straw bonnets. Perhaps this room put such fancies into their heads.

'The mistress don't sleep overmuch,' she replies sadly, hovering on the threshold. 'We're not always successful getting her to bed. I've known her spend the night downstairs, but I discourage it as much as I can, for 'tisn't good for her health.'

'No, indeed.'

There is no looking glass that I can see. A wardrobe lurks in the corner, and I must be right about the gowns in storage, for it radiates the scent of rosemary as strongly as a kitchen garden.

'She don't like to bathe if she can help it,' Mrs Quinn explains. 'Water turns her all queer.'

The look we exchange informs me that Mrs Quinn is aware of the irony. Why a woman who dislikes water should live on the cusp of the ocean, heaven only knows.

'When the mistress do go to bed,' she continues, 'I'm afraid 'tis necessary to lock the door. She's prone to wander, otherwise. Can't have her trying to get back down that steep staircase in the dark. She needs spectacles, you see, but she won't wear them. If we're not careful, she'll fall and break her head.'

A sensible precaution, of course, but it does not sit easily with me. I cannot wonder that Miss Pinecroft is reluctant to retire to bed if she knows she will be detained like a prisoner.

'I understand, Mrs Quinn. I will make certain to lock the door.' I nod to reinforce my words. The ghost of my headache wails. 'Now, I should very much like to meet Miss Pinecroft herself.'

She stands aside to grant me passage back into the corridor. Then she closes the chamber, locks it. The brass dial turns to sixty-seven.

I wonder what she is locking it against.

Returning to the staircase, we descend sedately, admiring the stucco. It seems a great pretension for a house that is not, after all, particularly large.

Set in an alcove is the statue of a man. I suppose he must be Poseidon, with his draggled beard and the seaweed artfully arranged to lend him some modesty. He stares at me as I pass, his plaster eyes blank.

'Do you know the history of this hall?' I ask Mrs Quinn. 'It appears to be straight from a ducal palace.'

She chuckles and pinks – no housekeeper is above a touch of flattery. 'Only what Creeda told me. 'Twas fitted out just before the mistress moved in, by a man with grand ideas. They got less grand as his money ran out. Then his fortune was lost at sea.'

I imagine the waves taunting him on his failure. Sir Arthur, too, was what the beau monde called 'nouveau riche': his wealth, as well as his knighthood, came from success in trade. But he had rather more acumen than the man who built this house.

Sir Arthur knew every item in his home, and its worth.

My tongue is beginning to feel dry.

As I gain the stone floor, I see that Merryn has kept her word and scrubbed my footsteps from sight. This time we turn in the opposite direction, away from the enticing odours of the kitchen behind the baize door.

There is nothing remarkable in this corridor; the usual little pier tables and prints that denote a lady's taste. Several doors stand ajar, leading, I imagine, to a dining room and a drawing room, but we do not stop at them. Mrs Quinn takes me right to the end of the wing.

This door is also partially open but no light spills from the gap. A twilit world awaits within, silent and still.

'Here we are.' Mrs Quinn hushes her voice.

My first thought is that we are disturbing something sacred. The room carries the air of an abandoned church, the same preternatural calm. Heavy, tasselled curtains conceal the view from the window, but they cannot muffle the sound of the sea.

I have never stepped inside a place so cold. It sucks the breath from me. There is no carpet or fire to add even a hint of warmth.

Dark mahogany panels the walls, yet this is only the background. Shielding the wood is an armoury of china.

Plates, sugar bowls, large, freestanding jugs either side of the ash-heaped fireplace. The mantelpiece is a series of shelves displaying vases, figurines and teapots. More china than I have ever seen in my life. There is a shelf of urns with matching lids, an arrangement of elegant cups too fine to drink from.

We walk right up to them, close enough to touch. Every piece is blue and white. No glass protects the collection.

'Good morning, Miss Pinecroft.' Mrs Quinn speaks gently, as if to raise her voice would shatter the display. 'I've brought someone to see you.'

She sits so quiet and still that I did not notice her as I walked past. Behind us, in the centre of the room is a wingback chair and upon it – or rather, being swallowed by it – is the frail figure of a woman.

Mrs Quinn was right; she appears far older than her sixty years. Her hair is not grey but a startling white. Wrinkles cover her face, so fine they might have been drawn with the point of a needle.

Palsy has marked her with a lopsided look. Invisible strings seem to tug at the corner of her mouth and the lid of her right eye.

Considering her afflictions, she is dressed tolerably well in a sage-green polonaise with a black belt at the waist. An outdated fashion, but she remains neat. I wonder, fleetingly, if she has retained this gown from her youth.

'This is Miss Why,' explains Mrs Quinn. 'Remember me telling you that I employed her to be your nurse and personal maid?'

I fall into a curtsey. My mistress's codfish eyes do not blink.

Mrs Quinn gestures that I might rise, rather than await a signal from Miss Pinecroft.

'I am very pleased to meet you, madam,' I venture. Ordinarily, it would not be proper to speak until she addressed me, but I sense that is not a formality to be adhered to here. 'Your household is beautiful. I am honoured to be a part of it.'

Ever so slightly, her head inclines. She is listening, but her eyes do not move from the china.

In their prime they must have been fine, blue eyes like a summer's sky. Age has watered them down and blurred their focus. With her mouth slightly ajar, the impression is that of an aquatic creature. The poor woman. My heart aches for her.

'It is very cold in here,' I say gently, taking a step forward. 'Shouldn't you like to have a fire built up?'

'No.'

I did not expect her to speak; I fight the impulse to recoil at the sound of her voice. It is so low and hoarse, it might have emerged from below ground.

'Miss Pinecroft don't generally keep a fire,' Mrs Quinn informs me.

I frown. On a day like this, with ice drawing ferns on the windows and the wind roaring outside, it seems utterly foolhardy. Even our breath is misting as we stand here watching the old lady.

And I suppose that is their problem: she is the mistress and they are not used to contradicting her. That is a nurse's prerogative.

'I understand that Miss Pinecroft suffers from occasional rheumatism? That will not be helped by the chill. Truly, madam, it is freezing weather. Will you not consider again, or at least take another shawl?'

There is a pause, and I think Miss Pinecroft will not respond. Mrs Quinn looks quite astounded at my effrontery.

Finally, the cracked lips part and mutter, 'Shawl.'

Slight as it is, the progress pleases me. 'That is a sound decision. I shall go and fetch it for you.'

It will be a relief to escape from this room to a warmer part of the house. I do not know what I shall do if I cannot persuade her to light a fire all winter. Her health will suffer, and so will my own. I cannot sit for hour upon hour in that room, without even a dram of gin to warm my blood.

What I would give for another glass of that heated wine.

Mrs Quinn prattles softly to the mistress as I approach the door. 'A nice shawl to warm you up, that's just the thing. We're lucky to have Miss Why. 'Twill be pleasant to have someone sit with you, won't it, while Creeda's busy with Miss Rosewyn?'

'Rose?' It is as if I have been yanked back from the threshold on a rein.

Mrs Quinn starts up. 'No, Miss Why. Rosewyn. 'Tis one of our pretty local names.' She hesitates. 'Miss Rosewyn is an orphan. The ward of Miss Pinecroft. Our kindly mistress adopted her.'

'Oh.' My throat seems full of my pulse; there is scarcely room to swallow. 'I was not aware of her existence.'

A child? Is that possible? I cannot see Miss Pinecroft exerting herself to visit poorhouses and take an interest in the orphans, much less anyone committing such a burden to her care. This is not an environment suited to a young person; even if the house had more warmth and spirit, its proximity to the cliff would render it hazardous.

But perhaps it was different before the apoplectic fit. Perhaps Miss Pinecroft was active in the neighbourhood, the kind of influential lady no guardians would dare to cross. I must remember that. The shell who sits before me is by no means representative of all the woman once was.

'Of course, you don't know about Miss Rosewyn. That's my fault, I didn't mention her.' Mrs Quinn seems embarrassed. She puts a hand to the chatelaine at her waist. 'Come now, what am I thinking to send you upstairs without your key?' She waddles away from the mistress. 'I've more to show you besides. Let's take our leave for a minute and come back with Miss Pinecroft's shawl.'

Glad as I am to quit the cold chamber, it seems melancholy to leave Miss Pinecroft there alone. I wonder who has dressed her, whether she has drunk the chocolate Merryn prepared.

'Just in here,' Mrs Quinn says, indicating a door to the right, which I did not observe previously. She leads me into a small room, more of a closet, where there is only space to stand one abreast.

Fishing in a drawer, she retrieves another set of keys. These are shining new, unlike her own.

'Here we are. Freshly cut for you. Now, Miss Pinecroft don't like her staff to be traipsing in and out of the china room; it's one of her private apartments, which of course you'll clean. Creeda's always looked after the collection, and very loath she is to have another body touch it. But her hands aren't what they were.' I place my own behind my back, hoping she does not see their tremors. 'When she read your character letters, and all those handsome things your employers said about how careful you were, she said you could have a go.'

I smile as if I am pleased, not appalled. All of that china! It will be a penance indeed to keep it clean, but it is not the work that troubles me.

Without gin, my hands will continue to shake.

'We keep some dusters, brushes and vinegar in these cupboards. The trick, I think, is to make sure the water's neither too warm nor too cold. Merryn can help you with that.' Mrs Quinn pulls a shorter key from the bunch. 'This one here is special to you. Opens our physic cabinet.'

She goes to a box on the wall, shows me how the lock turns.

The cabinet opens, and my heart begins to flutter.

I see hartshorn, lavender oil, soda ash, calomel and the range of dried herbs I would expect. There is a fleam and bowl for letting blood. A plaster iron lurks in the corner. But these are not the cause of my agitation.

Gleaming at the front are three large bottles of laudanum.

'I kept it stocked,' she informs me proudly. 'Visited the apothecary myself so we'd have enough to last us through winter.' Following my gaze, she adds, ''Tis for her pain, not that she complains of it much. But she feels it, I know. And a drop of laudanum helps settle her when she takes one of her turns.'

I daresay it does.

Part alcohol, part opium: the River Lethe must have flowed with this bitter, forgetful liquid.

It could calm any nerve.

It could steady a hand.

Chapter 4

And so I have begun my new position with theft.

By the light of a single candle, I fill my hip flask with laudanum. The slosh of liquid is alarmingly loud. I am certain someone will hear it, or detect the spiced scent, but I am alone here in my small physic cabinet. The night is still. Only the sea refuses to slumber.

My first day's tea allowance is all used up in replacing what I have taken. It makes a passable substitute for the reddish brown laudanum. With only my hands and the bottles illuminated by the candle's glow, I can watch the preparations like a dumbshow, pretend it is detached from me and someone else commits the crime.

This will *not* be the pattern for my employment here. Come Lady Day, when the roads are in no danger of being blocked and I have my first quarter's salary from Mrs Quinn, I shall pay her back with twice the amount of opiates I have borrowed. Yes, borrowed. It is a loan, regrettable, but necessary.

When it is done, I close the cabinet and turn the key in the lock, feeling as if I am concealing a filthy secret. How weary I am. Weighted with that exhaustion that settles deep in the bones, and yet, if I were to lay down my head right now, I know I would not sleep. I would toss as the sea is doing.

Does it have memories, too? Can it recall the cargos it has swallowed: spices, silks, even human souls? I hope so. It would be frightening to think the water indifferent, unchanged by all it held within its depths.

A floorboard shifts above me. My pulse quickens, but there is little to fear – I have every excuse to be where I am. I pick up the hip flask to hide it away, but even the cool feel of it in my palm is enough to make my mouth water. Two drops – just two, as I took in my childhood fevers. I place them carefully upon my tongue and feel the muscles in my shoulders relax. It is not gin, but it will do.

With the hip flask safely tucked inside my apron, I loop my finger through the silver candleholder and leave the physic cabinet. Shadows snake down the corridor. It feels eerie in this house at night, as though it is waiting for something, something I am not meant to see. When I heard the floorboard creak, I thought it was one of my fellow servants stirring. But there is no trace of them except the lingering odour of pork fat from our dinner.

Earlier I met our cook Mrs Bawden whose face closely resembled the ham she was dressing. The other maid, Lowena. The much famed Creeda did not appear. Could that be her, pacing above me? Mrs Quinn made her sound like a figure of ridicule, but at this time of night I do not find myself inclined to laugh. I would rather not meet an old crone riddled with superstition until the sun is firmly in the sky.

There is one unsettling elderly lady I cannot avoid. Guilt prevents me from looking her in the face as I enter the china room and stand before her chair.

In truth, I do not know what to do with her. Usually, a mistress will tell me of her pain and troubles, give me a problem to solve. But with this statue of a woman, it is all guesswork.

'Do you wish me to fetch you something before bed, Miss Pinecroft? May I warm you some wine? Mix some Black Drop?'

There is no response.

I think I will quilt a cap with herbs for her. Such a garment, warmed and placed upon her head at night, would surely stimulate the brain. It is too late to start on it now.

'Please, madam. How may I help you?' I ask wearily.

She raises one shaking finger and points at the china behind me. 'Keep it nice.'

She is not in full possession of her faculties, but I find I am too tired to conceal my irritation. 'I meant medically.'

With only half a functioning mouth, it is difficult to interpret the expression she pulls. If I did not know better, I would say she was laughing at me.

My temper nearly snaps. It is late and it is cold. The windows cannot be well glazed, for the candle flame wavers as if knocked by a breeze. My index finger, curled around the holder, is starting to feel numb.

'I believe it is time to retire, madam. Allow me to assist you.'

She shakes her head.

'Yes,' I counter. 'I am your nurse, madam, and I will not have you catch your death of cold on my watch.'

Setting my candle upon a table, I go and place my hand on her arm. I fully expect her to yield now she knows I am not to be trifled with. But as I gently tug at her elbow, her wrinkled hand clenches around the armrest, anchoring her in place.

'Madam!' I exclaim.

I tug harder.

Her face is set in quiet determination. Two wrinkles between her eyebrows deepen.

I am pulling her arm harder than I should. I do not seem able to stop. For all her height, she is not stout, and the flesh has wasted away. Surely I can overpower her? Half-carry her, if needs be.

No. She deserves more dignity than that.

Changing tack, I release her arm and seize her around the waist. She adopts the ruse of an infant and falls limp.

'Madam!' I say again, panting. 'Be reasonable!'

'Must ... keep watch.'

Watch over what, exactly? I turn my head briefly and regard the faintly luminous outlines of the china behind me. There is nothing else there. Even if there were, Mrs Quinn told me my mistress would not be able to see it clearly without spectacles.

As we are past the bounds of common politeness this evening, I dare to openly contradict my mistress. 'You must *sleep*.'

All at once she meets my eyes, and I let go of her as if she has burnt me. There is something so cold, so overwhelmingly tragic in that watery gaze. 'Bad things ...' she whispers, '... happen ... when I sleep.'

I shiver. 'Whatever can you mean?' She is silent. 'Do you suffer from nightmares, madam? I could sleep in a truckle bed beside you; my previous mistress often—'

'No.'

I am tired and sick from lack of gin. I cannot endure this much longer. 'But, madam—'

'Leave.'

With a cry of frustration, I seize a taper, light it from the candle and stride out of the room.

Let her stay there, if it pleases her. It is her health that will pay the toll, not mine.

The taper is weak and anger blurs my vision, but I find the bedchamber Mrs Quinn showed me earlier. It is warmer than downstairs, though not much. I blow out the taper and undress by the light of the moon.

Merryn is already asleep in bed. I am grateful for her presence, her body's small supply of heat.

I lie on my back, staring up into the darkness. All day I have yearned for repose. Now I have the chance, but my body has journeyed beyond it. It is too tired even to sleep.

Gradually, my breath regains its rhythm. Although my heart still pounds, it slows, becomes like the steady toll of a bell.

Whatever have I done?

Scolded my mistress. Practically insulted her person. Left her in a fit of temper with nothing but a candle to see her through the night.

All on my first day.

Shame tingles in my limbs, but I am too cowardly to climb out of bed and put it right. All I wish to do is curl in on myself. Weep.

I picture my new mistress in the lower regions of the house: watching over china plates with her blue tortured eyes; her poor old bones a prey to the merciless chill.

In the west wing, another floorboard creaks.

It is going to be a long night for us both.

PART TWO

Hanover Square

Chapter 5

My position at Hanover Square was by no means my first, although it was a significant step up. No one could wish to be associated with a finer master than Sir Arthur Windrop. Newly knighted and newly married, he was making a stir in society with his beautiful young wife. *Her* credentials were not equal to his, but the newspapers were surprisingly forgiving. Lady Rose possessed grace, and an air of fashion that instantly smoothed over any embarrassment of birth.

I did not receive a kind welcome when I arrived at the redbrick mansion with its black iron railings. Our housekeeper, Mrs Glover, did not permit me to rest after my arrival like Mrs Quinn, nor did she bring me warm wine. Indeed, she scarcely allowed me to remove my shawl. She was a poker of a woman, tightly laced into a dress of deep brown with ruffles at the sleeves. Black mittens covered her hands and upon her head rested a cap of exquisite lacework.

'Ah, Stevens,' she said – I went by my real name in those days – 'Good. You will join me in my room for tea at nine o'clock tonight.'

She did not trouble to tell me where her room might be. This was a difficulty of no small importance, for the servants' quarters at that residence were bigger than the entire ground floor of Morvoren House, what with the scullery, larder, boot room, butler's pantry and servants' hall.

Mrs Glover had neither the leisure nor inclination to show me about herself. Instead, she steered me towards a woman with a profusion of curls at her forehead, arrayed in a dress suited to mourning. The fabric was expensive, fine-napped, trimmed in ribbon. It must have been a cast-off from her mistress; I thought it rather poor taste for her to wear it while about her duties.

'Stevens, this is Burns. Burns is the personal maid of Mrs Windrop, Sir Arthur's widowed mother. Burns has been taking care of Lady Rose since her marriage. She will inform you of your duties.'

Burns raised one cochineal-stained eyebrow and I could tell she thought me a very inferior type of person. I seemed to shrink and thicken by her side. My sole aim had been to appear neat. Burns was something else, she was *smart*.

'Lady Rose did insist on selecting her own maid,' she sighed with a shake of her head.

I spent that morning trotting after Burns, thrown from wig to wall as the saying goes, watching her actions. Rarely did she deign to explain or speak to me beyond a scold: I had set out the items on the dressing table incorrectly; I should not touch that without first washing my hands; I did not need to be taking an inventory of my mistress's gowns quite so soon – did I plan to steal something?

A spiteful harridan that woman was, yet on the first day I stood in awe of her. Burns, the butler, the footmen: they all seemed to exude the wealth of the household they belonged to. I feared I had made a terrible mistake in coming here.

Mid-afternoon, there was a distinct clop amidst the cacophony of hooves that rang in the square outside. All heads shot up from their work and feet began to move.

'What is it?' I asked Burns.

'Are you deaf? It's the master's carriage. They are back from the china showroom.'

Nerves squirmed in my belly as I followed Burns's quick step to the entrance hall. I had only met Lady Rose briefly, following my interview with Mrs Glover; Sir Arthur I had not seen at all.

When the footman opened the door, my mistress stepped in with the dust and light of the street. She was even prettier than I recalled. Pink tinged her cheeks as she laughed, echoing the feathers and flowers in her poke bonnet. Her style of beauty would not please all; with her large, dark eyes and voluptuous lips, it was rather full-blown. But her figure was soft and curving, her hair fashionably dark, and she possessed what my *Guide to the Toilette* called a 'carnation' complexion, where neither the rose nor the lily predominates.

She turned to her husband, who followed close behind, and tapped him lightly on the arm with her shut fan.

Sir Arthur's appearance was more stately: tall with well-shaped calves. His face was square and handsome. His expression tended towards gravity.

Burns moved forwards officiously, ready to divest Lady Rose of her outside things.

'No, not you,' she chided, holding up her fan. 'My Stevens should be here. Where is Stevens?'

With burning cheeks, I crept out from behind the pillar and dropped into my best curtsey. Lady Rose bestowed a smile upon me. It was the first I had received all day.

'There she is! Charming.' She addressed her husband as I took her bonnet, gloves and jacket, 'Did I not tell you she was charming, Artie?'

'Indeed, I hope you will be happy in our household, Stevens,' Sir Arthur replied with a benevolent air.

I kept my chin down towards the floor, not only to avoid Burns's glare, but to conceal my fierce blushes.

My own mother had never described me as 'charming'. With a plain, somewhat fleshy face and mousy hair, I was exactly what a lady's maid ought to be: unremarkable, designed to blend into the background.

'Thank you, sir,' I managed to say.

Lady Rose strode towards the stairs. 'Come, Stevens, we dallied longer than we intended to; we were so pleasantly detained at the warehouse. You must dress me for dinner.'

I followed, cradling her spencer jacket like a newborn. It was a little dusty from the streets, but that would brush out.

Lady Rose's suite of rooms was on the second floor of the house. A lighter, airier space I never did see. Without Burns breathing down my neck this time, I was able to appreciate the little decorative touches. All was arrayed in pale lemon, except for the furniture, which was painted white. A dome spread over one wall, draping silk-fringed curtains either side of a Grecian couch bed. Vases full of fresh flowers were dotted here and there.

'Do you like it?' she asked. 'My husband had it all fitted out for me. Is he not a dear? I have never met a man with such exquisite taste.'

'It is very elegant, indeed, my lady.'

I placed the bonnet on its stand and the gloves on their stretchers. Having cast my eyes over Lady Rose's gowns, I knew which to recommend for dinner. But before I could list the merits of crimson silk, she seized both of my hands in her own.

'Oh, Stevens, I am so glad that you are come!' Her voice dropped an octave, losing some of its polish. 'Another day with that odious Burns would make me scream. She is my mother-in-law's creature, you know.' Releasing me, she dropped onto the stool before the dressing table. One hand swept across the surface, knocking the combs and brushes askew. 'There! I did that every time she left the room to frustrate her. She was so particular about the arrangement – it must be the very mirror of Mrs Windrop's! As if I should follow the patterns set by a stuffy old lady.'

I did not hazard a smile. She was winning, girlish, not at all like my previous employers, but half of me feared this was a test. 'I did attempt to lay out the silver-backed set a little differently, my lady. I thought the hand-mirror should be easier to reach on the right, and that the pin tray could go just there ...'

Lady Rose propped one elbow on the table and began to twirl the short curls at her forehead. 'Oh, you may do as you wish with it, Stevens. For my part, I only want these rooms to be a place of refuge. Artie is so very dear, but as for the rest of them, they are quite insufferable.' She smiled back at me in the glass, artless as a child.

It was reckless of Lady Rose to talk so candidly in my hearing. She could have no conception, beyond our previous short meeting, that I was not every bit as stuffy as the others.

For an occupation, I moved behind the stool and began to unpin her hair. It came down in gentle waves to the small of her back. There was a good weight to it; I should be able to coax it into all manner of styles. Picking up the brush, I continued, 'If you have not a preference for a dinner dress, my lady, I should recommend the crimson with flounces. As for your hair, may I—'

'I am going to bathe first,' she cut in. 'The streets were hatefully dusty today. You will find the hip bath just next door. But yes, the crimson will look very well. My emeralds will set it off.'

'Will your hair have time to dry before dinner if we wash it?' I asked anxiously.

'No, you are right. Brush it out and pin it up, I will try not to get it wet.'

By the time I had gone to the kitchen, filled pails with steaming water and carried them upstairs to the dressing room, my fingers were slick. They refused to cooperate with the buttons on Lady Rose's diaphanous muslin dress. The material adhered to her skin where she had perspired, but there was no odour to it – or if there were, it was lost in the fug of steam and the orange blossom mixed in the bath.

'Oh, this gown is always a torment,' she sighed, placing her hands on her hips. 'It is the style, you know.

I have heard of ladies being sewn into and cut out of them!' She laughed and the movement produced an arch in her back. The buttons finally slipped free.

'Well,' I said in relief, 'we shall not need to take the scissors to this fine muslin.'

White and sprigged, it retained the warmth of her. I laid it carefully on the chaise longue. It looked like a girl fallen into a swoon.

Somehow the stays were easier; the laces yielded to my touch without protest. Lady Rose stood before me in only her shift, and she would wear that to bathe.

'Come and help me in,' she ordered.

Leaning on my arm, she descended into the water. Her shift bloomed then clung to her legs like a winding sheet as she sat down. When I turned to hand her the wash-ball, two hints of palest pink had appeared where the material stretched over her breasts.

They appeared full and round. About her stomach also, an intimation of ripeness. Might these be the early signs of breeding?

I had served a lady, Mrs Farley, through pregnancy before. There would be gowns to let out and a variety of orders to place. My mind reeled as it considered the responsibilities that would fall upon me.

'Will you refill my snuffbox while I dine, Stevens? It is in my reticule, upon the bed.' She paddled her hands in the water, unconscious of my scrutiny.

'Yes, my lady.'

There was no labour in beautifying Lady Rose; nature lent me a helping hand. But she announced herself delighted when she stood before the cheval mirror and admired the hair I had styled *à la Sappho*, with a green ribbon threaded through to complement her necklace.

I hoped aloud that Burns would see it.

'I hope she will choke upon it,' agreed Lady Rose.

The rooms seemed quiet and forlorn after she had left. They were mine now, to tidy and take pride in, but I felt ghostly in them; something passing through like the stain of breath upon a mirror.

Nothing stirred the bathwater, yet I saw ripples of light, playing upon the ceiling. My pail lay upon the floor. Gently, I picked it up and scooped it through the water. The warmth had faded. Nothing of Lady Rose's body heat remained, only her scent. I held out my hand, inspected my wet fingertips.

I do not know how long I squatted there. I am not sure at what point I released the pail and let it sink. I only remember the relentless *drip, drip* as I cupped the water into my hands and let it trickle away.

Then I stood and removed my clothes.

Nobody could enter through the locked outer door. No footfalls or speech sounded in the corridors. Yet as I slipped one foot into the water, I had the strangest sensation of being watched.

Easing myself down, I closed my eyes and inhaled. Thought how it must feel to be Lady Rose: to have a person to dress you, to pour your baths. She was pleased with me. Called me 'her' Stevens. I thought of her eating, showing off her hair to Sir Arthur, asking how he liked it.

But when I opened my eyes, the enchantment melted away. My body, so inferior to that of Lady Rose, hunched beneath greying liquid. Shame heated my cheeks. I could not understand how I had come to commit so profligate an action.

Rising quickly, I climbed out of the hip bath. My feet squeaked wet upon the floor. Drips trickled down my arms to form pools.

Bundling up the used towels, I scrubbed at my skin with a kind of desperation.

How much time had passed? Suppose I had missed my appointment with the housekeeper? Or if Lady Rose should return to her rooms and find me? I should be in disgrace on my very first day.

Puddles covered the floor, the towels lay in a tangle. My heart beat fast, panicked.

When I drew my clothes back on and tidied my hair, I did not appear to be cleansed by my ablutions.

I had never felt more mired in dirt.

Chapter 6

Looking back, those first weeks seem idyllic, but I know that they were not. Each day began with a tight chest. I passed the hours in a state of happy anxiety, feeling that I held something wonderful, precious and terribly frail in my hands.

For all my delight in my mistress and my new position, there were certainly provocations. Chief amongst them was Mrs Windrop.

Sir Arthur's mother was only a woman, it is true, but so tall, wide and imposing that she gave the impression of being legion. People called her looks aristocratic. In truth she had an aquiline, predatory nose and a flabby chin. How a handsome, seemingly genteel man like Sir Arthur came from her I will never know. Her late husband, I conjectured, must have been henpecked to death.

Sir Arthur was Mrs Windrop's only child, all she had left in the world, and perhaps that went some way to explain his endless patience with her. But it seemed to me she rode roughshod over both him and his wife.

Despite Sir Arthur's marriage, his mother retained possession of the housekeeping keys; she kept the accounts, saw to the staff, unlocked the tea caddy and all of the presses, as if Lady Rose simply did not exist. When questioned, she claimed she was merely helping to ease her daughter-in-law into her new role – of course she would pass the responsibilities over when Lady Rose gained more experience.

I expect Sir Arthur believed it, but any woman could see the insult this treatment implied.

One day, early on in my time at Hanover Square, I was disturbed from making Lady Rose's bed by a repeated banging on the back door. I seldom heard deliveries come and go, particularly as my mistress dedicated her mornings to piano practice, but this barrage lasted so long it forced its way into my notice.

Balling a pillowslip into my hands, I walked out onto the landing and peered over the balustrade. Lady Rose's music floated around the parquet floor and marble columns of the entrance hall like so many butterflies seeking a place to settle. But I could not enjoy it. That knock was an unwelcome percussion, jarring the tune.

'Where can the footmen have got to?' I complained, starting down the stairs.

I had not taken four steps before Mrs Windrop threw open the double doors and powered into the hall. I must confess, my courage failed me when I saw the displeasure that galvanised her large frame. Before she could spot me, I ducked down and squatted on the step, hidden behind the balustrade.

'What is that?' she demanded. 'Where are my staff?'

The banging stopped.

Shortly after, two footmen entered the hall from the other direction, carrying boxes. They did not have my luck; there was nowhere to hide and Mrs Windrop seized her prey immediately.

'What do you mean by letting that fellow beat a tattoo on my door? Is this a household or a drum shop?'

The younger footman tried to retract his head into his collar like a snail. 'I'm sorry, Mrs Windrop, madam, I was moving furniture for one of the house-maids when—'

She cut him off with a motion of the hand. 'Save your excuses for the butler, boy. I will not have this household appear tardy or backwards to any caller, be they gentleman or tradesperson. Do you understand?'

'Yes, madam.'

'Now, who was it? What have you there?'

'It is not addressed to—' the younger footman began, but his companion hurriedly spoke over the top of him.

'A delivery, madam, from the warehouse of—'

'The china!' she exclaimed without waiting for him to finish. 'It is the new service for our little assembly, of course. They would *insist* on visiting the warehouse without me. Well, let us see what kind of job they have made of it.'

With the bustle of setting down the boxes and winching them open, I saw my opportunity to escape back upstairs and took it.

I thought little of the incident as I went about my duties. Mrs Windrop had no right to open the boxes, but it was of a piece with the rest of her behaviour. However, just as I sat down with my needle to repair a tear in one of Lady Rose's petticoats, I was startled by the most terrific scream.

All of the work fell from my lap. I started towards the door, hearing raised voices, but as I began to recover my senses, I realised that the cry had not been one of pain or fear. It was the way Meg would scream, if she caught me wearing one of her gowns without permission.

There were sobs, slammed doors. I took a breath to prepare myself for whatever horror awaited, when the door was flung open and Lady Rose charged into the room.

Tears had stripped the cosmetics from her skin, and the hair I had so carefully arranged was tumbled down her back. Her hands clutched, of all things, a china dinner plate, as though it could preserve her life.

'Oh, *Stevens!*' she cried.

All the conduct books stressed that I should maintain a respectful distance from my employers, avoiding familiarity. But I could never dress and undress a person, brush their hair and wash their face, without contracting some feeling for them. And the eloquence of Lady Rose's looks would undo even the greatest stickler for propriety. I did not think – I embraced her.

She placed her head upon my shoulder and sobbed.

Gradually, I coaxed her to sit upon the chaise longue and administered her smelling salts. They stemmed the flow of tears, but her bosom still heaved and she breathed with her mouth open, as if she could not get enough air. With a gentle touch, I began to ease the plate from between her rigid fingers.

It was a pretty piece: a white background busily decorated with Prussian blue. The scene appeared Chinese in design. A pagoda surrounded by trees occupied the right-hand side of the plate. To the left was an expanse of water, spanned by a bridge. Three figures stood upon it, seemingly crossing, while a single boat floated beneath. At the top of the circle, before the thick blue border began, two birds flew. Something about it was familiar; I thought perhaps I had seen the design before.

Lady Rose followed my gaze and let her fingers fall slack.

'Do you ... like it, Stevens?' she asked in a small voice.

I took the plate fully into my hands and apprised it anew. It was perhaps a little over-decorated, unlike the simple floral pattern we currently used. The reliance on the colour blue was also striking. It took the eye a second to adjust. 'I think it very pretty. Has it a name?'

'The Willow pattern.' She shuffled along the chaise longue. 'Here. Sit beside me. I will tell you the story of it.'

I hesitated, but the way Lady Rose spoke to me levelled the distinction of rank. She might be conversing with a sister. I wondered if she had siblings at home. None of them had called upon her in the time I'd worked there. She seemed terribly isolated.

I brushed my skirts and sat down.

'Now,' she began, wiping at her cheeks. Her voice remained hoarse, but she was trying to sound composed. 'There was once an old rich mandarin whose daughter was exceedingly beautiful. He was a proud man and arranged for her to marry a duke. But his daughter did not love the duke. She loved the humble gardener.' She pointed at the plate. 'There are the trees where the lovers met. Here is the wall the mandarin built, to try and keep the gardener out. The wedding was due to take place on the day when the blossom fell from the willow tree. The duke arrived to claim his bride, bearing a large box of jewels.' She offered me a watery smile. 'But the daughter would not obey her father. She took the jewels, found her lover and fled. See? On the bridge. She is carrying the jewel box. The gardener has a staff. And there is that horrid mandarin, chasing them with a whip.'

'They will escape in the boat,' I guessed, running my fingertip over the design.

Lady Rose sighed. 'That was the plan, Stevens. But the mandarin's soldiers caught the lovers, and they killed them.'

I stared at her in horror. She very nearly laughed at the expression on my face.

'It is not the end of the story, you goose! Look.' She indicated the birds, flying together at the top. 'The gods took pity, and transformed the lovers into a pair of beautiful doves. Now they fly together, forever, entirely free.'

There was an air of wistfulness as she said this. I considered the plate and went over the story in my mind. It did not take a great deal of penetration to understand why Lady Rose would be drawn to such a tale. She played the part of the lowly gardener in her own marriage. Mrs Windrop wanted a richer bride for her son, but Sir Arthur, in perhaps the only act of filial disobedience in his life, had followed his heart. I recalled the way Mrs Windrop had stormed into the hall and ordered the footmen about. I did not have to stretch my imagination far to picture her as a mandarin brandishing a whip.

'I think,' I said slowly, 'that I may have seen this pattern before. But I did not know it had a name, or a story.'

I wished my words back instantly. A curtain seemed to fall over Lady Rose's face, erasing all the joy her tale had brought.

'You have hit upon the problem, Stevens. Of course you have seen it before. Everyone has.' She dropped her head into her hands. 'How could I have been such a dolt?'

'Whatever do you mean?'

'Artie let me choose. I was delighted to finally have a choice! But they will not let me pick again, now.' Her eyes began to swim. 'I always loved that story, Stevens. And the blue is so charming! But it is cheap. Cheaply produced, made by transfer, she says, as if I could possibly know ...'

Emotion strangled her voice. Holding the plate in one hand, I patted her back sympathetically.

'A tasteless, shabby attempt at gentility, my mother-in-law calls it. China anyone might own. She said she would rather be seen dead than serve her guests on such plates, and I have to tell you, Stevens, I was very nearly ready to oblige her.' She did not see my smile. 'I daresay you think me prodigiously shocking.'

'My lady, it seems to me that your nerves have been sorely tried,' I said gently. 'It is an ... upheaval, marriage. And then you have been tiring yourself with preparations for the assembly. Your piano practice ...'

She sighed, closed her eyes. 'I *am* tired, Stevens. I am very tired.'

Once again, I thought of the night she had bathed and the hints of pregnancy about her person. Tearfulness and lethargy supported my theory.

There was a tap at the door.

'Rose?' Sir Arthur, concerned.

'Leave me in peace, Artie!' Her voice splintered as she called out. 'I cannot bear it, not now.'

There was a moment of silence, then we heard his footsteps retreating.

Lady Rose opened her eyes. 'I have failed him. He did try to take my part, but ... That old harridan is right. I do not want to make him appear vulgar in front of his guests at the assembly. He has risked so much for my sake. I could not stand it if others began to think of me as his cheap bride ...'

'Some milk thickened with rice,' I suggested, rising to my feet and placing the plate carefully upon her dressing table. 'And some chamomile tea. That will soothe you, my lady.'

'Yes, I daresay it will. Thank you, Stevens.' She nodded, as if she were trying to shake sense into her head. 'I am being terribly mawkish. I am sure I shall feel more secure in my marriage once I have given Sir Arthur an heir. Mrs Windrop is bound to move away when we have a family of our own. Children are the cornerstone of all solid unions, are they not?'

I curtseyed and left the room to fetch her victuals. I did not like to tell her that in my mother's profession, children were snatched away with more regularity than husbands, and there was no law or sacred vow that could make them stay.

Chapter 7

On the day of the assembly, hothouse flowers arrived in great swathes of colour. The housemaids spent hours polishing the crystal; Mrs Glover was here, there and everywhere. Anticipation crackled in the air like the static before a storm.

Usual duties fell by the wayside. Everyone scrubbed, fetched or cleaned until their backs ached. But all the while, we kept our spirits. There was a sense of being part of something bigger than ourselves, a thrill in knowing that our master's success depended upon us. And no matter how hard we laboured, there was something to cheer us along: music beneath the clatter. Lady Rose playing Handel on the Broadwood over and over again. Her performance was without flaw.

Standing before the cheval mirror that night was a lady born: her skin powdered ivory and kissed with rouge at the apples of her cheeks. Elderberries had darkened her eyebrows and lashes. Against the pale gold sarsenet of her overdress, her hair appeared richer than ever, a glorious nut-brown. Coating my hands in pomade, I made the final twists to the curls at her forehead before applying sprigs of fresh flowers.

'Oh, Stevens,' she gasped, clenching and unclenching her hands at her sides. 'Do you think I will do?'

I thought her much finer than the company below deserved.

Gently, I pushed a curl from her brow. 'I think the colour becomes you very well, my lady. I hope you are pleased with my work.'

'Pleased?' She showed her teeth, pearl-white against lips stained with rosehip. 'You have been a treasure. Whatever would I do without you?'

I turned away to hide my grin; I feared it would make me look ridiculous.

'I do not recall being so frightened in all my life. Not even on my wedding day. You would not credit the butterflies in my stomach, Stevens.'

I did, for they were fluttering in my own.

Carriages crowded the square and jammed half of George Street that night. I lost count of the number of linkboys I saw dashing past the window. Sounds of chatter and clinking glasses swelled from the *piano nobile*.

I could have asked the footmen for a report of my lady's performance. Concealed in the servants' hall, I might have heard the odd note and caught the faintest echo of her voice. But that was not good enough for me. The image of her sitting at the piano was as clear as a painting in my mind: the golden dress reflected in the polished wood, her full lips open in song, holding the company spellbound.

I could not rest until I had seen it with my own eyes.

On the pretence of visiting the privy, I left our quarters and crept upstairs. Marks already scuffed the floorboards that we had polished with such care. Someone had stepped in a splash of wine and trodden it across the Turkey rug.

All the company were gathered in the drawing room. Their conversation made a relentless buzz. Cutlery clattered – the last of the supper disappearing. No one could hear my footsteps, or the creak as the double doors parted in the smallest crack.

I peered through with one eye, searching for Lady Rose.

Her cheeks were set like alabaster and I was not sure it was entirely the work of my bismuth powder. Tension gathered at the corners of her eyes, as if she had the headache.

Mrs Windrop eluded my spying eye, but Sir Arthur's tall person was visible. Red grazed his nose and cheeks – the result of too much Madeira. It was unusual to see him carefree and felicitous. As he laughed with his neighbour, he looked years younger. He had every right to be happy with his wealth, his knighthood and his fine wife; it seemed that he was truly allowing himself to enjoy it for the first time.

Which made what followed all the worse.

Still smiling, Sir Arthur stood and thanked the company for coming. 'Shall we not have more music? I have a great desire for a song. Lady Rose, can we persuade you?'

She managed to appear reluctant, casting her gaze down and smiling sweetly, as if she had not rehearsed weeks for this very moment. 'I am fortunate to have such an exquisite instrument. Perhaps the young ladies might appreciate the chance to play it.'

The spinsters mimicked her downward glance, as a lady is taught to, but with less conviction. I saw one redhead flexing her fingers in anticipation.

'Ever kind, ever thoughtful,' Sir Arthur replied warmly. 'But they look for you to light the way, my love.'

Until she rose to her feet, I thought it the usual act of modesty. Yet the way she held herself, the square set to her shoulders, told another story.

Pain.

How did Sir Arthur not observe it?

No one else knew her, no one else cared enough to watch her every gesture. They were so used to seeing ladies dissemble that they missed the faltering steps she took towards the pianoforte. They failed to notice how violently the music sheets rustled when she arranged them.

I saw her gulp, poise her fingers over the keys.

Then I saw the blood.

Just a spot, the size of a guinea, where the sarsenet met the piano stool. Other eyes might mistake it for a drop of red wine. But I recalled her words about butterflies in the dressing room, took in the sweat beading her brow, and my stomach plunged in horror.

She began to play.

Non lo dirò col labbro, the aria she had practised a thousand times. Not a lengthy song. Perhaps she would make it through. Her fingers worked automatically, faultless.

But the spot spread.

I do not believe she knew what was happening. This was simply another inconvenience she must work through to appear perfect before her mother-in-law and those who said she was not good enough for Sir Arthur.

My brave mistress. She bowed slightly on her stool, causing me to drive my fingernails into the edge of the door. If I had not done that, I would have run straight to her.

Perhaps I should have.

For as her voice rose, fragile, wavering, another patch of red appeared on the white muslin, loud as a scream. Someone must see it now, I thought. They must stop her.

But she went on singing.

She must have felt the warmth in her lap. I could practically feel it in mine, and the pain. One key clanged, discordant. Heads raised.

A low whisper began to circulate. I was vaguely aware of Sir Arthur rising to his feet. But my gaze remained upon my lady, the way she regarded the key as if it had bitten her. Her eyes seemed to cross.

She slipped sideways from the stool and went crashing to the floor.

A lady screamed.

Such was the commotion that no one remarked me barrelling into the drawing room, where I had no place to be. I reached Lady Rose's side at the same time as Sir Arthur. But while he wrung his hands and called her name, I was on my knees, checking her head for injury.

Brown locks tumbled from their pins. The flowers lay squashed beneath, where the base of her skull met the floor. Mercifully, I found nothing more than a small bump upon her scalp; the only blood was leeching down her dress.

One of the young ladies caught sight of it and cried out like a ninny-not, 'Blood! She's dead, she's dead!'

Hysteria erupted.

Everyone was up, moving in blind panic and of no earthly use to Lady Rose. I was surrounded by a mass of knee breeches and swishing skirts.

'Your coat, sir,' I hissed up at Sir Arthur.

'What?'

'Give me your coat, to cover her.'

Blinking, he stripped the garment off and thrust it at me. 'What's happening to her, Stevens?' he asked desperately. 'Have you salts, can you bring her back to herself?'

Rather than draping the coat about her shoulders as I usually would, I arranged it carefully to cover the growing red stain. I could not bear for others to gawp upon it.

'I believe, sir, it would be kinder to restore her once she is in the comfort of her own room. Will you help me to move her?'

'*Me?*'

I could not keep my temper then, but spoke through gritted teeth. 'I should prefer it if the other servants did not see her in this condition. It is *your* child that she is losing. Sir.'

How little the rich understand. He lay with her twice a week – I knew, for I changed the sheets and sometimes found him asleep next to her when I arrived with the morning chocolate – but he had not noticed the changes to her figure. I do not believe he even comprehended where the blood was coming from until I spoke those words.

For an instant he swayed, and I thought he might faint too. 'Of course. I shall take her head and shoulders, Stevens, if you can manage with the feet.'

Ladies are always heavier than you expect. In a dead faint, her limbs flopped out of control. Sir Arthur clamped one hand beneath each armpit and cradled her head against his stomach; I took hold around her ankles, trying desperately to make sure the coat stayed wrapped around her waist. The guests parted for us instantly.

I caught sight of Mrs Windrop by the door of the drawing room. I do not know which emotion I expected her countenance to convey, but I was not prepared for her flaring nostrils. As if Lady Rose had done this on purpose, spoilt the party like a child who cannot be trusted with nice things.

'A physician, madam.' I threw the sentence at her with full force. It seemed to rock her back on her heels. 'She requires a physician. Perhaps you might send for someone.'

I do not know if she was the one responsible for the man who did finally arrive, an hour later. By the time Sir Arthur and I had carried our precious load into the corridors, all the servants were moving. The ladies' screams must have shivered down the walls and alerted them.

A footman carefully took Sir Arthur's burden from him, but the master followed us closely up the stairs to the rooms I had tidied just hours before. Our presence disturbed the clouds of orange blossom, added a coppery tang of blood.

Pushing the waiting nightgown aside, I laid her feet on the bed and removed her shoes. One of the housemaids built a fire on my direction. The footmen left once they saw I was preparing to strip our mistress and wash her legs.

Sir Arthur remained.

'Will she wake?' he demanded.

'I do not like to rouse her, sir. She will panic to see the blood. We had better wait until she is clean and comfortable, and the company have left ... It will only distress her to know the party was not a success.'

He exhaled. 'The company. I had forgotten ... My mother will have to see to that.'

'This will be unpleasant, sir,' I admitted. 'It may be better for you to step outside.'

Sir Arthur shook his head. 'I will not leave her.'

So I began the weary task of removing the outfit I had constructed with such care. Lady Rose was heavy and lumpen, a sack of vegetables in my hands. Her skin was clammy to the touch. The maid in me was already considering how to wash out the bloodstains. Nothing would avail. Like the evening, the gown was ruined.

Such fine hopes she had nurtured for this assembly. And although only a monster could view her without pity, I doubted gossip would record the incident in a kindly light. Of all the places, of all the times for this to happen. How would she raise her head in society again?

I would have to sustain her. I should be her true friend, where others fell away.

'My poor Rose,' Sir Arthur moaned. 'Only look at her, Stevens.'

I did. The vibrant colours of earlier had been erased. In the nightdress she appeared small, vulnerable. I found myself handling her with the same reverence as I would a corpse.

'I cannot bear to see her so,' he sobbed and raised a hand over his eyes.

I held my tongue, did not tell him the truth.

Could not tell him that to my eyes, this was when she was truly beautiful: at the moment of fragility, when she required only me.

Chapter 8

In the days that followed Lady Rose's miscarriage, I retained sole possession of her. She could not endure anyone else – not to change her bed or mend her fire, not even to fetch up her food tray. Sir Arthur she did permit, but he was not the same man who had watched me wash her. Faced with her tears he was stiff, awkward.

'I have failed him, Stevens,' she would sob into my arms after he had left. 'He knows that I have failed him.'

I scarcely knew how to deny it. Blameless though Lady Rose was, there could be no doubt that the fiasco had damaged Sir Arthur's standing. Like a porcelain figure, a wife was prized for smoothness and lustre, degraded by the slightest flaw. Lady Rose had been … chipped. We could not recapture that air of promise and glamour she once exuded.

Enquiries were made after her health, but not so many as I expected. Visitors stayed away.

Deep within me vibrated the old fear: that I had somehow caused this disaster. My tainted presence falling over my mistress like a cloud. But even my mother, who was apt to blame me for much, did not seem to think Lady Rose's plight out of the usual way. Miscarriages were common in her line of work; her letters were full of practical instructions to restore my mistress to health. She wrote out a receipt for me: a broth made with knuckles of mutton, spring water and hartshorn.

No amount of nostrums, however, could repair the emotional fissures. Only I saw them. When I insisted on taking Lady Rose for air in the carriage, she looked utterly terrified.

'People will see me,' she gasped. 'They will whisper.'

She was right. The *beau monde* were out in flocks upon those breezy summer days, gossiping behind their fans. Instead of sunlight, we saw the glint of a thousand quizzing glasses turned in our direction.

My mistress leant her head upon my shoulder in the carriage, as if the weight of her mind and its thoughts was more than she could support.

There must be somewhere I could take her. A single place in this great City where she could find peace.

I recalled how she loved the story of the Willow pattern about the lovers fleeing across a bridge. And just that morning, I had been reading her poetry from Mr Wordsworth.

'I have an idea.' I rapped upon the roof. 'Driver, take us to Westminster Bridge.'

When Mr Wordsworth composed his famous lines, he found the City in repose. It was not so upon that day. Traffic clopped steadily over the stone arches. Sails fluttered from a mass of boats and ships upon the river. Arm-in-arm, we struggled alongside other pedestrians to find a vantage spot unpolluted by dung.

As we stopped and looked out, the world seemed to open up like a casket. Towers and domes were silhouetted against the brightness of the sky. Fields stretched far into the distance. The abbey shone with a kind of hazy radiance I had only seen in paintings.

It gave me hope. This time, I thought, I will stay in my position. I will coax my mistress back to health and nothing else will go wrong. I will feel needed, secure. Lady Rose will love me. She will love me forever.

Lowering her head from the glare of the sun, she considered the water seething silently beneath. 'Did you never think of jumping in, Stevens?'

I almost laughed. 'Into the Thames?'

'Yes.'

I shook my head at her, sure this was her idea of a jest. The rim of her bonnet obscured her expression. 'That would be a very foolish thing for me to do, my lady, considering that I cannot swim.'

'No more can I.'

She spoke calmly, matter of fact.

Sunlight glanced off the river, dazzling my eyes. From this distance it appeared cool and glassy. With dust swelling up from the road behind us, the idea of water was inviting. I had heard of young bucks leaping into the Serpentine in the height of summer, emerging to scandalise the ladies with their dripping shirts. No doubt that was what Lady Rose meant.

'It is not at all safe,' I cautioned. 'It is not like the shallow areas in the sea where they take the bathing machines. The current is strong, the waters are rough.'

'What would they do to me?'

'They would toss you about. Chill you.' I put a hand upon her arm, a nurse once more. 'Promise me you will never attempt it, my lady. With all the refuse in the river you would be torn. Cut to pieces.'

She turned then, looked me squarely in the eye. 'Sometimes, I think I should like to be.'

Chapter 9

I had been fond of my previous mistresses. Of course I had. I wanted them to adore me. But with Lady Rose it was something else: something greedy, all-consuming.

As the months passed, I found ways to make her smile. Cowper's translation of Homer from the circulating library, marzipan from Gunter's. Gradually, she lost the wild and hopeless look I had seen on the bridge.

She still refused to venture out into society, but this pleased me; we spent the days instead reading and sewing together like sisters. In all honesty, she showed me more affection than Meg had ever done. No doubt this was what Mrs Windrop meant when she complained about her daughter-in-law's low breeding. No one born to her station would ever treat a servant with such familiarity. It was dangerous, she said. It bred 'ideas' amongst the lower orders.

She was right in that one respect.

Like any lonely person I trusted too quickly. Let my heart believe it had found a home. At night I would tear myself away from Lady Rose, ceding the ground to Sir Arthur, but I kept her in my dreams. And in the morning, when I awoke, I would hurry to fix her chocolate.

One day, I took up the Willow pattern cup, only to find her already awake and out of bed, standing before the press in her nightgown. Its doors were thrown open and she was rummaging inside.

'I fear you are punishing me, my lady,' I teased as I entered the room and set the chocolate down on the dressing table.

She looked quite startled. 'You, Stevens? Whatever would I punish you for?'

I smiled. 'Is this not the method you took with Burns? Disrupting her careful ordering?'

'Good heavens.' Lady Rose glanced from me to the press and back again, sheepish. 'I did not stop to consider. Is there a pattern to its arrangement?'

But when she saw me chuckle, she began to laugh herself.

'If there is a particular item you require, my lady, perhaps it would be best if you ask me to fetch it. That is my purpose, after all.'

She threw up her hands and huffed. I was glad to see some of the life returning to her. 'It is no use. I wanted to surprise you, but you see I am completely ineffectual without your help.'

'Surprise me? I do not believe anyone has ever given me a surprise.'

The eyes she turned upon me grew tender. 'Have they not, my Stevens? Then I feel all the more churlish for bungling it. Come here, please.' I went to her side. She laid a hand upon my shoulder. 'Do you remember a travelling dress? Fawn-coloured. Perhaps it was made of nankeen, but I am not certain.'

I was able to produce it at once. Fawn-coloured but poplin, not nankeen, and fitted tight about the bodice in the style of a riding habit. Dark blue frogging ran the length of the outfit, terminating in a broad band around the hem to catch dust. I had never dressed Lady Rose in it – I understood it was one of the gowns from her wedding journey.

She clapped her hands together. 'That is precisely the one. What is your opinion of it, Stevens? Do you like it? Is it not prodigiously handsome?'

I said it was.

'You shall have to take it in, of course. But I think it shall do very well. It is exactly designed to bring out the colour of your hair and your eyes.'

'My …?' The question died as she pushed the dress upon me. It smelt of her: orange blossom. A textured surface like skin. To think she had beheld such a beautiful item and seen me in it. 'You want *me* to wear this?'

She nodded, beaming.

'Are we … going on a journey?'

'No, Stevens. We have *been* on a journey. A very dark and disagreeable one.' Her brow tightened, the smile dropped from her face. 'I want you to have this for your own as a pledge that I shall never forget. Nothing shall erase the memory of the one who travelled by my side when others would not.'

Tears filmed my eyes; I looked up to see them on Lady Rose's lashes.

'It is too costly,' I stuttered. 'I cannot. It was my duty ... my pleasure. I do not require thanks, my lady.'

'But you have them, all the same.'

It seemed as if my entire life had been building to this: recognition, affection and an assurance it would never fade. Now that I had them, I was not sure what to do. Somehow, it was still not enough.

Lady Rose leaned forwards, kissed my cheek.

I thought my heart would explode.

'Now take the dress to your room. Put it away before Mrs Windrop sees. She never gives Burns her gowns until they are at least two years out of style. The last thing I need is another homily on my *extravagance*.'

'Yes, my lady.'

I emerged from her suite of rooms wearing an irrepressible grin and a small fortune draped across my arm, the finest gown I should ever own. There could be little occasion to wear it outside the secrecy of my own bedchamber, but it pleased me to possess something of hers.

It was not until I reached the passage leading to my room that I saw Mrs Windrop, standing in an open doorway. Watching me.

Hers was a gaze of fury. Full of outrage to see an exquisite garment, paid for by her son's money, in my grubby servant's hands. Or so I thought, at the time.

Now I wonder.

Wonder if she was not viewing me as I was, but looking into the future, like the witch that I fancied her to be.

Perhaps she saw that same gown, stained with blood and pushed to the bottom of a trunk.

Chapter 10

Sir Arthur resented our intimacy. He wanted his wife to cleave to him, as she did to me, but quite how he expected this result only he can answer. It is a rich man's way, I suppose: to anticipate reward for a fractional amount of effort.

The day after his mother had seen me with the travelling dress, he summoned me to his library.

I entered with some trepidation, for the room was unfamiliar to me, painted in a dull olive green with an Axminster carpet at the centre. It had all the accoutrements of a gentleman's library: the bookshelves crowned with busts, a spinning globe, decanters of whisky-coloured liquid. But it all looked rather too new, too much like a stage set at the theatre. Sir Arthur did not appear at home behind his desk. For the first time, I saw him as the aristocracy did: a tradesman playing at gentility.

'Ah, Stevens. Do sit down.'

The chair was made of leather. It squeaked as I put my weight upon it. I felt a flush of mortification.

'How is your mistress, Stevens?'

'Much recovered, sir. She has taken several airings in the carriage with me this week and is returning to herself. But it would be wise not to push her too far. She remains somewhat delicate, at times.'

He passed his tongue over his lips. His face seemed a little leaner than usual. 'Yes. My mother does not recall being indisposed for so long on similar occasions, but as you say, my wife is … fragile. I am most anxious that nothing should occur to distress her.'

'I trust it shall not, sir. You may rely upon me. I have some experience in nursing nervous, as well as physical, disorders.'

He raised his eyes to mine. A challenge bristled there. 'I have been reacquainting myself with your nursing experience,' he said, moving a paper on his desk. My character letters lay before him. 'I did not see your references, originally.'

'I gave them to Mrs Glover when first we met.'

'Yes.' He waved a hand. 'I let my wife employ her own maid as she pleased. But I would not be a responsible husband if I did not make my own enquiries now, would I?'

'No, sir.'

I itched to point out that I had been in my position for many months, and this dilatory effort hardly made him a model spouse. Naturally, I did not.

'I understand that your first mistress, a ...' He fumbled amongst the papers, '... Mrs Wild. She passed from this life, did she not?'

I bowed my head. 'Yes, sir. God rest her soul. She was an elderly lady. I had been in her service for two years ... The event was somewhat expected.'

'Her sons certainly praise your care of her throughout her indisposition.'

They were nice young men. It was always a pleasure when they paid a visit, which they were scrupulous enough to do each time their mother took a bad turn. I had hoped, at the time of her death, that they might move me into one of their own households. I was not so fortunate.

I returned to the Registry Office, and that had led me to Mrs Farley.

'Your next employer,' Sir Arthur went on, 'is particularly eloquent about your attention to her children. Little Robert, it seems, was a favourite of yours?'

'They were all dear children, sir. But Robert was the best of them. Perhaps that is why ...' My voice caught, remembering that cherubic face. 'I often told Mrs Farley he was too good for this earth.'

He scrubbed a hand across his chin, watching me. 'Yes ... because he died too, did he not? And you were a prodigious comfort to Mrs Farley in the years that followed.'

Tears pricked at my eyes. 'I hope I was, sir.'

'And you left the position because …?'

'My mistress was widowed and remarried. The children were sent to school and the household retrenched.'

His expression did not change. I wondered how Lady Rose could be married to a man of so few emotions. 'So that leaves us with Miss Gillings.'

A rare creature: a spinster who inherited funds. At forty, she still held out hope of catching a husband.

'Miss Gillings was an excessively kind mistress, sir. She treated me more as a companion than a maid. It was my honour to accompany her as chaperone to a selection of parties. I was very sorry to leave her service.'

'She left *you*, it seems,' he returned. 'For Naples. A better climate. Quite a perilous journey, in these times. Was she so very desperate?'

'The matter of her health became pressing, sir.'

'Yet she did not take you with her? Despite all your skills?'

This was a sore point. I tried not to show how it ruffled me. 'I should have gone, had my mistress requested it, but I do not believe she could justify the expenditure. Besides, sir, my father may have objected. I am his only unmarried daughter. Neither he nor my mother would wish me to be so far away.'

His eyebrows lowered. 'That is touching. I was not aware you were close to your family. I do not see you leave the house to visit them, even on your half-days.'

He had caught me out: my parents would gladly see me as far away as the Antipodes, if it caused no embarrassment to them. Only Meg seemed to care, and with her it was the habitual, weary concern of an elder sister rather than true love.

'No, sir. I keep myself available, in case I am required. My duties must come first.'

'Indeed. Well, happily it appears that your last mistress Miss Gillings survived on the Continent without your company. To judge from the hand she writes, I might fancy her returned to full health.'

'That would be a great pleasure. I hope it is the case.' It smarted to have all my failures read out before me. Any other master would be delighted with these unimpeachable references, but Sir Arthur was not. From the tone of his voice, I could tell he nursed the same suspicion I did: that I was hexed, an omen of bad luck. I shifted in my chair, eliciting another farcical squeak. 'May I ask, sir, to what all these questions tend? Have I dissatisfied you in some way?'

Sir Arthur steepled his fingers. 'No … I do not believe there is any cause for complaint.' How carefully he worded it. 'You seem quite as dear to Lady Rose as you have been to all your previous mistresses.'

It did not sound like a compliment, coming from his lips.

'I am very fortunate in my position.'

'All the same …' He gathered my character letters into a pile and bound them with string. 'Vast as your experience is … I believe I shall consult a midwife, should my lady find herself with child again.'

'Very good, sir.' Offended pride clipped my voice.

'That will be all, Stevens.'

He did not look up, did not see the way I clenched my jaw. It took a Herculean effort not to slam the door behind me.

Chapter 11

Anger has ever been a failing of mine. When it surges, it sings in my veins like a dram of gin. Any action seems possible, reasonable. It is only afterwards, when the fire fades, that I see the dark soot-stain of what I have done.

I thought I had conquered it in time for Lady Rose's next baby. Reconciled myself to the idea she would prefer the child's company to mine. Because after all, a baby would be a part of her: a girl with her heart-shaped face, or a boy with her melting brown eyes. Perhaps I could love it, too.

I would be there throughout its upbringing, and – who could say? – perhaps it would grow to favour me above the other servants. Perhaps it would call for me before its mother, as Robert Farley had done.

I could make it need me.

So after she missed her second course, I dedicated a few weeks' free time to sewing a complete set of baby clothes: barracoat, swaddling band, clouts and pilchers, two bonnets in hollie-point lace and a quilted gown. As the garments began to take shape, so did my affection for the stranger who would wear them. I grew impatient for chubby limbs to fill out the sleeves, a soft skull to place inside the caps. My tired fancy conjured up images of a baby that cooed and gurgled, a baby happy to be passed from its mother's breast to me.

It was on a Wednesday that everything began to unravel. Shortly before they struck the dinner gong, I tied off my last stitch and folded all the tiny clothes into a linen parcel which I secured with ribbon. If I took it down right now, my lady would have time to open it before I changed her dress. But I hesitated.

Unaccountably, my stomach came alive with nerves; I felt vulnerable, as if I was exposing part of myself in this gift. Showing, perhaps, how truly devoted I was: that I would sacrifice my leisure hours, sacrifice sleep itself, to make her smile.

Hugging the parcel to my chest, I took a breath and set off towards my lady's suite.

As I approached the door, I became aware of voices murmuring behind the wooden panels. The words were muffled.

I knocked.

'Oh, that will be Stevens.' My lady's rich tones rang clear now. 'Enter, Stevens.'

With some trepidation, I turned the knob. Entered the bedroom to see ... myself.

Or in fact a better version of myself; the woman I might have been, who had always eluded capture.

A dignified bearing. Hair of a darker colour tied neatly into a chignon at the back of her head. Her face rested, solemn, but the features were softened at the edges by a prettiness mine lacked. She stood with hands lightly clasped by her waist and her shoulders held high, carelessly highlighting the excellent cut of her plain navy gown.

'Stevens,' said Lady Rose, 'this is Mrs Friar.'

Friar nodded to me, pleasant enough. I did not know what to do with myself. The parcel of baby clothes seemed a ridiculous thing to be holding. I put it aside hurriedly on the bed, my practised speech all forgotten.

'I am pleased to meet you, Mrs Friar. Excuse my interruption. Will you be dressed for dinner, my lady?'

'Heavens!' Lady Rose looked down in dismay at her plain clothing. 'I had quite forgotten. Any gown should do. Did you let out the blue satin? I will wear that.'

I moved to the press to search out the gown, astonished that Mrs Friar did not seem to be going away.

Behind me, she cleared her throat. 'May I ask what you usually dine upon, Lady Rose? It may be wise to make some adjustment.'

'Nothing very exciting for today, Friar. Mutton, I believe. My mother-in-law Mrs Windrop takes the menus in hand, you had better speak with her.'

'As you wish, madam. And I would take it as a great favour if you declined any wine with your meal. Many liquids can be pernicious – I would not have you take anything stronger than barley water.'

Lady Rose caught my eye; hers widened, seemed on the point of a comical roll. 'Indeed? Well, of course, I shall do exactly as you say.'

'I will leave you to get dressed, madam. But Stevens,' I started, nettled by Mrs Friar's familiar use of my name, 'no stays. Jumps, if you must. I should prefer no constriction at this point.'

With that, Mrs Friar left the room.

My lady's lips twitched with amusement. 'Is she not impressive? Such assurance. She makes one feel quite safe.'

I smoothed out the blue satin, feeling as if I had gone mad. 'Yes … But if you'll pardon me … Who *is* she, my lady?'

Her laugh rang shrill. She moved over to the bed and slipped off her shoes. 'Well might you ask! She simply arrived this morning like an apparition. I had not the slightest idea she was coming.'

This hardly answered my question. Distractedly, I lay the blue satin down on the bed beside the bundle of baby clothes. What should I do with them now? My plan had all gone awry. I knew her moods and humours; she was not in the frame of mind to receive the present – or at least, not to give me the reaction I craved. To see her open the parcel without interest and put the clothes quietly aside would destroy me.

Holding my tongue, I began to unfasten my lady's dress.

'I never saw a woman like Mrs Friar,' she went on. 'I hear the nurses in hospitals are drunken frights, are they not? Then, of course, there are the useful apothecaries and good midwives like your own mother, but this Friar ... I think she has the air of a physician. Do not you? They tell me she assists one of the fashionable *accoucheurs* ... I cannot recall his name. I am glad we did not end up with *him*. You will call me outmoded, but I cannot abide the idea of a man interfering in these things. It is intrusive, indelicate.'

A sour taste crept into my mouth. 'Mrs Friar is here for the baby?' I slipped the gown from her shoulders and there it was, starting to show through her stays. I felt something in my own stomach, an abscess of jealousy quickening, growing.

'She tells me she has treated a number of women who have previously been ... disappointed.' A catch in her voice. 'The "lowering treatment" as she calls it, works wonders. How clever of Artie to find her! And to know, without even asking me, that I should not like a male *accoucheur*. He is terribly dear, Stevens. I pray I shall repay his attentions with a sturdy son. I could not bear—'

'Sir Arthur sent for her?' I had never interrupted my lady before.

Lady Rose peered over her shoulder, surprised. I noted one hand lay proudly on her small bump. 'To be sure, Stevens. Who else would do so?'

'I did not think ... We said ...' Betrayal was a bitter mouthful to swallow. She was speaking as if the baby had nothing at all to do with me. 'It is a surprise to hear, my lady, that is all. I thought him still in ignorance. You did not tell me you had made Sir Arthur aware of the pregnancy yet.'

'Oh.' Her lips parted in a little circle. 'Goodness. Did I not?' She shrugged her shoulders, as though it did not matter. 'How silly of me. I must have forgotten to say something.'

*

Looking back, my mind is clear enough to see that she was not unkind to me. She treated me a good deal better than most mistresses ever would. But that was the rub. With the 'interesting condition' she became a mistress again, gaining consequence each day. And I was no longer a sister, a friend, a confidante; merely a maid.

It was the 'lowering treatment', I believe, which had such an effect upon her moods. It seemed a barbaric procedure, not at all like something my mother would recommend. The day after Mrs Friar arrived, I came upstairs with my lady's morning chocolate, only to find that the blasted woman was already with her.

'Good morning,' I said.

Lady Rose glanced at me with her accustomed languid smile. 'Oh, good. Thank you, Stevens.' She put out her hands for the cup, but Mrs Friar's voice arrested them.

'What is in there?'

'Drinking chocolate.'

Mrs Friar shook her head. 'No. That will not do. Do not give her coffee, either. Some tea I shall permit – without sugar. I find the best things are fruit or herbal tisanes. I believe Her Majesty takes an orange tea. Now, *there* is a woman who has delivered many children safely to term.'

Lady Rose pursed her lips. 'Well, I suppose you had better take it back, Stevens.'

I left the room quietly enough, but I fear I made a terrible stomp going down the stairs. Burns was just emerging from the kitchen with Mrs Windrop's tray of tea and toast.

'You must take more care,' she tutted. 'The place for galloping hoydens is out on the street.'

Her sneer lingered as I poured the chocolate away and began to clatter the tea things about. The scullery maids shied out of my path.

Mrs Friar made me appear foolish without even trying. All I had learnt from my parents, the workings of the human body, seemed provincial in her presence.

When I returned with the cup of tea, I paused outside Lady Rose's door, listening to them talk.

'I fear you will ask me to forsake my snuffbox next.'

'No, madam, providing it is used in moderation.'

'To think that I did so many heedless things!' Lady Rose exclaimed. 'With my last child ... I was not certain, you see. But now I fear I must have hurt the poor creature, eating and drinking and riding about in the carriage as I did. Nobody warned me.'

'No, indeed. You were not to know, madam. Only those conversant with the very latest discoveries would be able to tell you. Our understanding of the child as it forms has changed.'

'Stevens's mother is a midwife.' I heard a strain in Lady Rose's voice. Not precisely distrust. Something worse: disappointment. 'It seems she must be rather a shabby one, for Stevens never said a word about any of this.'

Pride throbbed.

'No one can know what they are not taught, madam.'

'True,' she sighed. 'It is a prodigious shame. I had started to think my maid rather clever about these sort of things.'

Chapter 12

It felt like Yuletide once we had mulled the wine. Of course we would not decorate the house until Christmas Eve, but already preparations were afoot. Mrs Glover had put in the order for the hog's head and decided where we would hang the bows of evergreen. The kitchen took on the fragrance of celebration: citrus, plums and cloves.

The gaoler – as I had come to think of Mrs Friar – would not permit my mistress a taste of the season's delights. Nothing sweet over the entire Christmas period, no rich meat and no assemblies either. While I would be rejoicing in Lady Rose's company, glad to keep her all to myself, she would feel forlorn.

I could not bear that. So, pouring a little of the wine into a long-stemmed glass, I sneaked out of the kitchen and went in search of her.

There were few occasions I found Lady Rose alone in those days, but I could be sure that her piano practice would remain unmolested by Mrs Friar. She was playing now, filling the house with carols. I followed her clear voice up the stairs, as I had that night of the assembly: stealthily, hoping no one could see me. It was brave of her, I thought, to return to that room and its instrument in her current condition. A superstitious woman might fear the same thing would happen again.

But she was singing of joy. 'While Shepherds Watched Their Flocks'. I had heard it a thousand times, even sung it once myself in a wassail, yet it fell upon my ears as a new-made creation. Pushing the door ajar, I peeped through.

The drawing room looked tired, the carpet spread once more over the floorboards. They had turned the piano to face a different direction. All I could see was the back of Lady Rose's neck and a scoop of skin before the buttons started on her muslin dress.

She must have felt the heat of my gaze for her hand faltered and a note rang false. Cursing beneath her breath, she leant back on the stool and shook out her cramped fingers.

'My lady,' I whispered.

'Stevens? Is that you? What do you do here?'

Creeping in, I placed a finger to my lips. The door clicked shut behind me.

She did not smile, as she used to at my arrival. In fact, she did not appear like her usual self at all. The baby had made her put on flesh, but her cheeks had lost their petals thanks to the 'lowering treatment'.

Last time round she had glowed, a flower budding, yet with this pregnancy she was drab as a caterpillar's cocoon. Mrs Friar had much to answer for.

'Forgive me for disturbing you, my lady,' I murmured. 'I just thought … while she is not here.' I stepped closer, proffering the glass. 'It does not really feel like Christmas without a sip of mulled wine.'

Its aroma lifted with the steam, berry-rich.

I saw her wet her lips. Tempted. 'I did not ask you for a drink, Stevens.'

'No. I merely thought you might enjoy it. It seems unfair to keep you from everything sugary or pleasant to taste. Especially while you are bled so regularly.'

She closed the lid over the piano keys. 'Mrs Friar has forbidden wine.'

'Yes. But Mrs Windrop has also forbidden a great many things, and that has not stopped us,' I wheedled. The glass hovered between us. With all my strength, I willed her to take it.

She averted her face. Would not look at the wine, lest she succumb. 'I find Mrs Friar's restrictions are administered with a much kinder intent than my mother-in-law's.'

'Perhaps they are, my lady. I hope so. But you do look very pale. Drawn. It seems rather cruel of her to use you so.'

Her shoulders set rigid. 'Mrs Friar is trying to help me protect this baby.'

She would not drain the glass, but in a strange way I felt she was draining me, drop by drop. All our past association seemed to be trickling away. I had always anticipated her needs, but now she was denying them, acting as if I offered not a treat, but a serpent.

'Surely one sip …' I smiled.

'I am surprised at you, Stevens. You, who know how I suffered.'

I crept closer. 'It was not wine that took your last child.'

'Do you know that? Truly? Can you swear with your hand upon your heart? For I cannot.' She wrapped her arms around her belly. 'I have no idea what did it. I trust Mrs Friar. I must follow her advice.'

'But I have never heard of such a thing before, my lady.'

My world narrowed to that one glass: it seemed that if only I could persuade her to take it, everything would be mended. I would endure Mrs Friar without a word of reproach for the length of the confinement – beyond, if required. Only let Lady Rose taste this wine and prove her regard for me.

'My mother is a midwife,' I tried. 'She knows the ways of a child inside the womb.'

'There are … new discoveries,' she spluttered, weakening.

'Nearly every mother consumes alcohol during her confinement. Why, I have seen wine fed to a newborn baby.'

'All the same, I will not. Please take it away.'

'Surely you don't think I would suggest any action that would harm—'

'Take it away!' She did not realise how close I was standing. As she flung out her hand to enforce the sentence, she knocked the glass from my hands.

I gasped. Wine swept across the floor. There seemed so much more of it than I had poured.

Lady Rose's lip trembled. For a moment she stared at the carpet, stained as if from slaughter.

'Clear that up, Stevens. Let us say no more about it.'

Then she turned on her stool, reopened the piano and began to play again.

That was the worst part: the music. Her way of reminding me that I was nothing: a mere interruption to her practice.

Humiliated, I dropped to my knees and began to gather the slivers into my apron. The glass had broken into shards that cut me.

I was glad. Glad to have an outward mark of what she had done to me.

When I stood, the fragments made a sound like grinding teeth. After I had disposed of them, I would need to come back with a bucket and mop to clean the spilled wine.

Lady Rose did not even raise her head from the keys as I left.

My eyes were hot. Burning with shame, pain and anger, I felt that if my gaze fell upon the Yule log, it would ignite at once.

But it was not a log I saw. It was her.

She was at the other end of the landing, oblivious to me, taking the staircase up to the servants' quarters. The path I often trod, between Lady Rose's suite and my own rooms.

Mrs Friar was echoing my steps.

Over her arm hung a swathe of pea-green. An old friend to me: the morning dress trimmed with yellow. I had washed it, pressed it and arranged it over Lady Rose. Now another held it with reverence.

Mrs Friar was no thief. I can say that much in her favour; she was too sensible, too measured. I wish she *had* stolen it. I could have forgiven that. But the fact that she was carrying a gown from Lady Rose's room to her own could mean only one thing.

My mistress had given it as a gift.

I was not special at all.

*

I hardly slept that night. It is no exoneration, but I feel compelled to describe the frayed state of my nerves. What follows is easier comprehended after a glimpse into the torturous hours I spent alone, weeping until my eyes swelled and I thought my head would crack from the pressure of my tears.

They left wet marks upon the travelling dress she had given to me. Fawn and blue. Half the night, I held it with the grip of one who was drowning. Then I thought of the handsome gown Mrs Friar had received and its costly fabric; how it had been a dress that Lady Rose wore, treasured. By comparison, the travelling gown felt like an insult. I threw it off the bed, but that was not enough. Only thrusting it inside my trunk at the bottom of the wardrobe afforded me satisfaction.

Perhaps I was ill. Feverish. I remember lying on top of the covers, even though it was a cold December. When I awoke, I took scarcely any breakfast. Burns, sitting at my side, did not remark upon it, but I know she saw. She saw more than I gave her credit for.

Thanks to Mrs Friar, the morning ritual of mixing chocolate was lost to me. Instead, I poured a glass of barley water and left the kitchen, climbing the stairs in a sort of haze. The marble pillars and chandeliers were there, as they had always been, yet the house that I had cherished seemed beyond my reach now. I held no part in it.

Only in the yellow glow of Lady Rose's bedchamber did objects resume their proper shape. It was a bright, frosty day. Even with the shutters closed, sunlight was leaking in.

It fell upon a chair. The parcel of baby clothes I had made and later hidden at the bottom of the press lay unwrapped there.

Hope sparked, ever so faint. Had Lady Rose found the gift and softened towards me? Mrs Friar was nowhere to be seen. Perhaps my mistress had told her to keep away, so we might talk this morning?

I loved her, you see. I wanted to believe the best of her.

For a moment I watched her at rest, eyes flicking gently beneath their lids. Brown marks powdered the underside of her nose. She had been taking more snuff of late.

I touched her arm. 'My lady, it is morning.'

She grunted, stirred.

Placing the barley water beside her bed, I went to the window and drew back the shutters. Everything was illuminated. My head began to ache from the glare of sunlight bouncing off the frosted rooftops.

I heard my lady sigh and heave herself up in bed. A clink as she picked up the glass. Still I waited, forcing my watering eyes to watch the street. Any minute now, I thought, she will mention the clothes. Thank me.

There was nothing.

She could not have forgotten. The chair stood right opposite her bed. It would be before her gaze now as she sat against the headboard and sipped her drink.

Silence pressed down upon us.

At last, 'Stevens.'

In that second of joy, I might have wept. She would apologise for all that had happened, I was sure. The spilled wine and the shattered glass would pass from us like a bad dream.

I turned to face her.

'Stevens,' she said carelessly, running a hand through her bedraggled hair, 'my snuffbox is empty. Be so good as to refill it.'

I swayed on my feet.

I do not know what would have happened next if Mrs Friar had not chosen that moment to knock at the door and enter without waiting for an answer. For the first time in my life, I was grateful to her. The distraction gave me time to move to the dressing table and turn my back on Lady Rose.

I thought I needed time to compose myself, but that was not true. It was a nerveless, dead creature that picked up the snuffbox from the table and placed it in her apron. Lady Rose and Mrs Friar were talking, but I heard nothing of their conversation.

Of course I had experienced casual cruelty from the gentry before. There was no particular reason this instance should strike me like a bolt of ice to the heart. But it did and it changed everything: transmuted Lady Rose from a woman I loved into a beast whose jaw must be bound.

Moving towards the door, I stopped and curtseyed. 'Will there be anything else, my lady?' The words might have come from an automaton. She must have heard the alteration in my voice, for she glanced at me. Her brow furrowed. She did not recognise me either, I thought. It was as though we had never met.

Mrs Friar spoke. 'It is cold today, Lady Rose. Perhaps a tisane would warm you?'

'Very well. If you please, Stevens.'

Those were the last words she said to me.

I do not remember descending to the lower regions but all at once I seemed to be in the kitchen's bronze glare with pans of water steaming around me. Logs smoked on the fire. Burns was there, making something for Mrs Windrop, but I was not really aware of her. Nor did I track the movements of my hands. They knew what to do.

Juniper, tansy oil, rue, pennyroyal. Women came to my mother to get their babies out of their bellies, yes, but there was more than one way to achieve that. Not all of them wanted to wait the full term. I had seen them come and go in secret: mothers who could not afford to feed another mouth.

Afterwards, she would need me again. Mrs Friar would leave in disgrace.

I poured the mixture into a delicate Willow pattern teacup, sliced some sugar from the loaf and mixed it in to disguise the taste. When the ripples subsided, I saw my face staring back at me.

Something inside stuttered. Call it conscience, my good angel, whatever you will. I cannot name it, I only know that I paused there before the smoking cup.

My fingers groped for the snuffbox in my apron. Its cool shape steadied me. Suppose I made the snuff first and carried both items upstairs together? It would give me a little time to think.

Wrenching myself away from the kitchen table, I left the tisane and went to the pantry.

I spread out a sheet of vellum and sprinkled it with violet water. As I began to grind and blend the ingredients for Violet Strasbourg snuff upon it, I seemed to wake from a dream, my skin hot and cold by turns. Had I really ... What in the name of God was I thinking?

I could not feed Lady Rose an abortifacient. I knew what a baby meant to her. Had I forgotten those desperate tears, the day she had stood on Westminster Bridge and yearned for the waters to take her? If she miscarried, Mrs Windrop and Burns would smirk, triumphant. Sir Arthur ... I was not sure how it would move him. But he suspected me, that much was certain. Poisoning my mistress would be playing straight into his hands.

And of course, Mrs Friar was no fool. How had I not considered that? Surely, she would investigate the tisane or at least be able to guess at its contents. There was little chance of my emerging unscathed with her watching my actions.

It had been an evil, stupid thing. A moment of madness. Of course I could not do it! I loved her. Truly, I did.

I tipped the snuff into the box and snapped the lid shut, as if that were an end to the matter.

A fresh tisane would need to be brewed; my lady would be impatient, ask what had taken me so long.

But I could endure her harsh words. Better that than to see her lovely face crumpled in pain and anguish.

Walking back into the kitchen, I went to the table, ready to pour the diabolical mixture down the privy where it belonged.

The Willow pattern cup had gone.

Foolishly, I wiped my eyes, expecting the view to change. It did not. I even crouched down and looked beneath the table. There was only dust and crumbs, no trace of my sin.

Sweat ran down the back of my neck. The fire felt outrageously hot.

A scullery maid must have cleared it away; that was the only explanation. Some officious girl who saw the cup there and thought it had been discarded. Well, she had executed my task for me. So long as the thing was gone.

With a renewed sense of purpose, I brewed something better for my mistress from peppermint leaves. My slick hands fumbled to perform their tasks. I still felt warm, a little feverish, as if I had survived a great ordeal. I suppose I had.

I daresay the tisane I botched together was of an indifferent quality. I never found out. For when I opened the door to the kitchen, Burns was standing on the other side.

She wore the black dress I had noted that first day. Her face did not match its sombre hues. She was vivid, alive with something thoroughly repellent.

'Excuse me,' I said.

A grin crept up her cheek. 'Did she ask for another one already?'

'Another …?'

She gestured at the cup in my hands. 'It seems your mistress has a taste for poisonous herbs.'

My mouth turned parchment dry. A low buzz started in my head. I stared, dumb, a partridge flushed out by dogs.

'I saw the ingredients,' she added maliciously. 'One of your receipts, was it? No need to write it down. I committed every step to memory … just in case someone should ask me what you put in that cup.'

'That was not for … I did not …' I wet my lips and cleared my throat. 'You are mistaken, Burns. I did not take that drink to Lady Rose.'

'No. But I did.'

I had only seen such exalting hate once before: at a public execution. Now I was there again, only this time the noose was around my own throat. The floor dropped away beneath my feet and I began to choke.

'Careless, to leave it sitting about like that. I said as much to Lady Rose. Of course she defended you, expected you had forgotten it in your haste to mix her snuff.' She glanced at the clock. 'She has probably finished by now. You had better go and collect the cup.'

I did the only thing I could: I flung the peppermint tisane in her face.

She was too shocked to cry out. I heard her gasp, then a sound like a nut cracking as the cup and saucer fell to the floor.

I pushed past her and I ran.

My skirts tripped me on the stairs. Half-crawling, I grappled my way, up and up, to the servants' quarters. There was no time to think of Lady Rose; it was already too late to stop her from taking the drink.

Opening the wardrobe, I pulled out my trunk and flung a gown and some caps on top of the travelling dress. There was a little money in my reticule, wages from last quarter and odd coins which Lady Rose had given me to fetch ribbons and bonbons. I had a hip flask for water and the full snuffbox. It was all I dared stop to pack.

I crammed a bonnet on my head, not bothering to fasten the ties. I could not be caught. I could not bear to see the hurt creasing her face when she found out what I had done.

Heaving the trunk under my arm, I barrelled out of the room and down the stairs. Any moment now, the footmen would come running, or the housekeeper would appear. Burns would waste no time in telling her tale, of that I was sure.

Without a backward glance, I raced past the marble pillars and out of the front door.

PART THREE

Protection

Chapter 13

I must have fallen asleep. Merryn no longer lies in bed beside me. It is achingly cold.

Only the promise of laudanum spurs me to sit up and gaze blearily around. Darkness reigns, but that means nothing in the winter. In all likelihood it is morning and time for me to wake Miss Pinecroft. If, indeed, she has not frozen solid in the night.

I kept my stockings on to sleep and am glad of it. Dampness has pervaded the room; I feel it on the floorboards and even on my trunk as my weary fingers fumble with the lock. Strange, how moisture can make the atmosphere thick and heavy. Everything smells of sitting water.

Despite spending a night wrapped in the folds of my clothes, the hip flask is chill and hurts my hands. Shivering, I put it to my lips. The bitter taste of opium, undisguised by the druggist's valiant additions of saffron and cinnamon, stops me from swigging it like gin. One sip shall suffice.

I have heard of invalids misjudging the dose and consuming such vast amounts of laudanum that they cease to respire. They simply drown in dreams. I think, perhaps, that I understand how they could make such an error.

One of my gowns is clean; I have only the three in total. The bloody travelling dress squats at the bottom of the box like a toad. Will the maids wash the laundry here or send it out? Either way the sight of my dress is bound to cause suspicion. Even if I explain how the stains came to be there, they will see that the material is costly, too good for me.

Merryn has left me water in the ewer, but the thought of washing in such damp conditions raises gooseflesh on my arms. Instead, I brush my skin and apply a dab of lavender before changing my shift.

Tiny pebbles of liquid shine upon the side of my trunk. I close the lid, pause. The same marks are upon the surface, like raindrops.

'Just what sort of unwholesome room has Mrs Quinn confined me to?' I mutter.

In answer comes the noise I heard yesterday: high and ethereal. For all its sweetness, it unsettles me, touches a nerve I was not aware I possessed.

Whatever can it be? Does it emanate from inside the house or further afield?

Kneeling on the bed, I push back the curtains at the window and search for a clue outside. Frost marbles the glass. Only black lies beyond. Just now, it feels as if there is nothing past that darkness. We are abandoned here.

Then I see the light.

Quivering, very faint. Almost as if it came from below the water.

Squinting, I rub the sleeve of my gown against the glass. It produces no effect.

The light dips and sways. It has the same strange, entrancing quality as the noise. I wish I could see it clearly.

Could it be fishermen out at sea? A lamp might explain the glow, but I would not be able to hear the men singing over this distance.

All at once, the light blinks out

I am left strangely hollow. The darkness is blinding without it.

Disconcerted, confused, I turn back to the room. And I realise that the sound has stopped also.

Everything is silent.

I shake myself, climb off the bed. Perhaps I did take a drop too much laudanum.

Either that or not enough.

*

By the time I arrive in the kitchen, Merryn has stoked the fire and begun to bake.

'Good morning,' I say as I stifle a yawn. 'I am come to wake the mistress. I believe that eight o'clock is her time?'

She turns to me. Her face is sprinkled with flour. 'Good morning, Miss Why. How deep thee do sleep! I was afeared I'd wake thee earlier, but there was no chance of that.'

She speaks good-naturedly and I cannot take affront.

'It was all the travelling that fatigued me, I expect. Tell me, Merryn, were you mixing chocolate for Miss Pinecroft yesterday? I should like to take her something hot.'

Something to make up for my heinous behaviour last night. I do not know how she will receive me this morning. If, indeed, there is ever a change in her demeanour.

'I make the mistress a cup every day.' Merryn nods at her caked hands and apron. 'Be about it soon ...'

'Please don't rush. I can do it.' I move to the cupboard she opened yesterday. Sure enough the pan has returned to its place, scoured clean. 'The chocolate can be my task from now on. One less chore for you to perform.'

'Kind of thee,' she says, returning to her dough. 'That'll just leave Miss Rosewyn.'

My hand quakes minutely as I set the pan down and find the chocolate cakes.

'If you like,' I venture, trying to sound careless, 'I will make two today. I do not object to carrying a cup to Miss Rosewyn. Although I should have thought that would be Creeda's responsibility. She is nurse-maid, is she not?'

Merryn grins at me as she kneads. Her birthmark flashes through the smears of flour on her cheek. 'Curious, an't thee? To see Creeda and the young mistress. Shouldn't wonder. She be a queer one right enough.'

My lips seem to have forgotten how to smile, but I try nonetheless. 'I should certainly like to meet Creeda. She did not dine with us in the servants' hall last night.'

'Never do. For all that talk of fairies, I reckon she be away with un herself.'

Now, what was the correct combination of spices? Cinnamon, nutmeg. Not cardamom. My eyes continue to search the labels for it, out of habit. The mixture smells wrong to me without that peppery kick.

'Merryn, I happened to look out of our window before I came downstairs. I saw the strangest thing. It looked like a fishing boat, far out at sea. Does your father really put out in such weather?'

A puff of laughter escapes her. 'Nay, can't be a fisher. Pilchards keep wide of this cove, don't thee know? Naught but seaweed out there.'

My pan of milk bubbles gently. I give it a stir. 'No fish in the cove? How strange. I wonder why that should be?'

Merryn shrugs, as if explaining such things to a stranger is impossible. 'Folk all have a tale. Mermaids, Father says, but that be fishermen's nonsense. S'pect the water went bad long ago. Could've been a body in the caves.'

'A body?'

'If the tide caught 'em,' she elaborates. 'Or a suicide. Body of a suicide'll scare fish off like naught else.'

Perhaps I do not wish to hear any more.

'I did not realise there were caves upon the beach.' Carefully, I pour the dark liquid into two separate cups. A dribble escapes – without thinking, I put out a finger to catch it and raise the tip to my mouth. The taste is sweet, deep. 'Well, it is certainly not a place for sea-bathing.'

Merryn chuckles again. 'Hope it weren't a French ship thee saw, Miss Why.'

I doubt even Bonaparte, with his thirst for invasion, would consider this desolate place worth capturing.

Placing both cups upon a tray, I turn and leave the kitchen.

My hands are better now, almost steady – fortunate, for brilliant white surrounds my passage through the entrance hall.

A smudge remains on the cup beside my left hand, and this vexes me. My finger must have smeared it as I stopped the chocolate from running. I never used to be prone to sloppiness.

I shall give the smudged cup to the child. She will not remark upon it.

Miss Pinecroft is precisely as I left her – slumped a little further down in the chair, perhaps. She does not appear to have moved all night. The chamber pot is empty and my footprints disturb a patina of dust that has settled upon the floor.

'Good morning, Miss Pinecroft,' I greet her cheerily, hoping to pretend last night simply did not happen. 'How chilled you must be! I have fetched some chocolate to warm you.' For a moment I hesitate, wondering if palsy will prevent her from taking the cup, but one withered hand gropes blindly towards me. I wrap her fingers around the warm china. They are like icy twigs.

'I think, perhaps, once you have finished, that I will dress you in warmer clothes. Then we might sit by a fire in your bedchamber. I could read to you for a while. Should that be pleasant, madam?'

Miss Pinecroft does not reply to my suggestions, only sips noisily at the chocolate through one side of her mouth. That is warm milk inside her, at least.

What keeps her here? She cannot be comfortable. The aspect is not pleasing. Some association of the mind, maybe?

My father told me that a person can survive the apoplexy without material damage to their faculties. Others succumb entirely. It is difficult to know how much of Miss Pinecroft remains – and how much of it she is deigning to show me. Perhaps I have upset her, after all.

I follow her gaze to the display of china. There is beauty in the collection, but no variation. Blue and white, white and blue. Monotonous. If there were a range of colours I might understand her attraction, especially on a grey morning such as this. Yet there is nothing.

What can she see that I do not?

Her watery eyes flick from side to side. Watching.

'Have you everything you need for the present, Miss Pinecroft?'

She nods.

'Then may I take a brief leave of you?' Shifting my footing, I proffer the tray in her direction. 'I should like to deliver breakfast to your ward. Miss ... Rosewyn.'

Miss Pinecroft studies a teapot with peculiar intensity. I wonder if she can make out its shape.

Beyond, the waves crash.

'Miss Pinecroft?' I repeat. 'May I go?'

She blinks, as if she had forgotten I was there. Then she nods once more.

Irritation fuels my footsteps back to the entrance hall. I cannot even say what has vexed me. What did I expect after last night's performance? For my new mistress to grasp both my hands as Lady Rose once did and tell me how glad she was to see me? If I am to help her it must be by degrees, a campaign waged with patience. The other servants would not have left her sitting in that china room if it was an easy matter to get her out.

Chocolate slops from the cup. Crying out, I come to an abrupt halt halfway up the stairs.

Nothing has marked the spotless floor, but there is a mess upon my tray.

What has come over me?

Something knocks against the inside of my fore-head. Not pain precisely, but an endless tap, tap of sorrow and need.

I think of what Merryn said yesterday: that fairies knock in the chimney before the whole house comes falling down.

There is only one thing I can do.

I must fetch more laudanum.

*

The chocolate looks cold. At least now I have the hip flask of laudanum concealed within my pocket where I can reach it at a moment's notice. I shall not be caught out like that again.

This is the path I trod with Mrs Quinn yesterday, past the brass pointer on the lock. Today I must go further, I suppose. There are not a great many doors. Miss Rosewyn must reside behind one of them.

My feet echo upon the wooden boards: a lonesome sound to match this lonesome place. It seems strange, to me, to give a house a name. Morvoren. As if it were not just bricks and pebbles but a living thing.

At the far end of the hallway, a door edges open. The maid, Lowena, emerges with a coal scuttle and brush. She is a raven-haired girl of a decidedly olive complex-ion. I thought, when we met briefly at the servants' dinner yesterday, that she would look more at home under a Mediterranean sun than shivering out here at the end of the world. She certainly has an accent different from the others, but I cannot place it.

'Good morning.'

'Miss Why.' Gathering her skirts, Lowena makes an awkward jump before acknowledging me with a nod.

Is she a child playing at scotch-hoppers? I have never seen behaviour like it. Perhaps Creeda is not the only servant in this house with queer ways ... Lowena must note my expression, for she smirks as she passes.

'Don't disrupt the salt,' she advises.

Whatever can she mean? Confused, I watch her walk down the staircase, swinging her scuttle, before I study the door.

She has left it ajar. There is no detector lock here. Simple wood, polished with beeswax, a brass handle that shines. At first glance, it is the most ordinary of doorways ... except for the thick white border on the threshold.

Salt? I cannot think why someone would sprinkle it there ...

But suddenly it does not matter.

Resonating from the room, sharpening my nerves, is the sound.

My cheeks lift, my feet move forwards, before I am aware of authorising them to do so. Such ardour and promise in that sound ... No, not a sound. At this proximity, I know it is a voice.

Someone within the chamber is humming.

Tentatively, I push the door open.

The hum quivers and breaks into words. 'Titsy tosty, tell me true, who shall I be married to?'

The room unfolds before me, holding a cold bluish light. In the centre of the carpet is a round table spread with a variety of feathers, pebbles and flowers. Sitting before it, tearing pages from a book as she sings, is the girl.

Only she is not a girl. Not a child, I mean.

I think that she is older than me.

The person does not match her song. Rosewyn has a bulk to her, a strange, shapeless quality like a woman made of snow. Her dress, cut short as a child's, with pantalettes visible at the ankles, does nothing to diminish this. Brown hair hangs loose down her back, tangled into elflocks. Only in her face do I see a hint of beauty. Small, fine features. Eyes of china blue that match the walls in the corridors. She has an open, amiable look. She does not glance up from her work.

'And who might you be?'

I start. It is a harsh voice, a seagull's voice. Another drip of chocolate runs down the cup as I turn towards the speaker.

She hunches in a chair close behind the door. Dressed in a black gown and a cap of old lace, she cuts a sinister figure, most unlike my mistress downstairs, although they must be of a similar age.

Her skin, stretched taut over sharp lineaments, reminds me of parchment. Most extraordinary are the eyes trained upon me: one blue like Rosewyn's, the other deep brown.

'Oh, you must be Creeda.' I sound brisk and jolly, but that is not how I feel. Her presence demands something. What, I cannot say. A curtsey perhaps, as I would give to Miss Pinecroft. I shall not grant it. Stepping deftly over the line of salt, I enter the room and stand before her. 'My name is Miss Why. I have taken the position of personal maid to Miss Pinecroft. I believed you were aware of my arrival ... at least, Mrs Quinn implied so.'

Rosewyn's chant floats into the silence between us. Creeda's glare pins my feet to the floor.

'What's your name?' Creeda demands.

Perhaps she is deaf. 'Did you not hear me?' I say a touch louder, 'I am Miss Why and—'

'Your Christian name,' she interrupts.

'Est— Hester. Hester Why.'

That gaze. I am naked before it. She can see the lies on my tongue, the laudanum flowing through my veins – I know she can.

'Very well, Hester Why. You've brought Miss Rosewyn her breakfast, have you?'

'Yes.' My tone has lost its assurance. How pathetic the chocolate appears now. Spilt and cold, growing a skin. I wish I had let Merryn make it.

'Give it to me.'

Before I can object, Creeda reaches out one gnarly hand and takes the cup. She looks at the smudge, looks at me, and then turns the rim until she finds a clean part.

Her thin lips seal over the edge and then work – silent, unlike Miss Pinecroft's. What can she be doing? Sloshing it around her mouth? Tasting it for poison? Good God. What a house of strangers and misfits I have wandered into!

'You may take it to Rosewyn.'

Frowning, I receive the cup and wipe its rim on my apron.

There is a fire burning in this room. The difference it makes to the atmosphere is remarkable. Irons hang neatly on their stand, the hearth is swept clean. A small jug of what appears to be cream or milk has been placed on the mantel.

Rosewyn, the girl – woman – I do not know what to call her – must be simple, for she is destroying that book with relish. On the floor by her side lies a doll the size of a small lapdog. Real hair, similar in colouring to Rosewyn's own, flows from beneath its straw bonnet. She is far too old for such toys.

As I approach, she opens her mouth in a beatific smile.

'Your breakfast, miss.'

She removes the cup from the tray and takes a large gulp. Her mouth puckers. 'It's cold.'

'I'm sorry, miss. I was detained. I can heat it over the fire if you would like me to?'

She shakes her head. 'I don't mind.'

She does – I saw the revulsion on her face. But she is being kind. Smiling again. Brown liquid clings to her lips.

'Are you a visitor here?'

'My name is Miss Why.' It is as if they know repeating this lie will tarnish my soul. 'I am a maid to your guardian, Miss Pinecroft.'

She looks me up and down, without impertinence. I take the opportunity to assess her also. The cotton of her gown is pink but strangely matt and ridged. Around her shoulder, large stitches are visible. My eyes flick to her sleeve. The hem is turned up at her wrist. Yes, that is the trouble: she is wearing her dress inside-out.

That is Creeda's concern, not my own. What with this and the tangles in Rosewyn's hair, it is clear the old woman is not discharging her duties. I wonder Mrs Quinn allows such negligence.

Rosewyn's assessment of me, it seems, is more pleasing. Taking my hand in her own, she gives it a firm shake.

'Charmed,' she says.

It slaps the breath from me.

She could not … Of course, she could have no idea. It is coincidence, mere coincidence, that she uses a similar word to the one Lady Rose did.

Creeda clears her throat.

I had forgotten her, watching. And had also forgotten the other old lady, frozen in place downstairs.

'Is there anything else I can fetch you, miss?'

Rosewyn shakes her head. 'No. But I've got something for you.'

Hastily, she bundles three of the thin ripped pages together and squashes them into a ball. This she offers to me with the air of a queen bestowing alms.

'For protection.'

Better to humour the poor thing, I suppose. Holding the tray by my side with one hand, I reach out and take the papers.

'Thank you, miss.'

Creeda's unmatched eyes follow me all the way to the door. 'Don't disrupt the salt,' she rasps.

I will not degrade myself and leap as Lowena did. Striding across the threshold, I brush a few grains with the hem of my skirt. Creeda begins to tut, but I shut the door upon her.

Well, Merryn did warn me they were quite mad.

Taking the ball of paper, I go to stuff it in my apron.

Stop.

A word catches my eye.

It is the name of Our Saviour.

Astounded, I smooth the crumples from the paper, but I already know what I shall see. The Gospel of Matthew. Jesus walking upon the sea.

My nausea returns.

Rosewyn is sitting in there, gleefully tearing apart the Holy Bible.

Chapter 14

'An't thee ever seen a bible-ball?' Merryn's bemused smile is tinged with pity. 'I thought folk had every manner of thing in London.'

We are sitting at the oaken table in the servants' hall, awaiting our dinner. Aromas of butter and warm fish emanate from the kitchen where the cook Mrs Bawden carves up her famous Stargazey Pie – a dish I have yet to sample. The family ate mutton. I have already spent half an hour pulping meat and forking it into Miss Pinecroft's mouth. What with that and the sacrilege before me, little of my appetite remains.

'Of course we had Bibles in London, Merryn, and Salisbury too. But we would never dream of desecrating them in this wicked manner.'

Mrs Quinn sits at the head of the table, as befits her rank. Rather than crying out aghast at the bundle of mangled Scripture I have produced, she appears embarrassed. Her eyes focus on a deep whorl in the wood of the table.

'We lived near Bodmin Moor when I was young,' Lowena tells me. To my eyes she is still extremely youthful, I cannot imagine what age she is referring to. I had thought, with her tawny skin and slight accent, that she might be one of the Spaniards fleeing from the Peninsular War, but clearly I was wrong. 'Everyone in Bodmin used to take a bible-ball with them on a long walk, especially after dark. They didn't mean any harm by it. They trusted its holiness to protect them.'

That is what Rosewyn said: *for protection*. I wish a few torn pages could save me from my fears.

'To protect them from what, Lowena?'

'There are strange things on the moors. Noises and mists, lights.'

'Lights?' I sit forward with interest.

'They seem to …' She wiggles her fingers above the table '… float. Will-o'-the-wisp. If you follow them, you end up in a bog. People we knew drowned that way, Miss Why. Drowned in mud.'

Her words conjure the sensation of soil on my tongue. Dinner seems a less and less appealing prospect.

'How dreadful. But you do not truly believe that fairies led them astray? It was just a terrible accident, surely.'

Lowena shrugs. 'No, not really. Could be anything. A trick of the eye. But Creeda and Miss Rosewyn, they'd believe it. They'd believe all sorts.' Her dark glance drifts to Merryn and sparks with amusement.

'We once thought we'd invent a fairy of our own and see if we could make them fear it ...'

She tries to tell me more, but the rest of her sentence dissolves under giggles. Merryn's shoulders shake. The memory is clearly a comical one, and I find myself smiling with them. Mrs Quinn rattles out a quick, 'Girls, remember yourselves!'

Then Gerren, the man who drove me from Falmouth, lumbers into the hall and the laughter stops.

He takes a seat at the other side of the table in silence. His jacket carries a fug of hay and pipe smoke. By daylight, he looks different. His wrinkles are like cracks in leather. I think it is exposure to the weather that has aged him, rather than long years. No one could suppose him a young man, but I would not place him far above fifty. He is certainly younger than my mistress.

Mrs Quinn pours him a drink. 'Get you warm, Gerren. It's a chilly day's work out there. A body'll catch their death.'

His thick lips twist, as if only women or delicate dandies would consider it cold today. 'Nay. Been too hard at un for that. But me nose smells snow. Won't be long afore I'm diggin' me way out to that horse.'

'True enough. I made Mrs Bawden salt some more pork so we've provisions laid by. Still, if it don't start by Monday, we'd better do a last run to town. Miss Why, you'd be welcome to join us and gather any bits you need.'

A spasm in my chest.

The plan does not commend itself to reason: I should remain concealed. A trip on the freezing pony-trap, squashed by the bulk of Mrs Quinn, is hardly an enticement to risk discovery. And yet ...

My mouth waters at the image of a dark green bottle filled with elation.

Just one bottle to see me through the blizzards. I shall be able to manage if I can procure just one bottle from town.

Or perhaps two. For certainty.

'Thank you, Mrs Quinn. That is a sound idea. I may well need to call in at the apothecary.'

Mrs Bawden shoulders her way through the door and plonks a dish in the middle of the table. I recoil.

This is surely not dinner. It is an aquatic graveyard.

Dead pilchards poke their heads out from holes in the piecrust. They grimace, as if they have been baked alive. Into each pained mouth Mrs Bawden has threaded a sprig of parsley.

Seeing my hesitation, Gerren supposes I cannot reach the pie. He spoons a wedge onto my plate with a wet slap.

Mrs Quinn forks a whole fish head into her mouth. The sound of her mastication makes my stomach turn. 'Oh, that's another thing, Miss Why,' she says as she swallows. 'I didn't tell you about tomorrow.'

'Tomorrow ...'

'Sunday,' she prompts.

'Of course it is.'

'We take Miss Rosewyn to church in the morning, but poor Miss Pinecroft isn't strong enough.'

More likely she refuses to leave her china collection. Her body was strong enough last night when it resisted my attempts to move her.

'I don't want to deprive you, Miss Why,' she continues, 'but I'd take it kindly if you stayed with her. I don't like to leave her unwatched.'

'Naturally.' I cut up my pie. It is better this way. I have no wish for my face to become familiar to the locals. We shall be content together: she with her collection, me with my opioid. 'I am quite willing to make sacrifices for the good of my mistress.'

Paper crinkles as the bible-ball slowly begins to unfold in front of me.

"'Tisn't a great loss, for our good curate, Mr Trengrouse, is sure to come and administer the sacrament to the mistress. Sometimes he'll pray with her or read a psalm. You see, we're not so heathen as you think.'

I cannot tell if this is playful or tart.

'No, indeed. I never meant to imply otherwise.' I still have not taken a bite of dinner. A pilchard leers on my plate, parsley dribbling from its lifeless lips.

This is not food, it is a *memento mori*.

I am the first to ask Mrs Quinn to be excused. The need for my hip flask is knocking, knocking again. She grants my request happily, seeing only loyalty to my mistress.

But as I rise to my feet, Gerren grabs my wrist.

I am so shocked that I cannot speak. His weathered hand feels as rough as a shackle.

'Forgetting aught, Miss Why?'

For the first time, I notice a band of dirty metal on his ring finger – is this man then a husband? At any other time it would be comical to imagine him acting the lover, but now I can only shrink away with distaste from that hardened, calloused skin.

'I beg your pardon?'

Mrs Quinn averts her eyes. The maids are absolutely silent.

Unhurriedly, he leans across the table and picks up the bible-ball with his free hand. 'Keep it. Keep ee safe.'

He was not this solicitous for my welfare on the journey here. I would have much preferred his help with my trunk than this pagan offering.

Why does Mrs Quinn not upbraid him?

'Nonsense,' I declare.

Gerren narrows his eyes. He is taking the measure of me, but I cannot see his conclusions. He proffers the paper again.

'It's maids they want. Healthy-like. No blemishes. I'm thinkin' they'll be after ee.'

'Now, now, Gerren …' Mrs Quinn begins, but she does not have the courage to finish.

I am unsure what amuses me most: that Gerren deems me young enough to be referred to as a 'maid', as the Cornish call their girls, or that he thinks I am without blemish. Then I catch sight of Merryn's downcast eyes, the movement of her throat as she swallows, and all the laughter drains out of me. No one would call her unblemished. She will have endured teasing and worse, living with a port-wine stain like that. I wonder how Gerren can be so unfeeling.

I snatch the bible-ball from him and pull my wrist free. 'Sir, I have lived to the age of two-and-thirty without meeting the requirements of a *human* bride,' I retort. 'I have no reason to fear a supernatural suitor.'

Turning my back on him, I stalk from the room, flinging the paper into the fire as I go.

Chapter 15

This room is always dark, but by candlelight it feels like a cavern. The china is strangely matt; the flames do not reflect in the glazed plates upon the wall. Only the odd varnished figurine throws out a glimmer.

For all I am weary, I am restless. Sighing, I pass to the window. Miss Pinecroft protests if I open the curtains, but I find I can wind myself behind them, and look out while she sits, still as death, with her china. I take a drop of laudanum, but it does not warm me. I feel more fatigued than ever.

Dusk has swallowed every inch of the sky. There is a peppering of stars, ice-bright. Somewhere below, the ocean soughs and moans.

Here, without the curtain acting as a buffer, the chill is worse than ever, but still I watch, seeking the light. It is nowhere to be found.

Perhaps I imagined it. I had just awoken, it might have been the remnant of a dream.

As for the sound ... Could it have been Rosewyn's voice? When I first heard her hum, I believed so, but now I am unsure. It is hard to credit that the volume of a hum would travel across the house to the east wing. Yet what other explanation do I have?

When I return to my seat by Miss Pinecroft, it feels marginally warmer by comparison with my station by the window. That is all that has changed. Everything is suspended, not even the candles flicker.

The curved lines beneath Miss Pinecroft's eyes look like flounces on the skirt of a dress; her other wrinkles resemble cracks upon a plate. All inanimate things. My new mistress has no more life than the china figurines.

I have tried. No one, seeing me at work today, could find anything wanting in my efforts. I talked to her of the animals in the stables, of wildlife in general. I read aloud. The first canto of *Childe Harold's Pilgrimage* may have inspired the general public, but it does not move her.

This is unknown to me. Always, whatever the circumstances, I find a way in. My first mistress prized me for my ability to seek out the best violet pastilles. To Miss Gillings, I was beloved as the only person who could colour her hair without leaving a trace of grey. That is my purpose: to be indispensable. But I doubt Miss Pinecroft would either notice or care were I to faint before her very eyes.

The clock chimes, making me flinch. It seems to ping around the chamber, impossibly loud. Ten of the clock. Miss Pinecroft does not blink.

'I will not leave you here,' I say suddenly. 'Not tonight. I am absolutely decided. It is too cold and I insist you retire to your bed.'

To my astonishment, she inclines her head. No words, no change of expression – just that: a dip of the chin.

Flustered, I rise to my feet and search in my apron for the key to her room. She must be conveyed now, before she has the chance to change her mind.

She does not have the appearance of one cowed. As I approach her chair, I realise that this is not exactly victory. I have not persuaded her: instead she is humouring me.

'May I help you to stand?'

I reach to hoist her from the shoulders, but she brushes me away. Her venous hands grip the arms of the chair. Gradually, painfully, she winches herself up. Her skirts rustle, as if her legs are trembling beneath them.

'Miss Pinecroft?'

Releasing her hold on the chair, she takes two lumbering steps forward.

It is excruciating to see her move: that unnatural, halting gait. She cannot maintain it for any length; taking my arm, she leans heavily against me.

Since she retains the same position, day after day, and refuses to bathe, I would expect my mistress to be ripe with odour. She is not. She carries the scent that seems to pervade the air at Morvoren House: that of rosemary.

I pick up a candle and we move like a funeral procession, out of the china room, down the corridor, to the entrance hall. How tall and cumbersome she is. I do not comprehend how she will ever make it up the staircase. There is no muscle to her. I steer her towards the banister and she clenches it so tight that bones shift beneath the papery skin on her hand.

We toil our way upwards.

She stops, snags, tugs me back. I try to bear her weight, but the soft fuzz of laudanum is creeping into my brain and spreading its warmth through my limbs.

Inside, I am as weary and worn as this old lady.

Her breath saws. I should moderate my pace, but I want this to be over as soon as possible. The candle shakes in one hand as I strain the muscles in the other, pulling her. Three steps to go. Two.

Both of us waver on the landing. If I did not have my arm around my mistress's waist, I believe she would topple back down.

We shuffle towards the west wing, no sign of Lowena and her coal scuttle. My candle casts a wavering shadow upon the walls. Our shades are bent, hunchbacked.

Brass glints on the door to my mistress's bedroom and warns me that I must contend with the wretched lock. I have not hands enough to support Miss Pinecroft, the light, and turn the key.

'Please hold that, madam.' My voice emerges as a whisper. 'I will not be a moment.'

Miss Pinecroft takes the candleholder in the feeblest of grips. She cannot keep it steady. Light trembles as I attempt to slot the key into its hole.

Drip, drip.

What was that? I look to my mistress, but her concentration is all on the candle.

It sounded like water.

After a pause, I hear it again. You would hear a pin drop, up here tonight.

Drip.

It cannot be rain, not a hollow drip like that. Rain would patter, continual. Unless it has somehow soaked into the ceiling.

I close my eyes, rely on my sense of hearing. No doubt remains: the dripping originates from inside my mistress's chamber. There must be a leak.

When I open my eyelids, the light is more erratic than ever. I turn the key to the right; there is a click, a whirl and the slightest movement on the lock as the wheel turns.

I push the door ajar.

Silence reigns within.

The sound of falling water has ceased.

Relieving Miss Pinecroft of the candleholder, I prop her upon my other arm and we inch over the threshold. I expect that something wet will land upon my head, but it does not. All I hear now are the waves.

My candle flame gropes, illuminates patches of wallpaper. Blue oak trees, a blue fisherman. The atmosphere in this room is ... strange. Like me, it seems to be waiting for the next drip.

Carefully depositing Miss Pinecroft on the edge of the bed, I use my candle to kindle the tinder in the fireplace into a weak blaze. It is so small that Miss Pinecroft does not raise any objection, and I tally this as another point conceded. I will make her well and warm despite herself.

But if anything, the chamber is rendered more eerie by the soft orange glow. Figures flicker on the walls and the sea gives them a voice.

'Let us get you into your nightgown,' I say, setting the candleholder down on the dressing table. It strikes me that I have not undressed Miss Pinecroft before.

Touching her is akin to touching marble. Veins stand out upon her liver-spotted skin. Even now she is watching, watching. Blue figures stare down at us from the bed curtains, and she stares back at them.

I prop her against the bolster and pull the covers up to her hips. Her hands rest on the sheets. She does not look like a person about to slumber: she looks like an effigy.

Dare I unpin her hair? A silver-backed brush lies on the dressing table, but its bristles are completely clean. Either it is rarely used, or someone has painstakingly removed every strand of hair. Perhaps I shall leave it for another time. She would appear twice as unsettling with those white tresses spread over her shoulders.

Passing to the window, I begin to draw the curtains. Rapid white flecks disturb the monotony of darkness outside. The first flakes of snow. They are come too soon! I curse inwardly as I watch them tumble over the cliff edge, taking my hopes of gin with them. I must not lose hold of myself. With a decisive swish of curtains, I shut the view out.

I think it will be a relief to move the candle's circle of light towards the bed and cast the *toile-de-Jouy* people into shadow, but it achieves little. Still, I feel that prickle on my skin, the weight of a person observing me.

'I have been advised to lock the door,' I tell her. Part of me wants her to know this is not my choice. 'For safety. I am told that you wander in your sleep.'

At first I think she will not reply. Then she says, very softly, 'Not … *me*.'

Shivers run down my arms. I imagine Creeda in her dark gown, stalking the corridors by night. But that is unlikely. My poor mistress probably does not even know what she is saying.

'Goodnight, Miss Pinecroft.'

My impulse is to kiss the sad old lady's cheek, but I check myself and pat her hand instead.

The tightness in my chest, the creeping feeling – both vanish with the closing of the door.

Reluctantly, I slip the key into its hole. She could barely walk without my aid. But I must follow the housekeeper's instructions. Losing this position would be ruinous. I dare not risk it.

Breathing a sigh, I turn the key.

Once again there is a click. The number beneath the dog's paw shifts.

Seventy-five.

I bring the candle flame closer. Flutter my lashes, just in case there is something in my eye. No. The number is clear, there is no mistaking it.

When Mrs Quinn closed this door, I could swear the dial moved to sixty-seven. I saw it. Even supposing the number should climb twice, once when unlocked, and again when locked, it should only be at sixty-nine.

Someone has been inside this bedchamber.

Only Mrs Quinn and I hold the keys. The housekeeper may well have had a valid reason for her intrusion: perhaps she heard the dripping, as I did. There are hundreds of reasonable explanations, and yet ...

The brass dog stares solemnly at the number. He would tell me if he could.

I place my fingertip on the dial.

All at once, my candle blows out.

Chapter 16

This morning, I arise with Merryn. How she can wake every day at this bleak, friendless hour is beyond my comprehension. Of course I have been up early in my years of service, but the timekeeping of a scullery maid is a thing apart.

Snow dances outside our window. Thank heaven, last night's drifts did not settle. There will be no obstacle to the servants attending church or the curate calling here.

More importantly, we can travel tomorrow. I may still obtain a bottle of gin.

God knows how it has come to this. Such feelings of fear and hunger that take hold of me! Ever since that fateful day in the free house at Salisbury. I was scouring their newspapers in search of a new position. Instead, I found Sir Arthur's advertisement and fainted, right there in the tap room. When I came around, there was something strong and cool pressing against my lips. The meaty landlord and his wife leant over me. 'Dram o' gin,' he said. 'This'll pick you up, girl.'

I clung to it like a leech. Have been clinging ever since.

Now the first thought that crosses my mind in the morning is drink. I am wild for it, like a girl in love. I only feel alive when the bitter-sweetness rolls across my tongue.

I have found myself a new mistress.

Merryn and I descend to the lower regions together. The echoing stucco hall appears ghostly and forbidding. I wonder how a girl her age summons the courage to walk this path alone each day.

Once we are in the kitchen and Merryn has coaxed the fire into life, our aspect is much brighter. Like a great, throbbing heart, it seems to awaken the house, lending colour to objects and a soft crackle to our ears.

I am relieved to discover Merryn has been collecting rainwater in butts over the past few days and we are not obliged to venture outside to fetch it.

She hoists the wooden lid off the water heater and begins to fill the copper vat inside. 'Creeda did prepare the water herself,' she tells me. 'But I see how she do it.'

This is the reason for my early hours: I am resolved to clean the china. Attempting such a task under Miss Pinecroft's vigil would be impossible, but while she is safely locked in her room, I shall try.

Merryn takes a taper to the fire and ignites the water heater's stove. We stand for a few moments and watch it. There is something rather unnerving about hearing the water start to bubble, deep within the bricks.

'I believe it needs to be tepid,' I advise, hoping to sound knowledgeable.

Before long Merryn has filled a pail. It steams gently; no doubt the chill of the china room will take off any excess heat. Thanking her, I grip the handle and begin my quest.

Never before have I seen the china room without Miss Pinecroft in occupation. I set down the pail of water and approach the wingback chair cautiously, as if she might have materialised overnight. Of course, it is empty.

The sense of freedom is intoxicating. I fling back the curtains, releasing a cascade of dust. No one is here to stop me from lighting the candles and kindling a small blaze in the fireplace. Why should I not work in comfort, for a change?

For an hour at least, I am mistress.

After fetching a few supplies from the closet next door, I return and smile at the room before me. In the firelight, the mahogany panels warm to chocolate brown. Illuminated, the china reveals delicate brushstrokes.

Where shall I begin? If this were a wardrobe, I would start by taking an inventory of all the items, ascertain the material and how best it might be cleaned. I see no reason not to continue with this method. Once I familiarise myself with the pieces and their quality, I will know which need the greatest attention.

Most importantly, I will memorise their positions. Heaven forefend Miss Pinecroft's watchful eyes should find something out of place.

This morning there is no need to hide my steadying drop of laudanum; I place it upon my tongue, savouring the bitter taste. Then I survey the collection with brightened eyes.

I had thought the large pieces standing either side of the fire were jugs, but they could be used to hold indoor plants. I peer inside to see clumps of dust settled on the base. Although they will take time to make presentable, they seem thick and hardy. I should manage not to break them.

The mantelpiece tells a different story. A pair of swans with delicate necks and vases that look as if they have upturned thimbles on top. On closer inspection, I can see they are designed to hold individual flower stems. These will require care. Holding them reminds me of touching Miss Pinecroft's skin: they are frigid and shell-thin.

Shelves rise above the mantelpiece, higher than I can reach. Perhaps my vision is softened by laudanum, but it looks as if the items further up are imperfect. A teacup with a wonky handle. One of the chamber pots shows fire cracks along the side. It is as if whatever warehouse they came from has been refining its art – but why would Miss Pinecroft buy their seconds?

To the right of the fireplace is a kind of open cabinet displaying lidded urns. As I walk towards it, my nose wrinkles at an odd, slightly musky scent. Evidently Creeda has not been as conscientious about the collection as Mrs Quinn would have me believe. The lowest shelf, about elbow height, holds six urns that must be older than the rest. The colour – still blue, of course – has not come out well. Two in particular are very poorly glazed.

I turn ninety degrees and move on to the racks that line the wall opposite the window. Wiping my sweaty hands upon my apron, I remove one of the plates.

Then I see the design.

I should have expected it. With so large a collection, and all in blue and white, it would be surprising if I did not come across the Willow pattern, but the sight of it strikes me like a physical blow.

It is all there, just as Lady Rose told me. The pavilion and its sprawling trees. A boat. A bridge. No doves, though. Some heartless painter has left out the lovers' happy ending.

I wonder if they are still using that other Willow set, so despised by Mrs Windrop. I touch the tiny blue figure of the bride with my fingertip. Perhaps even now Lady Rose is echoing my actions far away in Hanover Square. Turning over the pieces and remembering me.

But something is not right. This plate does not tally with my lady's beloved story. Here is the bride clutching her box of jewels. I see the humble gardener with his staff. But the third figure is missing. There is no mandarin following them, brandishing a whip.

I walk along the row of plates, frowning. All the other Willow designs show three people upon the bridge. Only the one in my hands is faulty.

I turn it over to see the stamp. The back of the plate is rougher than the surface, somehow unfinished. At the centre the name 'Nancarrow' is written in an arch; the words 'Bone China' form a swag below. In the middle of this word-circle, as if to illustrate the point, is the etching of a skull.

I have never heard of this factory. Perhaps it closed; after all, they could not render the Willow pattern correctly.

I have let minutes slip away in my reverie. There is little time for anything but a perfunctory wipe over the plates before floorboards creak upstairs. The other servants are rising.

The water in my pail serves to douse the fire. I pinch the candles out, pull the curtains back into place. A smoky, charred scent lingers.

'Tattletale,' I mutter, and hope Miss Pinecroft does not notice it.

Barely eight o'clock and already I am weary to my bones. Soon will come the headache, the shakes, the cool sweat. This time I do not count the laudanum drops as they fall into my mouth. I find I do not care.

On the staircase, I pass Creeda. I am not minded to give the hag any more acknowledgement than a nod of the head, but she stops and watches me ascend.

'Hope the water wasn't too hot,' she growls. 'Not on the urns.'

I walk on as if I have not heard her. But as I go to unlock my mistress's door, I notice my hands are quaking in spite of the laudanum. She has unsettled me.

How did Creeda know what I was doing?

At least Miss Pinecroft's room appears more genial this morning. The shepherds on the wallpaper have lost their odd flickering quality. Still, I cannot say I like the jumble of blue and white swirling all around me, and I do not like the way in which I discover my mistress.

She looks as if she has seen a ghost.

I doubt she has slept. Her hair remains firm in its pins. There is a little urine, very pale, in the chamber pot, so she must have moved, yet I swear the coverlet is smooth, exactly as I left it.

'Good morning, madam. How are you today?' I ask with false cheer.

Of course she does not reply – I hardly expect it. I open the curtains and the window shutters. Droplets of condensation run down the glass.

Outside, the sea is a mass of froth. Ice sparkles prettily on the frosted grass and the twigs of the ash trees. It reminds me of Merryn about her baking, dusted with flour.

Today, I am in charge of dressing Miss Pinecroft and I vow to do it in a suitable manner. No more shivering in flimsy gowns. If she is to sit in that china room, she will do so wrapped against the chill.

After a few tries, I find another of my keys opens the wardrobe in the corner.

Sheets rustle as Miss Pinecroft straightens up in bed to watch me.

Is she really so protective of this paltry collection? It is scarcely worth locking away. Half a dozen gowns hang in linen pouches. Each pouch contains sprigs of rosemary. If you ask me, the dresses are not worth even that protection. They are outmoded and plainly coloured, made of indifferent material. More hardwearing than pretty. There are no redingotes or pelisses to bundle Miss Pinecroft up in. Whatever she spends her money upon, it is certainly not clothes.

In the end I settle upon a woollen gown in dark blue, a nice thick linen fichu and a brown cloak with a hood. Her stockings are all clocked cotton. I apply two pairs. She may not be fit to be seen in society, but at least she shall be warm.

Miss Pinecroft offers no comment upon my choices. Perhaps she cannot even see them clearly. It seems to be a relief to her when I close the wardrobe and the whole business of dressing is done.

Staggering to her feet, she leans upon my arm as she did last night, although her movements appear stiffer. That bedchamber cannot be salubrious, shut up tight with condensation and rosemary needles: it needs a good airing. After we shuffle out, I leave the door ajar.

We gain perhaps three steps before pain sears up my arm.

'Lock.'

Startled, I look down to see Miss Pinecroft driving her bony fingers deep into my flesh. The blue watery eyes are alive with an intensity I have never seen before.

'Lock the door.'

I dare not disobey.

The golden dial shows the number seventy-nine.

*

Church caused a bustle in Morvoren House – the first I have seen since my arrival on Friday. Miss Rosewyn galloped down the stairs in high glee, an oversized child expecting a treat. How she can reconcile her attendance with the destruction of Scripture remains a mystery to me.

Creeda followed her charge like a mourner behind a hearse. Clenched by her side was that elaborate doll I glimpsed yesterday. It wore a new gown. A tiny imitation of the coral silk adorning Miss Rosewyn.

Mrs Quinn, Mrs Bawden, Lowena and Merryn were also decked out in their Sunday best; even Gerren wore a neckerchief and smart jacket.

'A brisk walk today!' sang Mrs Quinn. 'We'll outrun that cold wind.'

To her and the maids it was a jaunt. But Creeda had a grim determination about her.

'Take Dolly,' she ordered Rosewyn.

I'd assumed Rosewyn refused to go abroad without her toy. Now I saw that this was not the case. She took the doll reluctantly from Creeda's hands, and rather than hugging it close, she held it limp. As a woman of her age should.

Mrs Bawden opened the door. Everyone exclaimed as freezing air rushed in; I could feel its chill, even where I stood looking out from the china room.

The maids tumbled outside, whooping and laughing. Mrs Quinn and Mrs Bawden followed amiably behind. But the trio at the rear were an ominous sight.

Rosewyn grinned foolishly, a rose between two black thorns. Gerren linked one of her arms through his; Creeda took the other. Each guardian looked solemn, determined somehow, as if they were facing down enemy fire. Beside Rosewyn's innocent joy it was terrible.

Now Miss Pinecroft and I are alone.

Church bells ring in the distance. The racing wind distorts them. I am better off here, anonymous in a dark room with an unspeaking companion. There is no disputing that fact. But in my heart, I wish I had gone with the others.

The smell of my earlier fire lingers. Miss Pinecroft's nostrils flare; she must know what I have done. I yearn to ask her why we cannot be warm, why we cannot have a little light. I doubt she would answer me. But the longer I stare into her face, the more I am convinced: I am not the only person who has seen and heard things within this house.

A bell rings.

I start to my feet, bewildered. Miss Pinecroft glances briefly at me before returning her gaze to the china.

The bell jangles again. It is coming from the entrance hall.

Warily, I steal to the door and push it open. Now there is a knock. I flinch, as if knuckles rapped against my body. Then I remember: the curate.

Half-tripping on my skirts, I hasten to the front door. Once I have lifted the latch, it blows in towards me, sending me staggering again. I must present a comical picture, for the first thing I hear from the young man outside is laughter.

'Careful! How she blows today.' He holds his wide-brimmed hat firmly over a spill of deep red hair. He is much younger than I expected, little more than a youth.

'Mr Trengrouse, I presume?'

'Yes. How do you do?' He bends in a bow, the flaps of his greatcoat whipping up behind him. 'You must be Miss Why. I was told to knock this week, so that I did not frighten you with my entrance.'

'I do not know why Mrs Quinn should suppose me easily frightened.' I stand aside and let him in.

He looks relieved to find shelter. In his right hand he clutches a Bible, dog-eared and much scuffed from overuse, but in a better condition than Rosewyn's.

I close the door behind him and shut out the boom of the wind. 'Allow me to take your hat and gloves,' I offer. 'You may wish to keep the coat. Perhaps you are accustomed to the temperatures Miss Pinecroft prefers, but I am still adjusting.'

His smile widens. He looks like a man who is always smiling, who cannot help it. 'Believe me, after the walk I have had, Morvoren House seems perfectly warm.'

He shakes off his greatcoat, removes his hat. The gloves take a little longer. He starts to hand them all to me in one messy pile.

'Thank you, I believe that I ...' All at once, the smile is knocked from his face.

'Sir?' I tug at his belongings but he clings to them, oblivious of my efforts. 'Sir, are you well?'

'Great God,' he breathes. 'It's you.'

Time seems to stop. He must have read the advert seeking my arrest.

I imagined I would cry out, faint or run. None of these things is possible. I simply stare at the warm brown eyes that bore into mine. Such handsome eyes to instigate my doom.

Mr Trengrouse releases his coat. Everything drops to the floor as he seizes my hand.

His hold is painfully tight. For a moment he stares at my fingers, their tremor. Then he raises them to his lips.

'God bless you! A thousand times, bless you!'

I think I have truly lost my mind.

'Did you believe that no one observed? I saw it all, although I was so struck with horror that I could not move a muscle. I, his brother-in-law! You put us all to shame.' He gabbles on, not just smiling but positively grinning now. 'Forgive me for not recognising you at first. Without your hat, and in the daylight ... But I should never forget your face. Someone said you must be an angel when you disappeared, so suddenly like that. I could not find you to thank you! Were it not for your actions, I'm sure he would have died. The leg should certainly have been lost. Our own physician confirmed it. And where would poor Polly and the children be, with only myself and a cripple to support them?'

I cannot ... My mind struggles, dulled by laudanum. Memories are surfacing from its black greasy depths.

'Do not be modest, Miss Why, I know it was you.'

'You were ... on the Mail coach,' I realise slowly. 'At Exeter, when the man fell?'

'My sister's husband! We rode together, on the roof. Upon my word, that was the most terrible night of my life.'

You would not believe it from the way he is beaming. My fear that night was correct: people noticed me. The consequences could be – very nearly *were* – dreadful.

'And … and the gentleman will recover?'

'It is our daily prayer. Time must tell, but our physician thinks him over the worst of the danger. He is still in Exeter, with my sister and our medical man. They do not think it advisable to move him yet.'

'I was concerned about the possibility of infection. That crack to the head … I wished to stay and assist, but the surgeon dismissed me and of course I had to take my seat …'

He grimaces. 'We were paid up until Falmouth, too. In the end I arrived home much later on the stagecoach, only to trade places with my sister. Her children fall under my care while she is away. Pity the poor little souls, Miss Why.'

'May I ask you to keep me informed of the patient's progress, Mr Trengrouse? I should like to know how he fares.'

'That I certainly shall.'

Together, we notice his hat, coat and gloves heaped upon the floor, and both laugh.

I stoop to pick them up. 'Please go on through to Miss Pinecroft, sir. I shall put these away and fetch you some tea.'

He seems to recall that he is my superior, clears his throat, straightens his waistcoat. 'Thank you. Thank you, I shall see you presently.'

The house feels brighter for having him in it. There is a lightness to my step as I make my way to the kitchen and begin preparations.

A drop of laudanum ensures my hands are quite steady to carry out the heavy tray with its pots, cups, urn and spirit lamp. This tea service is blue and white like the collection, but it is Wedgwood jasperware, quite affordable. To my eyes, it is prettier than the produce of Nancarrow Bone China.

I find Mr Trengrouse already reading aloud to my mistress, his chair much closer than I have ever pulled mine. It is a poor light. His head is bent over the page and he does not look up at my entrance.

I have never seen hair quite like his. When people talk of 'chestnut' horses, they are usually describing an orangey hue, but this is exactly the colour of a conker from a chestnut tree: the same deep, burnished red threaded with brown. It becomes him.

If I had a mistress with that colouring, she would truly be a challenge to dress.

Miss Pinecroft listens passively. The curate's presence seems to soothe her; her posture is less rigid, almost relaxed. The wrinkles on her face soften to creases.

I set the tea tray down quietly. Mr Trengrouse finishes his reading and Miss Pinecroft croaks 'Amen', although it is not called for.

'It is good of you,' I say, 'to come out like this for the parishioners with poor health.'

He smiles again, leans his hands upon the closed Bible. 'It is my duty. And it is always pleasant calling here. There are a few cottages with sick inmates I must attend later, and they will not be able to offer me tea.'

This is my signal to begin serving. The tea leaves are good, fragrant. I take a steaming cup to my mistress, which she receives with an ill grace, evidently irritated that I have disturbed her devotions, and then one to Mr Trengrouse.

'Will you not sit and drink with us?' he asks.

I waver. Accepting would hardly be proper, but refusal seems rude. Were Miss Pinecroft an ordinary lady, I do not suppose Mr Trengrouse would dream of asking me, but she will slurp at her tea in silence, unable to make conversation with him.

'How kind of you. I shall fetch another cup.'

He is pleased.

'Do not forget that you are a member of this parish also, Miss Why,' he says as I sit beside him with my tea. 'I hope that you will stay and pray with us, once you have taken refreshment?'

Without looking to Miss Pinecroft for permission, I nod.

'You have not had the opportunity, I suppose, of seeing the area much, Miss Why? You have no acquaintance here?'

'None whatsoever. I am recently come from Salisbury. My mistress's life is much retired, and that suits me.'

'Then you are new to Cornwall entirely,' he announces.

'I am.' Blowing on my tea, it occurs to me that he may know more about Creeda and the strange ways of this house. Mrs Quinn might take umbrage when I scoff at fairies, but surely a man of the church, even a Cornish church, will not hold truck with such superstition? 'Already I have offended a servant or two by scattering their lines of salt and refusing to carry a bible ball.'

'Ah!' he throws back his head, apparently delighted. 'The folklore and the little people. Fascinating, is it not? My mother was not native to this area either; she used to collect up the local stories in a great book. Many places have their tales, but Cornwall is prolific, I believe.'

Miss Pinecroft slurps at her tea.

'I was unsure how you would view such fancies, given your profession.'

He cradles his cup thoughtfully. 'The Methodists abhor them. For my part, I cannot see the harm, providing one does not get carried away. With a head of hair like mine, Miss Why, you learn to view super-stitions facetiously. And people are so fond of the stories. Some even make reference to Christianity.' His eyes light with a memory. 'My mother told me one that I often think about. It says that when our religion arrived on these shores, there was a group of elders who refused to convert from their pagan ways. Unable to receive salvation, they were not yet bad enough for hell, so they were doomed to shrink, smaller and smaller each day, until they finally disappeared. An ingenious explanation for fairies, do not you think?'

My glance flicks to my mistress. She is ill at ease. This topic does not please her; she chafes under Mr Trengrouse's playful tone.

I swallow my mouthful of tea. 'It is excessively diverting. But I cannot help thinking these ideas could be dangerous, if truly believed. Not everyone is so fortunate as to have your education; they may not see the tales for what they really are.'

'True enough,' he admits. 'We had a to-do a few years back with a fisherman's babe. It thrived to begin with, but after a few weeks it failed to suck. Folk put all kinds of notions into the mother's head. Said it was not her child any longer but a changeling, unable to eat human food. Our vicar Dr Bligh was obliged to speak very plainly, I remember, to set her straight.'

'That is precisely my meaning. Surely Dr Bligh deplores such beliefs in his parishioners?'

He sees that I am in earnest and arranges his expression accordingly. 'Well, Dr Bligh is a more learned man than I,' he says with modesty. 'He has studied much. He has spoken with professors. And it is his opinion that the bad fairies – not the useful ones who clean houses and such – well, that they are real.'

My eyebrows climb.

'I do not mean he thinks to see winged creatures frolicking around toadstools,' he adds hurriedly. 'No, it is more complicated than that.' He raises the cup to his lips and drinks as he considers how to explain. 'His belief is that fairies, or goblins, mermaids, pixies, ghosts – all of them – are the same at heart. Creatures of the devil. Enchanting, whispering in ears that are eager to listen.'

Some of his mother's fondness for storytelling has passed on; he speaks the last words with dramatic relish.

'How frightening, Mr Trengrouse.'

Miss Pinecroft slurps more tea.

'I daresay he is correct. That is what the Enemy would do: manifest itself in the image of what we most desire. Or,' he goes on pensively, 'those that we have lost.'

Waves slap against the cliff face. I close my eyes briefly, picturing them rushing headlong to the place where they break and scatter. What we desire and what we have lost. Are they not always the same?

Something snaps.

Both of us jerk to attention, aware once more of the woman in the wingchair whose house we sit in, whose tea we drink.

'Miss Pinecroft?'

She is staring at the china urns, thin-lipped.

To my horror, I think she has shamed herself. But then I realise the patch upon her lap is spreading, fed by sepia drips.

A lightning bolt streaks down the centre of her cup. Jagged, black.

My mistress has gripped the jasperware so hard that she has cracked it.

PART FOUR

Forty Years Ago

Chapter 17

Stalactites pointed down at Louise like an infantry of bayonets. She could not take her eyes from them, even though her spectacles were beginning to mist and obscure the view.

At her heel, Pompey tilted his head, first left and then right, puzzled. How must this cave appear to the poor dog? The way sound echoed, the flickering rock pools, the scent of damp stone. His senses would be overwhelmed.

But Papa, for his part, seemed delighted. 'See how far it stretches back?' He gestured, throwing his hand and his voice towards the pitch dark of the cave. 'There will be room for half a dozen at least, perhaps ten if we are fortunate.'

'Why not start with a small number?' she suggested. 'It may always be increased if we enjoy success.'

Her caution seemed to irritate him. 'Early intervention is vital. I wish to save as many people as possible, Louise.'

Her name resounded in the rocky space. Pompey muttered.

Louise bowed her head. Papa had not used to snap like that. 'Of course, Papa. Of course.'

One of the four Cornishmen accompanying them lifted his lantern and sent shadows flowing over the stone like water. 'Don't belong to me to say,' he whispered to the fellow beside him, 'but I shouldn't like it. Living beneath the earth.'

His companion was dressed in a worn coat of dark brown, nearly the same shade as the rocks. He did not take the same care in moderating his voice. 'Naught different from a body working in the mine. Though how that's supposed to help an invalid, I can't tell ee.'

Papa closed his eyes, inhaled heavily. 'Gentlemen, gentlemen. You have spent your whole lives here upon the coast. You no longer remark how fresh and cleansing the air is.' He breathed in again, as if to demonstrate. 'It will work wonders upon the lungs. And look.' He pointed to the mouth of the cavern. Outside the day was mild and springlike. 'The sun cannot penetrate this shadowy space. It remains damp.'

The Cornishmen swapped blank glances. Pompey's claws clicked against rock as he paced unhappily back and forth, listening to the distant boom of the sea.

Louise stepped forward, clearing her throat with a touch of self-importance. 'It is a counterbalance, you see. The phthisis – or consumption, as you know it – is dry and hot; it needs damp and cool humours to treat it. There is nowhere on earth like a cave for cold moisture.'

Papa nodded approvingly. She felt the accustomed glow in her chest. After all the years she had spent looking up to him, learning from him, her desire to impress had never faded. Papa was a great man. He had studied in Edinburgh, attended at the Royal Bristol Infirmary and been selected by Lord Redfern to act as personal physician to his noble family. He had done everything she would have liked to do, were ladies permitted the chance. But alas, other cares fell to her lot.

Cares such as these hard, unyielding stones. It was a woman's place to administer comfort, and somehow she had to achieve this within the confines of a cave. Although she understood the theory behind her father's venture, she could not help a traitorous suspicion that an invalid might feel better laid up in bed with feather pillows, for the short term at least.

'I shall require some time to make the accommodation more suitable for the men,' she told her father. 'They cannot sleep on rock, ill as they are. Shall we not construct something a little more homely for them, Papa?'

'They are used to the infirmary at Bodmin gaol, my dear. You will receive no complaints.'

Louise remained doubtful, but said nothing. After the calumny Papa had suffered, it would be unforgivable to have his own child question him.

Bending down, she picked up Pompey and held him close to her. He was a great deal more amenable to this treatment than her little brother Francis had ever been. Snuggling deep within her arms, he let out a sigh. Louise knew, in the instinctive way she knew many things about her dog, that he also regretted the move from Bristol.

Papa began to ask about transportation, access routes for supplies, and the local men answered. She let the words recede from her ears until they joined the rush of the sea to become a remote, meaningless babble. She would let Papa deal with the intricacies of the plan. He needed the distraction. Grief burnt within him, as bright as the delirium that had consumed their family. Occupation – any occupation – would do.

For herself, she appreciated a chance to gaze about and think. Peaceful time spent in solitude – or even better, with her dog – was always her most effectual balm. Once more her eyes were drawn to the stalactites. How spindly they were. Like wax that had melted and set. Louise had never considered 'underground' to mean anything but dirt and worms: the three narrow plots in the churchyard and the soil that had filled them. But here were secrets she would never have guessed. So much space. The walls were marbled grey, brown and a curious copper colour. A kind of bony structure, holding up the world she walked upon. It was good to know that something did. Of late, it had felt as if everything sure and supportive had crumbled to dust.

'My daughter will attend to all those needs,' Papa explained. 'She will launder the clothes and prepare the food for them once I have located suppliers.'

Forcing her attention back to the men on the other side of the rock pool, she found they were all watching her uncertainly.

'Dr Pinecroft, sir?' It was a fellow who had not spoken before. He removed his hat and turned it in his hands. There was a hole the size of a farthing in the side. 'The men from Bodmin … they be rough, unmannered fellows. Worse than folk in Bristol, I should say. Shouldn't let un near my daughters, sir. Mightn't be safe.'

Papa bristled, as he did now under any hint of criticism. 'I am perfectly able to judge the best course of action for my family, thank you. Men with phthisis will be weak and languid, more interested in drawing their next breath than offering any insult to a young lady.'

Pompey grumbled in his throat.

She could see the men eyeing her, willing her to speak out against Papa's plans. They did not understand. How could they?

Papa stood apart from the others. Clean shaven, better dressed, his chin thrown up in defiance. So brilliant, dashing … and terribly alone.

In need of defence.

These days it was not enough to be Papa's pet, the undisputed favourite of three children. His mainstay had gone and he needed Louise to become ... another person. A rope to bind the flotsam of their family together.

She would do it. God help her, somehow she would do it.

Louise drew back her shoulders. 'No doubt it seems a bold move, gentlemen,' she said, with as much gaiety as she could muster. 'So it is. But as Dr Pinecroft is always telling me, there can be no advancement in natural philosophy without risk. Only the intrepid make great discoveries. And I am willing to brave any inconvenience if the work may be of benefit to humanity at large.'

The hard lines in Papa's face relaxed. A trace, just a glimmer of the father she had doted upon crept through.

'We are going to find a cure, my good men,' he insisted. 'With the pure air and the right treatments we will eradicate consumption. It has taken enough from this country. After my experiments are perfected, no more families will lose their loved ones to its cruel grip.'

The men lowered their eyes. No doubt they had all seen people die of the disease. Almost everyone had. It was not selective in station, gender or age.

Another form of it, the scrofula, had even plagued the King's family. Were it not for visionaries like her father, mankind would struggle through such illnesses forever, never finding relief.

''Tisn't … dangerous, sir?' The man with the threadbare hat made one last timid effort. 'The disease? Don't it spread?' He met her glance and quickly dropped it once more. 'I … shouldn't like thy daughter to catch it.'

The man might as well have placed a candle snuffer over Papa's eyes. The light vanished.

'She has not caught it yet,' he said.

*

Why *had* Providence spared her? With Papa it was obvious: he was a great man who would do great things, even cure this disease if possible. But Louise …

Picking up her skirts, she began to climb the steep track that led from the beach to the back of the stable block. Pompey gambolled at her heels, glad to be released from the cave. His paws were caked in damp sand. So were her boots. It was just as well she had always clothed herself in plain, hardwearing fabrics; no modish gowns would have survived the ravages of the coast.

Her sister Kitty would have despised this place. She had been the beauty of the family, an avid studier of fashion plates. Every outfit Louise had worn in Bristol drew her playful abuse for its dull colour or its lack of trim. It had vexed her at the time. Now she would give anything to hear Kitty's voice again, even if it spoke unkind words.

As she rose higher, the wind swept downhill and combed the hair back from her face. The view was magnificent. The shoreline stretched to her right, far into the distance, making it difficult to tell where the ocean ended and the sky began. Waves rolled luxuriantly, flashing white crests. Where the foam lapped upon the beach, she could see a sandpiper questing for insects.

The natural world in all its beauty.

They were fortunate to be here. Such a fine house, cheaply won, an ideal location for Papa's experiments; so much opportunity to study the glories of the coast. She should feel grateful.

She was *trying* to feel grateful.

Pompey streaked ahead of her, his little legs a blur. Thank God, she still had him. It was possible to love Pompey without complication. The only pain he caused was when she remembered the day of his arrival. How ecstatic the children had been, how a much younger-looking Papa had immediately named him after the dog in the book he was reading to Louise: *The History of Pompey the Little.*

She had always shared a special relationship with Papa. Was that the real reason God had spared her: to comfort and assist him? A dismal realisation. She would so much rather be rescued on her own merit.

She reached the stables out of breath and aching in the legs. The youth her father had employed, Gerren, whistled from within. Pompey cocked his head.

'Come along, boy. Dinner will not cook itself.'

They ought to have a maid, of course. Especially in a grand house like Morvoren, with that entrance hall dripping in stucco. Papa had not thought to replace Alice. But perhaps that was *her* responsibility now, along with the orders and the accounts – a book she hardly knew how to complete, as she had no idea for how much money Papa had sold the Bristol property and his practice.

Mama would have known what to do. If only Louise had listened to her while she was alive. She recalled minutely the anatomy Papa had explained, the collection of bones that made up a human hand. But what use was that knowledge now, as mistress of a house?

The ash trees swayed gently, rocking the black velvety buds on their twigs. It was a relief to quit the uneven grass for the relative smoothness of the gravel path that led to the front door. She would need to order some sturdier boots – though from where, she could not fathom. It would be hard enough securing a butcher to deliver out here.

Pompey reached the entrance first. He snuffled loudly as he paced back and forth, nose hard against the bottom of the door.

'I merely said the word *dinner*,' she teased. 'I have not served it yet, silly dog. You will not be able to smell it.'

But clearly, he could smell something. Whatever it was made him whine.

Louise opened the door. Pompey pushed inside, nearly knocking her off balance.

Entering, she unwound her shawl and closed the door behind her. The entrance hall was still filled with boxes spilling their protective lining of straw and the bundles of the linen she had so carefully embroidered with numbers. Now that the rooms were papered, she could begin moving them all to their rightful places.

A fresh beginning, Papa had said. Chambers without the lingering presence of those they had lost. But if that were the case, why were the rooms decorated in Mama's favourite colour, powder blue? Why did the bedchambers bear the pastoral scenes *en vogue* in France that Mrs Pinecroft had been eyeing in the wallpaper catalogues? Well, men did not know about these homely things. To tell the truth, nor did Louise. Perhaps if Papa had burdened her with the task, she would have acted in the same way and relied upon the taste of her late mother.

Pompey yipped, calling her attention away from the boxes.

His paw prints tracked across the floor, towards the staircase. Louise followed them with her eyes, up to the iron banisters – and jumped.

Standing on the first step was a girl, holding a rectangular casket.

She did not have the demeanour of a housebreaker; she was too calm for that. Still, her attire verged on the untidy side of respectable: a thick linen shift with a collar, more grey than white, topped with a shapeless red dress and a man's coat far too big for her. Dried mud coated the hem of her skirts. Her hair, which was dark and wavy, fell without restraint to her shoulders.

'Can I ...' Louise started, feeling absurdly like an intruder herself. 'Is there something I may assist you with?'

The girl bobbed a curtsey. 'Please, miss. I'm Creeda. Come from Plymouth.'

Hers was a strange voice, unusually harsh. Pompey reared up and planted his paws against her leg. The girl shied away.

'Creeda from Plymouth,' Louise repeated. 'I am afraid I do not—'

Just then the door opened behind her. Papa strode in, windswept.

'Ah! Good, she is here.' He removed his hat without the least sign of perturbation. 'I engaged a maid, my dear. Credence?'

'Creeda, sir.'

'Yes, Creeda. And you have brought ...' He pointed his hat towards the casket she held. 'Excellent.' Pompey trotted over to Papa's feet and whuffed, as if demanding an explanation for this intruder. Papa laughed. 'Easy there, old chap.'

'A maid,' Louise said slowly. 'That is very fortunate. I was just thinking how desirable it would be to employ some help. But … did you say you came from Plymouth? Is that not a great distance from here?'

Creeda was casting her gaze around at the stucco. 'Yes, miss.'

'But coming from Plymouth,' Papa explained, 'she has also been able to bring a gift.'

'For whom?'

'For you, naturally.' He softened. 'I may be distracted, my dear, but I do not forget … You are mistress of a house for the first time. The circumstances are not as we could wish, yet still it is an occasion to commemorate.' Depositing his hat on the newel post, he reached out for the casket, which Creeda presented with another curtsey. 'Here, now. Our maid's family runs a porcelain factory up in Devonshire. Did I not tell you they have started mining the West Country clay nearby? See how white it comes up.' He opened the box and held it before Louise. 'What do you say? Is it not fine?'

It was: delicately wrought, painted as blue as the cornflowers that grew in the valley. A pot, two tea bowls, a pair of coffee cups and their saucers, one jug for the milk and a lidded basin for sugar. No ecru marks stained the bottom of these pieces. How Mama would have coveted them.

It was Mama's preference, again.

'This is delightful, Papa.' She took the box from his arms. It was much lighter than she expected. 'Thank you for your kindness.'

He regarded her tenderly. 'Every mistress requires her own tea service. You have become a woman, my dear.'

By necessity, not choice. This was a gift chosen to suit Mama. Louise only possessed it because Mama was dead.

But she could not let Papa think that his present had made her unhappy.

'I will take it through to the kitchen,' she said. 'I was just about to prepare dinner. Creeda, perhaps you can assist me? You will be wanting refreshment yourself, I think, after your journey.'

'Yes, miss, thank you, miss.'

'Capital. Become acquainted. I shall see you at dinner.' Flashing a smile, Papa bounded up the staircase.

Louise watched him stride along the landing to the west wing. He had always applied himself to medicine with energy, but he had never been a *bounding* sort of man in Bristol. She did not like to see this strained fervour in him. The desperation beneath it was all too apparent.

Sighing, she turned to her new maid. 'Follow me this way, Creeda.' For the first time, she noticed that the girl staring back at her had heterochromia: one blue eye, one brown. It hardly lessened her sense of strangeness. 'After dinner I shall have to consider where you will sleep. Forgive me, I was not informed of your arrival ahead of time.'

'That's all right, miss. You weren't to know.'

Louise led the way to the east wing, where she had recently cleaned out the kitchen. The box made a gentle chink against her hip. She *did* like the crockery – who could not? The workmanship was exquisite. Papa was sweetness itself for thinking of such a gift. Had he presented it to her on her wedding day, she would probably have been delighted. And yet ...

Perhaps that was part of her discomfort: the idea that she would not marry, now. For even if she were to meet a young man out here at the ends of the earth, however could she bring herself to desert Papa?

And then there was the disparity between this gift and the many others she had received over the course of her life. The time was that he would present her with samples of the *Materia Medica* or some odd pickled organ from his old colleagues in the dissecting rooms, knowing her fascination with such things. While Mama lived, he had seemed keen for Louise to flex her intellect. But now ... now, this present implied she was only required to make tea.

The kitchen was a long, narrow space without a window. It had a curved brick fireplace and a profusion of hooks which would serve nicely when she got around to unpacking all of the pans. Most useful of all was the water heater in the corner. Laundering for Papa and the consumptives was going to be a formidable task, even with Creeda's help.

Louise placed the tea set carefully on the table that occupied the centre of the room.

Pompey tapped his front paws in the little dance he always performed in anticipation of food.

'Impatience,' she scolded. 'Creeda, would you go through to the cold larder there? I have saved some offal; please give it to the dog in a bowl.'

Was that reluctance she saw in the maid's face? It lasted only an instant; Creeda obeyed without a word.

Louise began to unpack her new things. The teapot had a heft to it, but the other pieces felt light as thistledown. The glaze was rather harsh compared to the porcelain she was used to, yet the painting softened that. It was an original design of floral garlands. She could not make out precisely which flowers were represented – they were certainly none she had ever seen in the flesh.

Pompey ran the length of the kitchen as Creeda emerged from the cold larder with his offal.

The maid winced. 'Good dog. Good boy.'

She set the bowl down warily, almost leaping away when Pompey fell upon it.

Louise was obliged to hide her surprise. Pompey was about as dangerous as a butterfly. 'I am sorry, Creeda,

I did not consider how used I am to the animal. Are you much frightened of dogs?'

Creeda looked at her quizzically. 'Oh no, miss. *I* don't mind them.'

She spoke with such an inflection that it made Louise wonder who *did*.

'He will not harm you,' she added, removing the last tea bowl from the casket. 'He was perfectly trustworthy with my infant brother. A soft old thing and a useless guard dog.' She considered the tea bowl. 'This set really is very beautiful.'

'Thank you, miss. I painted that.'

Louise's head flew up in astonishment. 'You?'

'Yes, miss.'

Well, why should a maid not also be an artist? It was no different from a daughter who also studied medicine.

'You have a talent, I think,' she said kindly. 'I did not recognise the species of flower, though.'

'They were flowers I saw, miss.' Creeda's unmatched eyes darted away to watch the dog.

Perhaps Louise was trying to distract herself from the grief that lurked, always ready to pounce, but she found her mind filling with questions. Why would a porcelain factory let such a talented decorator go? It seemed an utter waste for a skilled worker to be reduced to domestic service, which nearly any poor girl could do. Even supposing Creeda had disliked the factory work, it was a family business. Had there been some disagreement?

It struck her that the girl appeared to have brought no luggage. She came with nothing but china. It grew more curious by the instant.

'You've ash trees,' Creeda said thoughtfully, still regarding the dog.

'Pardon?'

'Talking of plants, miss. You've ash trees around the house. I noticed them coming in.'

'Yes. The pattern of planting is rather inconvenient. Although the house is recently built, it is not of our design. I do not know if we should have the trees removed ... We possessed only a physic garden in Bristol, I cannot claim much knowledge of botany beyond its medical use.'

Creeda shook her head. 'It's hard to cut down an ash tree, miss. They say their roots reach to the underworld.'

Louise nearly laughed, but she saw the maid's face was deadly serious. Those odd eyes did not blink.

'Do they really? I had not heard that saying. What other folklore do you know, Creeda?'

Creeda's back straightened, as if here was a topic she might converse upon with authority. 'It's not folklore, miss, it's the honest truth. It's unlucky to cut down an ash tree, because of what they represent: the past, present and future, all as one. There's a ... timelessness to them.'

Absurdly, Louise's cheeks grew hot. She felt embarrassed for the girl and her foolish tales. Where had a maid learnt such nonsense? There could not be many ash trees in a port like Plymouth. Perhaps Creeda had read it in a book. But again that begged the question: what was a girl with knowledge of her letters doing washing plates and emptying chamber pots out here?

'How diverting, Creeda. Well, perhaps I will leave the ash trees alone. We have enough to do without adding landscaping to our worries.' She began to lay the fire, chiefly to make herself feel less awkward.

But rather than helping her at her task, Creeda continued to stare.

She should say something. Scold. Just how did one go about upbraiding a servant? She had never had cause to do it before. She had always been the placid daughter, the agreeable child. If only Mama were here ...

'I reckon you'll have another use for the ash tree,' Creeda's voice dropped to hushed tones, as if she were speaking of the dead. 'A fine young woman like you.'

Louise's cheeks were still warm from the previous blush, but she felt them flush again. 'Excuse me?'

'If you put ash leaves under your pillow, you'll dream of your future husband.'

Louise's throat tightened. 'I do not mean to marry,' she managed eventually. 'Would you please pass the tinderbox?'

And of course it was true. Her views of future happiness had never depended on a husband, unless he was a doctor she could assist like Papa. But there was something rather awful in having the choice taken from her. To have *I will not marry* changed to *I may not*.

Creeda handed her the tinderbox. Young as they were, her hands had a sandpaper roughness to them. 'Don't be so sure, miss. I can tell these things.' She nodded, looking much older than her years. 'Aye. I wouldn't give up hope. There may well be a man in your future, yet.'

Louise remembered poor Papa, the vulnerability on his face as he presented her with the tea set.

'My place is here,' she said shortly. 'And I do not consider this an appropriate topic of conversation for a maid and her mistress.'

Creeda gave a slow smile and set about her work.

Chapter 18

Cowards. The lot of them: measly, self-serving cowards.

He turned the pages of the medical journal faster and faster, sending a pile of letters neatly addressed to *Dr Ernest Pinecroft* sliding to the floor. No matter how hungrily his eyes scanned the print there was nothing, nothing, nothing. With a cry of frustration he reached the last page and slammed his hand down upon the desk. Another quarter of the year passed, and no one dared publish on phthisis.

He began to pace the small room he had devoted to his work, at the far end of the west wing. Astonishing, how quickly a new house could fall into disarray. Strewn across the floor were the stock ties he had torn from his neck at the end of each day. Books lay splayed open on every available surface and his pipes were tipping their burnt-out ashes into his inkwell. There was a tumbler, somewhere, hidden in this chaos, but since he could not locate it quickly, he took a small nip of brandy straight from the decanter. As he wiped his lips, he noticed for the first time the incongruity between the heavy oak-wood desk he had removed from Bristol by water and the elegant blue-and-white paper decorating the house. A large masculine smear across something female and delicate, like tobacco staining an evening gown. Well, what did it signify? *She* would never see it.

He threw himself down on his chair, still cradling the decanter. His wife would have known the words to put him in a better mood. She had been there, leaning over his shoulder, whispering in his ear, for more than a score of years. Now she was silent, just like his peers.

It had never been fashionable to devote oneself to the study of phthisis. *Foolhardy*, his friends would say, for everyone knew the disease was incurable. But Ernest could not accept that damning statement, and it enraged him that others would swallow such dross. What kind of a *healer* simply threw up his hands and said there was nothing to be done? He swirled the brandy around its decanter, watching the light play upon the liquid. 'All diseases began as incurable,' he muttered.

And that was another thing. If consumptives were doomed from birth, unable to be saved, how was it he had incurred such scorn? You could not, in good sense, brand a disease as unbeatable and simultaneously blame a man for not being able to treat it. But that was what had happened to him, all the same.

The light reflected off the glass and caught on the mourning ring adorning his smallest finger. Her hair, plaited with that of the two children. He could scarcely tell one from the other. Letters were engraved beneath the glass: L for Louisa, C for Catherine and F for Francis, but this felt like a falsehood. Catherine had been Kitty from birth and Louisa, his dearest wife, he had always called Mopsy.

That was what she resembled: a mopsy, a pretty child. Always slender and fine boned. So innocent with the roses in her cheeks and the sparkle of her eyes, and yet mischief would suddenly possess her elfin face. He sighed, set the decanter down precariously on the desk. He should have noticed from the start. But he was young then, he had not even completed his studies when the discovery of little Louise necessitated their marriage. He saw only Mopsy's enchantment, not that she was what others would call the 'consumptive type'.

Was *that* it? A certain type of person, selected by the disease with almost religious predestination? There could be no doubt that Kitty and Francis resembled their mother, whereas Louise was the spit of him, a feminine version of him, save for her mother's blue eyes, which blinked owlishly behind her spectacles. He riffled through the papers and found again the list of prisoners en route from Bodmin gaol. Men ranging from their mid-twenties to sixty years of age, serving hard labour for their crimes. Their existence rather

belied the theory. He would be a good deal surprised
if these ruffians and vagabonds resembled his dainty
wife in any shape or form.

Indulgence, one colleague had said many years
before; Ernest forgot his name now. At the time, talk
of phthisis had meant as little to him as it did to the
other physicians. Whoever the fellow was, he had been
convinced that the disease was brought on by pamper-
ing – the sufferer was consumed, as it were, by their
own consumption. And this was ... interesting. For
Ernest could not deny that he had always given his
wife whatever his pocket would stretch to. Then there
was Kitty with her rage for gowns and gimcracks, no
matter how exposed the new fashions left her skin.
And Francis was a baby, the desired heir born so long
after the girls; of course he was petted.

Ernest clenched his teeth, swallowed hard. It was an
answer, but not the one he wanted: that his love had
killed them.

He thought of Mopsy reclining on the soft pillows
of her bed. He had fed her dainties, trying to coax her
back to health, pulled a swansdown coverlet over her
narrow shoulders. He should not have plumped those
cushions for her. He should have laid her on a rock.

And that was what the convicts were going to get: a
short, sharp shock. Something to force the blood out of
its current erroneous patterns and start it flowing naturally again. No one could accuse him of overindulging

them. They would live more as nature intended and by God, he would make the treatment work.

Work – yes, work! That was the greatest protection against the blue devils, those low spirits that plagued him. He should not have allowed himself to become distracted by the past. Eagerly, he scooped the letters up from the floor and began to crack their seals. His enquiries to nearby towns and villages had been met with welcome. It seemed there were any number of local grocers and butchers who felt they could help him supply a nourishing but digestible diet to his patients; and many carpenters in need of work ready to construct huts. His plan to erect a dam for safety from the tide was confirmed as feasible. He would have to tell Louise …

While he read, Pompey nudged the half-closed door open with his nose and trotted in. The little scamp saw the scattered correspondence on the floor as a game; he began to paw through it. Ernest paid him little heed – the letters were dirty and crumpled anyhow and could endure a few more scuffs.

But after some minutes had passed, the dog's shuffling noises seemed to change. There was a rasp. Teeth against material. Ernest threw his current letter on the desk and leaned back in his chair.

'What have you got there then, old chap?'

Pompey wagged his tail proudly, as if he had exposed a great treasure. In fact, it was a cloth-bound volume of folklore Ernest had picked up from a stall in Falmouth.

'Ah, yes.'

Leaning down, he patted the dog on the head and retrieved the book from his mouth. Two medical cases at once. He never had been one to do things by halves.

The book was undamaged and only slightly damp from Pompey's attentions. Ernest gave the pages a cursory flick, finding more amusement here than in the medical journal. The rot people came up with! *Bucca* in the coves, *Knockers* in the mines. But one could almost understand how the stories had formed, in the days before medical knowledge. He knew there were healing properties in the soft, fresh air that entered the caves – an ignorant person might well attribute such powers to magical creatures. He must not scoff at these ideas. Treating his patient's theories with derision would only alienate her – he needed this book to understand her way of thinking before he could change it with the force of his own mind.

And perhaps at heart the two maladies he was tackling were not so very different. Some had observed a correlation between the consumptive's health and their state of mind, after all. Emotional well-being could stay the disease's ravaging hand …

He let his own hands droop, lowering the book onto his lap, and stared at them. Ink-stained, paper-cut. Marked with the many ways in which he had tried to divert his attention away from that mourning ring pinching on his right hand. No, he thought wearily, such a theory could not be sound. For his wife had been light of foot and quick to smile, his son a babbler of the happiest kind. They had been more like the creatures in these foolish fairy stories than people inclined to melancholy.

He threw the volume to the floor, narrowly avoiding Pompey.

No, if it was misery that laid a person vulnerable to phthisis ... It would have taken him by now. Him and Louise, both.

Chapter 19

Louise had been dreading their arrival. The terrible pallor and sunken cheeks, the eyes that glittered like sunlight upon the ocean. Worst of all, the cough. Sometimes she awoke at night, thinking she had heard that dreadful tearing sound in Kitty's throat, only to find herself alone.

Would it be different, from the chest of a man? More guttural, perhaps. If Louise had her choice, she would have gone the length of her life without finding out. But here she was, shortly after dawn, dressed and waiting for Papa by the front door. If he did not cower in the presence of the disease, neither would she.

She was well prepared as usual, with paper for observations, one pencil in hand and a spare tucked behind her ear, underneath her cap. But Papa arrived unshaven, his stock loosely tied. Smudges beneath the eyes suggested he had not slept well – or he had spent the night poring over medical treatises again. 'They have come. I saw the carts go down, from the window,' he told her. 'Let us meet them.'

Louise hoisted up a smile. 'Do we need to take anything with us?'

'Only your notebook for this preliminary inspection, and I see you have that to hand. Did you change the water in the leech jar this morning?'

'Yes, Papa.'

'Good.' He nodded. 'Good. We will have need of them later.'

A stiff March wind charged over the clifftop and flattened the grass. Already signs of spring were showing: the gorse and rosebay willowherb coming into bud, and strands of cow parsley emerging from the hedgerows. The sky had yet to follow suit. Currently, it was a veil of dirty gauze, devoid of any blue.

The track steepened and Louise took hold of Papa's arm. His kerseymere sleeve felt damp to her touch, as if he had sweated through it. Her chest tightened another notch.

There was so much at stake. Both of them knew, yet neither would speak of it; just as they did not voice their dread of the memories these men would inspire. Louise had to compromise all her understanding and support into the pressure she applied to her father's arm.

She could still picture the blankness that had swallowed his face when, after ten years of patronage, Lord Redfern had sent for another man to attend upon his gout. How on the street, the next day, a lady in a poke bonnet had whispered to her companion, 'A fine physician, upon my word, unable to keep his own family alive!' and they had both pretended not to hear.

Sea mist welled up as they descended to the beach, its thickness clouding her spectacles and muffling the relentless pound of the surf.

'Be careful,' Papa warned. 'The stone will be wet underfoot.' He took her hand. His glove had already turned clammy and cold, disturbingly like the palm of an invalid.

Together they negotiated the pebbles and rocks, jumping down to the sandy part of the beach, which sucked at their shoes as they walked. Dark shapes were apparent up ahead.

Disembodied male voices floated down the beach. Louise tensed her shoulders, braced for the sound of a cough.

'Courage,' Papa whispered. 'Have courage.'

She could only nod.

The wind made a scouring sound as it blew through the cave. As they walked past its mouth, Louise turned her head to look inside. She had always been tall and well built, but the cave made her feel small, humble beyond measure. She could not shake the feeling that there was a vast presence inside looking back.

They had arranged for some wooden huts to be constructed and a small dam to keep the waters back at high tide. Moisture dripped from somewhere, echoing as it hit the surface of a pool.

'Ah, it is the surgeon from Bodmin.' Papa was looking straight ahead and accelerated his pace, tugging Louise along with him. He sounded all business once more. 'Make haste, my dear, I must speak with him.'

The man was standing beside a wagon heaped with cane chairs, pots, pans and bales of straw. One glimpse told her he was not cut from the same cloth as her father – she had not supposed a gaol surgeon would be. He wore a bent three-cornered hat and his own rat-coloured hair was tied up in ribbon beneath. Slung around his waist was a sword belt and tarnished scabbard. Louise wondered if his charges had ever given him occasion to use it.

'We're just glad to be rid of 'em,' he was saying in a tired, deep voice to the driver of the wagon. 'Infection will spread through a gaol quicker than crawlers. And o'course there's no hospital hereabouts as will take a contagious disease. '*Tis* contagious – I don't care what they say.'

'Let us hope this will be a second chance for them. A reclamation,' her father called. The man turned confusedly. Papa removed his hat and bowed. 'Mr Jeffries, I presume?'

'Aye. Dr Pinecroft, is it?' He gave an awkward imitation of the doctor's obeisance. 'Well, 'tis a novel concept ee've got, I'll give ee that. Although we've miners enough coughing up their lungs in this district, I doubt *they'd* see the sense in living underground.'

'But the cases are not similar in any respect.' A touch of heat from Papa. 'The mineworkers are sweltering in galleries, inhaling nothing but dust. My patients here will have pure air, clean surroundings, gentle exercise and a nourishing diet.'

Louise cleared her throat.

'Ah, forgive me. Mr Jeffries, my daughter, Miss Pinecroft.' She curtseyed. The man looked somewhat taken aback, but sketched another bow. 'A capable nurse. She is fully conversant with my theories.'

'*Vis medicatrix naturae.*' She smiled. 'The healing power of nature.'

'Almost, my dear. Strictly speaking, that is the body's natural ability to heal itself, which we also hope to capitalise upon. Given their condition in life, it is likely that these men will be sturdier and more resilient than the patients we are used to.'

Mr Jeffries raised his eyebrows in her direction. 'I daresay they will, miss.'

She did not allow her smile to waver. It irked her how everyone, save for her father, envisioned her as too delicate to countenance a group of criminals. No doubt they would prove uncouth. But she had wiped streams of blood from her own mother's mouth, watched the life fade from Francis's big blue eyes. After all that, did Mr Jeffries really think a few curse words were likely to undo her?

'I believe,' she said brightly, 'that these men have agreed to participate in the trial on the understanding that their crimes will be pardoned, should the treatment prove efficacious.'

'Just so, my dear. An extra inducement for us to succeed. Lives will not only be saved, but changed.'

Mr Jeffries grimaced. 'I suppose ee'd better meet 'em, then.'

It would not do to take Papa's hand now, so Louise clasped both of hers before her stomach and inhaled a deep draught of salt air. She might not be afraid of the men, but she could not be quite so confident about the disease. It had been many months since she stood *vis-à-vis* with the wraith of consumption. This time, she would not let it win.

Five men of varied height were lined up beside the shore, iron gyves fastened around their ankles. There was little need for that restraint. All were skeletal figures incapable of flight and their fetters only served to chafe their painfully bony joints, rubbing the flesh raw. One, on the far left, she took for a man of Eastern descent, but it was difficult to distinguish the colour of either hair or skin while both were heavily engrained with dirt. Louise took off her spectacles, rubbed them with her handkerchief and reapplied them. A tall, bearded man shivered before her in the morning mist. He wore ragged, filthy clothing, despite his illness. Small wonder he showed no signs of improvement at the gaol. She was glad she had sewn so many new shirts against their arrival.

'You have records of their height and weight, Mr Jeffries? They were not included in the correspondence.'

'I do, sir. I'll send them on.'

'Good.' Papa rested his chin upon his hand. 'Louise, write down my observations as we inspect them.'

The first man, who gave his name as Seth, was older than the others and troubled with a squint. Louise could not be sure whether or not he was leering at her. In her estimation, he had contracted consumption quite recently; the flaccid, wasted muscles of his calves were the only hallmarks of the disease.

Papa looked at what she wrote and nodded.

'Won't keep me down, Doctor,' Seth averred through feeble vocal cords. 'Got through the Seven Years' War, I'll be damned if this makes the end of me.'

Papa patted his shoulder and declared that he had the right spirit.

Michael, the heavily bearded man, they could not view with the same degree of composure. Fever was written in every line of his body. Sweat plastered the shirt to his narrow chest, which looked all the thinner because of his height. In his prime, Louise supposed he had been sturdy, the kind of man used to manual labour. Now he did not seem to know where he was. Gently, Papa placed an ear against his chest to listen to the lungs.

He did not dictate anything to her this time – she based her notes on the dark expression that clouded his face.

Third in line was the youngest, perhaps five-and-twenty, going by the name of Harry. He was at what Papa generally termed the 'dazzling' stage. Hectic colour flooded his cheeks. He was willowy, rather than emaciated, and his green eyes sparkled like emeralds. She could not take her eyes from them.

Mr Jeffries called the following man Tim. He was too exhausted to speak even his own name. Illness had drained the skin; he appeared to be made entirely of bruised wax. No hair remained upon his head, and although this was hardly the fault of the disease, it served to make his impression all the more pitiful.

Papa gave her a single shake of the head.

Chao was the last man. Perhaps he had always been slender, but even beside the other patients he seemed outrageously thin. Had he tried, he could simply have slipped his feet through the gyves and walked away.

Papa greeted him kindly, like the rest. 'And how long have you been afflicted with this complaint, my good man?'

Chao opened his mouth to answer. What emerged was a cough.

She heard the fluid in it. Hacking, scraping, hurting her own throat with its force. Her pencil pushed through the damp paper. She was back in Bristol, spoon-feeding fennel root and ginger in water that refused to stay down.

Papa turned his head away and looked out to sea. His hands were balled into fists.

It was a marvel they had come so far today without hearing this. But the reprieve had not helped, had not enabled Louise to prepare herself. The emotions were every bit as acute as she had feared.

Ignorant people always fancied that ghosts appeared as shrouded ghouls. Anyone who had suffered loss could tell them differently. Sounds and smells haunted with more persistence, dragged you backwards in a way that nothing else could.

Chao spat a glob of blood onto the sand. The same colour of scarlet-red, no matter who the sufferer. For a moment Louise stared at it, transfixed.

'Rest yourself.' Papa returned his attention to the man, his face set in a perfect mask of cordiality. 'There will be time enough to discuss this later. We must settle you in, procure you some refreshment.'

He put a hand on Chao's shoulder. Only Louise saw the tremor in it. She had no doubt that Papa felt exactly as she did, but he was forced to prove himself, lest he lose all professional reputation, along with his family. After what he had endured! How was that possibly just?

If you put a string under that amount of tension, it would be sure to break.

She might break, if Chao coughed again.

The surf rushed in, bubbling around their feet, and washed the blood away.

Chapter 20

As a bachelor and a medical student, Ernest had spent the night in some unsavoury situations, to say the least. But as the sun touched the horizon and began to bleed across the sea in streaks of crimson and gold, it occurred to him that he had never slept in a place as strange as this before.

The lanterns were burning low. All the twinkles and shimmers that had crossed the cavern walls during daylight had fizzled out. Now long shadows scurried over rocks and human faces alike, seeking dips and hollows. Such gaps were not wanting in these unfortunate men. The deep eye-sockets, the sucked-in cheeks – each were perfect wells for the darkness to spill into. His current patient, a man named Tim with no hair, seemed transformed into a gargoyle.

'Today has been a great exertion,' he told the man, as he settled him on his straw pallet. 'And your previous conditions were uncommonly draining. Tomorrow, we shall help you regain your strength. Light, nour-ishing victuals and equally light exercise.'

Tim moved his head on the pillow, which was probably all the acquiescence he was going to get. Considering the fellow had not been able to swallow his broth supper, it was a wonder he possessed the energy to keep his eyes open.

If that blasted surgeon from Bodmin, Mr Jeffries, were here, Ernest would string him up. What did he mean by sending him such woeful specimens? Beggars could not be choosers, but he had hoped a fellow prac-titioner of medicine would comprehend his need for patients not yet *completely* ravaged by the disease. And while Ernest would not expect prisoners to be treated softly, he was appalled that the men's health had been neglected to such an extent in the gaol. They were not, after all, murderers.

Thankfully, he had taken Louise's advice and made the caves a little more comfortable for them. If the phthisis *was* caused by overindulgence, at least Bodmin gaol proved that spartan conditions were definitely not its cure.

He left the door to the wooden hut open so that he would hear any sound of Tim's distress during the night. He did not anticipate much sleep, but he was used to that. Often, in the early hours of the morning, he would lie awake and hear Louise crossing her own room, fetching a book or going to her escritoire. Neither of them had regained the trick of undisturbed slumber after those long nights of caring for their family.

Removing his coat, he folded it and laid it upon a level slab. That would serve as a pillow, if the straw ones were too flat for him. The air was rather chill, but there were plenty of blankets, and he was by no means averse to cooling the general temperature of these men.

On the other side of the cave, Louise bent over the youngest man – Henry, was it? Maybe Harry. The lantern light reflected in her spectacles and turned her eyes into discs of gold. He felt a flush of pride seeing how tall she was, how robust against the slender man. Not quite the beauty Kitty had been, perhaps, but with a charm of her own. Fully grown. His heart seemed to stumble in his chest as he reflected that Louise's mother was about the same age when she gave birth to her.

Louise handed her patient a gallipot. 'Here. It is camphor. Apply a little to your chest and your back before you try to sleep. It will help.' She mimicked Ernest's own authoritative tone, he noticed. He could not help but smile.

Leaving Harry to follow her directions, she withdrew. Despite the encroaching dark, she managed to pick her way over the slimy stones towards Ernest.

'You were born to the wrong sex, my dear,' he told her. 'If you had been able to serve as my apprentice, I would be losing my patients to you by now.'

He had meant it kindly, but he heard the bitterness that crept into his voice. Such talk was meaningless – he had no patients left to lose.

'Everything I know, you taught me, Papa.'

He considered her, as she stood half concealed by shadows. During the terrible nights of illness, they had whispered together many times in such poor light. In the dark, she seemed hardly his child at all but an indispensable part of himself, following his directions, supplying his missing thoughts. 'And so it will not surprise you to hear these patients are worse than I expected. You will require all of your learning to help them, and I ...' he trailed off. There were not enough words to convey the activity his mind was buzzing with. 'I will work harder. I shall find the cure.'

His daughter carried a habitually worried expression behind her spectacles, but he saw it deepen, carving two lines between her eyebrows. 'The man I was speaking to. Harry. He seems stronger than the rest. And the Chinaman's appearance is very slender, but I note that he is still alert.'

'Yes. That is true.' He stroked his chin. Stubble had grown there without his realising.

There was undoubtedly a difference in the patients. Poor Tim clearly had the galloping consumption that had taken Kitty and Francis so quickly. But the men Louise had singled out seemed to echo the gradual decline of Mopsy. Almost a different, more refined version of the illness. Did this mean, then, that there were two strains of the same disease? Not just one but *two* impossible cures to find?

He placed his face in his hands and rubbed it hard, as if it would restore will to the flesh.

'It is late. Off to bed with you, my dear.'

Louise pursed her lips. 'Are you sure I should not stay, Papa? You will need some help ...'

'No, no.' In truth, he would like to keep her with him, but he would not have his precious girl sleeping on rocks, surrounded by knaves. 'I know I have a tendency to set propriety at naught, but I must draw the line somewhere, Louise. Your mother ... she would never forgive me.'

She gave a tight nod. 'I will fetch you in the morning.'

'Of course. I will come up to the house and we shall take breakfast together.'

'You do not require my assistance lighting any fires?'

'Not tonight. I believe it is mild enough, and the men need cooling down.' He peered over her shoulder. The sun was nothing more than an ember gasping above the waves. 'I *had* hoped your maid might come down to accompany you back to the house.'

The corner of her mouth quirked, as if she had some secret amusement. She leant in and kissed his cheek. 'I shall do perfectly well alone, Papa.'

Removing a lantern from its hook, she began to walk with it swinging gently at her side. For a moment her shape appeared, clear as cut glass in the mouth of the cave, and then she was gone.

It felt as if she had taken all the light with her.

After a final check on the men, he lay down and attempted to get some rest. Perhaps the moon was full tonight, and maybe there was a frosting of stars, but inside the cave he could see none of it. Everything was black as a mole's pelt. He stared upwards for a while, equally disconcerted and fascinated. You would not find a darkness so absolute in Bristol. It seemed to press on him like a living thing.

Ernest closed his eyes and scarcely noticed any change. One of the men muttered.

He was tired, but he had learnt this meant nothing to his busy mind. It was occupied in recalling medical lectures from years ago. Briefly, it alighted upon his other patient. He had scarcely seen her. Tomorrow he must make the time … She had not come down to the cave. Was that due to an excess of domestic work, or did she have another reason? Not all girls were like Louise; some shrank from illness. And hadn't he read something … yes, something in that folklore book. Fairy Caves. Pixie's Parlours.

He shifted on his slab. Under the cover of night such stories did not appear fantastical.

The stone amplified every sound. A distant drip. The sea, gurgling against the sand. When the wind blew it made a high, keening note like a chained dog.

For all his isolation, he did not feel quite alone. There was that indefinable sensation ... a lingering. As if someone were watching him through a window.

He opened his eyes. Black, still black. Louise was right, he should have lit a fire and ordered another pallet for his own use. The temperature was dropping.

He passed a hand across his eyes, as if it would help matters. Somebody was there, he was sure. One of the men. They might have stumbled from their hut in search of aid. But where were their footsteps? All he could hear was that drip.

'Ernest.' Right against his ear, the breath hot on his skin.

He cried out and jerked into a sitting position. Who was that?

Who was *she*?

His heart thundered. He reached out with both hands, grasping, trying to feel. Stone. Cold, hard stone. There was nothing, no one beside him.

He could hear himself panting. The short, shallow gasps of fear. It was impossible to slow his breath while it remained so dark – there was nothing to anchor him.

Pull yourself together, man.

A dream. He must have fallen asleep and imagined ... He had overtaxed himself. All that worry was manifesting itself in strange fancies. But he was awake now. He was certainly awake, and cold.

How he wished for Louise.

The thought of her steadied him. He remembered her childhood nightmares – worse than Kitty's had ever been, as if the poor girl had some prescience of the horrors she was going to witness. He had calmed her so many times. How had he done it? What did he say? *Take a deep breath, count to ten …*

'One,' he whispered, 'two …'

A strangled scream.

He sprang to his feet.

'Hello, there!' he cried out into the emptiness.

His words echoed with nowhere to land.

He must walk, must make his way to one of the huts, but it was hard to force his legs to obey. They did not want to step forward into a wall of blackness. It went against all good sense.

Stop being such a fool.

Haltingly, he managed to take a few paces on the uneven rock.

'Help me!' A male voice this time, not the one that had whispered in his ear. He took courage, headed towards the sound.

Shapes appeared in the darkness. A smudge of yellow that must be a lantern – he *knew* he had left some of them burning. He had never meant for the cave to grow this gloomy at night. The wind must have snuffed the other flames out.

With a wash of relief, he saw the door to a hut and a puddle of light spilling across the threshold. He was grounded again. A physician. He felt ashamed of his folly, but the devil take him if that hadn't been the most vivid dream …

The hut belonged to Chao. Louise dubbed him a Chinaman, but the voice that called out was as English as roast beef.

'Doctor! Get 'em off me! Get 'em off!'

Ernest took the lantern from its hook on the wall of the hut and bent down beside the man.

Chao's face was beaded with sweat. His eyes had the appearance of smeared glass.

'Calm yourself, man. You are feverish, nothing more.'

Chao stared about him with his mouth ajar. 'But they … where did they go?'

Patiently, Ernest swept the length of his frail body with the light. 'See here, there is nothing on you.'

'But I felt …'

'You have thrown your blanket off in your sleep,' Ernest pointed out. 'The cool air must have tickled your skin and caused you to dream.' He picked the tangled blanket up and handed it to Chao, who snatched it under his chin like a child. Fear and emaciation left him looking utterly harrowed.

Suspicion and wild visions were all part of the illness, of course. He debated giving Chao some laudanum to help him sleep, but that might lay his troubled mind open to stranger phantasms still.

'Let me find the barley water. Miss Pinecroft left some by each door. A drink will restore you to yourself. Are you in any pain?'

Wordlessly, Chao shook his head.

When Ernest handed him the tankard, Chao sipped at it meekly enough, but still his dark eyes darted around the confines of the hut. It was on the tip of Ernest's tongue to ask him what he thought he had seen, but he judged it better to let the vision pass from his mind.

How could other physicians be content to let people suffer like this? Phthisis was a trial not just on the body but on the mind and the spirit. It was monstrous. He *must* find the cure. But the sea air, which he had set so much store by, seemed already to be working against him: dousing his lamps, irritating Chao's delicate skin and whispering ...

Gingerly, he touched his ear.

Chao spluttered into his tankard. 'Doctor?' he croaked.

'Yes, Chao.'

'I'm tired.'

'I should say so,' he replied. 'You look absolutely hag-ridden.'

A tremor passed over the man's slender frame. Perhaps it was too soon for him to laugh off the experience.

'I don't think ...' Chao glanced down at the blanket, embarrassed. 'Inside, you see, there's a lot of people. Chained in the cell. All cooped up together, we are. It's what I'm used to.'

Ernest supressed a smile. He knew what the convict's pride would not let him admit.

'Ah. An oversight on my part. I did not consider how difficult it would be for you to adjust to the change. It is a natural reaction of the body. It senses danger, although there is none.'

'Right.'

'Suppose,' Ernest added conversationally, 'I were to sit in here for a spell? Just until you fell asleep again. Your body might register my presence and allow you to rest easier. That is what it is used to, after all.'

He could almost see the tension leaking out of Chao's shoulders. The blanket dropped from the bony hands that had gripped it for dear life. 'Well, Doctor … If you think it's a good idea …'

'I do.'

Gratefully, the man settled down in his bed.

Ernest sat on the floor and pressed his back against the wooden wall of the hut. An improvement on the stone slab, at least. The lantern sat by his feet, bathing him in its warmth and light. He could still hear the stray drip, but it was softer here, less insistent.

He smiled wryly at his situation. In the forty-two years of his life, he never dreamt he would spend the night in a makeshift hut with a convicted criminal, but he found himself glad to do so now.

If he were honest, he was even more relieved than Chao.

Chapter 21

'Underground?' Creeda spoke the word as if it meant perdition. 'He's put those poor sick men underground?'

'Not precisely. They are staying inside the caves for a while. Constant exposure to the sea air will prove beneficial to their diseased lungs.'

It was certainly proving beneficial to the laundry, hung out in lines before the house. White linen snapped and bellied like the sails of the ships in Bristol harbour. It would dry in no time, and that was just as well; Louise had thought little Francis made much washing, but his clouts were nothing compared to the demands of five sick men.

Having sweated over the tubs for hours, Louise and Creeda were treating themselves to a stroll upon the cliff. Mounds of thrift grew unchecked here while moss campion hugged the soil.

Pompey scampered ahead, yapping for joy. Gulls scattered at his approach.

'Excuse me, miss.' Creeda's hand twitched, picking at the wicker basket hung over the crook of her arm. 'Did you say *caves*?'

'Yes, Creeda. There are caves on the beach beneath the house. That was the main inducement for my father to purchase the property. He has had this colony in deliberation for some time.'

'I didn't know.'

'Did you not? I was certain my father would tell you there were diseased men, possibly infectious men, in the vicinity of your workplace. It is not like him to omit such information.'

'Oh. Well, aye,' Creeda replied. Louise could only see her brown eye, peering down at the empty basket. With her hooked nose, she looked rather like a bird from this angle. 'I knew about *them*. Just … not the caves.'

The wind boomed, trading cannon shot with the sea.

'Is it …' Creeda went on hesitantly. It seemed Louise's earlier scold had been heeded, for the maid was certainly speaking with more care. 'Forgive me, but is it a good idea, miss?'

'It is an excellent notion,' she responded in a voice that brooked no argument. 'My father is a brilliant physician.'

'Yes, miss.'

They could not afford to lose against death a second time. Papa's professional reputation had already suffered two mortal blows – the loss of his family and Lord Redfern's patronage – it would not weather a third.

The caves had to work. They *would* work.

She looked sideways at Creeda and felt a twinge of sympathy for her. The girl was young – about Kitty's age – alone and far from home. She had enough to be afraid of, without worrying about the men. Perhaps Louise could help allay her fears.

'Tell me, Creeda,' she said softly, 'what bothers you about the caves?'

'It's ...' Creeda wet her lips. 'It's the things that live in them, miss.'

Louise remembered standing by the mouth of the cavern, that sensation of being watched. 'Crabs? Nesting seabirds? I do not think there is anything else that might live—'

Pompey began to bark. For an awful moment, it sounded like an echo of Chao's abrasive cough.

Both girls looked up to see the dog's tail wagging furiously. He snorted and pawed at the ground before him.

'What has he found?' Louise groaned. 'I must not let him eat it, he will be sick.'

Quickening their steps, they came up behind Pompey.

Louise seized his collar. 'No! Leave it!'

As she pulled him away, she saw what he had been nosing.

It was a collection of bones, bleached by the sun and picked almost clean. Whatever had expired had been dead for some time. There were no flies or maggots. Grass grew up around it in a little circle, as if to lend the deceased some modesty.

After her father's tales of the dissecting room, Louise was past being frightened by macabre sights. But she was surprised to see Creeda kneel fearlessly beside the skeleton and begin to inspect it with no sign of distaste.

'A hare, most likely.' Creeda picked up a bone and turned it over. Bristles of tan-coloured fur snagged on the end. 'Or some sort of rabbit.'

To Louise's astonishment, she placed the bone inside her basket.

'What are you—'

'For the factory,' Creeda explained, reaching for a rib. 'It's our special composition. Six parts bone ash, four parts Growan stone, four parts clay.'

Pompey strained beneath her grasp. Louise scooped him into her arms and continued to watch her maid as she gathered up the bones. The skeleton was mainly intact. Birds had carried away the majority of the flesh, but a dark ribbon here and there gave a hint of putrefaction.

'You mean to send those bones to your family in Plymouth?' she asked, astounded.

'Yes, miss, after I've boiled them and cleaned them up. Gerren found me a seagull yesterday; I'll do that too. You'd be surprised what you can boil down. A whole carcass, if needs be. Makes the china strong.'

Ladies in Bristol had looked askance at Louise for her medical learning; even asked her, over tea, how she could withstand such ghastly subjects. Now she longed to go back and tell them that the very bowls they held in their hands were made of animal skeletons; that their prized sideboards were filled with nothing but bone!

'I had no idea they could be used in such a fashion. But surely the slaughterhouses in Plymouth can provide bones for the porcelain factory?'

Creeda paused, holding the remains of the skull aloft. She caressed it with a fingertip. 'You'd be surprised, miss. There's demand for good bones. Ask Dr Pinecroft.'

'Whatever do you mean?'

'Those resurrection men. They don't just sell corpses, miss. Sometimes the flesh is too rotten, so they flog what they can.' Creeda sighed, packing up the remaining bones like some morbid picnic. 'Father made a pot once, after they come round. I don't know what he bought, but they weren't animal bones. Not them.'

Louise felt sick. She had an image of her family's graves in Bristol, so exposed and unprotected. Dissecting corpses to further medical science was one thing, but this ...

'Could anyone truly be so wicked?' she whispered.

Creeda shrugged. 'It's a memorial, of sorts. China's prettier than a skeleton.' She glanced towards the coastline. The wind blew out her dark hair. 'They mine the china clay near here, don't they, miss? Who knows? Perhaps I'll make some china of my own, one day.'

Pompey whined. Louise buried her face in his fur for comfort and walked away. In Creeda's voice, the words did not sound like an innocent aspiration.

More like a threat.

*

Louise trod the familiar path down to the beach where her father was already at work. Some of the men were out and about on this blustery morning, making the most of the sun as it flitted between fast-moving clouds. Old Seth sat on a rock, drinking milk from a pewter cup. Chao stood at the edge of the water, letting the surf play over his bare feet. One of the shirts Louise had sewn billowed around his wasted frame. The plan was to start the men on a regime of sea-bathing once they had rallied a little strength, but she could not envision the Chinaman taking part in this. He was so slight, the tide would carry him away.

She approached the entrance to the cave. Some lamps hung suspended from nails driven into the rock. By their light, she saw her father, just inside the opening, listening to Harry's chest.

The young man offered a wan smile. Today his lips were crimson, flecked with blood.

'Good morning,' she said. 'How are you feeling? I trust the camphor brought down your temperature?'

He nodded, reluctant to speak while the doctor listened. She noticed the distinct three-sided bite on his wrist, which showed Papa had been removing his diseased blood with leeches.

Harry reminded her of the apprentices who had trained under her father in Bristol: eager, polite young men with just that little spark in their eye to suggest they could misbehave, given the chance.

It was a daily struggle for her to remember that all these men had been arraigned and incarcerated for crimes.

Papa pulled away from Harry and appraised him. 'Hmm. Have you drunk your milk today?'

'Yes, sir.'

'Good man. I want you to go and walk slowly on the sand, take in some of that fine air.'

'Glad to.' Harry tugged his forelock. 'Miss,' he said to Louise as he passed her.

A hardened criminal indeed.

A cough echoed from the back of the cave, punctuated by a steady dripping. Papa rubbed the bridge of his nose, thinking.

She felt awkward, a trespasser. It was always so in the morning. The men banded tightly together, as if something had taken place in the night that she could not understand. But she comprehended all too well: the nights were the worst for consumptives. The fever, the restlessness, the gasping for breath. She had seen it all and she should be down there, helping Papa to nurse them through it.

'How do you progress?' she ventured.

He turned away, not meeting her eye. 'It is too early to tell at present. I am sure the air will prove salutary, but I am not willing to trust to that alone.' He began to pack the jar of leeches and the tongue depressor into his mahogany chest. 'We both know the dangers of such complacency.'

'Papa, you did everything you could—'

'Not everything,' he insisted, growing slightly hoarse. 'I did not take them to a better climate. Italy has many advocates, but it was so difficult to travel with ...' The top of the box slammed shut. She saw him trying to form the F for Francis; he could not bring himself to do it.

Her own chin trembled. Dear God, she thought, do not let him see me cry.

Another cough rang out.

'However,' he added tightly. Both his hands remained flat on the top of the mahogany chest. 'I begin to suspect it is the sea voyage, and not Italy itself, which offers relief to the phthisical patient. Look at the lower classes. Neither the sailor nor the fishwife suffer. We will find the cure in the ocean water ... in the air. How your mother would have loved this air.'

Louise swallowed and tried to turn the subject. 'I did not see Michael or Tim outside. Do they keep to their beds?'

'Yes.' Still he did not look at her. 'The moisture retained in the rock has done something to lower their fevers. The emetics are also jarring Tim's humours back into balance, but Michael ...' He exhaled. 'Michael stands in need of your nursing. Perhaps you could help him to drink his milk.'

'I will do it directly, Papa.'

She picked up a cup and made for Michael's hut.

The wooden door was damp and spongy to her touch. It creaked when she pushed it open. Michael made a confused noise that was not quite language.

'Hush, now. It is Miss Pinecroft.'

The atmosphere inside was oppressive. A natural, stony smell rose from the cave and mingled with the tang of wet wood. But these were the pleasant scents. She tried to focus upon them, rather than the effluvia and stale exhaled breath.

Michael lay on a straw-stuffed mattress. He had sweated through the sheet and his clean shirt. A brimming pot at his side showed the purges had worked, at least.

'Water,' he panted.

He looked haggard, the flesh hanging from his cheekbones. Droplets of blood and vomit were sprinkled in his beard.

'We should prefer you to drink milk this morning.' She took a rag from her apron and ran it over his brow. 'It is most effectual at building up the strength.'

He groaned.

She imagined the disease sitting thick on his lungs, like tar. How could it waste a strong, tall man like Michael and leave her, a slender girl of barely twenty, untouched?

Sitting Michael up, she leaned his weight against her shoulder and began to spoon the milk from a cup into his mouth. After only two swallows, he erupted into a coughing fit.

She felt it spray her cheek and closed her eyes. Michael gripped her so tight that it hurt. She thought of the catch in a fisherman's net, twitching and gasping on the deck.

She opened her eyelids and saw why Michael had not been able to take in air. His lungs were brimming with something else.

The blood spilled over, dribbling down his lips into the cup of milk. She watched red ribbons twist through the white liquid, and all at once she was holding a cup fit for the devil's table.

Hastily, she set it aside and tried to dab Michael's mouth. When she brought the handkerchief away, all

the red he possessed seemed to come with it. The hue
of his lips now matched the pallor of his skin. Even his
gums were anaemic, shrivelled.

It took all her fortitude to keep her distress from
showing on her face.

'We will try again later,' she said briskly, rising to
her feet. 'In the meantime I will obtain a feeder cup.
Such a vessel will make the process easier.'

He wheezed for a moment before replying. 'A ...
pap boat. Like a ... damned baby.'

Little Francis flashed before her eyes.

Turning on her heel, she left the hut.

Papa was still standing in the same spot, his fingers
at his lips. This was the way he would listen, intent, as
a patient described their symptoms.

Only no one was there.

'Papa?'

'Louise! Did you ...' Confusion suddenly clouded
his brow. He glanced quickly behind him. 'Did you
just arrive?'

'I have this moment come from Michael's hut.'

'Oh.' He sounded disappointed. Again that furtive
glimpse over his shoulder.

She considered showing him the cup of blood, but
his distraction was evident. She set it down on a rock,
glad to have it out of her hands.

'So you did not ... Never mind.'

'Is something amiss, Papa?'

'Amiss? No, no.' He ran a hand down the length of his face. 'In fact, I have had an idea.'

She nodded encouragingly.

'You recall me saying that smoke inhalations have relieved the symptoms of asthma?'

'I do, Papa.'

'And this disease shares characteristics with the asthma: the difficulty breathing, the tightness of the chest. Surely strengthening the lungs in general will help fight against one aspect of the illness.'

'So you propose to give the men pipes?'

'I do.' He drew back his shoulders, a touch more confident. 'But smoke is not the only treatment that has helped asthma sufferers. They have also derived benefits from stramonium and *digitalis purpurea*.'

'Foxglove?' The word popped from her; the cave took it up and bounced it back, mimicking her amazement.

Papa waited until the echo faded away. 'You are right to be surprised. Of course, the plant can prove poisonous. But in small doses, it will promote the absorption of air.'

'And slow the pulse.'

'Just so. We will regulate the hectic flow of the men's blood. They have an overfullness of blood, at present.'

His face had unfolded. The muscles of his jaw looked more relaxed; there was something of the old gentle set to his brow. Her parent returned to her.

Surely she must encourage this, or anything that gave him purpose?

'I will layer the tobacco with stramonium and digitalis,' Papa decided. He seized her hand and pressed it in his own. 'Then we will work to combat the fever and the wasting. It will be a cure, Louise. We will achieve it. These men shall live to enjoy their freedom.'

She had read *Pharmacopoeia Extemporanea* more times than she could count. Without going back to consult the pages, she knew the composition it recommended for such inhalations: pistachio peels, hyssop, horehound, even orpiment. There was no mention of smoking the leaves of foxglove or stramonium – a plant the common folk called Devil's Snare. This must all be her father's own genius.

'It is a bold plan, an admirable plan,' she began carefully. 'If we could only be certain ...'

'Courage, Louise! Trust me,' he said.

She did not realise, until that moment, that she had ever stopped.

Chapter 22

Ernest awoke at the first glimmer of dawn, when the gulls began to screech. He did not object. Sleep, when it came, was no relief. His wife flitted through his dreams. Not as she had been in life but radiant, transformed into an angel. A mirage he could not touch.

That image remained in his mind as he returned to the house and spoke with his patient before she began her daily tasks. He realised that his own grief was giving him a unique insight into Creeda's troubled world. He could comprehend, when others could not, how the demands of sensibility might have caused her to weave elaborate stories for comfort.

Such as her tale of 'changelings'.

'Sometimes they swap,' she had told him, as matter of fact as if she were asserting the time of day. 'See, they get the sickly fairies, ones that are of no use, and they put a charm on them.'

'What kind of charm?'

'One to make them look like us. So you could be gone, taken away underground, but there'd be a fairy in your place, wearing your own face. No one would know,' she added, her voice tight and afraid. 'No one would even know to come and find you.'

Swapping the sick for the healthy. An ingenious concept. He almost wished he could do the same.

'And you believe that these sickly pixies—'

'Fairies, sir.'

'Pardon me, fairies. Do they die?'

She shrugged. 'I expect they would. They can't stomach our human food.'

He thought of his men on the beach, struggling to consume the milk and broth he had brought them. What would she make of his consumptives, if she ever braved the caves? 'But in your mind, the person concerned is not actually deceased? Although their double expires, they remain … in fairyland?'

She nodded. 'Under the ground. Where I was.'

A consolation. Almost a blasphemous, mangled concept of heaven: to believe that your loved one lived on in a world separate from your own. But the similarities with orthodox religion ended there. The differences were stark and decidedly lunatic.

'There is no method, I suppose,' he had asked almost jokingly, 'of switching back?'

'Water,' she replied at once. 'You banish the fairy with water or fire.'

'You kill them,' he said flatly.

'Yes, sir.'

An altogether more pleasant exchange took place at the end of the interview. He left her with her daily ounce of distilled vinegar, and in return she handed him a small wooden casket. 'Your order, sir.'

He opened the lid. Inside were two small vases. Cobalt blue flowers surrounded the rims, but the curved bodies were a fretwork of strange vines, intricately twined.

Mopsy would have adored them.

And she would have been pleased too, he thought as he climbed the stairs, that he had procured another present for Louise. Towards the end, she had always been pestering him to leave her and tend to the children instead.

'Louise has them in hand,' he would say, loath to part from her.

But she would lie back on her mountain of pillows and fix him with that infinitely wise look. 'Do not neglect Louise. Intelligence is no guard against distress. She may be capable, but that does not mean she is coping.'

A highly womanish thing to say, but he had heeded it nonetheless.

He stopped outside Louise's bedroom and was reaching for the door handle when it struck him that perhaps he should knock. She was a young lady now, after all ... But he could not quite bring himself to swallow that, so he entered the room boldly as usual.

The ash tree outside the window was bursting into leaf. Morning light filtered through the branches and gave everything a greenish underwater tint. Louise sat at her dressing table, wedging some extra hairpins through her cap.

She did not pause in her toilette or show the least surprise at seeing him.

'Sorry, Papa, I fear I am running late. I meant to be at the caves an hour ago. Creeda did not wind my clock.'

'It is of no matter. I wanted to speak with you.'

'And I with you.'

Her dressing table was very sparse, he noticed. None of the lotions and powders Kitty would have thought necessary. And then there was the room in general. It was neat as a pin. He thought with shame of the chaos that reigned inside his own chamber. How devilishly tricky it was without Mopsy to keep things in order.

Louise reached for her spectacles. 'What have you there in your hand?'

'A gift.' He smiled and laid the box down on the dressing table. 'It occurred to me that my last was perhaps not fitted to our current circumstances. We are hardly likely to receive guests for tea! I hope you will like this better.'

She opened the casket and withdrew one of the vases.

Ernest had thought the vases were identical to the *toile-de-Jouy* in which he had decorated the rooms, but now he saw the paint was a darker blue, the colour the sea turned when you were beyond the shallows and venturing out of your depth.

'How exquisite.' He was disappointed to hear the detachment in her voice. Her smile did not reach her eyes. 'I can pick the wildflowers that grow on the cliff and display them.'

'Precisely.'

Louise looked at the base of the vase and saw the Nancarrow factory stamp. Her smile faltered. 'Another from Creeda's family?'

'Yes. I asked Mr Nancarrow to send a pair that your maid had decorated herself.'

She let out a slow sigh. Despite the cap she wore, he could see the worry bunching in her forehead.

'You ... do not care for them?'

'Oh, Papa!' she cried. 'It is only ... Forgive me, Papa, it is not the present that is at fault. It is ... Creeda.'

'I see.'

Damn him for a blockhead, he should have foreseen this. How long did he think he could keep it secret from her? She had her mother's penetrating eyes; they saw everything.

'I do not mean,' she explained haltingly, setting the vase down, 'to question your judgement. Creeda is a very diligent worker. I can see how on first application, she might appear ... However, I am sorry to tell you that I have observed the girl closely and reached the conclusion that she is not suitable to work inside our home.'

His temples tightened. Why did he not plan for this eventuality? So many thoughts were blazing through his mind: the caves, the smoke, the phthisis … He needed time to consider his words. But there Louise was, blinking up at him, expectant.

'Would you care to explain your reasoning, my dear?'

Louise wet her lips. 'I did not wish to tell you. It seems unkind, akin to gossip, and yet … Well, I shall give you some examples. First, she collects animal bones from the clifftop and boils them clean. Not for soup. She just boils them, in our kitchen … And then, she is always trying to give me handfuls of ash. She says it will protect me from … something or other.'

'That is certainly peculiar, but—'

'You have not heard the worst of it. Last night, I happened to mention her heterochromia. I cannot even recall what I said, it was a careless remark about her eyes. But she told me that she was not born that way. That, if you can credit it, her aunt found her on the factory steps one day and her eye had turned from brown to blue.'

He tried to chuckle. 'Impossible, of course, but Creeda is not to know that. Perhaps it is merely an anecdote her family have passed on.'

'I would agree with you, except for what she said next. Papa, she …' Louise dropped into a whisper. 'She thinks she uses her blue eye to see into fairyland. I am afraid that she is quite mad.'

Bizarrely, he felt a spurt of irritation with his daughter. It passed; he held up his hands in surrender and sat down on the edge of the bed. 'I know it, Louise. Her mind is not sound. That is why she is under my care.'

'Papa!' Just one word, but it made him wince. The reproach – no, worse than that. The *disappointment* in it. 'She is a patient of yours? You did not tell me!'

'I told you she came from the factory to be your maid, which is true. I exchanged correspondence with the Nancarrow family. They heard of my imminent arrival from their workers at the nearby clay setts. You see, Creeda's behaviour had been causing difficulty at the porcelain manufactory. Her family wished for her to be watched by a professional. Away from wagging tongues.'

Louise swivelled round on the stool. 'But Papa, you are no mad doctor.'

'No,' he admitted. 'That is exactly the point. Should you like Creeda to have her head shaved and rubbed with vinegar? To see her chained and doused with ice water?'

Her mouth fell open. 'Truly, she … she is a young girl, to suffer from delusions,' she stammered. 'What can she be – fifteen, sixteen?'

'Kitty's age.'

Louise was silenced.

Ernest noticed his hands were shaking. He tried to take a breath, but his throat was painfully tight. 'Louise, I want you to imagine for a moment that you are a woman, not advanced with the experience of a great many years, responsible for the well-being of a small child. A child, shall we say, of about five. This poor little creature has endured a travail, the likes of which would fell grown men. Naturally, the child seeks to find meaning for her suffering; she wishes to know what has caused it and yet … How do you explain such depravity? The meaningless cruelty of the world, when she is obliged to go on living in it? How are you to tell her when you scarcely know yourself …' He stopped, aware he had grown excessively animated. Louise was staring. He gulped another breath. 'Now, if you were this woman, would you relate the cold, immovable facts as you understand them to the child? Or would you not rather couch them in terms she is more likely to comprehend? A fairy tale with wicked imps, for example. Something altogether more … palatable.'

'I do not understand you, Papa.'

His darling girl. He wanted to shield her from this. 'My dear, I am speaking of Creeda's aunt. I am afraid she was put in this very position when Creeda was abducted in her youth. The child went missing for an entire year.'

'Good God,' she said with quiet feeling. 'Abducted by whom?'

The twisted blackguards who paid for such things. Many had come to his door with their chancres of venereal disease, exclaiming that even lying with a child had not cured them. It had taken all his restraint not to run them through with his lancet. They might pollute those poor children, but he was damned if they were going to sully the innocence of his own daughter.

'That remains unclear. But one of the brutes had an attack of conscience and fetched her back home.'

When Creeda spoke of her rescuer, she described snowy white skin and a red mouth like a wound. Rather like a consumptive. Or a whore, powdered and rouged.

He felt a reluctant admiration for this brave prostitute. In all likelihood, her madam would have beaten her to death for saving the child.

Louise had turned very pale. 'Merciful heavens.'

'Creeda did not know her mother. She looked to her aunt to explain her experience and I am afraid that … It was ill advised, but understandable in the circumstances. The aunt told Creeda that she had been taken away by the fairies.'

'And the poor girl still believes it,' Louise breathed.

'Yes. That is the reason for her somewhat – indecorous – behaviour. The Nancarrows pay me well to watch her, but that is of no consequence if she causes you distress.' He twisted his fingers together. The mourning ring glinted. Hair trapped beneath glass. 'Do you want me to send her away, my dear?'

'No.' Louise rose sadly to her feet. 'Good gracious, no. She is an unfortunate soul. We must help her, Papa.'

His kind girl. He only hoped his ability was equal to her compassion.

Chapter 23

Pompey took a liking to the stables, where he could spend his days agitating the chickens penned just beyond his reach. Louise went to collect him as evening began to descend on Morvoren House.

To her fancy, the sea sounded kinder in the twilight. No longer impatient, chopping this way and that, but respiring softly, as a child in slumber. There was comfort in it. She longed to be off her lonely clifftop, walking barefoot on the stretch where stones gave way to sand.

How pleasant it would be to simply wander, with no companion save for her faithful dog, and breathe in the fresh sea air. Let her troubled thoughts wash away with the tide.

Pushing open the door to the stables, she found Gerren climbing the ladder to the hayloft. He held one lamp in his hand; another hung on a nail beside the cows.

'Where is my rascal, then?' she called.

At the sound of her voice, Pompey came scampering across the hay-strewn floor, his tail wagging.

'Been fixin' to drink milk from Betsey, missus,' Gerren drawled. 'Had to fetch un a dusting.'

Louise knelt down and let Pompey clamber onto her. 'Oh dear. I trust you were not too harsh on him?'

But she knew Gerren was soft-hearted towards the animals; he had a calm manner that drew them to him. Besides, he was a skinny whip of a thing. Eleven years old, or twelve at most. He lacked the strength to cause any real damage.

'What do it matter, missus? Beast don't mind a word I say, dustin' or no.'

She laughed for the first time that day. Was it odd that she envied Gerren and his night here amongst the animals, breathing in their tang and the sweet warmth of hay? Despite the modern comforts of her room and the decorations Mama would have adored, it still did not feel like home.

However, the landscape was a different prospect. She loved the untamed beauty of Cornwall. How it rose, fell and curved. Its vital breath. Even the granite and moorland were not wholly bleak; here and there were flashes of vivid colour. Mines pocked the county like a honeycomb, yet they did not spoil it.

Towns were all very well, but she knew she would struggle to return to one now. How artificial it would feel. She belonged out here, where the only order was that of nature itself.

'Tell me, Gerren,' she said, as she fondled Pompey's silky ears. 'Were you bred in this area?'

'Aye, missus.'

'And is there a stretch of beach where one might walk, unmolested, without the tide cutting them off?'

The lamplight flickered on his face. 'Away from the caves?'

'Yes,' she said emphatically. 'As far away from the caves as possible.'

*

Never before had she committed an act of such daring. To walk alone, by night, with only Gerren's lamp to guide her! But she did not experience the thrill of misbehaviour; there was no shortness to her breath and her pulse came steady. There was a calmness to this beach on the north side of the cliff. As silver moonlight played upon the water, it was impossible for Louise to feel anything except serenity.

Even Pompey appeared pacified, trailing behind her. He did not caper after the waves. Once or twice he cocked his head at their two shadows, thrown against the cliff face by the lamp, but that was all. Smells absorbed him: millions of tiny nuances to which Louise was insensible and always would be.

She held her lantern higher. Clumps of seaweed lay upon the beach. A few puddles remained where the tide had been and gone and their still water reflected a sprinkling of stars. Who could imagine Creeda, or anyone, facing horrors in a place like this? It was beautiful, eternal. She regretted their cave on the other side of the cliff. An ugly scar on the landscape, marring the peace with sickness and death.

Pebbles tinkled down behind her. She heard Pompey's paws scrabbling over shale. What was the little scoundrel about now?

She swung the lantern around. The dog was facing the cliff. He looked as if someone was offering to throw him a ball: backing up before darting forward, impatient. Had he seen a bird nesting in the rocks? No matter how high she raised the lamp, she saw only the rough stone. But Pompey's gaze remained fixed.

'What are you doing?'

He planted his feet square. A growl rumbled in his throat, and suddenly he barked.

The sound that answered him took her breath away. It was like branches breaking, but there were no trees here, only the valerian growing in the rocks.

The rocks.

One thudded down, dark as a lump of coal. It landed with a spray of pebbles beside the dog. Everything was sliding, melting. A landslide.

'Pompey!'

He whimpered.

'Pompey, run!'

Another creak.

She could not move, could not tear her eyes away. She would have to watch. She would have to watch another one die.

Black spots crowded into her vision. There was a great whump, and she felt a gust of wind sweep over her, taking her glasses with it.

It was impossible to see clearly now. As she squinted, one of the shadows seemed to expand and lengthen into something tall and thin. Pebbles stung her arms. The last thing she saw before a cloud of sand engulfed her was the dark shape, falling over Pompey.

*

Pain rang at her elbow. Coughing, she wiped a hand over her gritty face. Sand was in her hair, on her lips, up her nose. The lantern had gone out. She let it drop.

Before her lay a small mound of rubble, indistinguishable in the gloom.

Pompey.

Tears tracked their way through the sand on her face. How had it even happened? Surely, landslides only occurred in heavy rain? The night was clear, if cool, the moon sailing free of clouds. It should not be possible.

It should never be possible for one person to lose so much.

Her spectacles lay half buried at her feet, their shape jutting through a thin layer of sand. She scooped them up. The frame was a little bent. A hairline scratch marked the left lens, but when she settled the wires back over her ears, she could see perfectly well. She was not sure if that was a blessing or a curse.

Louise took a deep breath, readying herself for what she must do. Then she heard the cough.

Her heart leapt. 'Pompey?' But it was not the shallow cough of a dog. This was deeper – a sound she knew well. The consumptive choke. It came again, harsher this time. Foolishly, she thought of Kitty. All the long-forgotten childhood stories of ghosts and spirits came back to her. 'Is ... is someone there?'

Pompey yipped.

The rush of hope shook her more fiercely than the landslide had done. Crying out, she leapt forward to the pile of debris.

Most of it was sand. She moved what stones she could and dug. First, she saw the shirt – one that she had sewn herself, drenched in mud. The man was lucky – he had caught the very edge of the cascade where the scree was thin.

'Are you hurt?' she spluttered through the sand in her mouth.

'Nah. I'm a hard nut to crack.' Despite these brave words, the voice that spoke them was strained and hoarse. Louise dug faster.

'Here.' She tapped the man cautiously, unsure which part of his body she was touching. 'This way is up. I am digging from here.'

He began to writhe. She heard him trying to dig, too, and the clink of Pompey's collar. At last she caught glimpses of the space within: a smaller, darker cave.

There was a scuffling sound, and Pompey's head burst from the hole she had made. His ears pricked up; he looked delighted with himself.

'Pompey!' She lifted him out, receiving a barrage of licks to her face. She ran her fingers through his matted fur, searching for a wound, but there was nothing. Not a scratch upon him.

The reason for that soon became clear. As she put the dog down and recommenced her excavations, she saw the man inside the little hollow was crouched on his hands and knees. He had thrown himself bodily over Pompey as the cliff crumbled, taking the force of it himself.

'Harry? Is that you?'

He turned slightly, wincing as he did so. 'Yes, miss.'

'What are you doing here?'

Her nails were cracked and the muscles in her arms were screaming, but she managed to move the last few rocks and haul the man up.

The sight of him terrified her. He had broken his nose and was half blinded with blood. His glistening, almost translucent skin had bruised purple and yellow like the flowers on the clifftop.

'Here, lean on me. Can you climb out of this hole? It is just a short way.'

He was not heavy, for a man. She felt the bones beneath his skin as she pushed him before her.

A sorry sight the three of them made on the moon-lit beach, spluttering, trellised in salt and sand. Their clothing was ruined. Pompey ricocheted between his mistress and his rescuer, keen to lick off every trace of their adventure.

The oily black waves rushed in calmly, as if nothing had happened.

'Come, let us wash your nose in the salt water. Careful, it will sting.'

He obeyed without question, letting her guide him to his knees in the surf and cup water over the wound. He did not flinch as she expected.

'What were you doing all this way from the cave? Does my father know you are walking about?'

'You're very welcome, I'm sure,' he replied sourly.

She cursed herself. 'Do forgive me. Of course I am beyond grateful that you saved my dog. Words cannot express ... But truly, I worry that you are hurt.'

His face twisted. 'Hurt? I'm dying. You know that.'

The wonder was that he could talk at all after taking such a knock to his weakened frame. Sharp collarbones rose up from the neck of his ruined shirt, reminding her painfully of the collection of hare bones Creeda had found.

'Have you so little faith in our treatments?'

Harry wiped the blood from under his nose. He looked more unwell by moonlight, without the flush and sparkle. 'They might give me a bit longer. But a cure for consumption? You'll sooner find a hen with teeth. I'll keep living each day as if it's my last – if it's all the same to you.'

Her shoulders were trembling. The shock, perhaps, and the chill of the sea.

'The span of your days will be shorter if you do not rest,' she explained, rising and dragging her sodden skirts with her. 'Why are you on this beach? Were you ...' Another shiver took her. 'You were not following me?'

Harry laughed and was instantly racked with a coughing fit. He doubled over, spitting something into the water before straightening up.

'No doubt the lads do follow you, miss. But I'm afraid I an't one of your conquests. It's the caves.' He pointed to a narrow cleft in the rock face, some two hundred yards behind her. 'They run all the way through, if you know which way to go. I come here often.' In an undertone, he muttered, 'God knows there's no sleep.'

The image of the cave at night rose up before her: the ghostly tendrils of pipe smoke, moonlight bouncing off the waves and playing in ripples on the ceiling. Disembodied coughs. Somewhere, deep within the cavern, that constant drip.

No wonder he wanted to escape.

'I will not tell my father,' she promised, looking down at him. 'About this beach, at least. But we will have to say something. These are not injuries you can disguise.'

He regarded her. 'I reckon I'm not the only one in trouble with the doctor.'

She flushed. 'Never mind about that.'

Harry struggled to his feet, ignoring her outstretched hand. Pompey jumped over the sea foam to beat his tail against the man's leg.

'Do you trust me with your dog?'

'Trust you?' she repeated. 'You saved his life.'

'Then leave him with me. I'll let him out of my hut in the morning, tell your da I saved him from the rocks. He's not to know the daft thing didn't escape from your house.'

A criminal, she told herself. This man is a criminal. But she couldn't believe it.

'That is tremendously kind of you.'

Harry shrugged.

'I do not …' She glanced doubtfully at the pile of rocks where the cliff had crumbled. 'I do not suppose you could take me back with you, through the caves? I have no idea of my way home …'

He was sickly, dirty and bleeding, yet still there was a certain light when he smiled, the crinkles that appeared beside his eyes and the gentle curve of his mouth. A spark disease would never quite quench.

'Well,' he grinned. 'I reckon you'll be owing me a few favours, miss.'

Chapter 24

Pompey placed his head on Louise's thigh, awaiting crumbs from her breakfast.

Papa tutted at him. 'You see the rascal is unabashed by his ordeal.'

'I cannot think how he came to escape,' she replied, feeling guilt prickle beneath her skin. 'I shall make certain to lock him up in future. And I will get to work on a cold compress for poor Harry's nose straight after breakfast.' She reached down from the chair and scratched Pompey's ear to hide her unease. It felt horrible to lie to her father, even over this trifle. But Harry had kept his side of the bargain. Papa never need know that she had been outside, brazenly wandering on her own at night.

As if he had read her thoughts, Papa went on, 'We owe Harry our gratitude, certainly, but he should not have been walking about at that hour. I am afraid I was obliged to read him a pretty stern lecture.'

Louise's shame climbed a notch. Another punishment he had endured for her sake – not that he was a man likely to be troubled by an upbraiding. She wondered what sort of life he had led before prison, and how he came to be so kind. There must be good in him. Pompey would not have been fond of him if he was truly a bad apple. Dogs could always tell.

'Perhaps this increase in energy is a sign of improvement,' she said awkwardly. 'But what do you say to the rockfall? Is it not uncommon?'

'Yes, miss.' She jumped to hear Creeda's voice beside her ear. The girl had entered the room noiselessly and now stood next to Louise's chair with a plate of hot muffins. 'Not just uncommon, that rockfall, but unnatural. I told you. They don't like dogs.'

Papa was drinking tea at the time, but Louise saw his eyes widen over the rim of the bowl.

'I do not gather your meaning, Creeda.' She shot her maid a warning look. 'You told me nothing. Of whom do you speak?'

'Of the fairies, miss.'

Papa put down his tea bowl, fingers still wrapped around the blue flowers. 'And it is your opinion, Creeda,' he said slowly, 'that fairies made – what? – an assassination attempt on our naughty little beast?'

Creeda swallowed. 'It is, sir.'

Papa gave a rueful smile. 'In this instance, you must admit the evidence is not in your favour. The cur is untouched – it is Harry who has a broken nose.'

Louise motioned with her hand. 'That will be all, Creeda.'

Creeda curtseyed and retreated with a foreboding expression.

Louise poured herself more tea, but she could not shake her feeling of discomfort. To think of something malignant, trying to hurt dear Pompey! It was just another of the unfortunate maid's many delusions, of course, and yet she kept remembering the way Pompey had stared up at the cliff and barked. How the land had cracked without rain, without warning.

If Harry had not been there ...

'I must beg your congratulations this morning, my dear,' Papa said as he bit into his muffin. 'Aside from our rogue Harry, the men slept soundly last night. I have observed an increase in vigour since the pipes were introduced.'

She was able to give the first genuine smile of the morning. 'I am glad to hear it! They were an excellent notion, Papa.' Absent-mindedly, she picked a crumb off her own muffin and offered it to Pompey. 'But what of Tim and Michael? I fear they fare rather worse than the others.'

Papa held up a finger. 'Yes, but that is because the disease is more advanced in them. It has had longer to grab a hold. Do not fret, I have a plan for them too, which we shall implement later today. It came to me last night, as I slept. Possibly at the same time that canine imp you are rewarding was attempting to kill my patients.'

How pleasant it was to hear him jest again. Were it not for the empty chairs at the breakfast table, she could almost convince herself they were back in old times.

'Do you truly think we will manage to heal them, Papa?'

'I do,' he replied emphatically. 'I can feel ... Oh, you will laugh at me, no doubt.' He shook his head, but a smile still played about his lips. 'I know this is right, Louise. Our fate, our calling, our purpose. After all we have suffered, this is what we were meant for. God is with us ... and your dear mother.'

His last words made her tea bowl rattle against its saucer. Looking into his face, she saw his eyes were ablaze with zeal.

'I do not say this to upset you. But I *feel* her, Louise, guiding me.'

Absurdly, Louise felt a spurt of jealousy. It was *she* who needed Mama's guidance. And she had felt nothing – save the great crater her mother had left behind.

'We do it all in Mama's name,' she said, as steadily as she could manage. 'She would be proud of you. Very proud. I know it.'

He looked down at the tablecloth. 'I fear I have alarmed you. Do I sound extremely fanciful?'

They had prayed for help from heaven. If it had come, she should be grateful. And she must bear in mind that Papa had been nursing late at night. Weariness could be a kind of fever. She knew all too well that when all you saw for hours was sickness and death, your musings could take the strangest turns.

In the distance she could hear Creeda washing up pans, and the steady beat of the sea. Was it her imagination, or had the breakfast set grown? There seemed to be more blue and white patterns, more Nancarrow Bone China. As if Creeda's past were slowly spreading across their table.

She reached out and took her father's hand. 'What will we do, Papa? What shall we do after we find the cure?'

'Oh, Louise.' He blew out his breath. His features grew rapt. 'Once I have slayed this demon ... What shall I *not* do?'

Chapter 25

Ernest was not used to being repelled by his patients. He had attended on countless deathbeds, births and post-mortems. But since they had shaved Michael's beard, the man's head appeared uncannily small upon the pillow. The neck supporting it was swanlike, the shoulders beneath steep and sloping. Put together, his body looked less than human.

A damned stupid thing to say, of course. It *was* human. When he scarified that narrow, heaving chest, it would bleed like any normal person.

'Water,' Michael gasped.

'I have only this milk for the present,' he said, pressing the pewter cup into Michael's slender hand. He noticed the fingernails, curved and misshapen. 'Miss Pinecroft shall fetch more drinking water down to us.'

'Water,' Michael repeated.

Such a thirst.

'Yes, my good man, it is the water that will cure you. Fine English salt water. None of these gentle, mawkish

Italian climates for us but something bracing, more invigorating.'

He began to unpack the cupping set from its mahogany box, the glass jars rattling and chinking. Did they remember the last flesh they had disfigured? That sweet, young skin. Francis did not bawl in protest, as any other infant would do. The poor child could not draw breath enough to scream.

Nauseous, Ernest passed a hand over his face. Blue devils. It did not do to dwell upon the past.

'Water.'

The most powerful element. He had seen it this morning as he descended from the cliff: gunmetal grey, rippling like a horse's flank. If he concentrated, he could hear it even now, sucking greedily at the sand. One had to listen closely in this cave. To hear the secrets hidden in its depths.

'Water,' Michael pleaded.

Creeda spoke of banishing fairies with water. She also claimed that was how the miners freed their china clay from the slurry, by bombarding it with water.

But water was not enough. He must have fire, too.

He polished his chosen jar and heated it above the lantern flame. Light swam in the glass, liquid amber. Ernest would have appreciated the beauty, if his mind was not set on the next stage.

He approached Michael with the scarifying knife and the heated glass. Sure enough, when he nicked the lily-white skin of the man's chest, it dribbled blood. Ernest exhaled, strangely relieved. What had he truly expected to see?

He placed the rim of the jar over the cut, fencing it in. Michael twitched and clenched his jaw. The hiss that came from his skin echoed the one issuing from between his teeth.

The sound was always the worst part. That and the smell. One could not help but think of pork skin, bubbling over a roasting jack.

Ernest watched the blister form with a vague feeling of dismay. Perhaps it was the dim light, but the sight he had seen a thousand times suddenly appeared brutish, primitive in the extreme. Was this medicine? Healing?

He recalled the days of observing chirurgical procedures at the hospital. Sawdust and an insufficient box to catch the washes of blood. Patients with handkerchiefs draped over their faces, as if in preparation for a shroud. So few survived. The chasm between mankind's advancements and the infernal cunning of illness felt wider than ever.

It would take a revolution to overcome phthisis. An entirely new way of thinking, like the men who had dared to open their minds and believe the world was not flat. His own brain was capable of such a leap. It *must* be. He could feel so much potential, burning within him.

Michael's moaning pulled his thoughts back to the present. That pitiful, sparrow-like breast was surely too frail to endure more blisters. There was a gentler method of drawing bad humours from the chest. He would insert a seton and let the skin weep.

Michael continued to beg for water. Ernest ignored him and began to fumble in his satchel for the necessary equipment.

Wind gusted into the cave, bouncing from rock to rock. The lamps flickered. It sounded like the dead whispering.

'Water.'

'Damn it, man!' he burst out. 'I have none. Be patient.'

Ernest tipped up his satchel and cast the contents on the ground. There was the needle and a spool of silk thread. It would be best to start with silk and move up to the bulkier India rubber in a few days' time.

'Lie back, Michael. The water is coming.'

Ordinarily, he would need to feel the position of the patient's ribs to ascertain the correct placement. There was no need for that here. Each one of Michael's bones stood out prominently. When Ernest threaded the silk cords through the skin, they seemed to become part of the man, moving when he breathed, burrowing ever deeper. Somehow, that simple, bloodless sight was the most revolting Ernest had beheld in his career.

'I am hoping for a discharge,' he explained as he finished. 'Once that begins, we will—'

'Blast your eyes!'

The shout that cut him off was followed by a scuffling. Someone whooped.

'Just try it, old man.' The responder was surely Harry, his voice vaunting and full of disdain.

'I'll knock your bleedin' head off!'

There was a crash.

Cursing, Ernest abandoned his work and left Michael's hut.

He had the sensation of walking into a country fair. Seth and Harry were wrestling in the ashes of the fire circle like common louts. Tim lay on his back, propped up by his elbows, looking on, whilst Chao smoked and cheered from the sidelines.

'Look sharp,' he said around his pipe stem, 'here comes the doctor! You'll be for it now!'

But the men did not stop.

Ernest's temper flared. Did his authority mean nothing, even to these men he had rescued from incarceration? He clenched his jaw – felt like a patient biting down upon the strap. 'Gentlemen! Come, come. You are not in gaol now.'

Seth jabbed at Harry's throat. The already bruised young man fell back, clutching his neck and gasping. Seth scrambled to his feet and spat.

'You keep your hands off my food. Got it?'

Blood trickled from the corner of Harry's mouth.

Ernest seized Seth by the collar.

'What have you done? What kind of imbecilic, degenerate ...' He pushed the man from him, disgusted. 'Is this sport to you? Is it?' He looked from one startled face to the next, hardly able to credit the depth of their stupidity. 'I am trying to save lives! Night after night I spend tending to you in this ... hole in the ground! And all you want to do is punch the remaining life out of each other!'

Seth's stubborn old mouth set into a line. 'He drank my milk.'

Ernest raised his eyes to heaven. 'Good God! And that is reason enough to kill the man! What do you lack? Do you think I could not supply you with whole pints of milk?'

Harry scowled. Though his left hand remained on his throat, he managed to struggle up to a sitting position. 'I didn't crib it.' His voice sounded like raked coals. 'You're losing your wits, you old coot.'

Only the strength of Ernest's glare stopped Seth from going for him again. Instead, he picked up a pewter cup and waved it in Harry's direction. 'What do you call that, then? Just upped and went on its own, did it?'

'Why the hell would I want your milk? Like the doctor said, there's plenty to go around.'

'Then stop filching it!'

'Now listen.' Ernest inhaled deeply through his nose. 'This must cease. For shame! Are you men, or a squabbling parcel of old maids?'

'But all us, Doctor!' Seth whined. 'We've all had cups go empty.' He pointed a dirty finger at Harry. ''Cept him. Old Jack Sneak there.'

Harry sneered. 'I an't sneaking your milk, dotard. If I wanted aught, you'd know about it. I could baste you easier than taking a piss. There's only one milksop here, and I'm staring right at him.'

'Why, you bleedin'—'

Seth launched himself forward. Ernest leapt at the same time, grabbing the back of the old man's shirt. But then a sound rent the air. Something high, crystal and sharp.

Chao clapped his hands over his ears.

Seth and Ernest fell to the ground, puppets with their strings cut.

'What ...' Harry gasped. 'What the hell is that?'

Ernest felt the ringing in his teeth. He fought his way out from beneath the old man's bony frame. Everyone was frozen, entranced.

Somehow the noise was as familiar to him as a well-loved voice. He knew he had heard it before, heard it in his dreams.

Cautiously, he rose to his feet. 'I think it is coming from Michael's hut.'

To his astonishment, the men shrank back. Chao bit his pipe and began to shuffle towards his own wooden home. For all their puff, they were cowards. What had they to fear?

He followed it.

Distantly, he was aware of Harry dogging his steps, the harsh grate as he cleared his throat.

The ringing swelled. As he crossed the threshold into Michael's hut, it nestled in the base of his skull. What could it be? There was nothing remarkable here. The space was as Ernest had left it: partially lit with shadows darting like minnows about the walls. Only ...

He frowned, puzzled. There *was* a change. The cupping set.

It was packed neatly away into its box.

Each jar shivered gently within the velvet lining of the chest. The lid remained thrown back, as if to display their tiny spasms.

A memory stirred with the sound. *That* was where he had heard it before: on the streets of Bristol. A performer begging coin, running the wet tips of his fingers over glass rims to release their song.

But there was no entertainer here. Only the cursed figure of Michael in the corner, confined to his bed, his skin sunk down on the trellis of his bones.

Ernest looked from the chest to the bed and back again, certain he would comprehend shortly. But all that came to him was a nervous twitch in the throat.

There was no conceivable way Michael could have risen and packed all the jars.

'Devil fetch me.' Harry lurked in the doorway, his eyes circular. Both men stared at the trembling cupping set together, in the profound manner they would watch over a corpse. 'Doctor, how can …'

'The wind,' he said shortly. He used that explanation to shield himself as he stepped forward and firmly closed the mahogany lid. 'Simply, the effect of the wind, blowing around the glass.'

Harry remained silent.

Self-conscious, Ernest placed the chest under his arm. 'This has been a damnable waste of a morning, Harry. Brawling and conjuring tricks do nothing for your condition. Go on, back to your hut with you. Oblige me by resting.'

Harry stroked a contusion on his cheek, thinking still. Ernest saw that his words had not convinced him. The man was no dupe.

'Didn't think the wind could make that kind of noise,' he said suspiciously.

'What else could it possibly be?'

But even as he scoffed, Ernest felt the motion, quivering in his armpit. He heard a drone, muffled yet certainly there, ringing on and on beneath the mahogany lid.

*

Last night Louise had negotiated the dark veins of the cave, holding Harry's hand. She knew full well that they led out to another beach on the other side of the cliff.

Yet as she approached the entrance to their little underground colony, she experienced the same uncomfortable sensation as always. There was the umbra: its depth, its immensity. She could almost imagine it reaching out and dragging her in, a pit ready to swallow her whole.

Placing her buckets of water on the sand, she pulled down her cuffs and scrubbed at the salt freckling her spectacles. Pipe bowls glowed in the darkness.

She loitered on the edge of the cave, reluctant to enter into that smog. The men had seemed pleased to receive tobacco, never mind what was mixed with it, but Louise hated the stuff. The way it clung to her skin, even her hair.

'Louise? Is that you?'

Taking a deep breath of fresh air to see her through, she stepped inside the cave.

Chao and Seth sat together on a rock, smoking and talking in whispers. Her father stood apart from them, jacket removed, his hands upon his hips. This morning's poise and confidence had deserted him. She did not like the tight knit of his brow, or the way he ran a hand through his hair. In Bristol, he had usually worn a wig, but the sea winds made that impractical here. Now he tied his hair back with a single black ribbon. It had a natural curl, which was not helped by his habit of rumpling it when perplexed. The wayward locks made him look rather frantic, not at all like the polished physician that had attended upon Lord Redfern.

'Papa?'

'Oh, it *is* you. Good. Michael has been calling for water incessantly.'

'The buckets are just outside.'

'And I see you also brought the balsam and wound water for Harry's nose.'

'I did.'

He turned from her, began to dig through the contents of his satchel. 'I have cupped Michael and inserted a seton. Tim will require a similar treatment. His fever ravings … the delirium … I have left him insisting that a hag sat on his chest and rode him all night. I cannot for the life of me begin to—' He jerked his head up, like Pompey when he scented a rabbit. 'What did you say?'

She frowned. 'Nothing, Papa.'

'Nothing?' He glanced furtively towards the back of the cave. 'Listen … There! Do you really not hear that?'

Louise closed her eyes and stretched her senses. There were layers of sound – the wind whooping softly, and the constant hum of the waves. Somewhere, distantly, water falling in its own slow, repetitive beat.

'I can hear a drip,' she offered.

Papa shook himself. 'Very well, very well. I must have imagined it. This morning has been testing, to say the least. See to Harry, if you please.'

She was loath to leave her father so distraught, but she knew disobeying his orders would only vex him more. Collecting her supplies, she made her way to Harry's hut.

The young man was sitting at the entrance, spine straight against the wooden wall. It was impossible to view him without a flush of gratitude. He had certainly taken a knocking for Pompey. The damage appeared even more alarming than it had last night; brown and purple mantled his face, blooming up to his eyebrows. He looked like a prizefighter.

'Good morning, Harry. How are you?'

'Tolerable.' A squashed voice, struggling through cartilage. It made her wince. 'And you, *Louise*?'

A good turn did not warrant the familiar use of her Christian name. 'My name is Miss Pinecroft,' she replied stiffly.

Rather than offending him, her pride made him smile. She noticed a missing tooth, high up towards the back. Had that shaken loose last night?

'Haughty as you like. And here's me, having lost my good looks for your dog's sake.'

She raised an eyebrow. 'Such as they were.'

He laughed and began to choke.

Louise went to assist him, but he held out a hand to stop her. It seemed Harry had his pride too.

She uncorked the wound water and soaked a clean handkerchief while he composed himself. There was fighting spirit in the young man. Afflicted with consumption, hit by a rockfall and still trading repartee? That *did* suggest they had caught him in time. Even if they lost Michael and Tim, just one cure would be enough.

'Sit still now,' she ordered, kneeling at his side. 'I will wash it and dress it with a balsam. I did intend to make you a cold compress, but I forgot we have no ice house here.'

'Such privations.' He mimicked her accent – rather too closely for comfort.

'Do not test me, sir.' She brandished the wet handkerchief. It reminded her of forcing her younger siblings into line; how she had needed to cajole and threaten at the same time. 'I can make this much more painful than it needs to be.'

Evidently he believed her, for he pushed the dark hair back from his face and tilted his chin up to the light. She had thought his eyes were green. At this moment they appeared grey, little chinks of slate. Cautiously, she began to wash around them. He did not close the lids.

His skin was rusty with dried blood and took a while to clean. He did not complain, just sat, as if for his portrait, letting her touch flow over him.

'Your nose may set a little crooked, I'm afraid.'

'Hardly matters, does it?'

'Less for a man, I suppose. And it will lend you a certain notorious aspect, which I understand is very desirable.'

'It won't matter because I'll be in my coffin.'

Her hands began to shake. She busied herself with the balsam to conceal it.

'I wish you would not speak like that,' she said sadly, 'as if all this were for nothing. We have high hopes for you, Harry.'

He turned away.

'Come here.' She began to smooth the balsam over him. It had a deep herbal scent. 'You might tell me, instead, what you will do with your freedom when you recover.' She saw the gentle motion of her hands soothed his temper, took a little of the anger away. 'I do not know how you ended up in Bodmin but—'

'No.' Less prickly now, just weary. 'Don't start that. What is it about you rich folk? Always after remaking someone. When I saved your dog, I just did it. No conditions, no fanfare. Done. If I live, I an't going to be a different person. I was a fence before I went in, and I'll be a fence if I get out.'

She was not certain she had heard right. 'A … fence?'

That curled his lips. 'So bloody innocent. You know, a fence. I take things in, melt them down, change them up. Pass it off as something new.'

'What kinds of things?'

'Hot things. Wipers, jewellery, silver jugs, all that.'

'Stolen goods?' Even she heard the note of disapproval in her voice.

He guffawed. 'How the hell do you think I ended up in gaol?'

Louise was not used to being spoken to in this manner. It shocked, but did not upset her. It made her feel strangely alive.

She *was* alive. Her heart was beating, her knees were aching and a man was swearing at her. After so long staring at death, she had begun to feel that she had stepped behind the veil herself.

She placed the lid back on the balsam and made ready to gather her skirts.

Then Harry spoke again. 'Who's Louisa?'

'What?'

He must have seen the way her face turned rigid, for there was a dart of panic in his eyes. 'The doctor calls you Louise. But who is Louisa?'

'It was my mother's name,' she said tightly. 'Why do you ask?'

Harry's mouth drooped. He looked sorry he had spoken. 'Doesn't matter.'

'*Why?*'

'He … says it sometimes. In his sleep. Or to himself.'

Unconsciously, Louise placed a hand on her chest. 'She died,' she whispered. 'They all died.'

Harry shifted awkwardly against the wall of the hut. He made a movement, as if he was going to clap her on the shoulder, but seemed to think better of it.

'Well, it happens. He an't an old man. Give him time, he'll marry again.'

Many daughters would fear such a thing. Not Louise. She would be only too glad to assure herself that Papa's life would move on in a different direction, but she knew him better than that.

'He will not. He ... You do not know how it was, between them.'

Harry looked down at his hands. 'Chough,' he muttered.

'I beg your pardon?'

'The choughs in the cliff. Did you never see them? Red beaks. We hear them all the time, down here.'

'I know the bird.'

'It pairs for life,' he told her. 'That's what my ma always said. Same mate, same place, every year. Always come back. Maybe your da's like that.'

She was afraid to speak lest the tears spill. The truth was, it was easier to take blows on her own account than watch Papa suffer. She had cried far more for him than herself.

'And what about you?' he asked. 'You and that damned dog?'

'I will assist my father,' she said briskly. 'He needs someone to serve as apothecary.'

'But for how long? He's not old. By the time he ... you know, joins your ma, it'll be too late to start a family of your own.'

'That does not signify. The hospitals employ nurses to live in all the time. They prefer an older lady without dependants.'

Harry sighed. 'High-bred lass like you, working in one of them rough places? Don't sound like much of a life to—'

'What is that?' Before she considered what she was doing, she seized his hand, pulled it under the lamplight. There was a blotch and a kind of scribble next to it, as if someone had drawn on him in red ink. '*That*? How long has it been there?'

He inspected it. 'Don't know. Could it have happened when the rocks hit me?'

'I would be surprised. It is more like a rash and that … that next to it is certainly not a scratch. A scratch could not twist itself so. Does it hurt?'

Pulling his hand away, he shrugged. 'Everything hurts. I've got the consumption, an't I?'

'Do not be so difficult, Harry. I am concerned. It is a very strange mark.'

'There're a lot of strange things in this cave,' he said darkly.

And at that, he got up and left her.

PART FIVE

Potent Liquids

Chapter 26

We must set off early to make our way into 'town'. Dawn trembles upon the horizon. The moon is still at large, refusing to be cowed. No clouds obscure its milky glow. It seems set to be a bright day.

Our pony is eager to be on the move. He paws the grass, breath pluming from his nostrils. Although his winter coat has grown thick on his rump, he clearly still feels the cold. One would need to be made of stone to ignore it. I am exceedingly lucky that Merryn has lent me her cloak.

Three people just about fit on the trap. The backwards seat, where I put my trunk on the journey down, will serve us for any packages we bring home. Gerren initially places himself in the middle, but Mrs Quinn is much larger, so he ends up pushed towards the right-hand side with me anyway. Even in the fresh, salty air, I can smell the tobacco on his coat. This morning, I do not mind. I am grateful for his warmth.

Gerren loosens the reins and the pony springs to life. The wheels wobble. I remember the winding road up the cliff and gulp.

Behind us, Morvoren House is shuttered and sightless. I gaze over my shoulder, keeping it in view until we sink downhill, deep into the darkness. Miss Pinecroft will still be there, in the china room. I hope Merryn will be kind to her in my absence, help her to drink her morning chocolate.

I have more potent liquids to pursue.

We do not take the Falmouth road. I am glad, for that would be an arduous journey. It crosses my mind to ask our destination, but the name of the town would mean nothing to me.

As we travel inland, a pink pearly light begins to wash up the sky and a very different Cornwall materialises before my eyes. Here there are no raw cliffs or craggy rocks, only hills sliding from green to gold. Hedgerows and stone walls tease the eye in every direction. Far away, the flues of tin and copper mines pierce the horizon.

This land is fertile; there are a great quantity of trees. Some have twisted to odd shapes in the wind, all of them are bare, and yet they give me the impression life is slumbering, just waiting to erupt.

The sound of the sea fades. I can still smell and taste the salt, but I no longer feel it shredding my cheeks. Sir Arthur's acquaintance would call such a landscape picturesque. They would marvel over its untamed romance. I prefer the formal gardens of London with their straight lines and patterns. What I would not give now to see a fountain or a trained and pruned privet hedge. Everything neatly controlled.

'Nearly there,' Mrs Quinn announces, making me jump.

From a distance, I see a hotchpotch of whitewashed houses surrounding a bay. Narrow streets twist uphill to more buildings, some of them rough cast like Morvoren House but much smaller. I push back the hood of Merryn's cloak. It does not appear so much a town as a large fishing village.

Entering the bustle of streets feels strange after my three days on the clifftop. Descending a steep lane, we pass a rope maker and a chair mender to stop outside an inn. Its walls are embroidered with the remains of ivy.

My spirits lift.

Mrs Quinn is already making her way down from the trap with a basket hooked over her arm, eager to be about her business. Gerren points to the stone church tower, close by the water.

'Back by two bells,' he says.

The inn will bait the pony, and it seems as if Gerren intends to spend his time in the taproom smoking. This is no cause for alarm – any manner of shops may sell me gin.

Together, Mrs Quinn and I make our way over the cobbles. A man drives sheep in the opposite direction. This is a busy village, a boat-making village, the housekeeper informs me. There are certainly signs of small industry: women mending nets, children dashing about with pails. Boats bob at anchor in the bay.

'Walk with me to save growing lost,' she offers. 'I'll show you about, but first I've to visit the bank for the mistress, and Mrs Bawden has a fancy—'

'Please, do not trouble yourself. I have an excellent sense of direction.' Seeing her mouth droop, I add hastily, 'I should only get in your way. I do so hate to make a nuisance of myself.'

Mrs Quinn hesitates. ''Tis your choice. Only wait outside the church when you're done, and I'll meet you there.' She hands me a small purse of coins and cups my fingers tight around them. 'Be careful. I shouldn't like you to fall in the way of any rough folk.'

I nod, as if she is very wise. 'I shall be cautious. Living in London certainly taught me that.'

Living in London has also taught me to appreciate this view of the sky: a great bowl overhead, clouds draped across it like lace on blue silk. I do not remember ever seeing so much of it.

I wander at random. A woman bundled up in a threadbare shawl eyes me warily. The butcher's boy stops to watch my progress, a parcel of bloody meat dripping in his hands. I raise the hood of Merryn's cloak over my face again. I daresay I appear strange to these people. Dressed simply though I am, my gown is a world apart from their mud-splattered boots and darned clothes. These people have known hard times. The wars have been kind to no one, and our Regent is not famed for his consideration of the lower classes. I see the cracks cut into their hands by salt, and remember reading of bread riots in Truro. Circumstances have improved, but not greatly.

For me, it is quaint to wind through this little village, up and downhill as the erratic cobbles dictate. Whether it is the freedom from Morvoren House, the bright day or the prospect of gin that charms me, I am certainly happier than I have been for a long while.

I locate an apothecary without much trouble. His premises are small and grimed with dirt at the windows. There is a seedy appearance to him. The bottles are dusty about the shoulders, the weighing scales tarnished. He sells a variety of quack nostrums, the Venice turpentine and syrup of maidenhair I need, and he can even supply my gin from under the counter. Once, I would despise such a man. Hester Why thinks him a capital fellow.

Uncorking the gin bottle with my teeth, I press it against my lips. I have spent laudanum-weary nights dreaming of this moment, but the reality is better.

I find a fence to lean against and watch a small boy selling packets of newspapers. He struggles to keep them from taking off in the breeze. It seems fitting that he is here. A newspaper started me drinking, after all. That advertisement, still hidden in my trunk. God knows why I have kept it. To feel wanted, perhaps, sought after.

I take another sip of gin.

It is unbearable to imagine Lady Rose out there in the world, despising me. But even worse is the possibility that she does not think of me at all.

In the distance, a church clock chimes. My time is running out. I decant the bottle I am holding into my empty hip flask; the other I wrap carefully in an extra shawl and place at the bottom of my basket. I need to cushion it as thoroughly as it cushions me. Mrs Quinn must not hear the telltale chink.

I nearly make it: go straight to the church and meet Mrs Quinn. But as I pass the boy, my footsteps slow. He pushes the salt-matted hair from his eyes and looks up at me with a world of hope.

Somehow my hand is already in my pocket. I have just enough left after buying the gin. Sick with anticipation, I press the coins into his print-stained palm.

The packet tears in the wind and the foolishly large pages beat frantically like the wings of a netted gull. I consider crumpling the newspaper into my basket and taking it up again once we are home. But that is a trial of patience my nerves will not stand.

I reach the society pages first. My eyes scan the print eagerly for news of her. A certain duchess has been seen sporting a new hat … One of the Prince Regent's outriders lost his way in the fog and fell into a ditch … There will be a musical gathering in the Queen's Concert Rooms …

And then comes the sensation of falling.

It is worse than that day in Salisbury. So much worse.

The boy swims at the edge of my vision. 'Miss?'

I have just enough time to set my basket down upon the cobbled pavement. Then the world turns mercifully black.

Chapter 27

They have all been exceedingly kind. That has only made it harder to bear. When Mrs Quinn clucked over me and wrapped her shawl about my shoulders for the journey home, I wanted to scream at her. Does she not understand that I deserve no tenderness? Does she not see the rot at my very core?

My hands shake worse than ever, and it has nothing to do with gin. Much as I try to hide my emotions, Merryn knows something is awry. I see it in her sideways glances as I mix the chocolate like an automaton.

'If thee an't well enough to work …' she begins.

'I am quite recovered, thank you.'

'Mrs Quinn says thee went down hard yesterday …'

'I had simply not eaten enough,' I snap.

Performing my duties is torture, but I would rather have them to focus on. If I were left alone in that salt-ringed bedroom with my newspapers, my snuffbox and my memories … I think I would drown myself in gin. Dram by dram.

I pour the chocolate into a cup that has two handles and a lid to keep it warm.

Merryn takes a breath, but I leave the kitchen before she can speak again.

When I am in the west wing, halfway down the corridor leading to the china room, a familiar scent reaches me: cardamom. I stop dead, my hands shaking on the tray. I have mixed the chocolate as Lady Rose would take it, by mistake.

It is all I can do not to break down in sobs.

After a few minutes, I regain something like composure. I balance the tray on one unsteady hand, open the door and step inside the china room. It is like plunging into a pool of icy water.

Never before have I felt a cold like this: sharper than any blade.

A violent gust slams the door behind me and I scream. Dust swirls in clouds across the floor. The curtains flail and I realise what has happened: Miss Pinecroft has opened the window.

This is too much.

'Confound it!' I cry, slamming the tray upon a side table.

I run to close it. Damp has warped the wooden frame of the sash and it initially refuses to budge. Shoving aside the billowing curtains with one arm, I pull at the wood until my fingernails crack. At last, with a great whoosh, it gives way and slides shut.

The wind dies. The curtains slap back into place. Outside I can see the ocean, writhing with glee, as if this were all a game.

'Of what were you thinking, madam?' I demand. 'All the care I take of you, and you wish to undo it! For what? What reason could you possibly have?'

I round upon my mistress.

Miss Pinecroft's spine is poker-straight. She clenches the arms of the chair. Her hair is blown awry and she looks terrified.

As if she is afraid something will rip her from her seat.

'Miss Pinecroft? What …?'

Glancing down at her hands, my stomach turns over.

Her wrinkled fingers have twisted themselves into the shape of birds' talons. Her nails are broken, worse than my own.

Gouged deep in the armrests are thin white lines. As jagged as the fissures in the jasperware cup.

*

What troubles me most is the fact that I screamed when the door slammed behind me, then I harangued my mistress in a manner deserving instant dismissal: I was loud and clamorous, but no one came. No one heard me above the tossing of the sea.

It occurs to me that if Miss Pinecroft should fall while I was out of the room, I would not hear her either. I would be too late to help.

And I *must* help her. Even if I achieve no other good. The thought steadies me. If I can be of use to this poor lady, who can barely hold her chocolate in her freshly bandaged hands, it will be my atonement.

I wish she would tell me what haunts her. Through a gap in the curtains, I glimpse steel-grey waves. Until now, I did not think there could be enmity in the sea, but it is there. Taunting my mistress.

Footsteps thud in the corridor and the door swings open, making us both jump. It is Rosewyn. Alone.

She offers a shy grin before toddling inside. The way she moves, her facial expressions: all are exactly as a child. She does not seem to belong in her body.

When she reaches the side of the wingchair, Rosewyn throws her arms around the old lady's neck.

There is a moment of tension; Miss Pinecroft's eyes bulge, her fingers grasp the armrests once more. I try to imagine her adopting Rosewyn when she really was a child – somewhere near forty years ago. Was Miss Pinecroft softer back then? Indulgent to the small, unfortunate girl? I think she must have been, for Rosewyn's affection is evident. She truly loves her.

'Good day!' Rosewyn kisses the papery cheek and seats herself on the floor.

'Hello, Miss Rosewyn,' I say. 'What brings you downstairs?'

Before she can answer, a heavy tread sounds by the door. Creeda stalks towards us, carrying the doll.

Rosewyn hunches her shoulders.

'You're not to go running off. Haven't I told you a hundred times?' Creeda's voice is sand-rough.

I clear my throat officiously. 'You needn't be alarmed if Miss Rosewyn decides to visit her guardian. She is quite safe down here with us.'

Creeda cocks an eyebrow above her brown eye. 'She is, is she?'

'Allow me to light the fire. I would not want Miss Rosewyn catching a chill.'

Both the elder women move, but it is Creeda's hand that nips my shoulder.

'Don't,' she decrees. 'Heat harms the porcelain.'

This woman. She irritates me like an itch at the back of the throat. She reminds me of Burns – but that maid was spiteful, openly malignant. Creeda speaks with none of her passion. It is her very coolness, her self-possession, that grates upon me. 'Nonsense! I never heard of such a thing. Why ... is not porcelain fired in a kiln, when it is made?'

She stares straight at me with those uncanny eyes. 'Don't presume to tell me. My family made this collection.'

I was not expecting that.

'Nancarrow Bone China,' I whisper.

She nods. 'Yes. Nancarrow was my maiden name. I got everything when the factory closed down.'

It is on the tip of my tongue to mention the error on the Willow pattern transfer, but I forbear and resume my seat.

'I did not know you had been married, Creeda.'

'I am married still,' she barks.

What man on earth would have the courage? I am about to make enquiries when I realise: Gerren. The band on her gnarly finger matches his.

What a pairing! I would be amused, were I less miserable. Creeda is the spider in the centre of a web, connected to everything. Even Miss Pinecroft follows her commands. Who, really, is the mistress of Morvoren House?

Outside, waves collapse into the embrace of the sea. Creeda proffers the doll to Rosewyn, who sulkily accepts it and places it in her lap.

'Come on. Stand up, let's be out of here.'

Rosewyn turns her doll over and begins to plait its hair.

'*Rosewyn.*'

'Perhaps you might adjust Miss Rosewyn's clothes, if you are taking her back upstairs,' I tell Creeda. 'They are inside out. It is not fitting for a lady to appear so, even before her family.'

'Maybe not, but it's right for this child. Her gown must be that way.'

I had thought it a failure in the old woman's eyes; that they might be weak, as Miss Pinecroft's are. Can she really be doing this to Rosewyn on *purpose*?

Rosewyn glances up, smiles and returns to her doll. She is natural – innocent. Fertile ground for any strange ideas this maid should choose to plant inside her head. It strikes me now that she is nothing but a doll herself, dressed and positioned to please Creeda.

What sins might she push this unwitting soul towards? Was it Creeda who urged her to rip apart the Bible?

Miss Pinecroft cannot defend her ward, but I can. I *should*.

'I am not from Cornwall, Creeda. Perhaps you might explain to me what possible virtue your people see in wearing their clothes the wrong way around?'

She considers me. Her hooked nose juts further forward than ever. 'I don't know, Miss Why, if you ever heard of people being pixy-led.'

'No, that is not a term I am familiar with.'

I imagine she is about to spin me a similar tale to the one Lowena recited at dinner on Saturday: floating lights, hidden bogs. As if the most dangerous hazard here were not the great clifftop, yawning where all can see it.

Creeda glances at the china. 'They ... want. Always more.'

'Who?' I ask, incredulous.

She deliberately misunderstands. 'Our people. We keep their race alive. They can't breed, you see. So they take us.'

Father told me once of the lunatics in Bedlam and their hideous fantasies. I never thought to see one in the flesh.

'Of course they're clever about it,' she continues. 'They know, by now, what moves us. I never hear of children tempted by succulent apples these days. It's deeper than that. They call out for help. They shout in the voices of our loved ones who have died.'

Miss Pinecroft tightens her grip on the armrest.

I cannot reply to this madness.

'Once they take you underground, you belong to them. But some people have turned back, before it was too late. They broke the charm by flipping their clothes inside out. So I protect my charge. I make sure Miss Rosewyn is guarded against them at all times.'

On the floor, Rosewyn finishes her plait and hugs the doll to her chest. It is the first time I have seen her show it tenderness, but she does not appear to be clinging to it with love: she holds on as one who is afraid.

'Fairies, you mean?' I scoff. 'Imaginary creatures, waiting to take us underground? Bosh! This is nothing more than folklore! It is no excuse to dress poor Miss Rosewyn in such a whimsical manner. Why, if it is so dangerous, do you not all have your clothes on inside out? Why do you suppose they would want only *her*?'

I expect Creeda to be offended, to shout back. But not a muscle moves in her face. She merely looks sad, a priest before unrepentant sinners.

'Don't you listen, Hester Why? They want offspring. A woman young enough to bear them.'

'They cannot be very powerful fairies,' I mutter under my breath. 'Barren. Stopped by backwards clothes and a line of salt.'

Rosewyn presses a finger to her lips and makes a desperate hushing sound. 'Shh! You mustn't speak of them that way!'

'They are not real, miss. I may speak of them in any manner that I choose.'

She shakes her head, solemn. 'They listen.' Her arms tighten about the doll. 'They listen and then they punish.'

Chapter 28

Eighty-six.

The lock clicks, but I do not remove my hand from the key. Cannot.

There is no doubting it this time. Candles burn in the sconces on the wall, flooding the corridor with light. Nothing could be clearer. The dial on Miss Pinecroft's bedroom door has turned all the way to eighty-six.

For a moment, I stare. Then I begin to laugh.

The entire house is mad. From the maids in the kitchen to the simpleton trapped in the nursery, it is all completely and utterly mad.

I walk alone in sanity – and I am the one foxed on a mixture of laudanum and gin!

The wind howls and ravens about the house, crashing the branches of the ash trees together. The waves roar back. They are wild creatures, these elements. They will tear one another apart.

Removing the key, I place it in my apron and stumble towards the east wing. Nausea treads upon my heels. It has grown steadily worse since my conversation with Creeda – if indeed, you can refer to that as a conversation. It was more like the ravings of a mad woman.

They punish, Rosewyn said earlier. Certainly, I am being chastised. But my foes are not fairies, jabbing with their tiny hands. The wretch that has brought misfortune upon me is none other than myself.

I open a door to find I have accidentally walked into the room Lowena shares with the cook Mrs Bawden. The housemaid sits on the edge of the mattress, tying her black hair in rags ready for bed, and my abrupt appearance makes her start. Apologising, I lurch back into the hallway to seek my own room. Am I really so inebriated? I must be. Yet my temples burn and my mouth is dry. That is usually a sign I have not drunk enough.

Another door gives way and this time I lumber into the correct chamber. The silvery moonlight is alive with shapes. My own shadow stretches, monstrous over the bed. Already the moisture is welling up and turning to vapour, I feel it cling to my arms, breathe against my cheek.

Falling to my knees beside the bed, I reach for the key to my trunk – but my trunk is already open.

The room spins.

Feverishly, I grope through the contents, past the bloodied travelling dress and the newspapers.

The snuffbox has gone.

A strangled gasp escapes me. I search again and again, my hands moving faster each time. I am about to tip the whole thing upside-down when it hits me: the travelling dress and Sir Arthur's advertisement were at the top of the open trunk. I did not leave them there.

Someone knows about me. They have read the advertisement mentioning the snuffbox and taken it for evidence.

I grab for the chamber pot and vomit. Little food has passed my lips. The liquid that comes from me is bile.

Why, oh why, did I keep the blasted clipping?

'Poor thing! What ails thee?'

I whip around as if stung. Merryn stands in the doorway, holding a candle.

Merryn.

Those bright eyes, those busy hands. I knew sharing a room with this girl should be my undoing.

Wiping my chin, I put the pot down and struggle to my feet. The world slants away; Merryn's candle dips and sways before my eyes.

'You!' I fling the word at her. 'How *dare* you?'

Her jaw falls slack. She gapes at me like an idiot.

'You have opened my trunk! Is it not enough that I must share my bed with a lowly scullery maid? Am I to have no privacy? These are my things. *Mine.* Keep your grubby hands off them.'

Merryn's shoulders start to quake. 'I never ...' she whispers, 'I never would.'

'Then who? Who else would be in my room, going through my personal property, but a scullery maid? Tell me, what is your wage, Merryn? Pitiful, I expect. You thought to supplement it with the snuffbox, didn't you?'

She looks frightened. 'I an't a thief.'

'You are a sneak! What did you think of the advertisement? Is it a fair description? Are you in a way to be *thankfully requited*?'

'Please, miss, I don't—'

'You must tell me what he gives you. Of course he did not write specifics – or did he? I do not recall, the words will be fresher in your mind, having read the advertisement so recently—'

'Miss!' she shouts. 'Thee be mistaken! I *cannot* read.'

A dreadful pause follows. Merryn's chest rises and falls. All I can hear is the sound of her laboured breath.

I am suddenly and terribly sober.

Of course she cannot read. No doubt Lowena cannot either. And it would take a good deal of heft to break the lock upon my trunk. Merryn's arms are thin.

'I ...' I begin, at an utter loss. I cannot take the words back. The moist air still drips with their venom. 'Merryn, forgive me, I do not know what ...'

A tear slides down her cheek.

I am a brute, an absolute brute.

This girl has shown me nothing but kindness.

'I am so sorry.'

Her bright face snaps shut. She blows out the candle and drops upon the bed.

In vain, my jumbled mind tries to piece the conversation back together. How much did I reveal? Whatever the actual words used, I have admitted to keeping a secret locked away.

Fumbling in the darkness, I pack the contents back into their rightful order, push the lid down tight. Silver gleams back at me. The lock is not broken, as I had supposed. There is no damage at all.

I have never left it unfastened. Never *would* – my life depends on its integrity. There is cunning at work here. Someone has picked the mechanism – perhaps the same person stealing in and out of Miss Pinecroft's room, turning the dial.

But who?

Try as I might, I cannot repress the image of fairies, their slender little arms groping through keyholes.

Merryn has turned her back to me; her body stiffens as I climb carefully into bed. It is excruciating: her hurt seems to prickle through the sheets.

Outside, the sea huffs and frets.

I know I will not sleep tonight. When I close my eyes, there is a number etched on the back of the lids. Eighty-six.

Chapter 29

Never did a weary slave bless heaven so fervently for the Sabbath day. They have all left the house: the lunatic Creeda, Rosewyn and her doll, Merryn with her dejected countenance. For a few hours, I will be free of their reproachful looks.

Only Miss Pinecroft remains, opposite me in her wingchair. Though she went to bed in her own chamber again last night, she does not appear to have slept. Her white eyelashes are stark against the bloodshot orbs beneath.

My own health remains poor. Breathing has become an exertion. Now, more than ever, I wish that Miss Pinecroft would allow me to light a fire.

I picture the fire in the kitchen, blazing merrily, its light shining on Merryn's face, and my stomach lurches with guilt. She has not spoken to me since Tuesday evening. Even in this house, amongst the friendliest staff I ever met, I have found a way to sour the atmosphere. Yet for all their kindness, one of them is against me. They have taken the precious snuffbox. They can literally hold my dearest memories and my life in the palm of their hand.

Mrs Quinn showed a good deal of curiosity about my luggage when I arrived, but surely, if she had seen the contents, she would have dismissed me immediately? The advertisement, the dress drenched in blood: these are not sights to keep concealed.

Mrs Bawden, Gerren and black-haired Lowena present themselves to my mind's eye by turn, but deep down I know there is only one suspect. Only one person in this house could have committed the vile act.

The curate knocks on the front door. When I open it, I am surprised to see the sky is metallic and sleet is falling; ice crystals bounce from the rim of Mr Trengrouse's hat.

'Come inside, sir,' I urge him, stepping aside.

'It is starting,' Mr Trengrouse tells me. He brushes spots of white from the shoulders of his greatcoat. 'The real snow has finally arrived. In a few hours, the paths will be impassable. I must not stay for long, Miss Why.'

I take Mr Trengrouse's coat, hat and gloves. They are colder even than my hands. 'At least stay for tea, sir. Drink something warm before heading back.'

There it is again – the smile that lights up the room. 'Thank you. You are all goodness.'

If only that were true.

He is more conscientious in his religious duties this week. He keeps reading to Miss Pinecroft as I blunder in with the tea tray, scarcely able to hold its weight, and prays while I prepare three cups. It is a pleasure to hear the lilt of his voice, educated, with only the slightest trace of the local accent.

Miss Pinecroft takes her tea from me with her bandaged hands. 'Take care,' I whisper. 'Please do not hurt yourself again.'

'Are those scratches from the broken cup last week, Miss Pinecroft?' Mr Trengrouse asks as I go to fetch his tea. 'Unfortunately, ailments do linger, the older we get. We are fortunate to have Miss Why looking after you. No doubt she will have you back to full health in no time.'

I pass Mr Trengrouse his cup. 'But are you unwell also, Miss Why? You look pale.'

I turn my face away. 'I am ... not myself.'

'Should you not go and lie down?'

Even if I did, I would not sleep. I have taken laudanum, but my head pounds as if I have not seen the bottle for a week.

Sitting beside him, I cradle the warm cup in my hands. 'I have my duties, sir.'

He watches me intently with those gold-flecked eyes. 'Whatever will my sister say if I allow you of all people to neglect your health?'

'Oh yes!' I seize the change of subject eagerly. 'Do tell me how they all get along at Exeter.'

'Better,' he announces happily. 'Much better. As you know, the progress is bound to be slow, but the physicians are pleased. It is only unfortunate that this snow will keep Polly away for another week at the least.' He sips his drink. 'Pity me, Miss Why, with my household of children. I shall be run ragged. Three boys and two girls, all under the age of ten.'

I picture Mr Trengrouse before a hearth with a gaggle of red-headed children about his knees, and wonder what it must be like, to share a love like that. A comfortable, steady affection that does not consume all it touches.

'I was ... very fond of a child once.' If I close my eyes I can still feel him, leaning against my leg, sense the small, hot hand that reached for mine. 'Robert.'

'One of my nephews is also named Robert.' He blows on his tea to cool it. 'I suspect your charge has grown into a fine young man by now. Alas, our Robbie looks set to be the worst kind of blackguard. Stealing apples from the orchards, always pushing his sisters.' He grins. 'He is but four years old. I have hopes of reformation.'

I cannot return his pleasantry. The child has bobbed to the surface of my mind. Not cherubic as he was in life: instead his cheeks are stiff, the eyes sunken. *Was* it my fault? Can I be such bad luck that I simply drained the life from him?

I take a breath, gather myself. 'I confess, it sometimes feels as if we have a child here at Morvoren
House. Do you know Miss Rosewyn?'

Something flickers in his face. He seems momentar-
ily unsure of what to say. 'Yes. Indeed I do. She is a …
pure spirit.'

Miss Pinecroft twitches.

'Can you tell me her age?'

His charm re-emerges. 'Really, Miss Why, a gentleman would not enquire.'

'Of course not. I merely wondered if there was
anything I could do to assist her. As a nurse. I presume
she has always been … well, I do not mean to say
deficient, for she is very bright, but … I received the
impression there was some … affliction. You cannot
tell me its nature?'

Mr Trengrouse regards me thoughtfully. At last
he says, 'It is true she is a little unusual. You haven't
encountered any problems with her, have you?'

'Problems? No. I believe she requires only kindness
and understanding.'

'I knew it,' he smiles. 'I knew the moment I saw you
at Exeter that you had a good heart.'

I nearly splutter a mouthful of tea.

He takes it for embarrassment, rather than the guilt
that it is. 'Forgive me for speaking so warmly. But you
see, others have been less sympathetic towards the
poor lady.'

I wipe my mouth. 'Who?'

Mr Trengrouse darts a glance at Miss Pinecroft. She is not drinking her beverage, but neither is she watching us. I wonder how the world must appear to her without her spectacles. Blurred.

As if she were underwater.

My throat grows tight.

'I say this in confidence,' Mr Trengrouse whispers. 'Mrs Quinn would prefer not to have it spoken of, but you are an inmate of this house after all. It's only just that you know.' He wets his lips. 'Your mistress has not always required a nurse. For many years her needs were ably met by Mrs Tyack —'

'I have never heard of this person.'

He blinks his brown eyes. 'Mr and Mrs Tyack. You do not call them that? Perhaps amongst the household staff they go by their Christian names.'

We both avert our gaze, discomforted at the reminder of our difference in station.

'Of course you mean Creeda,' I say hurriedly. 'Do go on.'

'Yes. Well … *Creeda*, as you say, only recently became unable to cope with all her responsibilities. A nurse was sought. Locally.'

My mouth tastes as if I have bitten into something sour. Even now, I cannot push down my umbrage. It hurts me to think I was not the first choice.

'I should have thought,' I say stiffly, 'that Mrs Quinn would have informed me if my position had been previously occupied.'

'Please do not be offended!' he cries, looking panicked. 'I do not say this to make mischief. It's a compliment to you. Other applicants for this role were horribly prejudiced. Your predecessor, for example, would not stay on account of Miss Rosewyn.'

I shoot him a quizzical look.

'It is true. She was an affected, hysterical miss. I do not mean to be unkind, but there it is. She said that poor Rosewyn frightened her! Can you imagine that? When all she had ever shown the nurse was her usual sweet affection?'

The strange history of my employment begins to make sense. Did I not wonder why Mrs Quinn should advertise so far afield? That she should be willing to pay the expense of my journey here by Mail coach? I remember how awkwardly she behaved when I first heard about Rosewyn. How she had omitted any mention of her from the correspondence.

If it were Creeda who had caused the issue, I would understand. Any young woman might take exception to *her*. But perhaps the last nurse was not brave enough to name the real culprit and made an excuse. She had the choice to leave. I do not.

Creeda will hold the snuffbox over me like an axe, ready to drop.

Tea slops into the saucer as my fingers quake.

'But *you*,' Mr Trengrouse is waxing on. 'You, Miss Why, are infinitely superior in both skill and moral fibre. It's obvious to me that you have no other goal in life but to care for your fellow man.'

Shakily, I raise the teacup to my lips.

Stop.

I want to drop it, to cast it away from me, but I cannot. My hands will not move.

'Miss Why?' His smile melts. 'Are you unwell? What a brute I am to have kept you talking, I did say that you looked pale ...'

I turn to him in mute appeal. Yet the confusion on his brow, the sheer lack of horror, make me tremble all the more.

He cannot see what I do. It must be a trick of the laudanum, the effect of too much gin, but it looks so gruesomely real, staining the china, reeking of iron and rust.

I am holding a cup full of blood.

Chapter 30

Turpentine, sage, vervain, comfrey and plantain: my father's 'arquebusade water' for cleansing gunshot wounds. Miss Pinecroft has suffered her injuries in a different kind of battle from the soldiers Father treated. No cannon or musket fire; the weapons are more subtle. I douse her cut hands, smooth on some balsam and wind them in lint. Can these really be the same scratches? They seem to reopen each night.

My mistress *knows*. Whatever it is, inside this house, or on those cliffs, she has seen it.

'Did someone hurt you?' I whisper.

Her thin shoulders tremble.

The china room may as well be buried underground. Even when I step behind the curtains, my view is that of a white barricade. There is no beauty in the purity; it is so white that it burns.

I shake as one with the ague. Shapes swirl and merge before my tired eyes; when I look at the porcelain figures, their cheerful faces are replaced with skulls.

Another glance shows me my error, but I cannot be sure that the death-heads were never there. I cannot be sure of anything at all.

Walking to the plate rack, I pick up the one with the faulty Willow pattern. The two figures on the bridge seem further apart today. Untethered, drifting away from one another. When I put it back, my fingertips are coated in dust.

'I need to clean the china,' I whisper, turning urgently to Miss Pinecroft. 'Is all this happening because of the china?'

She stares straight at me. For the first time, I see a real woman behind those cold blue eyes.

'Tell me!' I drop to my knees beside the armrest and clutch at her shawl. Surely, there is a part of her, a small part still awake that can answer me? 'The music, the dripping – do you hear it too? What about the lights?'

Shakily, she places a hand on top of my head.

'What do you see in the china, Miss Pinecroft? Is it blood? I saw a cup of blood ...'

'Him.'

I fall back as if she has hit me. Her hand still hovers, mid-air.

'A ... a fairy?' I stutter.

'Him,' she rasps again.

And then I hear the song.

It drips into the ear, siren-sweet. This sound could lead me through fire; it could lead me to the ends of the earth. I feel it in my very marrow.

'What is …' I gasp.

But Miss Pinecroft has departed as quickly as she arrived. Her blue eyes fog over, she turns towards the china display and I have lost her once more.

She cannot hear the music.

I must know. Everything within me yearns for an answer. Juddering to my feet, I begin to follow the sound.

The stucco hall rings like a crystal glass. Poseidon stands in his alcove and his expression is triumphant. Entranced, I mount the stairs, not pausing even to lift my skirts.

Can it truly be a thing of horror that radiates this sound? I remember what Creeda said of the fairies – how they sweep people away to their land flowing with honey and milk – and I think: why resist? Do people really fear being transported from this cold world to one of sunshine and song?

At the top of the staircase, I turn towards the west wing. The melody runs right through me, a thread pulling tight. At the end of the hallway, Rosewyn's door stands open.

I do not want to break the charm. With infinite care, I place one foot in front of the other. My steps make no sound. Only the sea pulses in the background, accompanying the song.

Elves of the night, enchant my sight
Your forms to see in moon and sunlight.

This is not Lady Rose's voice, but there is a taste of it, a shadow. As if she might be using the lips of another.

With this spell and with this sign
I pray thee forward my design.

My pulse spikes. This is not right. The sweetness is turning, like milk in the sun.

Yet still it draws me onwards.

I cross the threshold to Rosewyn's room, treading in salt. The fire burns high.

She sits at her table, as I saw her before, crooning over a small item in the palm of her hand. There is a flash of pink and gold.

For a moment, it seems I am dreaming. But then she glances up and I am awake, ripped from the spell as if I have been doused in freezing water.

Rosewyn is holding my lady's snuffbox.

'Put that down! Put it down this instant!' I scream, actually scream at her, torn by anger and terror. She blinks at me, her lower lip wobbles. There is no song now, only the crack of flames.

Blinded by fury, I stomp over and snatch the box from her grasp. Rosewyn cries out.

'Please God, please God.' I search for marks. There is nothing. It remains pristine, warmed by Rosewyn's touch.

I close my eyes and try to breathe.

How has this happened? What can it mean? That it was *Rosewyn* who picked the lock on my trunk, went through my things?

I thought her soft-brained and innocent. But she has shredded the Holy Bible to pieces, singing of elves and spells while she does it. The last nurse feared her. Is the salt in the doorway to keep something out … or to keep her in?

I open my eyes to see her flushed, her cheeks slick with tears.

She too is afraid.

I clear my throat, attempt to soften my voice. 'Miss Rosewyn … Wherever did you get this?'

Miserably, she points to the door.

'In the east wing? In my room?'

'No, just *there*.' Her throat bubbles. 'Past the line of salt.'

I follow her finger and see Creeda, framed by the open doorway. She has crept up on us like a cat.

Hurriedly, I drop the snuffbox into my apron, but it is too late. She has seen it.

The unmatched eyes flick from me to Rosewyn and back again.

'They do leave her gifts, sometimes. They're always trying to tempt her out from where it's safe.'

'I didn't cross the salt,' Rosewyn whines. Creeda glances down at the white line scattered like spindrift, and raises a sceptical eyebrow but Rosewyn points at me. '*She* did it.'

Creeda bends. A joint cracks. Ignoring it, she begins to sweep the salt back in place with her hands. 'You should know better, Hester Why.'

I shift uncomfortably. Even after all I have seen and heard, doubt is leaking back in. This is *my* snuffbox, my secrets are at stake. If human agency is involved, I need to know.

'Who leaves Miss Rosewyn gifts, Creeda?'

She does not look up. 'The little people, of course.'

'Well, this was not theirs to give. It is mine. A ... very dear person gave it to me.'

Creeda snorts. 'They won't mind about that. All they do is take.'

A log pops on the fire. Glancing over to the mantelpiece, I see the little jug of milk or cream still in place, its contents freshened.

'Oh, that,' she says, as if she has followed my gaze. 'That's to distract them, should they get inside. Same as the doll.'

Rosewyn seems to notice she is not holding the toy and snatches it up from the floor, eyeing Creeda timidly.

'What about the doll?'

'A likeness of the child. It confuses them. They don't know which one to take.'

Having finished her task, Creeda unfolds and steps cautiously over the line of salt into the room. She does not dust the granules from her hands. They cling to her palms.

A dull throb beats at the base of my skull. I wish I had seen a phantom, or even a wretched fairy. At least then I would know what to believe.

'Are you saying that pixies have opened my locking-box, taken an item out and left it here for Miss Rosewyn to ... what? To tempt her away?'

Wearily, Creeda sits in her rocking chair. 'Pixies and fairies are different, Hester Why. The sooner you learn that, the better. Now if the little people have some reason to be going through your things and tormenting you, that's none of my business. But I know they seek the child. Always have. They think she belongs to them.'

The old trick: blaming an affliction upon the supernatural. A child without the use of its legs, a harelip, a woman with the mind of a girl like Rosewyn.

'Miss Rosewyn is not a fairy,' I assert. 'She is not touched by them. It is a malformation of the brain, or else some imbalance of humours ... The surgeons have not quite confirmed the science but—'

'Hold your tongue, girl, I'm not saying she *is* a fairy, only that the fairies claim her.' Creeda starts to rock. The castors of the chair bump against the floor. 'She came into being in the world that they rule. She was conceived underground.'

'How could you possibly know such a thing? Miss Rosewyn is an orphan Miss Pinecroft adopted—'

'Don't you tell me what I do and don't know about this child!' Her growl does not disrupt the rhythm of her chair. 'Didn't I cross her cradle with iron, rub salt onto her gums? It's been the work of my life to guard her. Nobody knows this child better than I do.'

'She is not a child!' I cry. 'Look at her! She is a woman grown.' Rosewyn does not act in support of my claim; she clutches the doll, watching us in miserable silence. 'What do you think you are about: keeping her in one room, her clothes in disarray, forcing dolls upon her? She may not have the full use of her faculties, but this is degrading. It is cruel.'

Creeda purses her lips, seemingly amused.

I must leave this room. These crazed women will be the undoing of me.

When I reach the door, Creeda's voice scratches, 'Lock it away with iron and oatmeal, Miss Why. Point the toes of your shoes outwards when you place them beside your bed. I told you, they're after a woman of childbearing age. Whatever happened to your bible-ball?'

Purposefully, I plant one foot in the salt. 'It was a *person* who unlocked my trunk last week. A meddling baggage of a person.'

She utters a low laugh. 'Believe that, then. Believe it if it gives you comfort. You will come crying for my help soon enough.'

Flicking the hem of my skirts in a shower of salt crystals, I storm from the room.

Chapter 31

Clearly, I can trust no one in this house.

I cannot lie on the thorny bed of Merryn's resentment; I cannot be under the watch of Creeda's evil eyes. Miss Pinecroft refuses to retire to bed – very well, I shall stay here with her. Keep her safe.

Only one candle winks. By its valiant light, I see my breath turn to smoke. The temperature is lower than ever. My gaze cannot help but dwell upon the fireplace and the heaps of ash that might relieve my discomfort. And then I realise: it is *always* full of ash.

Where does the ash come from, if she never lights a fire?

Perhaps I shall discover tonight.

I have brought my trunk and a blanket down to the china room with me. No one shall invade my privacy again if I can help it. Even the laudanum bottle has been interfered with, the tidemark lower than when I left it this morning. I cannot imagine Merryn dosing herself, but Lowena? Who can say?

She is dark, mysterious. I do not really know her. Or perhaps it was Creeda, drawing on the opium's power to manifest her fairies.

Miss Pinecroft pays no mind to my rustlings with the trunk, but when I wedge it firmly beneath my chair and spread the blanket over me, she begins to flutter. Her eyes are small, darting fish, torn between me and the china.

Candlelight renders the collection strange. Shadows spread, darkness trickles down the plates.

'Go to bed,' Miss Pinecroft orders.

I shake my head. 'I am your maid. I will remain with you.'

Maybe it is the poor light, but I think her chin trembles. As if she yearns for this secretly: company, through the long, cold watches of the night.

'Dangerous,' she croaks.

'If you do not consider sleeping downstairs a danger to *your* health, I do not see how it can be to my own. I am many years younger.'

Miss Pinecroft inspects the curtains, drawn tight against the closed windows, and the racks of plates and the shelf of urns. What she searches for, I cannot say. She glances up at the ceiling. The briefest of actions, but it tells me she has swallowed Creeda's poison: she too believes Rosewyn is in danger.

Perhaps she is. Rosewyn, Miss Pinecroft and I: we are all of us in Creeda's power now.

Gradually, my eyelids droop, my limbs grow heavy. Exhaustion wraps its arms around my neck and everything solid drifts away.

At the edge of my consciousness, I can hear the clock tick. My pulse slows to its rhythm.

I haven't been able to rest peacefully like this for a long while. No visions of Lady Rose rise to torment me. I can scarcely recall her face. The sweats and pains that plague my body when I do not drink seem a distant memory.

Was it not terribly chill earlier? The ice has lost its claws. In fact, I can feel sunlight feathering my cheek, playing over my shut eyelids. It is achingly pleasant.

Until, of a sudden, it is not.

Something has shifted and the current has turned. There is a sensation of intense strangeness, like that inside Miss Pinecroft's bedchamber; the same prickling, the same conviction I am being watched. I hear a quick, hissing breath.

Snip.

My eyes fly open. They cannot make immediate sense of what they see. Our candle has guttered but another looms close to my head. Something glints. An old face hovers above, shadows sinking into the wrinkles.

'Creeda!'

My breath extinguishes the flame.

She is standing with a pair of scissors in her hand. Dropping the smoking candle, she snatches something up off the floor; it is too dark to see what.

'What on earth do you think you are doing?'

Miss Pinecroft observes us; the whites of her eyes shine. She says nothing. She has watched Creeda bend over me with a sharp metal object, and she has not said a word in my defence.

'It *was* you, wasn't it?' I rage. '*You* opened my trunk, made me think that poor Merryn—'

'It's for your own good!' Creeda mutters and turns on her heel.

She escapes from the room, her dress billowing like black wings in the darkness. A bat, I think. A witch, a mad woman.

My heart will not stop pounding.

Miss Pinecroft sighs and shifts in her chair. Her focus returns to the china: pale shapes, bone-white in the gloom. The china that Creeda's family made.

'What was she doing with the scissors?' I demand. 'What did she take?'

Nothing.

'For the love of God, Miss Pinecroft, I want to help you! Please speak to me!'

Only my own voice echoes back. Miss Pinecroft is spellbound.

The skin about my temples tightens. *Spellbound.* There is something in that. Creeda's pagan ways, her people manufacturing the china.

Can a woman control a house, a family, through something as brittle as porcelain?

I turn my head to inspect the plates, now small moons hanging against the wall. My hair brushes against my neck. I push it back. Pause.

Now I know what Creeda took.

She has cut off a lock of my hair.

PART SIX

A Broken Man

'A little to the left. Turn the honeypot. No, the other way. There!' Ernest stepped back to admire the display of china Creeda had assembled. Mellow spring sunlight reached through the window to caress each piece. 'Capital!'

'The *mode* is to put them on a sideboard, sir,' Creeda said.

That was what his wife had craved too: a sideboard full of fine china. No doubt her taste was superior. But to his mind, such presentation took away from the colours. When natural light could catch it, the white background was luminous and pearl-like. The blues sang: mazarine, Prussian, one the shade of Bristol glass. By God, he wished she could see it.

Did she see it, somehow?

'There is no sense in limiting myself to a sideboard when I own such large, empty rooms.'

'Empty rooms in the mermaid house,' Creeda muttered, turning to the window.

It did not do to let these asides go unchecked. Lunatics, given an inch, would soon convert it into a mile. 'I beg your pardon, Creeda?'

Creeda did not trouble herself to face him. Her gaze remained fixed out at sea. 'Sorry, sir. No offence. I was just saying, the man that built this house. He called it after the mermaids.'

'Morvoren? Is that what it means in the local cant? I was not aware.' He rubbed at his forehead, feeling the strain there. This practical chore was meant to be a respite for both of them: distracting Creeda from her mania and him from his overtaxing work in the caves.

So far, it had not been a success.

'They didn't take too kindly to him using their name, did they?'

'Come again?'

Creeda stroked the curtain. 'The mermaids, sir. Didn't you hear? Both the man's ships and all their cargo went down at sea. He was near ruined when you bought his house.'

'Of course I was aware, Creeda,' he replied wearily. 'It was a stroke of luck on my part. A mere Bristol physician would not have been able to afford an establishment of this quality, had the owner not been forced to make a hasty sale. Naturally, I pity the man, but this has always been the way of it for merchants. Not a day went past in town when the coffee houses were not ringing with news of some disaster or the other. But you seem to be implying that the wreck was some kind of ...' He stopped for a moment as his brain finally caught up with him. 'Wait. How did *you* hear of this story?'

Creeda was not the kind of girl to blush. She merely lowered her chin. 'People tell me things.'

'People from your father's clay mines,' he finished sternly. 'How many times must I repeat that you are not to set foot on that property?'

'I don't *go* to the mines!' she flared. 'I never would. But the people who earn their living there, they talk to me at market. And they're not like the decorators at the factory. They know things.'

'You are not to associate with them. Mr Nancarrow stipulated that his employees were not to catch wind of ...'

He ran a hand through his hair. What use was all his work if these miners were filling her head with superstitious hocus-pocus the moment he had emptied it? Perhaps his methods had been too gentle. Though he could not condone the savage practices of the Bedlam doctors, their theory was correct: the mad must be dominated. Forced to submit to the overpowering logic of their physician's mind. Only in all good conscience, he could not say that he had been the model of logic recently.

Once again he heard the strange, hollow music of the caves. It sounded like that instrument Mr Benjamin

Franklin had invented: the glass armonica. Had he not thought, when the jars began to ring, just for the briefest moment, that maybe *she* ... But he was over-stimulated. Working too hard. Everything would return to its right course, once he hit upon the cure.

'Do you hear me, Creeda? No more talking with the miners. I insist.'

Finally, she turned. He could see from the set of her mouth that she was not won over yet. Was that the malady of her mind, or the stubbornness of a girl her age? 'There has been some good come of it, sir,' she pleaded. 'One gave me weed.'

'Weeds?' He repeated, perplexed. 'As in herbs?'

'No, sir. The discoloured clay no one wants. Weed's what they call it. I've been playing about, throwing it – after my duties are done, of course. Seeing what I can do. You said I should busy my thoughts with practical things.'

'Yes! That is precisely so!' In his relief he seized upon it a little too eagerly. 'This is the only transformation that should concern you: mere clay and water into something exquisite. That is *real* magic, Creeda. Human endeavour. Have you continued to paint?'

With a shy smile, she crept towards the china display and pointed out an unglazed vase shaped like a pagoda. 'This here's one of mine. Father sent it undecorated for me, but it never looks as good when you paint it after the firing.'

He squinted at the design. Not the Chinoiserie pattern he would expect on a piece of this nature – of course, the girl would do nothing predictable. It was a native flower. A familiar one.

'Digitalis!' he exclaimed happily. 'Why, did you copy this from my supplies? I distil it in the alembic. Foxglove.'

'Fairy bells,' she corrected.

Hell and damnation, did the child never relent? Why the deuce could Creeda not pick gowns to fuss over like Kitty, or better yet, something useful as Louise had done? To give one's life over so completely to the fantastical ... His irritation was matched only by his fear for her.

'Creeda,' he remonstrated, as gently as he could manage. 'You know this must stop. If I cannot show your father some improvement ...' He opened his hands, as if he could display the madhouse and all its horrors there. Then a thought struck him. 'Tell me this: if you fear fairies so, why do you seek to keep them in your life? Why paint their flowers, read about them, if it gives you pain? Even supposing they *did* abduct you, which I am far from allowing ... Would it not be better to forget?'

She returned his look in that unnerving manner of hers. The expression of her blue eye was always different from the brown one. Harder. 'Do *you* forget, sir?'

For a second, he was speechless.

'I see them everywhere now,' she went on, 'I can't help it. They opened my eye.' She laid a finger on her cheek under the cornflower iris. 'It's a new way of seeing. Of looking. Like those men you tell me discovered how the blood flows, or how miasma spreads. Please, sir. I know you understand. Don't you see everything differently since they ... went?'

He should have been furious at such impertinence. He knew it, but did not feel it. She chilled the anger within him.

'Papa?'

The door squealed on its hinges.

His daughter stood on the threshold. She had entered without knocking as he had done, so many times.

Suddenly, he was conscious of how close he stood to Creeda, and how the china display resembled a strange sort of shrine.

Louise had implored him not to buy any more china. She had said they had no use for it.

'Louise.' He drove his hands inside his pockets to hide their fidgeting. He felt like a fool.

How much had she heard?

His daughter's face betrayed little. It rarely did. Whether she was rolling pills or standing in the hell of a consumptive's sickroom, her features remained faintly troubled. But there was that crease between her brows. Deeper, these days. Soon it would be there permanently.

Her cool eyes moved behind her spectacles: from him to Creeda, to the china. Assessing. Silently condemning. It was a sickening sensation: to have his own child stand in judgement on him. For a moment he saw her as a woman, fully grown, beyond his recognition.

'Papa,' she said firmly. 'It is time for you to go to the caves.'

Chapter 33

Louise hovered on the beach, a tureen of gruel growing steadily heavier in her arms. Surf licked at the heels of her boots as it rolled onto the sun-warmed sand. Standing here, the hole in the cliff face was nothing but a gaping void. It seemed absurd to imagine that people, living breathing people, would dwell within.

She found herself wanting just one more minute. Another moment in the fresh air, where the waves masked the sound of retching and coughs. It was not like her to fall prey to such weakness. She was flustered, that was all. Hard work would set her right. Heaving up the tureen, she took a deep breath and marched across the sand.

A volley of choking greeted her at the mouth of the cave. No men sat together swapping stories by the fire pit.

Only old Seth limped up to her, bowl in hand. 'You're a sight for sore eyes.' His voice was like gravel. 'Starvin', I am.'

Hurriedly, she set the tureen down. 'Please, help yourself. Where is Dr Pinecroft?'

He shrugged, more interested in the gruel. She noticed the marked way in which he favoured his left leg as he moved. This was a new and alarming development. Could it be that the disorder had spread to his hip?

'What of the other men? Do they keep to their beds? It sounds as if someone is very unwell.'

Seth ignored her, lifted the lid from the tureen and scooped his bowl in. Tattoos marked his stringy arms, their ink faded and creased. It was as he removed a brimming bowl and began to rummage in his pocket for a spoon that Louise noticed something else winding between the black patterns.

The same red mark she had seen upon Harry, weaving across the skin like crimson thread.

'Come here—' she began, but a cry cut her off.

'They've got me! They got me!'

She ran. It was not easy on the damp, stony surface. She tripped and stumbled, splashing through the shallow rock pool, but her urgency was not misplaced. As she drew nearer to Chao's hut, she heard Papa's voice.

'Hold still, man!'

The door stood ajar and both Chao and Michael were lying on their backs while her father knelt between them.

He made no endeavour to conceal the anguish on his face. 'Louise! Thank God that you are come. Something has happened, something strange, I cannot ...'

'They marked me!' Chao choked. 'I saw them come in the night and do it.'

Papa extended a hand to restrain him. It was covered in dried blood.

'Whatever does he mean?' she asked.

'This mark ... It is on Michael, too.' Papa shook his head. His hair had come loose from its ribbon tie and fell chaotically about his face. 'I changed his silk setons for ones of India rubber, and when it was done I saw ... Well, come and see for yourself.'

Releasing Chao, he crawled from the narrow space between the patients to the door of the hut. Louise helped him to stand. With unwashed clothes and his skin streaked with dirt, he might have passed for one of the convicts himself.

'I have never seen anything like it,' he confided. 'In all my years of physic, I never ...' He broke off, coughed.

Her blood turned cold.

'Sit there, Papa, on that rock there. You are exhausted. I should have been here with you, caring for them.'

He let her push him down, but continued to gesture while he coughed. 'The mark ...'

'Very well, I will go and look at it.'

She had to hitch her skirts up and fight her way into the cramped hut. The smell was indescribable. Both men appeared to have soiled themselves. Scarlet trickled down the side of Chao's face.

'Miss!' He tried to sit upright. 'Miss, look what they did to me!'

His shirt was unfastened at the neck. A mass of blotches were spread over the skin. Chao pulled the material up to show his stomach. It was covered in the same wild red scribble as Seth's arm.

'Their little feet,' he gasped, rubies bubbling from his lips. 'Like blades. They danced on me. *Danced.*'

The image was appalling. She reached for a cloth and carefully wiped the blood from his mouth.

'What do you mean, Chao?'

'I saw them,' he insisted.

'Saw what?'

His lips trembled beneath her cloth. 'The things that live underground.'

Next to her, Michael spluttered painfully. The man was in a terrible state. Papa had exchanged the silk setons under his ribs for bulky rubber ones that tortured the skin. Pus was draining down the tubes unchecked. She did her best to clear it, but it swelled up anew from underneath. At least there were no blotches or scrawls near the wound. Yet Papa said he had seen something ...

Awkwardly, she assessed the rest of his visible skin. There. That wobbling line, paler and pinkish, traced on his feet.

'Things that live under the ground,' she murmured as the realisation broke.

Papa was wrong to say he had seen nothing like this. He had seen something *exactly* like it, although less severe.

'Papa!' She struggled up and through the narrow door. 'Papa, I know what it is.'

He was still sitting on the rock, elbows propped on his knees, eyes fixed on the ground.

'Worms, Papa!' she cried triumphantly. 'It is just an infestation of worms.'

He stared at her in astonishment. All at once, something seemed to break, and his mouth fell open.

'Papa?'

'Worms. My darling girl. Of course! *Worms.*'

He began to laugh. There was something terrible in that laugh. Bitter.

No matter how hard she attempted to smile, her cheeks would not obey.

'Damp, moist conditions,' she explained quietly. 'The diarrhoea that accompanies the malady. It is an ideal environment for the hookworm to thrive.'

He had taught her that himself.

She remembered each and every lesson. A younger man, with no grey streaking his hair, sweeping her into his arms and sitting her upon his lap to explain what he was reading. The smell of him, sharp and clean, and the rumble of his voice as she laid her head against his chest.

Papa had survived the consumption, yet somehow she was losing him all the same.

'What would you recommend?' She pressed him. 'Rue and alum? Santonica clysters?'

'Yes ... all of that. We must endeavour to keep everything clean. Bring a jar of burnt alum and some rosemary, would you? I will ...' He waved one hand vacantly, '... fumigate.'

'Yes, Papa.'

He hung his rumpled head.

A broken man. That was what one of the apothecaries back in Bristol had whispered, after it happened. She had never believed them until this moment, would not have dreamed Papa capable of making an error, let alone one so amateur. Every surety in her life seemed to be crumbling away.

'They were right,' he told the ground. 'Even gouty old Redfern. They were right, and I was not. How blind I have been. How damnably proud.'

'I do not understand—'

'They said this disease was beyond my ability, and they were correct. I am a gentleman's physician, no pioneer. I should have confined myself to leg ulcers, quinsy and gout.'

'No. That is untrue. You have not slept—'

'I doubt I will sleep again. God!' He slapped his hand against the rock, making her jump. 'It was to be our purpose, Louise! The *one thing* to make sense of it all. I was so sure ...' He stared towards the back of the cave. She saw the muscles in his jaw clenching and releasing. 'We suffered, but I thought we were called ... There was a reason ...'

He trailed off into silence. The wind whistled through the rocks.

'Papa,' she said urgently. 'What are you staring at? Papa! Look at me!'

He did. And now she wished he would not. Being held by his gaze was like being held in the grip of a fever.

'Worms, Louise. I failed to detect something as simple as worms.' He laughed again, a horrible, gasping sound. 'When I think of your mother ... of little Francis. What else might I have missed?'

Chapter 34

Harry was the last to be treated with her rue posset. He had not emerged from his hut the entire morning.

Louise knocked upon the wooden door, nervous about what she might find inside. But Harry opened it straight away, upright and dressed. His eyes gleamed in the low light. Even now they were better acquainted, she could not be certain of the exact colour of his irises. They were changeable, like the ocean: mutable depths of green, blue or grey.

'Louise.'

'Miss Pinecroft,' she corrected, less firmly than usual.

'Please, come in.'

Why did it feel different to be alone with him? She nursed the other men without a thought, only turning away when Papa was obliged to administer the clysters. But as she negotiated the step inside the hut, she felt self-conscious. Perhaps it was the similarity in their ages.

'You need to drink this,' she said, proffering the jug. 'I have sweetened it with honey, so there is no need to pull that face.'

'What's it for, *Louise*?'

She gritted her teeth. 'That mark I saw on your hand. It is the worm. We need to purge you of it.'

He held out both palms to her and turned them over. 'Don't trouble yourself. See? I don't have it any more.'

'Not on that hand, but what about the rest of your body?'

He smirked. 'Do you want to check?'

'Why must you be so—'

'I'm sorry, I'm sorry,' he laughed, sitting down upon his cane chair. 'There's no sport in this place. Let me joke and look at a pretty girl for a minute, would you?'

'I have not the time,' she replied shortly.

His smile faded, and his face became solemn once more. 'You can sense him, can't you?'

'Whom?'

'Death.'

Louise swallowed. She *did* recognise this strange, charged atmosphere: she had felt it while watching Kitty sleep. A presence, where none was to be seen.

But that was folly. They were all starting to sound like Creeda.

'I've never been white-livered,' Harry went on. 'Death don't scare me much. Things look brighter. Livelier. They do, when you know you're going to lose them all.' He shrugged. 'But I'm stuck here in this hole. Time's running out and the only beauty I get to look at is the ocean … and you.'

She glanced away, touched in spite of herself. 'This cave is better than a prison, Harry. You should count yourself lucky.'

'I do,' he said softly.

His wooden cup lay in the corner on the floor. She bent and scooped it up, filling it with posset from the jug.

'Here.'

Harry grimaced but took the drink, their fingers touching briefly.

'How are you so brave?' he asked suddenly.

She snatched her hand away. 'What?'

'For a maid. You …' For the first time, he appeared unsure of himself. He lowered his eyes to the posset. 'Down here, day after day. Don't you fear you might … catch it?'

Her muscles stiffened as she remembered Papa's cough. But healthy people *did* cough occasionally. What with the smoke, and the stench, it was perfectly natural …

'I am not sure that I can catch consumption, Harry,' she sighed. 'I was the only one of my siblings who did not sicken. Perhaps I have a resilience to it. And there are even physicians who say that consumption is not infectious at all, but a tendency we are born with.'

He shook his head. 'Hell of a risk to take.'

'Well, I am not "white-livered" either.'

Harry grinned. 'No, you an't.'

Perhaps something of her disquiet showed on her face, for Harry became intensely interested in his drink. She watched him to make sure he swallowed it all.

His forehead was still marked with bruises, and his nose crooked at an angle, but for all that he was peculiarly attractive, marked with the beauty of a dying thing. Sharp cheekbones, enhanced by the wasting. Wine-red lips and burning eyes.

His throat bobbed as he downed the final drops of the medicine.

'Not so bad for the rest of them, is it?' He wiped his mouth with the back of his hand. 'They've lived. Especially Seth. I would have liked to see battle. Had a wife. Maybe a brat to bounce, too.'

'There was little chance of you achieving any of those things in gaol,' she reminded him.

'Ah, but I wouldn't have been in there forever. A brand and six years: that was my sentence.'

'You might not be *here* forever, Harry.' She took the cup gently from his hand. 'I will admit the treatments have not progressed as we planned, but you are looking stronger than the other patients. If I had to place a wager on a man likely to survive … it would be you.'

He did not smile. Did not even look at her. 'That's kind of you, Miss Pinecroft. But I know where I'm headed.'

'None of us can presume to know—'

'You think it's deep underground here,' he said bitterly. 'But it an't. There's another space, even darker, six feet under the soil. Who's going to keep me safe from the worms then?'

*

Fire and water. Ernest possessed them both now. Flames capering, malicious and gleeful in the stone circle; a tripod above them, supporting the bowl of water and rosemary. Fire and water to rid yourself of fairies, of worms.

They were banishing nothing. Only bringing memories back.

Rosemary had been the scent of their wedding day. Her clothes smelt of it, her hair. She carried sprigs in her bouquet. 'Rosemary to bind us,' she had said.

And they were bound, still.

The water started to bubble, tinkling against the bowl like a fall of rain.

He tore leaves of rosemary between his fingers and threw more in. Thought of the rosemary and the lavender he had used to conserve the three bodies until their burial. He had seen them laid in that churchyard himself, but he knew his family were not truly there. That was mere bones and flesh.

They had been taken from him and yet ... He felt them. Always. They were not gone, so where were they? He considered the ring on his finger, the remnants of them trapped behind glass. Just as he was. Seeing them, hearing them everywhere, never able to reach ...

It seemed his blue devils had finally won.

One by one, he took up the pamphlets and trea-tises on the ground and fed them to the flames. Stray words stood out. *Phthisis ... Balsamic ... corrects acrid Ichor ... stuffed Bronchia ... dissipates crude Tubercles ... lungs strengthened with cold ...*

Everything he thought he had known. How quickly it curled and blackened.

Ash left to the wind.

His cheeks burned from the heat. The scent of rose-mary soared, spiralling towards the back of the cave. Cleansing. He wanted to bathe in it until every inch of guilt was scrubbed clean.

He had been proud. Worse: headstrong. So cocksure and confident, telling Mopsy all would be well. Until he found himself dressed in black, staring glassy-eyed at the one surviving member of his family, he had not truly believed that he could fail.

But now this business with Louise ... Watching his own daughter outgrow him. She, a woman, more able, more perceptive. She put him to shame.

He felt a desperate clenching inside, knowing she would slip through his fingers. No more would she raise her blue eyes to him with that trusting look of devotion and utter faith. He had failed her as thor-oughly as the rest of them.

The paper did not burn cleanly. Smoke puffed out, smothering the blackness. Pervading all. Sitting on his chest, heavy like clay.

Somewhere, distantly, the cupping jars trilled. He had grown used to it now.

Kneeling down, he took the last few scraps of paper, scrunched them into a ball and threw it into the heart of the flame. It uncurled, crackled.

There was just one item left. A slim volume, bound in cloth. Ernest picked it up and brushed off the cover. Folklore.

He had forgotten this. He must have gathered it in the great bundle from his desk.

Another failure. Creeda was no better. She remained as convinced of the existence of fairies as ever. He envied her that certainty.

Hesitantly, he held the book towards the flames. Pulled it back.

He remembered that day in Falmouth. Yearned to be again the man who searched its stalls and purchased this book. A man focused on the future, envisioning a new horizon where consumption was no more.

Much as he tried, he could not swallow the idea that it was truly over. How could it be that he had wanted it so much, worked so hard, and still not found the cure?

He had believed greatness was within him. Still believed. It was his destiny to go where others would not. If only he could turn the key, unlock the answers ...

What was it Creeda had said? *A new way of seeing.*

Ernest raised his eyes, searching.

He could see nothing through the smoke.

Chapter 35

Morning light stroked Louise's closed eyelids. Sound crept back into her awareness: waves frisking, the squall of gulls. She had always risen from bed and dressed of her own accord, rather than waiting for a servant to wake her, but today she was weary.

Watching Papa suffer tired her in a way nursing had never done. Sometimes she thought the bond between them ran so deep that she felt every one of his pains. Yet the way he looked at her recently, the strange, rapt expression of his eyes ... It threatened to undo all that had been in the past. Losing that special relationship was a prospect more horrifying to her than any mortal disease. She could not part with him. Not Papa.

Pompey shifted his weight where he lay at her feet. His first stirrings of impatience, reminding her it would soon be time for his food. Papa would be up from the caves, expecting his own breakfast, and she would have to accompany him back to that terrible scene ... But Harry would be there.

His smile.

She found the energy to open her eyes.

The blue dimity curtains were still closed around her bed, tinting the space with sapphire hues. Louise could take no joy in the effect. She felt as though she were drowning.

She pushed herself up against the pillows and heard a rustling crunch. Pompey raised his head.

'What ...?'

She reached behind her. Nothing. Her hand groped beneath the pillow, found something scratchy and rough.

When she drew the object out, she saw it was part of an ash tree. A few twigs and their long, slender leaves. Pompey padded over and sniffed at them as she stared in tired bemusement.

How had they got there? It could be no accident. They were neatly cut. Who would put ... She sighed. Creeda, of course.

Did she not have enough to concern her without the maid's foolish tricks? No doubt it was well meant. She remembered now, speaking to Creeda on the day she arrived. How Creeda told her to put ash leaves under her pillow to dream of her future husband.

'But I dreamt of nothing,' she whispered to Pompey, handing him the twigs to chew. 'Nothing at all.'

It did not signify. She had never really expected, never *wanted* ... She must be very tired still. There was moisture in her eyes, and a dead weight in her stomach.

Angry with herself, she pushed her plait over her shoulder. It was time to stop moping. With more force than was necessary, she threw open the curtain to the bed.

Screamed.

Her father stood there.

Or something like her father. A cruel, brutal imitation of him.

He wore no stock, no waistcoat. His shirtsleeves were rolled to the elbows. Dirt and dried blood mottled his arms. There was no pretence at fastening back his hair now; the ribbon had vanished.

'They were taken!' he cried.

Pompey growled.

'Taken,' he muttered again, putting his fingers to his lips. The nails were bitten and tipped with dirt. 'It makes sense. They were getting better. They *were* getting better.'

Tentatively, Louise climbed out of bed and placed a hand on his shoulder. He was burning up. 'Papa, you are unwell. You must rest. Go to bed. I will see to the men.'

'Men!' he scoffed. Hectic colour suffused his cheeks. Beside them, the rest of his face was as white as marble. 'Are they? I made them well ...'

Making him sit on the bed, Louise put on her spectacles, threw a cloak over her shift and pulled on yesterday's stockings. Her hair was quickly bound up and concealed beneath a cap – it would have to do. Jamming her feet into some slippers, she put her head around the door and bellowed for Creeda.

Papa was still mumbling. 'A switch. That must be it. They waited, waited until I cured them, and then traded the men. I *succeeded*, but ...'

Louise went to him and clasped his hands. There were tremors in them. She had heard rambling like this before. Not the exact words, but the tenor. *Any minute now*, she thought, *he will cough*.

She could not endure it. Could not even let the understanding enter her mind – she held it at a distance, hovering on the brink of a precipice.

'The sudden decline ...' he went on, addressing no one. 'And Louise. Louise said the mark vanished from Harry's hand.'

'Louise is right here, Papa.' She knew he did not hear her.

Both Creeda and Gerren appeared in the doorway.

'Dr Pinecroft is unwell.' She was amazed how serene and authoritative she sounded. 'I need you to put him to bed and make him something to eat. Beef tea, if you can.'

Papa shook his shaggy head. 'No! No food.'

'You must try, dear Papa.'

He broke into a wheezing cough.

Louise closed her eyes. Harry had asked if she was afraid of catching consumption; she realised that the answer had always been no. *This* was what she had feared; this was the worst that could possibly happen.

And it had.

'I will care for him,' she said, her voice firm despite the tears that started to flow. 'I will make him well. Gerren, fetch me ... But the men!' She gasped. 'They are down there in the caves, suffering ...'

'They switched them while I slept ...' Papa choked.

It was like being torn in half. What would Papa want her to do? Although it revolted her every feeling, she knew. He would say that the men were his work, his good name. He would desire them and his reputation to be saved above all else.

'I must go to them,' she breathed. 'If only for a little while. Watch over him, Gerren. Promise me you will run down to fetch me if there is the slightest change in his condition.'

Gerren hesitated. 'To the fairy cave?'

'*Promise me.*'

He nodded. 'Aye. For ee, missus. Anything.'

She took one last look at Papa, sitting deadly still beneath Pompey's nosing and fussing. Then she ran from the door and down the stairs as fast as her feet would carry her.

*

The beach wore a different aspect that morning. Louise felt she was seeing it for the first time. The grey rocks, hazed with moss and the droppings of birds, were ancient, unyielding as death. How arrogant it was for a mortal to strive against nature's order. How utterly hopeless. The sick would die; the tide would come in.

Her slippers squelched on wet sand. That terrible cough reverberated off stone, warning her away. But even if she returned to the house, it would be there, awaiting her.

She stepped into the cave's shadow. It reminded her of a tomb. She had taken only four steps inside when Harry appeared out of the darkness and seized her shoulders. 'Louise!'

This time, she did not correct him.

He looked half wild. The bruises on his face had paled and the swelling around his nose was reduced, but that only served to display his panic more clearly. The dilated pupils, the strained brow: everything was suddenly and achingly human.

'The doctor, he just—'

'I saw him.'

'He just upped and left!' Harry exclaimed. 'Left them to die.'

'He did no such thing. I am here, I will do whatever needs to be done.'

He released her shoulders, seeming to notice that she was not properly dressed. It was not a leer that crossed his face, but something softer, something made of confusion and longing.

She wrapped the cloak more tightly about her. 'Who ails?'

'Tim's blisters have gone green. The stink ... And Chao. You can't ...' He placed one hand on the back of his head. 'Louise, I heard the rattle in his chest. I think he's done for.'

'There must be some way.'

'I cleaned them up as best I could and gave them that – what is it? The white stuff.'

'Calomel?'

'Just a bit of it in brandy.'

She saw the misery of the last few hours etched into him, but it was comforting to know she was no longer alone in her torment.

'You have been helping them,' she realised. 'Looking after the others.'

'I told you, I'm a fence. Not a monster. But I don't know the things you do. They need a nurse.'

Grabbing her hand, he led her across the slippery rocks towards the hut that had belonged to Michael. Michael was not in it now. All four men lay stretched out on the stone.

'Couldn't keep running between huts,' Harry explained. 'And the smell – I thought they might be better where the air could blow it away?'

She squeezed his hand, sensing his need for reassurance. 'You did right.'

But who could say whether that was true?

Bending beside Seth, she remembered his words about the Seven Years' War and wondered if there had ever been a battlefield equal to this. Tim had lost complete control of his bowels. None of them seemed to recognise her. Fever shook their limbs, while their eyes were vague and glassy. Seeping wounds – the wounds her father had purposefully inflicted upon them – showed the burnt crust of gangrene.

For the first time, she felt thoroughly powerless. There were too many of them and she did not know where to begin. She could bathe their brows, she could give them water – but that was all. Harry might not be a physician, but his instinct was right. Death had made his mark.

From nowhere, Seth's gnarly hand shot up and seized her cloak. He pulled her close, so close that she could taste his bitter breath. She must have screamed, for the sound ricocheted through the cave.

'Louise.' She did not realise he had known her name. 'Louise, don't let me die.'

The rocks, the patients – everything seemed to blur, as if someone had removed her spectacles. These were not Seth's words – they were Kitty's. The same look, the same words, the same inexorable cough. She was going to faint.

'Let her go!'

Hands grabbed beneath her armpits, just in time.

'Sorry,' she mumbled. She could not hear her own voice, so she said it again, louder. 'I am so terribly sorry.'

It was like a magic lantern projection: one moment she was swooning against Harry, the next someone had changed the slide and she was bent over on a cane chair, her forehead pressed to her knees. Her spectacles sat crooked on her nose.

'Drink this.'

She uncurled, ever so slightly. She remembered holding a cup such as this for Michael, that day early on in the experiment. The way his blood had dripped into the milk and turned it red. A poisoned chalice.

'No!' A wave of dizziness went through her.

'Easy! It's only water. I cleaned it out.'

Reluctantly, she allowed him to coax the rim between her lips and tip the cup. The water tasted stale, but it did make her feel better.

She lifted her head.

'Not so quick,' Harry scolded. 'An't you ever dropped before?'

Louise blinked as the world before her undulated and finally settled. They were inside a hut. This one, though, was not piled with filth. Perhaps it was Harry's own.

'No, actually, I have not. I am not prone to fainting fits.'

She turned to him, expecting to see contempt in his face, but there was none. He looked as if he might pass out himself.

'It's enough to set anyone off,' was all he said.

Barely knowing what she did, she reached out and took his hand. It felt warm, alive, responding to the pressure she applied.

'The way Seth spoke ... It reminded me of my sister. My sister went the hardest of them all. They say consumption is a kind and gradual death, romantic somehow. It was not so for Kitty.' She should not be saying these things to someone with the disease, but she did not seem able to stop. 'My little brother left softly enough. With Mama there were gasps. Her hands, clawing at the bedsheets as she fought for breath. But Kitty ...'

Kneeling down beside her chair, Harry took her in his arms.

There was an instant when she stiffened, the respectable Miss Pinecroft still. But then she heard the men outside, their lungs working like bellows, and pressed her face deep into the linen of his shirt.

'What am I going to do, Harry? What on earth am I going to do?'

Beneath all the terrible odours of the cave, she caught the essence of him, something musky and masculine and real.

'Nothing to be done. We can't save them.'

Four lives lost. The last dregs of Papa's reputation would go with them. What then? Humiliation would kill him if the consumption did not. She was only twenty years old, but when she thought of her future it was like staring into a deeper darkness. This hated, diabolical disease. Why could it not just take her, along with everyone else?

Harry's shoulder hitched against her cheek. 'I thought I could tough it out, tried to make myself ready. But when I see what it's doing to them ...' His voice cracked. 'Maybe I'm white-livered after all.'

She tightened her grip on him, her fingers burrowing into his back. 'You might not ... Perhaps ...'

'Don't,' he whispered. 'It's useless. We both know it.'

Louise released him and sat back. He looked so young kneeling beside her. What a waste it was. Such meaningless, breathtaking waste! All these lives destroyed and nothing gained, no cure discovered, no cause furthered.

'The thing is ...' He struggled. She saw his eyes filling with tears. Blue, today. A clear, flawless blue. 'Now it comes to it ... I don't think I ever really lived.'

She leant forwards and pressed her lips to his.

It was a second before he responded. But then his mouth was moving, warm and soft, belonging a hundred miles away from this awful place.

Her heart began to throb, insistent. It was beating still. She was here, for now. Harry was here.

They clung to one another for dear life.

Chapter 36

A persistent drip awoke Louise from her sleep. Beneath her head was a hard, cold slab that sent twinges of discomfort down her neck.

She was in the cave.

She started up with a cry, groping for her spectacles. What time was it? Impossible to tell from the weak light in the hut. She might have been out for hours. She could not believe herself. Had she really slept while the men suffered outside?

That was not all that she had done.

She turned to look at Harry. He slumbered on, his back to her. She had a sudden memory of his skin moving against hers, and shivered.

A moment of madness. Desperation. Yet she felt more ashamed of deserting the men and Papa, even for a short time, than of taking comfort in his arms.

She thought that she would feel altered, afterwards, but there was no difference. No difference in the least. She brushed down her skirts and climbed to her feet with a wince. All the value that was put upon virtue and there was so little to the act. Now she knew.

Faintly, from beyond the walls of the cave, came the slap of water against rock. It sounded playful, but that was a deceit. The cliff face suffered; that was why it looked so stern. Wave after wave, blow after blow, relentless, interminable. The sea gradually ate away at the cliff's defences, the same way misfortune was chipping away at her own.

One of the men spluttered.

They needed help. She reached out to Harry, shook his shoulder to wake him.

Something was wrong.

She snatched back her fingers. Their sensations, their feel for temperature must be at fault. They must.

Holding her breath, she touched him again. He did not feel like flesh. His shoulder was icy and solid.

She pulled at him and he rolled over, a dead weight. Glazed blue eyes stared beyond her. The lips, which she had so lately kissed, were no longer red, but grey and lifeless.

It could not be. It could not possibly be.

'Harry,' she said.

She did not expect a reply. Yet still she kept shaking him, saying his name.

'Harry!'

He was the one patient able to function. The healthiest. He had shown no signs of decline.

'My God,' she gasped, realising. 'I killed you.'

Jerkily, she pulled on her cloak and stumbled towards the door. Her body felt numb, would not listen to her commands. What had she been thinking? In a moment of selfish weakness she had seen him as a man, not an invalid; she had overtaxed him and now ...

The other men's coughs hit her. She swayed slightly, watching them writhe and twist. All alive. How could they be alive when Harry ...

She had not heard him die. She had been right there, and she had not even woken up. He must have passed without a sound. Not like Mama, not like Kitty ...

'Oh God.' Her knees went slack again, as if someone had cut the tendons behind them, and this time there was no Harry to hold her up. She grabbed at the wall of the cave, scratching her hands. 'Papa.'

Until that moment she had thought only of her own loss. But these men were dying. Harry was already dead. Her father's experiment was utterly doomed and she would have to convey the message. He would hear the death sentence of his career from her own lips.

She must fetch help for the men.

Somehow she persuaded her legs to walk. She had lost her slippers. Scattered pebbles on the beach pressed into the soles of her feet, but that seemed too trivial a thing to concern her. Fresh air blew cold against her face and she realised it was damp with tears.

She had never been one to despair before, but as she reached Morvoren House, she was aware of being broken at last. There was no feeling of relief, even at the prospect of rest for her sore and aching body. For a moment she paused outside the door, trying to catch her breath.

It swung open.

Papa stood there in his nightshirt. He had pulled breeches over it without properly fastening the buttons. His legs were stockingless, his feet bare.

'They kept me from my duties,' he raved. 'Drugged me with something ... Where are the men, Louisa, where are the men?'

'Louise.' Her mouth could barely form the name. 'I am Louise.'

When she left, he had been paddling in the waters of the fever. Now he was fully submerged.

He reached for her chin, pulled it up and stared into her face. His fingers gripped her with surprising strength. 'Louise,' he repeated. 'Louise ... But she did not ...'

She must not let him push past her. If he reached the cave and saw Harry ...

She had meant to tell him the truth, but she could not, not while he was like this. She must protect him from it. Even if she had to write to another physician for help with the men, she would spare him her own painful knowledge.

She put out an arm to block his passage. 'Creeda!' she shouted. 'Gerren!'

They emerged from the west wing.

'Why was he left unattended?' Louise demanded.

'I am well,' Papa interjected, 'I am perfectly well, I must just—'

'Didn't expect him to wake,' Creeda confessed. 'Gave him that much laudanum ...'

Pompey hurtled down the stairs, attracted by the sound of voices. Papa recoiled.

'Get him away. Get the cur away!'

Nothing born of delirium should surprise her, but this did. Papa adored Pompey. She had never thought to see him cringing from the dog's advances.

'Gerren, take Pompey to my room.'

'But ee said—'

'Do it, Gerren.'

Louise could feel them slipping: the men, Papa, the servants; each one a rock tumbling from the cliff. Why was everyone so useless? Why would no one help her?

'Please, Creeda,' she said desperately. 'I must get him to his room. Help me move him.'

'The men ...' Papa objected.

Little did he know that one of them lay dead, somewhere below his feet. Presumably, there would be no family to claim poor Harry's body. The gaol would not pay the expense of burial.

What was she going to do?

Somehow, they heaved Papa up the stairs and back into bed. He was still talking, talking all the while about lights and trades, and heaven knew what else. Louise seized the laudanum bottle from the medicine chest and administered two more drops to his moving lips.

Gradually, his eyelids wavered and fell. The breath rumbled in his chest. She stood watching him, conscious of the time and of his life slipping away.

She wished it were her instead.

'Creeda,' she whispered, needing to say the words. 'Creeda ... Harry is dead.'

Papa's face twitched. But surely he could not have heard her?

'Dead,' Creeda echoed. She sounded as if she did not quite believe it. '*Is* he, miss?'

'It was me.' She closed her eyes. 'My fault. I made him ... I pushed him too far. I killed him.'

Something warm settled on her shoulder. Creeda's hand. 'No, miss. That can't be true. You said he was getting better.'

'He was! I thought ...'

Forgetting herself, she turned to the maid and sobbed into her arms.

'Who do I report it to? What shall I do with the body? I do not—'

'I'll send Gerren to town,' Creeda soothed. 'The man was a convict, wasn't he, miss? I'm sure they won't take much bother about him. The number of poor folk who die every day ...'

Creeda's gown smelt of rosemary. There was something comforting in that herbal scent, something redolent of her mother. 'But the body ...'

Creeda drew a breath. 'You leave that to me. I know what to do.'

The solace in those words. She hungered to believe them.

'Only ...' Creeda's fingers tightened on her back. 'Miss, are you really sure he's dead? The experiment has failed?'

Louise could not erase the image of Harry lying there on a cold slab of rock, his sightless eyes fixed beyond her. Blue eyes. Had they not once been green?

'I am certain he is dead, Creeda.'

'Not ... changed?'

She did not know whether to laugh or cry. In the midst of all this disaster, Creeda was Creeda still.

'No, Creeda.' She withdrew herself from the maid's arms. 'You never saw Harry, did you? He was ... just a man. A good man.'

Creeda pressed her lips together. 'If the men die ... you and the master will be leaving us. Going back to Bristol.'

Fresh tears slid down her cheeks. They could never return to Bristol. But how could they remain here, living in the grave of all their hopes? Seeing every day the places she had walked with Harry, the gap on the cliff where the rocks had fallen ...

'It is too early to consider that. I can plan nothing until Papa is well again.'

Creeda's eyes ranged over Papa, tossing and turning in the bed. 'The master isn't himself. What if he decides to send me back to Plymouth?'

Louise lowered her head into her hands, trying to clutch everything together. She had always prided herself on her courage and sense. It was as though she had spent a lifetime being calm, just waiting for today. Knowing that nothing she endured would be truly worth panicking about, until this.

'I told you, Creeda, I cannot think of it now. Leave us, please. Just leave us and ... tell Gerren to set out at once. We need doctors. Anyone who can come. I cannot leave those men alone in the caves.'

Was that a tear Louise saw gleaming in Creeda's brown eye? She did not look eerie now. Just a girl, petulant in her fear of being returned home to ... whatever treatment Mr Nancarrow deemed necessary.

'It's the caves you should have left alone in the first place,' Creeda muttered bitterly. She slammed the door behind her.

For the first time, Louise had to admit that Creeda was right.

Chapter 37

Sleep had restored him. Fully restored him – he felt like one of the actors at county fairs who dropped their crutches in miraculous recovery after taking a quack's nostrum.

Ernest sat up in bed. His shirt was plastered to his skin, but his mind had never felt so clear. The fever had refined him. He had sweated out all of his impurities.

A new dawn showed Louise asleep in the easy chair with her long legs curled beneath her. Her cap sat askew and her spectacles had slid to the end of her nose. Even in slumber, those lines of worry remained carved in her face.

His dearest child had endured so much. But she would not have to fret any longer.

Rising quietly, he pulled on his stockings, breeches and boots. Soon he would be dressing like a gentleman again: the powdered wigs, the shoes with buckles. He might even invest in a gold-topped cane. Anything was possible.

He could not wait to see them all bowing and scraping to him. Stuttering apologies in the wake of his great achievement. Imagine Lord Redfern's chagrin! He almost laughed aloud.

Poor Louise was so exhausted that she failed to stir, even when he stroked her cheek. Only her eyelids flickered, as if she were avidly watching the outcome of some absorbing dream.

'No more nightmares, my precious,' he whispered. 'Papa will put everything right.'

Only the small blue shepherds on the wallpaper watched him creep from the room and close the door.

No fires were lit. The shutters remained closed. But Ernest was unaffected by either the dark or the cold.

Pompey rose from where he was lying on the landing and sidled up to his master, sniffing at the dried sand on his boots. Of course, it was all falling out as it should: he must take Pompey with him. They did not like dogs.

Ernest wrinkled his nose as he considered the cur's tangled fur, his wet, questing snout and the small tongue that darted out to lick his boots. Strangely, he did not seem to like Pompey that much himself.

'Come,' he whispered, and the dog obeyed, trotting with him down the stairs and into the hollow entrance hall. Stucco loomed from the walls, white as a consumptive's calcified chest.

It all made sense now: each and every paradox the illness had presented. Why it touched rich and poor alike. The doctors had been looking at it with blinkered eyes. Searching for answers in wrong places. But Ernest was here, at the end of the world, and he could see it all.

Creeda had not locked the front door. He stepped out into a wakening day with Pompey at his heels. The salt air carried the freshness of potential. Here and there a clump of gorse flared out from the clifftop, brimstone yellow. He began to walk.

The fine weather they had enjoyed since the end of February was turning into something colder and brighter. Every object presented sharp, clear lines. The shore was washed clean, the sky the vital blue of a vein. It was as though he was viewing the world through a microscope.

Sails bobbed on the distant horizon. Ships taking the clay, the tin and the copper to other shores. All the secret, hidden treasures of Cornwall. But he had found the rarest of them all.

The stones that grated beneath his boots finally gave way to sand. It yielded to his steps, taking every impression. Ernest glanced over his shoulder just the once, to see the prints he and Pompey had left.

The final leg of a long, arduous journey.

The cave rose up before them. The sea pulled at the shore, the glass armonica sang and Ernest smiled.

His family had not died in vain.

He had finally found a way to quash the blue devils, once and for all.

*

When they laid out the dead, they placed coins on their eyelids. Sometimes stones. Anything heavy that would keep their inanimate pupils from gazing into a world in which they no longer belonged. *Perhaps it has happened to me*, Louise thought. *Perhaps I am dead.*

It was not just her eyes that felt weighted. Every shred of her ached. But that obstinate flicker of life remained, the one that refused to let even consumption quench it.

A clock in the corner ticked by the seconds while her eyelids remained closed. Papa had been fretful at nightfall, but now he did not stir. No coughing, no mumbling, no tossing in his bed. She thought of Harry, passing noiselessly from the world while she lay beside him. Her stomach clenched.

She did not want to open her eyes. Did not know what she would find.

Another minute passed. She could not even hear Papa's quiet breath. Pressure built behind her ribs, forced itself up her throat.

What if she just stayed there? What if she never let herself see?

Claws scratched at the closed door.

Her mind was racing with memories of Papa: his wise eyes, the reassuring smile, the comfort of his embrace. She must keep them. No matter what terrible grey version of him stretched out in the bed, she must hold onto him as he was. She was the only person left who could.

Pompey whined and scratched again.

It would be better to face the truth quickly. Like pulling a tooth or ripping off a bandage. *Courage, Louise*, he used to say. *Courage*. She forced her eyes open.

He had gone.

The bed was empty, its covers thrown back to reveal a sweaty stain on the mattress and the pillow left at an angle. Louise gaped at it.

Dawn had broken without her realising. The window sash was raised, letting in a thin stream of air. There was no conceivable way he could have climbed out of it. The gap was too narrow, the drop too high.

The door jolted as Pompey jumped against it.

Papa must have glided out silently and shut the door behind him.

She struggled to her feet. What a traitor she was, what an absolute fool! How had she managed to drift off when Papa needed her? She opened the door and Pompey spilled in, jumping at her legs with urgency. He had come to fetch her, she realised. This could not bode well.

'Where is he, boy? Help me find him.'

He streaked straight along the corridor and thumped down the stairs.

Louise followed, calling breathlessly for Creeda as she went.

The maid emerged from the west wing, holding Louise's teapot and a dusting rag.

'Where is Dr Pinecroft? Did you not see him? Hear him?'

Creeda paled. 'Has he gone?'

Pompey was pawing at the front door.

'Come with me,' Louise demanded as she crossed the hall to stand behind her dog. The bolts were already drawn back. Papa must have gone down to the beach, to the men. To Harry ...

Panic rolled in like a storm.

She opened the door and pulled Creeda, who was still clutching the teapot, outside with her. Pompey shot between their legs, and round the house.

How innocent the scene appeared. Light touched the clover flowering on the cliff. The sun burnt far above the horizon and the day had begun in earnest. A soft breeze blew through the ash leaves and there was a gentle green scent in the air.

Anticipating the direction of their steps, Creeda attempted to turn back. Louise tightened her grip on the maid's arm and forced her on.

'Don't make me go,' Creeda pleaded. 'Not to the fairy cave!'

Louise felt a pinch of sympathy but it was distant, as if it were being experienced by someone else.

Pompey did not bark. That was the eerie thing. As they half-ran, half-fell down the track, they saw him standing on the shore, his ears raised, the wind ruffling through his fur. Bearing witness.

Louise followed his gaze a little further out to sea.

'Oh God.'

A dark hump lay in the water. Foam seethed around it, fluttering the edges. In a few more steps she could see the knotted hair and the unravelled hem of a shirt. It was a man. A man face down in the shallows.

'Papa!' she screamed. 'Papa!'

She began to run.

Damp sand snatched the shoes from her feet, but she did not stop. She tugged Creeda with her, all the way to the water's edge, where she was forced to drop the maid's arm and hold up her skirts. The waves kept trying to shove her back. She struggled to keep her balance, but she managed to wade knee-deep, close enough to touch the clammy, swollen skin.

It was not her father.

Water inflated the loose shirt and breeches that hung about the withered frame, pushing the man in her direction. Swallowing her horror, Louise grabbed hold of his sleeve cuff and began to drag him towards the shore. He was heavy – far heavier than he looked – and her wet skirts made it feel like she was walking in shackles, but the tide was working with her, now. She saw the shoreline coming closer, Pompey and Creeda poised at its edge.

'Help me,' Louise cried.

With an absurd amount of care, Creeda set the teapot down beside Pompey and paddled towards her.

Together, they heaved the man over to face the sky.

It was Michael.

The consumption had not carried him off. His jaw hung open, slack, revealing smashed teeth and a mouth stuffed full of sand. He had not stumbled out of the cave and fallen into the water to drown. Someone had done this to him.

Louise stared at the corpse, sure her vision would suddenly clear and reveal a different picture. If she could only concentrate, surely this must change? No one could want to *kill* Michael ...

'Miss.' Creeda's hand on her shoulder, demanding her attention. Angrily, she brushed it off. 'Miss!'

She looked up. Creeda's hair lifted on the wind. She looked like a saint: stern, pitying, righteous. She pointed behind Louise to where Pompey still gazed, transfixed. 'I ... I told you he wasn't himself, miss.'

Slowly, Louise turned.

There were more. Two protrusions from the ocean, two more human rocks. And just beyond, a third that still thrashed and scattered water.

Old Seth.

Papa was holding him down.

Her feet carried her forward before she authorised them to do so.

Veins stood out on her father's arms and forehead. His features were distorted, goblin-like. He thrust down on the transparent back of Seth's shirt, a satisfied grimace appearing as the old man's motions became steadily weaker.

Pompey barked.

It did not break the spell. Papa swivelled his head to watch them, but he was a stranger still. A blood vessel had burst in his right eye, streaking the white with red like a gory egg.

Louise sobbed. 'Stop it! Let him go, P—'

She could not finish. Could not call this creature *Papa*.

'Changelings!' he bellowed over the roar of the surf. The air of self-congratulation turned her stomach. 'They were changelings.'

Seth twitched and grew limp.

Papa discarded him the way he would a used bandage. Coughing, he began to wade towards her.

'It was all as Creeda said! Dirty creatures, sickly, fairy stock.' Staggering up the shore, he threw his arms wide. Water dripped from his sleeves like blood. 'Oh, they wanted to drag me down, to ruin my reputation along with everything else, but I have bested them. Fairies are a poor match for a man of science! See,

Louise! I have found the cure for all ills! I have saved our men!'

'You *killed* them!'

His smile wavered. 'No. No, I destroyed the fairies, Louise. They tricked us ...' His body heaved with another cough. 'But I have found the solution. They are gone now, and they will be forced to send our men back. Healthy men.'

'Our men are dead!' she screamed. 'They were people. *People*, and you have killed them!'

There was a moment with only the rush of waves and a chough calling.

Something hardened in his jaw. 'You do not believe me. My own daughter!' He ran a hand through his wild hair and gave a harsh, bruised laugh. 'God, I thought you were my equal, but you are not. Your mind is too narrow to grasp the advance of our discoveries. You are just like those damned old college fograms, standing in the way of progress.'

Even after all she had seen and heard, these words cut her to the quick.

'You are very sick ...' she tried to explain. 'The fever ...'

That bloody eye bored into her, its pupil sharp and black as a poker. 'No. No, I am not the one in need of treatment. How foolish I was not to see before. You reek of their glamour. My *real* daughter would have believed me.'

He sprang. Louise stumbled back, her wet skirts tangled around her legs. He was coming for her and he would drown her, too.

She began to run away but she was slow, painfully slow; her soaked dress pulled her back and she could hardly breathe for tears. Pompey and Creeda were not far off. If she could only reach them …

'Help me!'

She tripped. Pain exploded in her foot where it had collided with a rock or some other debris; she hardly knew what it was, for the next moment she was scrabbling in the sand.

'Help!'

White flashed past her. She heard a growl and then a shout of pain.

Pompey. Pompey had come to her rescue.

Painfully, she climbed to her knees. Red speckled the sand. Pompey had driven his teeth into Papa's calf and clung on with the strength of a bulldog. He was not large, but Papa couldn't shake him off. The pair of them flailed, inseparable.

It was only as Louise hauled herself to her feet that she noticed the teapot on its side, without its lid. That was what had tripped her. Not a rock or seaweed but china. She remembered how Papa had given it to her, a lifetime ago.

'Get off me, you damned cur!'

The man who looked like her father knelt on the ground, his murderous hands buried in fur. Papa had cossetted Pompey from a puppy, taught him tricks, fed him scraps from the table. Now he had his fingers around his throat.

The dog's paws flailed as he let out a strangled whine, his brown eyes bulging in panic. Papa began to squeeze.

She did not think. She picked up the teapot, ran at her father and cracked it over his head.

She should not have heard the sound, not with the waves lapping, the cry of the gulls and Pompey coughing at his sudden release. But everything seemed to shatter with that pot.

A warped mask glared up at her, astonished. Shards of china were driven deep into its temple. It fell back, hard – or perhaps she did. It happened too fast for her to tell. The last things she saw were those white porcelain chips and the blood, welling like an ocean beneath.

Chapter 38

Louise's hand hurt. That was the sensation that pulled her back to consciousness. It rested on the arm of a chair. Small white fragments, like the teeth of a tiny creature, were embedded in the knuckles. She watched with strange detachment as blood oozed from her skin.

Through her left eye, the image was clear. But in the right it doubled, quadrupled, splintered into a thousand pieces. It took her a moment to realise it was her spectacles: the right lens had cracked.

The chair she sat on was made of horsehair. It moulded to her body, cradled her. She wondered if she should try to stand, but the desire evaporated before it was fully formed. She felt sewn in. Carefully contained. One false movement would ruin the balance.

Pompey mumbled at her side. He was staring opposite, at the empty hearth and the china Creeda had displayed upon it. Reaching up to her face, Louise removed her broken spectacles. Without them, she could not discern the individual shapes, only smudges of blue. Cool, elegant blue. It doused the red that threatened to spread across her mind.

'Did everything ee asked, Creeda.' It was Gerren, his voice distant, like everything else.

There was a gentle scratch inside her head. Gerren ... he should not be there. Had she not told Creeda to send him to town? She tried to remember, but could not. Memories slipped through her hands like sand. It did not matter. Nothing mattered, now.

'Smashed the dam,' he went on. 'When the tide come in, happen it'll look like an accident.'

'It's only the doctor they'll mind.'

'Rock might've hit un,' he suggested. 'Swept by a wave and ... bam!'

She flinched.

'They shouldn't ask too many questions,' Creeda assured him. 'It's no wonder to have a group of consumptives die. It's only the doctor's head we'll need to explain, and he was living in a cave full of convicts. If the coroner won't believe an accident ... Well, it won't take much to persuade him one of them criminals hit our master.'

Once, Louise would have told her that the coroners were not medically trained. That even if they suspected murder, it would take a rich and interested party to pay before they sought prosecution. But her worldly knowledge no longer seemed important. It felt like a story she had read long ago.

'Loss of blood, were it?' Gerren asked softly.

'Think so. Who can know? It wasn't human, Gerren. At the end there … that was a fairy.'

The idea did not seem so very unlikely to Louise now. There was certainly something, peopling the silence; she could feel it, as surely as she had felt death prowling around the men.

'Their bodies.' She sounded listless, unlike herself. 'What will you do with the bodies?'

A hand stroked her arm. 'Hush, now.'

'The money it would cost to bury them all …'

'There's more than one way to dispose of bones, miss. I know just what to do.'

Of course she did. Creeda *knew*. She knew all the things Louise did not.

'He is dead, then. My …' She trailed off. She had not noticed before that this room resembled the cave, when the light was shut out. Dark brown walls pressing close. The gloom and the chill. She had loathed that cave, but now it made her feel better. It reminded her of being with Harry.

'Miss, it wasn't your father,' Creeda insisted. An edge of panic crept into her voice. 'Don't you see? They got the men and then they came after you. They wanted you and me.'

Louise exhaled. Even that was an effort. She wanted to see them, to see the fairies dancing. The pretty, dainty fairies she had read of as a child. Not cruel and savage like that man on the beach.

'Has my father been taken by the fairies, Creeda?'

'Yes, miss. I'm afraid he has.'

Her ribs seemed to scrape against her heart. 'And I'll never see him again.'

'Well ...' Creeda took a breath. 'I don't know about that. Maybe you will. I came back, didn't I? One of them brought me back.'

Back from under the ground. Could it happen? She did not see why not. Everything else Creeda had said had come to pass.

'You could ... stay here,' Creeda went on, tremulous. 'In this house, close to the cave. Just in case. But you'd need me here. To protect you from them.'

She could not imagine parting with the girl now. Could not imagine a future at all. Vague images of chains and straw flickered in her mind. That was right. Creeda had been threatened with incarceration in the madhouse. As if that would help her.

She thought of medicine and it was like mourning for a lost love. A sweetheart whose true colours gave only disillusionment. Mama, Kitty, Francis, Harry, Papa ... physic had not saved a single one of them. It had left her with nothing, not even faith in the science that had once been her passion.

'Will your father not come to fetch you away from here?' she asked wearily.

'Not if you write,' Creeda pleaded. 'Not if you tell him you're a nurse, and you'll care for me now the doctor's gone. He's got plenty of money, he'll keep paying for me …'

Louise sighed. 'I will write whatever you wish. Sign whatever you want me to.'

'We'll look after each other, miss. We'll wait for them to be returned. What do you say?'

Louise did not blink. It was not only china that lay before her. It was a choice.

She could believe that Harry was gone forever, his life a pointless waste; that her beloved father, driven mad with grief and illness, had committed the gravest of sins; and that she had murdered both. There was no heaven, no forgiveness, for any of them.

Or there was Creeda's way. She could believe they were coming back. Stare deep into the china and picture two men blinking, stumbling into the light and the welcome spray of the waves.

'I will wait,' she said. 'I will wait as long as it takes.'

PART SEVEN

Pixy-Led

Chapter 39

I did not believe Miss Pinecroft when she said it was too dangerous for me to spend a night in the china room. Now that morning has come, I wish I had listened to her.

I retch into Miss Pinecroft's chamber pot again and again.

A spell. It must be a spell.

Creeda has done this to me.

The muscles of my stomach heave, beyond my control. How they burn. Either side of the chamber pot, my hands appear soft and bloated. I drive my fingernails into the floorboards as an anchor.

Every spell requires a lock of hair. That was why I found Miss Pinecroft's brush picked clean. The crone must be controlling my mistress, somehow, causing harm in subtle and insidious ways through the power of hair.

And now she has mine.

'Hester?' It is Miss Pinecroft. Through watery eyes I peer at her; the lady and her chair are nothing more than a blur to me.

I cannot answer her.

Dawn dribbles beneath the curtains, pale as death. It grazes my hands but does not light the china room. Nothing, it seems, can illuminate this infernal chamber and its paganism.

I close my eyes and focus on breathing.

The tide draws breath with me, lapping in and out.

Gradually, my insides cease their bubbling. My belly settles. Exhausted and giddy with relief, I fall back onto my haunches.

Floorboards bump upstairs. I hear clattering down the corridor and realise it must be Merryn, going to wake the kitchen from its slumber.

Should I tell Merryn?

Once, I might have done so. But if my behaviour has not already convinced her I am soft in the head, this story will do it. I can picture myself streaking into the kitchen, dishevelled and gaunt, rambling about Creeda cutting my hair for witchcraft.

Can she be a witch? Both Merryn and Lowena mock her, yet no harm has befallen them. I recall my own brew, mixed in the cold white-tile kitchen of Hanover Square. There was no dark magic involved there. The fault was entirely human.

Scrabbling to my feet, I lurch towards the door.

Miss Pinecroft releases her breath.

The corridor rocks. With every step, the floor tilts in a different direction, but somehow I manage to stagger on, through the white haze of the stucco hall and beyond.

Heat reaches out and takes me by the hand, leading me to the kitchen where the fire spits.

'Merryn.'

She jumps as I haul myself into the room. How young she looks. I realise now that Merryn does not hate me for my previous outburst: she is frightened of me.

She shrinks close to the wall, no informant ready to run to the magistrate; just a poor girl who does not want to be shouted at.

'I need water. Hot water.'

She nods, mute.

Leaning against the doorframe for support, I watch her work, aware of the unsightly birthmark upon her cheek. Is that why she was hired here? Because she is a girl the fairies would not wish to take?

No, that cannot be. Mrs Quinn hires the staff, not Creeda. Although she told me with her own lips that Creeda read my reference letters … Creeda needed to approve of me cleaning the china.

How far does the clawed hand of that woman reach?

The water heater hisses.

I thought I had run here to save my own skin, but perhaps there is a higher purpose behind my arrival. Only a person like me can spot Creeda's tricks, stop her. Maybe this is how I will make amends.

The pail Merryn warily places on the floor is scalding hot, but I do not wait for it to cool. Seizing the handle, I totter back the way I have come.

Water slops and spills. I pay it no heed. The hand that holds the bucket is no longer as white and dead as it looked beside the chamber pot; it is steamed red.

Since the moment I arrived eleven days ago, I have heard nothing but entreaties to keep the china room cold, to wash the plates with tepid water. I will not play their games any more. We will have flames and heat and cleansing steam: I will smoke this evil out.

Miss Pinecroft turns in her chair to see me stumble across the threshold. It is the first time she has done so.

'Hester?' she whispers.

I think I might be sick again. Swallowing down the bile, I pull a cloth from my apron and hold it against my mouth. Nothing comes.

'Hester?'

'I have left it long enough. I am going to wash the china.' I lower the cloth and plunge it into the searing water.

Pain bites instantly, but it is satisfying, somehow reassuring, like a steadying drop of gin. Gin ... I have not taken liquor for many hours. My body craves it, yet the thought of putting anything past my lips now ...

Later. There will be time for everything else later, once I have broken the hateful woman's spell.

Determined, I step up to the rack and remove the first plate. *Nancarrow Bone China*. I scrub furiously, front and back. The skull leers from the base, knowing.

The next plate. The next. I am not taking the time to dry them but slam each back into place. Water drips like tears onto the floor. My wet thumb squeaks against the varnish.

'Careful,' Miss Pinecroft gasps.

I hear movement, as if she is attempting to stand.

What has Creeda hidden here? What is her secret – and why can I see nothing of it?

Excitement and fear quake through me. Only with great difficulty do I manage to pick up another plate. This one is familiar: the Willow pattern with the missing figure.

No.

Two missing figures.

Blinking, I reconsider the bridge. It is no mistake: there is the man with the staff, standing alone. Reddish brown speckles the place his bride once occupied, flecks of something dried onto the plate.

Shakily, I pass my cloth over the spots, leaving a slick trail. Down, down, run the droplets, snaking their way from the painted bridge to the white void representing a lake.

And there it is.

The missing figure, the one that I looked for, is in the water. She has jumped off the bridge.

A bead of water magnifies the head, bobbing just above the surface. Blue painted lines indicate ripples around the body as it thrashes. Little use in that now. The stones in her pockets will weigh her down: I know, for I have read the report. I have seen this so many times in my nightmares.

I reel backwards, desperate to put space between myself and this terrible sight, but my hands have set rigid and will not release the plate.

Look what you have done, Esther. Look what you have done.

I stumble into something; there is a crunch like bones.

'No! No!' Miss Pinecroft cries hoarsely. 'How could y-y—?'

Whipping round, I see that I have dislodged one of the urns off its shelf and it has smashed. The lining, revealed at last, glows curd-white.

There is liquid. Thick and dark, like honey. It spreads, slowly forms a viscous pool. Rosemary needles are sprinkled through, but they do nothing for the stench.

Little wonder Miss Pinecroft did not want a fire in this room. Heating such a monstrous potion would make its stink unbearable.

'What on earth is this?'

It is not just rosemary caught in the liquid. There are nail clippings. Pins. A lock of human hair.

I cannot help it; I retch.

Miss Pinecroft makes no noise at all.

It is as though lightning has struck her. She stands before the chair, one arm extended to point at the urn, but she cannot support it. Her hand droops; everything seems to droop.

Her palsied mouth works, unable to catch words. Then it clamps shut. The blue eyes bulge.

Without a sound, she drops.

'Miss Pinecroft!'

Now my fingers do fall slack against the plate. It smashes to the floor. I do not care. I am on all fours once more, turning my mistress over, cradling her head.

'Help!' I scream. 'Fetch help!'

Merryn and Lowena tear into the room together. They take one look at the mess, the china scattered like broken teeth – and they freeze.

I see myself through their eyes: drink-deprived, retching, grovelling uselessly over the woman I swore to protect.

'Help me,' I plead.

Merryn begins to cry.

Chapter 40

Once, I would have revelled in this: the hushed panic of the sickroom where I reign supreme, other servants hurrying in deference to my orders. A chance at last to use my costly palsy water. But I do not experience that gentle hum of satisfaction, deep within my bones. I feel no sense of purpose. Instead, there is something else. A tightening, a dread.

The blue people on the walls and the bed hangings seem to crowd together, whispering. I cannot hear the drips as I once did. It is hard to hear anything above the knocking of my heart.

Another drop of laudanum slides from the bottle and down my throat. It softens nothing. My eyes are pinned open and forced to behold the agony I have caused through my carelessness. There is no doubt in my mind: if I had not broken the urn, Miss Pinecroft would not have suffered the fit.

She is stiff upon the bed, her lips ghost-pale. I dribble the palsy water between them: lavender and malmsey wine, herbs, the same spices I use in her drinking chocolate. It only trickles from the corners of her mouth.

No physician will come to aid me. Gerren has set out on the indomitable pony for help, but I hold no hope of his success. Icicles hang from the window and the glass is marbled with frost. Every now and then, snow huffs through the chimney and makes the fire hiss like a cat. Gerren will be lucky if he is not lost in a drift himself.

His wife does not seem overly concerned; at least, not for him. I hear her at the end of the corridor, admonishing Rosewyn.

'Hold it tight! Tight! I am locking the door. Don't you even think about moving.'

There is a slam, the click of a key turning in a lock.

Hairs stir on my arms as Creeda stalks closer. The door to Miss Pinecroft's chamber is open wide. Weak as I am, I will not be able to protect my mistress against the witch.

Is this what she wanted all along? Did she hex me on purpose so I would break the china? It would make a dreadful sort of sense to eliminate Miss Pinecroft and rule the house through Rosewyn, who must now surely inherit.

'She's been blinked.'

I twist round at the sound of Creeda's voice. She stands on the landing, a good few paces from the door. The emotion on her face startles me.

I expected triumph. Something malign, sinister. But there is no mistaking the expression written there.

Creeda is terrified.

'It is an apoplectic fit.' I sound withering in my derision, far more confident than I feel. 'I understand that she has suffered them before.'

In answer, Creeda gestures at the brass lock on the door.

Ninety-nine.

'Blinked,' Creeda repeats. 'Even you, Hester Why, must see it. Something's going in and out of that room at night. Feeding off her.' She shoots one anguished glance at Miss Pinecroft before turning and clomping down the stairs.

A moment later I hear her again. 'Leave that! Leave it be. Go on with you.'

Buckets clanking, the skitter of maid's feet. Whatever monstrous objects she hid within the urn, she does not want them touched.

I take my mistress's hand. It is limp and cold as a dead fish. 'What is happening?' I beseech her. 'What can I do for you?'

She is inscrutable as always. For once, it is not her fault.

This apoplectic fit has damaged her nerves more severely than the last. Already I can see the alteration: slackness all over the body and the candles in the brain gradually winking out. There is no saying whether we shall get her back.

I wish it were the season for lady's smock. That would be the best herb to use. But the frost has devoured everything and there is so little at my disposal. I should have stocked the cupboards against this. That is what I am paid for. How uncaring I have been, how flagrantly selfish. I should have thought of more than my precious laudanum.

But there is one person in this house who requires even more help than Miss Pinecroft.

From behind the walls, Rosewyn whimpers softly. Not for others to hear, the noise flows down the corridor towards me rhythmically, perfectly even in volume and in pitch, as though it is something she does not control, as natural as her own heartbeat. I wonder how many hours she has spent thus. Alone. Waiting.

'A moment,' I whisper to Miss Pinecroft, patting her hand. 'I shall be gone for just a moment.'

Leaving the door to Miss Pinecroft's chamber open, I creep to Rosewyn's room. My footsteps fall as softly as they would in church. I do not want to startle her. This morning's screams and uproar will have scared her enough.

It is only when I reach the locked door that I realise how canny Creeda has been. Her line of salt fills the gap between the wood and the floor exactly. She did not put a grain out of place when she closed the door. How many years of measurement and practice would that take?

I sink down, peer instead through the keyhole. Rosewyn sits on the floor, knees hugged against her chest, slowly rocking. It reminds me of the day I took the Farley children to see the poor caged beasts at the Tower Menagerie. It is heartbreaking.

'Miss Rosewyn,' I whisper.

She moans.

'Come here. To the door.'

She does not even look towards it. Her hands fly up to cover her ears. 'I mustn't listen to you!' she wails.

'It's me,' I say, louder. 'Miss Why.'

A pause.

'Miss Why?' she repeats. Her hands remain clapped to her ears. 'You were angry at me.'

'Pray forgive me, miss. I was not truly angry. I was … frightened.'

'I am frightened,' she bleats.

'I know.'

Slowly, she unfolds. Taking a quick survey of the room, she scuttles across the floor on her hands and knees until she is sitting right before me. Her blue eye peers back through the keyhole.

'You must not upset yourself,' I continue soothingly. 'All that noise downstairs … It was nothing to be scared of. Miss Pinecroft came over unwell, that is all. It was a shock and something broke.'

'Was it fairies? Did the fairies hurt her?'

'No. I was there the entire time. I saw nothing.'

How I wish that were true. It is still printed on my mind: the faulty plate and the painted figure thrashing in the water. But Rosewyn has no need to hear of that.

'I want her,' she moans.

'Soon. I will take you to visit your guardian as soon as I can ...' Helplessly, I work the door handle. What is to be done? I may be a thief, but I am not one by trade. I cannot pick a lock.

We are interrupted by the sound of a latch and hinges squealing. Wind gusts from the entrance hall below. I jump as Miss Pinecroft's bedroom door slams shut.

I hear boots. Gerren's voice muttering something, and then Mrs Quinn, much louder.

'Lord bless you, Mr Trengrouse! You'll have caught your death of cold. Come inside, quickly!'

Has Mr Trengrouse really trudged all the way back through the snow with Gerren?

'How is Miss Pinecroft?' he pants. 'Does she live?'

'Yes, sir, but the fit has weakened her. She don't seem to know us.'

'Poor lady. I fear I shall not be of much use – you have Miss Why, after all – but I would pray over her, if you will let me.'

'We'd take it kindly, sir. Come, give me your things. I'll dry them before the kitchen fire. Goodness, they're frozen stiff. Let me fetch you some tea. 'Tis so good of you to come, sir.'

I climb to my feet. 'I will be back, Miss Rosewyn.'

Her whimper rises once more as I walk away.

Back in the *toile-de-Jouy* chamber, my mistress lies motionless, the blink of her white lashes the only sign she is still alive. Her breath is grainy. Full of sand.

Mr Trengrouse taps gently on the door and enters, bringing the scent of frost with him.

This is the first time I have seen him without a smile. It has not been an easy journey for him, that much is clear. Snow forms a tidemark at his knees; his boots are coated in a thick white crust.

'Miss Why.' He bows. 'I am so terribly sorry that this has happened. I came as soon as I could.'

I clench my hands around the band of my apron, feeling like the imposter I truly am. I hate for him to see that I have failed yet another mistress. Up until now he believed I could cure anything: the angel who leapt from the coach to save his brother-in-law.

'Who is watching the children?' I ask.

'My housekeeper, same as when I come on a Sunday.' We stand shoulder to shoulder, looking down on Miss Pinecroft as if she were already in her coffin. 'She thought I had lost my wits to come out in this weather.'

'You are all goodness, sir. I doubt anyone else would rush to our assistance.'

Miss Pinecroft stares up at us. God forgive me, she reminds me of the pilchard in Mrs Bawden's Stargazey pie.

'Dr Bligh would be here too, but for his age. He cannot ride through the snow.'

Although my mistress is often silent and still, there are people who care for her well-being. It makes me feel as though I am being slowly crushed. *I* was the one meant to protect her. Didn't I vow to make amends for my past? Yet here she is, stretched out and gaping like a landed fish.

My own incompetence sickens me.

'Please, Mr Trengrouse.' I grab at his sleeve. 'I must talk to you. I need your help ...'

His face registers alarm. 'Of course. I shall help you in any way I can.'

After a brief hesitation, I dart to the door and close it. This is not proper. I should not be behind a shut door in a bedroom, with a man, but I cannot risk being overheard.

'Whatever is the matter, Miss Why?'

'It is this house!' I burst out. 'Oh, Mr Trengrouse ...' The sight of his dismay causes me to stop and gather my breath. 'Forgive me, sir. I have not slept. I am so afraid for my mistress and poor Miss Rosewyn. *You* have compassion for Miss Rosewyn, don't you? You said yourself ...'

Gently, he takes my shoulder and guides me to the easy chair. 'Yes. I am very fond of Miss Rosewyn. But what's all this? Has she distressed you in some way?'

I sit down heavily. 'No. Creeda has. Creeda is keeping her prisoner! Even now she is crying behind a locked door. Surely, such measures cannot be warranted?'

Mr Trengrouse frowns. His gaze flicks between me and the figure in the bed, torn.

'Please try to calm down, Miss Why. Are you sure there isn't some mistake? Perhaps at times Miss Rosewyn is too boisterous and can be a danger to herself.'

'It is not that,' I insist. 'It is cruelty. Can we not appeal ...' My head swims. No doubt the guardians who signed Rosewyn over have long since perished, and she is not a minor, but there must be *someone* responsible for her welfare? 'I am sure no charity would wish to see Miss Rosewyn in such hands. Can't you tell me where she was adopted from?'

'That all took place long before I was born, Miss Why.'

'But there must be records. Was she on the parish? As the curate you must at least have a list of the places nearby that care for orphans.'

He bites his lip, will not meet my eyes. 'That is the crux of the problem. There are no such institutions around here, Miss Why.'

I do not understand. He is shifting his feet in embarrassment and keeps glancing at Miss Pinecroft, as if to ask for her permission.

'She came from *somewhere*. Would Dr Bligh know?'

Mr Trengrouse releases a slow sigh. 'Dr Bligh ... Dr Bligh was here at the time, yes.'

'Then I will go and ask him.'

He puts out a hand as I attempt to rise from my seat. 'In this weather, with your mistress so unwell?'

'It is a matter of urgency.'

'Please, Miss Why.' His voice gets louder. 'It is ... delicate.'

I stare at him. He squirms under my scrutiny. I feel guilty for pushing my advantage, but I cannot help myself. 'Please, sir, tell me what you know. You owe me a debt. Or at least your brother-in-law does.'

He hangs his head, thinks. 'I *shall* tell you,' he decides. 'In confidence. Only please promise me you will remain calm and stop all this talk about running outside.'

'You have my word.'

He exhales. His brown eyes flick back towards the bed before he comes round to the side of my chair and kneels beside me. 'I do not wish to speak slander,' he whispers. 'Remember that gossip is rarely true. But Miss Pinecroft does not seem long for this world and ...'

I nod impatiently.

Still he struggles. 'You see, Dr Bligh was acquainted with Miss Pinecroft, briefly, when she was a young woman. They met to arrange the burial of her father – the plaque is still in our church. Even then her health was not strong. She didn't venture out much, except with a small dog. He says that she had a squint.'

So her obstinacy over her glasses is of long standing.

'Then, as now, she was a woman of few words,' he continues. 'I believe her father died with some sort of shadow over his name. After the funeral she shut herself away.'

'So how would she have learnt of Rosewyn's plight to adopt her in the first place?'

'Ah ... That is where it becomes rather unclear. There was no warning of the child's arrival. Only Mr and Mrs Tyack worked at Morvoren House back then. I don't suppose anyone local would have learnt of Miss Rosewyn's existence, had Dr Bligh not become concerned and decided to call. He was sent away pretty sharp, but he gathered that the dog had died, Miss Pinecroft had suffered a fit and there was a baby in the house.' He pauses. 'It pains me to say this, Miss Why. I don't wish to shock you. But I understand – that is to say, that Dr Bligh never heard of a wet-nurse being summoned.'

I catch sight of the blue chair beneath my skirts. China blue, like Miss Pinecroft's eyes, like Rosewyn's ... Understanding rushes upon me. I have often reflected that I do not know who my mistress was or what she did in her youth. There must have been a fall, an indiscretion.

Rosewyn is her daughter.

I regret promising to stay calm. This is my saving grace. I may have failed Miss Pinecroft, but I can still help her daughter.

I can see it all so clearly now. How the birth must have brought on Miss Pinecroft's first debilitating fit, leaving Rosewyn in Creeda's clutches. Rather than taking on the role of housekeeper herself, Creeda employed others – people she could intimidate and control – so that no one would interfere with her monopoly over the child. She has cultivated the heir so that when Rosewyn inherits, she will do whatever Creeda wants.

Unless I put a stop to it.

'If this is true,' I say slowly, mindful not to sound indelicate. 'If I understand you, sir, then protecting Rosewyn is vital. She is a gentlewoman's daughter and should be treated as such.'

'But we have no proof,' he reminds me softly. 'And even if we did, the revelation would ruin the good name of mother and daughter alike. I don't even know if Mrs Quinn would stay on here if she thought there was anything … disreputable about the family. Please promise you will not breathe a word of it.'

'It is our secret, sir. But I can assure you that Creeda's actions are more reprehensible than any hushed-up scandal.'

I turn it over in my mind. Mrs Quinn is the only person in this house with the authority to remove a member of staff now that my mistress is incapacitated, yet I cannot imagine her dismissing anyone, least of all Creeda. How can I make her see the injustice taking place right under her nose? Convince her that it was almost certainly Creeda's strangeness, not Rosewyn's, that made the last nurse quit?

It is a dangerous game to play. The newspaper stashed away in my trunk flutters before my eyes. If, as I strongly suspect, it was Creeda who broke the lock and read it, she may counter my accusation with one of her own.

I swallow.

Mr Trengrouse offers me his hand. 'Come, Miss Why. We'll find a solution. But for now we must think of poor Miss Pinecroft. Let us pray together.'

He helps me to my feet and escorts me over to the bedside. Miss Pinecroft is just as I left her, but my perception of her has changed. My fancy irons out her skin, travels up to tint the white hair that spreads over her pillow like a thick cobweb. Trapped inside this body is a young woman who had a pet dog, a lover, even a child. She may be cold like a porcelain figure, but there is warmth within.

Has she heard us, whispering about her? Can she hear me now?

I stroke her hair away from her ear, lean down and press my lips to it.

'I will help your girl,' I whisper. 'Do not fret. This time, I promise you, I will not fail.'

Chapter 41

Hour laps over hour, and Miss Pinecroft's condition does not change. I am the one who grows worse.

I have brought my trunk back upstairs. I thought that my hip flask and the clean taste of gin would help me, but it doesn't. Alcohol merely confuses the passage of time. I could not say how long I have sat here in the chair beside her bed, my back aching and my eyes filled with those endless patterns of blue.

Even when I look away, there is no comfort. The newspaper I bought last week is spread over my lap, open at the vital page.

'A rash and melancholy act.' That is what they call it. No doubt they wished to spare Sir Arthur's feelings. But if it was a fit of lunacy, as the coroner's court declared, would Lady Rose have gone to that exact spot on Westminster Bridge? Would she have weighed all her pockets down with stones?

It was the baby, I try to tell myself. The loss of another baby that unbalanced her, and that was mainly Burns's doing, not my own. But the voice of conscience will not be silenced. It says I might as well have stood behind her and pushed her into the water with my own two hands.

She was a kind mistress. Why had that not been enough for me? I could have spent my life in her service. Watched her flourish, and her children after her. I did not need ownership to adore her, I could have done that from afar. And in her own way, she would have loved me.

But I always wanted more.

You ought to give things to the one you love. Not take, as I have done. The snuffbox and the dress are the least of my spoils. I took her child, her servant and confidante, her trust. She had no family to comfort her. Only Mrs Windrop's barbed glares and the awkward ministrations of Sir Arthur.

I weep in silence.

There are so many I have failed to save. Old Mrs Wild. Robert – God, dear little Robert Farley! Miss Gillings survived, but that was no thanks to me. I killed Lady Rose and I am responsible for the fit that has felled Miss Pinecroft.

Am I truly cursed? Why do I damage all I touch?

Snow paws against the window, pleading to be let in. Gradually, the sound calms me. Reminds me of something ... Not a person seeking entry.

Rosewyn, trapped in her room, trying to get out.

Unsteadily, I gain my feet. They are cold and numb. Miss Pinecroft sleeps, one vein pulsing through the onion-skin of her neck. I may leave her for a moment.

In the corridor it is brighter. A few of the candles are lit, but night has not yet fallen. Outside, the iron-grey sky bleeds into the pewter waters below. It is unclear where one ends and the other begins.

I suppose it must be late in the afternoon. Somewhere, one of the maids is brushing a hearth. Beneath the scrape of her brush I hear another sound.

Hairs stir on the back of my neck. It is not the angelic singing from before – this is human, raw. A tune I know well by now: the sound of a female crying.

I follow it to the staircase. Rosewyn sits halfway up the steps, bent over on herself. They have finally released the poor thing. Her hair covers her face in a tangled curtain, her gown – still inside out – is crumpled and showing her calves. It is a childish posture, but there is nothing immature about the sobs heaving from her chest. They sound like those of a full-grown woman. She *is* a full-grown woman, I remind myself.

Carefully, I sit down beside her on the cold marble step and place a hand on her shoulder. She tucks herself in tighter, a hedgehog curling in on itself.

'Take comfort, Miss Rosewyn. I know you are worried for your … guardian, we all are. She has been very ill but I will do everything I can. Perhaps now you would like to come upstairs with me and visit her?'

One red-rimmed eye peeks through a gap in her hair. 'Do you have her?'

'I beg your pardon?'

'Did you take her, because I had your snuffbox?' She wipes her nose with the back of her hand.

'I do not know what you mean, Miss Rosewyn.' I look around, noticing her isolation. 'Where is Creeda?'

A fresh wail breaks from her lips. 'Don't tell her! She'll be so angry. I am meant to keep it with me, always.'

'Are you talking about your doll?'

'I had her,' she sniffs. 'I was tired, I needed to sleep. She was right under my arm. But when I woke up …'

'She must be somewhere in your bed. Shall we go and see?'

'I looked!' she retorts, indignant. 'I looked *everywhere.*'

Her voice echoes back at us.

Creeda emerges from the corridor leading to the china room. She looks older than she did, that beak of a nose dominating her face. If she is surprised to find us sitting here, she does not show it.

'You don't have your doll, Rosewyn.'

Rosewyn flinches. 'I lost her!' she gabbles. 'I lost her, but it wasn't my fault.'

Creeda drops her head, as if she has the weight of the world on her back. 'Then it's as I feared.'

Surprised, perhaps, by the quiet tone, Rosewyn peeps up beneath her fringe. 'You are not angry with me?'

'Angry, child? No. This is what we had the doll for. We gulled them. They've taken her and not you.' She releases a long sigh. 'But they'll realise. They'll come back.'

I feel Rosewyn's shoulder shiver against mine.

'For goodness' sake,' I hiss. 'It is a lost doll. It will probably turn up in a press or beneath a bed.'

Creeda grips the iron banister and begins to mount the stairs. Her smile is bitter, carved into her cheeks. 'Come, Miss Why. You've seen them, haven't you?'

My skin crawls at her proximity. 'I saw *you* cutting off a lock of my hair at night.'

She nods, unashamed. 'A protection charm.'

I place an arm around Rosewyn's shoulders. Can delusions be infectious, I wonder? They carry no effluvia but they seem to spread gradually, wine in water, changing the colour of a person's mind.

'I believe Miss Rosewyn *does* need protection, but it is not from goblins and ghouls.'

Creeda turns both eyes on me. It is the blue one that expresses her indignation. 'Don't you *dare* interfere with—'

She is forced to stop when Mrs Quinn waddles through the baize door. Despite the earlier chaos, our housekeeper looks her usual cheerful self. Her only concession to Miss Pinecroft's illness is that she has taken the ribbon out of her cap. 'What's this, then?' she asks. Then she sees Rosewyn's tears and my sombre face, and her mouth opens. 'Oh no, Miss Why. Don't tell me the mistress ...'

'No,' I say quickly. 'Miss Pinecroft is sleeping. I came down to comfort Miss Rosewyn.'

Rosewyn places her head upon my shoulder. My chest feels as if it may crack. At last, I am truly needed.

And she needs me to have courage.

'Miss Rosewyn is distressed, Mrs Quinn, and I cannot wonder why.' I take a breath. 'I regret to inform you that Creeda has been mistreating her.'

Mrs Quinn looks as if I have struck her between the eyes.

'Mistreating?' Creeda gasps. 'All I ever did was protect her!'

My own mind is not sound; I am the last person entitled to laugh at this unfortunate, deranged woman. But perhaps that is why I hate her so much. I see in her the damage a maid can do to her mistress. I see elements of myself.

I stare the housekeeper squarely in the face. 'Look at her, Mrs Quinn. See how she is dressed. Her hair. Does she appear well cared for?'

Rosewyn's breath is hot against my neck. She presses in to me, whimpering like a dog.

'But ...' Mrs Quinn blusters. 'Miss Why, Creeda has cared for Miss Rosewyn for a great many years ...'

'That does not make what she is doing right. Mr Trengrouse agrees with me. What gives Creeda the authority to lock a member of the family in her room? For pity's sake, do you not hear the girl crying at night?'

Creeda moves uncomfortably. She is divided, I think, like her eyes. Two sides at war with themselves.

'For safety,' Mrs Quinn falters. 'Isn't it, Creeda? Like Miss Pinecroft and her wandering. Miss Rosewyn needs special care. She's never been quite so … sharp … as others.'

My temper snaps. 'Neither have the staff of this house,' I retort. 'For it seems they will swallow anything. Miss Pinecroft does not wander at night! She never moves from the moment I leave her. And we *do* leave her, in her state of health, sitting unwashed in a room with no fire! God above. Do you wonder that she is so ill? Freezing day and night surrounded by whatever foul liquid Creeda keeps in the urns.'

Poor Mrs Quinn. She has spent her employment afraid to say *boo* to Creeda, but now I am here, speaking with the passion of an avenging angel, and she does not know who to fear the most.

'You just … being from London. You don't understand,' she says. 'There's nothing in the china. Is there, Creeda?'

'Urine,' I declare, before Creeda can answer. 'It *was* urine, was it not? Ask Lowena and Merryn, they saw it too. Urine, nail clippings and human hair. Was that *my* hair, Creeda? She took some, Mrs Quinn, while I slept.'

'That wasn't yours!' Creeda brays. Her hands clutch at her head. 'It was mine. To protect me. The newer servants are higher in the cabinet.'

Mrs Quinn has gone very pale.

'Your bottled spells do not seem very effectual,' I scoff. 'They have done nothing to help Miss Pinecroft.'

'I don't know. I don't know any more,' she mutters. 'I thought I knew their ways. But I'm getting old. Maybe I don't remember it all.'

'Creeda,' Mrs Quinn exhales in astonishment. 'Are you saying ... All this Miss Why tells me about bottled spells and stolen hair ...'tis *true*?'

Creeda lowers her hands, offers a sly, defiant smirk. 'Why do you suppose the fairies don't bother *you*?'

Queasily, Mrs Quinn reaches up to pat her cap. Whatever hair Creeda stole from her must have been cut long ago, but she still checks. 'I can't ... I don't know what to make of this. Whatever would the mistress say?'

'She can say nothing!' I cry. I know I am being cruel, but Mrs Quinn has buried her head in the sand for years. Only a violent tug will pull her out. 'Miss Pinecroft has long been incapacitated, and she pays *you* to keep things in order.' I gesture at Rosewyn, trembling and tear-stained. 'This is not order. This is what happens when you are content to merely laugh along with the maids. Don't you think it's time you started taking your responsibilities as housekeeper a little more seriously?'

It is as though I have slapped her. Mrs Quinn sways gently on her feet.

Too much. My thudding pulse begins to falter. She will dismiss me on the spot.

It is some minutes before the housekeeper gathers herself to speak.

'Creeda,' she says eventually. Her voice is dangerously quiet. 'I think you'd better move to Gerren's room. Until I've looked into this.'

'You can't keep me away from—'

'I can,' she replies coolly, and I am proud of her.

'The child needs—' Creeda begins, but again Mrs Quinn cuts her off.

'I'll stay with Miss Rosewyn tonight.'

With a fresh sob, Rosewyn clings to me.

'No!' she cries. 'Miss Why. I want Miss Why!'

I thought I had heard her sing before, but this – this is true music.

'Miss Pinecroft is unwell,' I try to explain. 'I must sit with her …'

Rosewyn's big blue eyes fill with tears. 'Don't leave me.'

'Very well, very well,' Mrs Quinn chides. She appears on the point of tears herself. ''Tis only one night. I'll get one of the girls to watch the mistress.

Miss Why can stay with you, Miss Rosewyn. And Creeda … Gerren's room.'

Creeda's whole frame trembles against the iron banisters. It is impossible to tell whether fear or fury makes her shake so hard.

'Now,' Mrs Quinn demands.

Her knobbly fingers ball into a fist. For a moment, I truly think she will do the housekeeper harm.

'You'll regret it!' she warns.

With that, she stalks up the stairs.

Chapter 42

I longed for this room. Downstairs, shivering by Miss Pinecroft's side, I thought that Creeda was lucky to sit in Rosewyn's chamber with the fire burning. But it is different by night.

A swimming mass of shadows covers the table where Rosewyn sits to draw, sew and pull pages out of her Bible. There is something forlorn in the scattered pencils and ragged collection of gull's feathers she has pasted to a piece of paper. These are not hobbies but pastimes: activities to speed the passage of hands around the clock. In gaol, they give the prisoners hemp to pick. I see little difference between the two.

The jug of milk glows on the mantelpiece. I have known ladies display items of pride in this place: invitations from the best society hostesses, silhouettes of their friends. In Morvoren House, the mantelpiece is a monument to Creeda's insanity.

For all my brave words earlier, I cannot pretend she is alone in feeling there is a mighty power here lurking, always out of sight. I sense it tonight. Waiting.

Or is that just a guilty conscience?

Rosewyn sleeps on her back. One arm curls across her chest, mimicking the familiar gesture of cradling the doll. My searches of the room have been in vain; I cannot find the toy, yet that is hardly proof of the supernatural. Mrs Farley's children were always losing things.

But Rosewyn is *not* a child …

There is so much I do not understand about this house and the woman who sleeps in the bed before me. Who was her father? I cannot make out if she is truly simple or just a victim of circumstance. Would she have been this fey and infantile if her mother raised her, or have the days locked up in this house with Creeda taken their toll?

I doubt the harm can be undone now.

I changed into my nightgown and said I would sleep on the truckle bed, but I cannot settle myself to rest. Sitting instead on the stool before the dressing table, I stare into the mirror. It is molten gold in the firelight. My face is limned in amber, strange.

What if *I* were one of Creeda's changelings? Cursed to wander from place to place, unable to belong. I would not know if I was swapped at birth.

Sipping at my laudanum, I think of the bottle in the cupboard that I replaced with one of weak tea. One thing substituted for the other, as simple as that. A taste would expose the fraud there, but with a person ...

Maybe that is why all my employers die.

Maybe that is why I can hear the fairies sing.

I hear them now: a high, pure note soaring above the sea's lamentation.

The bottle of laudanum drops from my hand and lands on the carpet. I watch the liquid flow until it is nothing but an empty vessel and a sodden mark.

When I glance up at Rosewyn, she sleeps on, no part of the heavenly choir. Yet she is touched. Blessed. An orb of light hovers at the foot of the bed.

It is the most beautiful thing I have ever seen. Painful in its loveliness. There is no fear, only an ache in my chest that moans, *This, this. This is what you sought, but never found.*

Slowly, it rises. It is like a dream. I am rising too, standing on my feet as if I have been pulled up by an invisible string.

'What are you?' I whisper.

It floats, heading towards the door.

I dash to open it, terrified that the orb will burst against the wood. I am just in time. The light glides past my face as it leaves the room, its warmth caressing my skin and eliciting a sigh.

How gently it wafts down the corridor. Helpless, entranced, I follow.

I follow it all the way to Miss Pinecroft's chamber.

I grope inside my apron for the key, but before my fingers touch the metal there is a click, a whirl, and the door swings back on its hinges.

Rosemary. Lemony and sharp, filling my lungs.

The light drifts to the wardrobe, where it hovers and quivers.

Deep inside my mind, a voice tells me to check upon my mistress, but it seems to speak in a foreign language. She feels far from me now, part of a distant land. Nothing matters. Nothing but the light.

Before I realise what I am doing, I am standing before the wardrobe, opening the doors. Miss Pinecroft's dresses hang ghostly in their pouches. The scent of rosemary is so dense that my head begins to ache. Rosemary can be medicinal, but I know instinctively that is not the use here. Nor is it to stop the moths. Rosemary for remembrance, rosemary to ward off nightmares. Rosemary to bind.

The light intensifies. My gaze travels down to its furthest reach, where faint rays of amber lave against the wooden base. There is the usual clutter of dust, forgotten shawls and odd shoes. Unremarkable, and yet I am scanning it eagerly, waiting for something to appear.

I drop to my knees. And then I see it.

The pallor of a skull.

I reach out. It is chalky, sharp at the edges. As I lift it to the light, it glistens and I realise it is not a fragment of bone at all but glazed china. Small blue flowers form a pattern that has faded with time. Other larger pieces lie tangled in a shawl. I spread it out on my lap. Needles of rosemary have dried to husks around the chips. Some are rimmed with a rust-coloured substance that I recognise at once as blood. Together, they make up a shattered teapot.

There is a gurgle from the bed.

Then darkness.

The light is extinguished, the singing melts into air.

Everything turns empty and hollow, cold as the soil of the grave.

Liquid bubbles in my mistress's chest. Frantically, I crawl towards her, the china falling from my lap and crunching beneath my knees. I do not feel it cut. I am only desperate not to be alone.

Her hand reaches down from the bed and latches on my shoulder, tight.

'Kitty.'

Reality rushes back. I remember where I am, who I am. 'No, madam ...'

'Mama?' Her chest sounds like water slapping against rocks.

Kneeling beside the bed, I search for her face in the gloom. I cannot see its lineaments, but I smell her sour breath.

'Remain calm, Miss Pinecroft. It is I, Hester. Can I fetch you something? I have an infusion made from horseradish, mustard and orange rind —'

Even as I babble on, I realise that it is useless. The labouring of her breath, the chest filling with fluid – I know what it means.

Her hand squeezes all feeling from my shoulder.

'Papa.'

There is a sound like pebbles rattling, then water draining away.

Miss Pinecroft's hand falls limp and she has gone, slipped between the cracks.

*

A shadow rises up the opposite wall. 'Who's there?'

I tremble, the dead woman's hand still against my shoulder. There are bumps, the sound of chair legs scraping against the floor. My mind seems to have lost all ability to function. My mistress is dead: that is all I can absorb. I have failed her and she is gone, gone forever.

'Who is that?' The voice repeats. There are sparks of light. I half expect to see the orb again, but this is no fairy. The woman is loud, afraid.

Then there is an orange flare and I see dark eyes, huge in terror. 'Miss Why?'

She moves her tinderbox to light a candle beside Miss Pinecroft's bed. It is Lowena.

From the look of it, she has been sitting in the easy chair on the other side of the bed all night. I stare at her, stupefied, unable to comprehend how she has been there the entire time. Did she not see the orb? Hear me open the wardrobe?

'What are you doing to Miss Pinecroft?' she demands.

Gently, I remove the wilted hand from my shoulder. 'She is dead.'

My words do not seem to strike her at first. It is only when she moves to the bed and sees the old lady that she gasps. She places two fingers against her mistress's throat, as if she expects to feel a pulse. When she does not, she cries.

They are noisy, unchecked tears.

'I did not …' I begin, realising how this must look. 'I thought that I heard something and when I came to check …'

But she is not listening. She is weeping fit to break her heart.

'I … fell … asleep!' Each word is gulped between sobs.

Surely, no one could sleep through all that? The singing, Miss Pinecroft's last whistling breaths – why, even the noise of my moving about the room ought to have alerted her.

Whatever Lowena might sleep through, it seems her tears have woken everyone else. I hear doors opening, footsteps. My eyes cast wildly around at the shawl and bits of broken teapot strewn across the floor, and the lifeless body in the bed. There is no way I will emerge from this scene in a good light.

But before I can flee, candles are bobbing towards us. Mrs Quinn in a lopsided nightcap, Merryn with her hair in rags, even Gerren half-asleep.

'I heard ...' I start again, gesturing helplessly at the corpse.

Mrs Quinn covers her mouth with her hand.

'I am afraid she has passed away.'

Lowena pitches towards Merryn. 'It's my fault!' she wails. 'I fell asleep and the candle went out. I let her die!' The pair embrace, crying.

'I do not believe anything could have been done,' I say, more to defend myself than Lowena. 'The attack was too severe ...'

Gerren leans against the doorjamb, ashen.

'I should never have left the poor girl sitting with her.' Mrs Quinn shakes her head. 'I should've done it myself. But we're all topsy-turvy with you in the nursery and ...' She makes an impatient gesture, as if it is my fault and not Creeda's. 'What brought you to this room?'

'I heard ...'

'Ah,' she sighs. 'That's the trouble. Lowena can't hear.'

I blink at her. Each time I think this night cannot become any more surreal, it surprises me. Just how much laudanum did I drink?

'What do you mean, she cannot hear?'

'She's deaf, of course.' Mrs Quinn replies.

'But ... that cannot be. She has spoken to me, she ...'

'She wasn't always deaf. Now she reads lips. But in the dark, with the candle gone out …'

That accounts for the accent I traced – no foreign influence after all, but the effect of not being able to hear her own voice. Clearly, the misfortune has done nothing to impede Lowena's other abilities – and yet the first unforgivable thought that comes to my head is that *of course*, something had to be wrong with her. There had to be some imperfection to stop the fairies from abducting her.

'What an ill-advised notion to leave a girl who cannot hear in charge of a sick woman!' I protest. 'How would she wake, if she could not hear Miss Pinecroft gasping for breath?'

Mrs Quinn bristles. 'I've had enough of your opinions for one day, Miss Why. Always creeping about, never staying where you're meant to be …' But as she looks at the pitiful figure in the bed, and poor Lowena, her temper drifts away. She shakes her head. 'I just don't understand how that candle would burn out. Look, there's still plenty of wick to it.'

'Candles are always going out. They—'

Gerren's smoky voice cuts me off. 'They snuffed un.'

We both look over at him, perplexed.

'Gerren,' Mrs Quinn says slowly. 'Where is Creeda?'

His mouth falls open. Snatching Mrs Quinn's candleholder, he plunges out the door.

Without thinking, I follow. He is surprisingly rapid, given his age. He takes the stairs two at a time.

'Gerren, wait! What is it?' I cry, trailing after him.

He simply shakes his head.

We reach the bottom of the staircase and turn left. I may not know his purpose, but I know where he is headed: the china room.

Waves boom in the cove beneath the house, loud as cannon shot. Nearer, faintly, I hear the drips again.

The flame of Gerren's candle flattens and winks out.

I can feel the wind that has extinguished it. Spitefully cold, just as it was when Miss Pinecroft opened the window. It must be open again. Although the door to the china room remains closed, it is fidgeting, twitching in its frame.

'Creeda!'

Gerren runs the last few steps and slams his shoulder into the door. Locked. He hits it again, kicks it. He is too old and exhausted to make it budge.

'Let me.' Pushing Gerren aside, I throw my full weight against the wood.

Something splinters and I am falling forward, my arms turning windmills.

Pain rips through the soles of my feet.

I cannot get my bearings. Such a confusion of sound: the ocean, the wind and a crunch like eggshells against the side of a bowl. Somehow, beneath it all, I hear the strangled anguish in Gerren's throat.

I stumble to a halt just inches before the mantelpiece and its display of china.

No. Not a display. There are no vases, figurines and teapots: the china has ... hatched. It is the only word I can think of.

Everything lies in fragments. Moonlight spills through the open curtains. As I suspected, the window stands wide, admitting the salt breath of the waves.

'Creeda.'

I turn to face the wingback chair and what I see takes my breath away.

Silver rays wash over one side of her, the side with the blue eye. It barely appears human. She has been scourged, raked with tiny thin lines like the teeth of a comb.

But she is still alive.

Gerren kneels, clasps her.

'Half in, half out,' he whispers. 'They nearly took ee.'

It cannot be. I have spent every day in this house decrying her words as nonsense ... But I can almost sense them: a procession of unseen people on the air, teasing the curtains to a frenzy, scattering the wreckage of the china.

'I have salve,' I ramble. 'Lavender, comfrey ... We must get her upstairs.'

Creeda's brown eye moves sluggishly to focus on me. Its stare is more dreadful than that of the other, bloodshot and scratched. Although her lips remain still, I hear her voice.

Rosewyn.

My heart seems to stop.

How long have I left her alone?

Shattered china covers my path to the door; I ran over it, barefoot, as I fell into the room. Picking my way back hurts even more. I track bloody prints down the corridor, into the white expanse of the stucco hall.

Even Mrs Bawden, the cook, is awake now. I see her descending the staircase with Mrs Quinn, dithering about what they are to do. How to fetch the lawyer in weather like this? Is it too unkind to ask the girls to wash the body? They say Rosewyn will not inherit directly. It will all be held in trust by the Tyacks.

I push past them. One of them calls after me, but I cannot stop now. A terrible suspicion is forming in my mind: that it was *true*. Every deed I have taken for madness, cruelty, vile superstition – perhaps all of it was true.

The sheet is thrown back on Rosewyn's bed. The mattress yawns, empty. She is not there, not in the room. Guilt doubles me over. It is my fault. Like a fool I left her and followed the light. If she is hurt …

My mind completes a frantic tour of the house, seeking a logical answer for where she may be. Would she go to my room to seek the snuffbox? Sneak down to the kitchen for sweetmeats? Perhaps she is visiting the animals in the stable? They are the straws a drowning woman clutches at. I grab them, all the same.

Dragging a pair of her stockings over my bleeding feet, I search the wardrobe for a dress. They are all far too short for me, and wide in the shoulders, but I pull one over my nightgown so that I may venture outside if necessary. I must find her before she comes to harm. Before Mrs Quinn realises I have lost her.

The servants' wing lies deserted. Merryn and Lowena are shut up together, weeping audibly. The room I once slept in houses nothing but the damp. Spinning on my heel, I take the stairs again, feet throbbing with every step. I can see the red prints where I have walked before. The sight of them makes me shudder.

In the west wing there is commotion: Mrs Quinn and Mrs Bawden have found the grim tableau of the china room. Ignoring their cries, I turn towards the kitchen.

Scents hang in the air: burnt fat, cinnamon. By day this space is cheerful and warm, the only part of Morvoren House that is. It feels as if its heart has stopped beating, leaving everything desolate. Rosewyn is not here.

Did I truly expect her to be?

Another life on my hands. She was innocent, kind. She trusted me.

Swallowing tears, I jam on a pair of Gerren's discarded boots and open the back door. Feathers of snow swirl. Despite them, the temperature has risen, ever so slightly. The icicles hanging from the ash tree drip. I start to walk.

A light burns in the stable block, guiding my way. My heart leaps. Gerren was sleeping in the house, he did not ignite this.

Rosewyn has childish ways; I can imagine her doting upon the animals and bidding them goodnight. *Please, please*, I pray, *let her be there.*

Gasping for breath, I reach the door. Push. It is unlocked.

Hooves stir against straw as I enter. The pony tosses up its head. A hanging lamp illuminates the space between the stalls and a broom, fallen from where it leant against the wall. There is no sign of her.

'Rosewyn?' I whisper.

Footsteps sound in the shadowy corner. They are not hers – they are too heavy, too firm.

Fear seethes in my stomach. I hold my breath as a tall male figure emerges slowly into the light.

Chapter 43

It is like the sea: the rushing and roaring in my ears, the undulating lines obscuring my vision. I open my mouth, but the words have run dry.

'Please don't be afraid, Miss Why. It is me.'

As my eyes adjust to the lighting, I see a dusty great-coat and red hair tangled with straw. Breath returns to my lungs.

'Mr Trengrouse? What are *you* doing here?'

He surveys my eccentric clothing as if he might ask the same question. A strange pair we make, shivering in the lamplight with chickens scratching around our feet.

'Did Mrs Quinn not tell you? The snow was too thick for me to ride home. Since there are no spare beds in the house, I was sleeping in the hayloft, but then I heard—' He stops and chuckles, struck by the absurdity of the situation.

I think I might cry. Suddenly the last few hours are a burden too great to bear. Shall I tell him of Miss

Pinecroft's death? He should probably be in the house, helping. But now I have found him, I do not want to let him go.

'You can ride a horse?' I demand.

All his amusement fades. 'Well … yes, Miss Why.'

'You could saddle it up right now?'

His grey mare snorts from her stall, as if in protest.

'I do not understand …' he begins, brushing off his coat.

'Mr Trengrouse, Rosewyn is missing. I have searched all over the house. She must be somewhere outside, in the snow.'

'Great God.'

In a moment he has retrieved the bridle from its peg. The mare tosses her head as he darts into the stall and slides the bit between her teeth. I too feel as if I have something cold and metallic in my mouth.

'What direction has she taken?' Mr Trengrouse asks urgently.

'I do not know …'

'There should still be footprints. Only Mr Tyack and I have been about outside Morvoren House today. The snow will hold her tracks.'

'The snow is beginning to melt,' I fret.

He heaves the cloth and saddle onto the mare's back, starts to tighten the girth. 'She will not have got far. Heat some blankets, start to make tea. I will have her back before you have finished—'

'But I am coming with you!'

My cry is so sharp that the mare flattens her ears.

'Coming with me?' Mr Trengrouse drops the saddle flap. 'Absolutely not. You will catch cold, Miss Why, it is not the weather for a lady—'

'Rosewyn is out there!' I cut him off again. 'If she can survive, so will I.'

He shakes his head.

He may be a man and my superior, but he is younger than me. I will not let him dictate. If he thinks I am going back inside Morvoren House to tell Mrs Quinn that I have lost my charge, he is mistaken. I cannot fail another mistress. This is my last chance.

'You saw me on the Mail coach, sir. You know I am no milk-and-water miss.' He opens his mouth, but I do not give him the chance to speak. 'Suppose Miss Rosewyn is hurt? If she needs medical attention and you cannot move her? What shall you do then?'

He flounders. 'Well, I suppose I would have to return here and—'

'Wasting precious time! And even if, God willing, no harm has befallen her, what makes you think she will agree to come with you? She knows me, she *trusts* me.'

His shoulders slump and I know that I have won.

*

Dawn is a crimson slash on the horizon. Morvoren House appears innocent and beautiful. Snow on the rooftop, ice laced around the pebbles. A mansion cradled like a jewel between the bare branches of the ash trees.

You would never dream of what goes on behind those walls.

The mare is warm and sweet-smelling. Her back is wider than I expected; it feels curiously alarming to jog along, astride, clutching Mr Trengrouse around the waist for all I am worth.

We have just gained the top of the slope when he reins back. 'Look. There, at the rear of the house.'

I peek over his shoulder. Putting the reins in one hand, he points at the window to the china room.

Someone has closed the sash. Beneath it, the snow is pocked, dotted, like a trail of freckles over the bridge of a nose. The marks straggle around the side of the house and away, off into the distance.

But that would mean ... Did Rosewyn climb out of that window?

Mr Trengrouse nudges the mare on and follows the tracks.

I rest my cheek against his back and try to make sense of what I have seen. In my panic, I'd assumed Rosewyn had been taken. Spirited away, without a trace. But that was not how Creeda described it. *Pixy-led*, she said. Just as that orb led me to Miss Pinecroft's bedroom.

The mare inhales and snorts. I feel it run the length of her body.

If Rosewyn was in the china room ... She must have seen what happened to Creeda. Panicked, and fled through the only available exit. The poor thing will be terrified.

Diamonds of moisture bead the mare's mane as it flutters in the wind. Though I will never admit it to Mr Trengrouse, I am thoroughly chilled. This winter has lasted an eternity. It feels like a spell that started with the poisoned cup in Hanover Square and will never, never break. I try to imagine the spring: the flowers, the birds, the whole world coming up for air. I cannot. It seems like an impossible dream.

The mare's hooves fall silent in the snow. Without my noticing, the sun has edged further across the horizon, setting the sea aglitter. It does not look so far away, now. If I reach out my hand, I think I could touch it.

'Great God.'

The words run up Mr Trengrouse's spine. My own grows rigid.

The mare comes to a halt.

A figure stands on the cliff edge, looking out to sea. Her unbound hair and the white skirts of her nightgown yearn towards the waves. One step forward would send her into the abyss, but she is perfectly balanced, halfway between life and death.

Rosewyn.

'She will fall!' Mr Trengrouse cries as he throws down the reins.

I am ahead of him, already slithering off the mare and stumbling through the snow. My throat aches to call her name, but I know I must not startle her.

The ground is slick and icy near the edge. Slowly, I make my way towards Rosewyn, marvelling at how she managed to do this in bare feet. The tips of her toes have turned blue.

'Rosewyn,' I whisper softly.

When she turns, her face is serene. As if she expected me, all this while. 'I found her,' she says.

'Whatever do you mean?'

She points down.

Cautiously, I peer. Her doll is spreadeagled on an outcrop of rock, its china face reduced to powder. I feel giddy and sick.

This must be where the caves are. For now, the beach is swallowed by the tide, as if it had never been. Should Rosewyn fall, she will plunge straight into the ocean – providing she does not hit the rock first.

'Never mind. Come away from there. We will get you another doll,' I promise.

Rosewyn shakes her head. There is a terrible rattle as pebbles fall down the cliff. 'Creeda told me never to go this far. But she can't stop me now. I'm going home.'

'*I* will take you home. Get on the pony and—'

'No.' She gestures to the chasm below. 'My other home.'

Her words chill my very bones. 'Fairy land?'

'You get there through the water.'

My eyes are fixed on her outstretched hand. If I could grab it, quickly, I might pull her back. I take a breath, muster my courage. And then I notice her fingernails.

They are broken. Bloodied and torn.

Rosewyn closes her eyes. 'She'll never lock me up again.'

Truly, I would not blame her. Forty years of captivity. Four decades of being kept as a child. Anyone might snap, smash their captor's beloved china and flee.

But Creeda is still alive. Holding the estate in trust.

She will claim she was attacked by fairies. And if I contradict her with my own suspicion ... Rosewyn will be branded worse than simple: she will be dangerous. I would be dooming her to another life of imprisonment elsewhere.

Gently, I pull her a step back from the edge. 'What would it take, Rosewyn? To stop Creeda from locking you away?'

She shakes her head. 'I don't know. She doesn't ... It's the fairies! We have to please the fairies. They've got men. Now they need a girl. A girl to make their babies.'

Lady Rose's stained dress flashes across my mind.

I push her back another step. 'But that does not mean it must be you, Rosewyn.'

Her lower lip wobbles. 'Can't you hear them calling me?'

I listen, but I do not hear fairies. I hear something else.

Non lo dirò col labbro. Lady Rose's aria, her pure voice.

My eyes drift from Rosewyn to the waves.

A humbling sight. That vast power and expanse, able to give life, able to take it. I have seen the ocean grey, ink black, once green as a mossy tree. This morning it sparkles blue. Spray leaps, playful and teasing, where once it was hostile.

'Your friends would be sorry to lose you, Rosewyn. You may not care for Creeda, but what about Mrs Quinn? Merryn?'

She hesitates. 'They can't stop the fairies.'

Mr Trengrouse is wading uncertainly towards us through the snow.

I turn back to Rosewyn and seem to see clearly for the first time.

The two of us, side by side. I am wearing her dress. It is not turned inside-out.

'What if someone went in your place?'

'Who?'

'Answer me. If the fairies got their woman, would Creeda stop?'

She sighs, as if I am naming an impossible dream. 'It would *all* stop.'

I guide her further away from the edge. The waves beckon with their clean white foam. Surely it could not hurt, to fall into their embrace. One might slumber, peaceful, in the untroubled deep.

Snow crunches behind us. There is a cry of 'Miss Rosewyn!' and then Mr Trengrouse engulfs her, clasps her arms to her sides.

Rosewyn wails. 'Please don't lock me up again!' She writhes, but he is strong.

'I have hold of her, Miss Why! We will …'

He keeps speaking, but I can no longer make out his face. The world is turning to water around me; ice beginning to thaw.

At last, at last. I can let go.

'Miss Why?'

I will drown out the past, I will make amends. Rosewyn will live free at Morvoren House and I … I will no longer hear my lady. No voices of the dead; only bubbles.

'Miss Why, come away from the edge!'

The sun is rising.

I look over my shoulder and smile. Strands of my hair fly upon the breeze to wave farewell.

Rosewyn stares in wonder, safe within her saviour's embrace.

'They need me,' I say.

And then I take the step.

Acknowledgements

Every so often, a seemingly innocent story idea turns into an absolute monster to write. *Bone China* has been one of these books. Fortunately for me, I have received the support and professional advice of a wonderful publishing team, all of whom deserve a tribute here.

First, my agent and dear friend Juliet Mushens. She is truly a legend and I cannot thank her enough. My brilliant editors, Alison Hennessey and Marigold Atkey, as well as their assistant Lilidh Kendrick, for their kindness and unstinting support. The shining gems of the Marketing and Publicity department, Philippa Cotton and Amy Donegan, who continue to dazzle me with their talent and enthusiasm. Also a heartfelt thanks to everyone else at Raven Books and Bloomsbury – it is a privilege to work with you.

I honestly would not have made it through the last year without my husband Kevin picking me up when I fell down. He earns the most important thanks of all for his unending supply of patience and all-round goodness.

I would also like to acknowledge the people, both living and dead, whose work has contributed towards the content of my story. The understanding of consumption, or phthisis, from the Georgian era until the discovery of the tubercle bacillus in 1882 was both confused and confusing. My 'radical' Dr Pinecroft wrestles with some of the theories debated during the Victorian era, and so after his time, but most of his reasoning is based on the work of Thomas Beddoes published in Bristol during 1799, the treatment undergone by George III's daughter Amelia between 1809 and 1810, *Primitive Physick* by John Wesley (1747) and *Pharmacopoeia Extemporanea* by Thomas Fuller (1710). It may interest readers to know that Dr Pinecroft's 'bold notion' of a cave colony also had a real-life inspiration. In 1839, the American doctor John Crogan opened a sanatorium for tuberculosis patients in Mammoth Cave, Kentucky, believing the steady climate would benefit them. His experiment ended in failure in 1843.

While bone china was being produced as early as the 1740s, the formula used by my fictional Nancarrow factory was actually discovered by Josiah Spode and introduced to the world in 1796. I do not mention the exact location of Morvoren House in Cornwall, since it is a place entirely of my invention. However, I drew inspiration from a visit to Carlyon Bay and Charlestown, the harbour of which was built specifically to ship china clay. Further west, one of the first china-clay setts was opened on Tregonning Hill – not many miles from Rinsey Head. Since writing this book, I have discovered the existence of the iconic house built on this clifftop location. Although it was constructed in the early twentieth century, it fits my image of Morvoren House wonderfully!

For Esther's household first-aid and cosmetic treatments, I am particularly indebted to two books: *Lavender Water and Snail-Syrup: Miss Ambler's Household Book of Georgian Cures and Remedies* (2013) and *The Duties of a Lady's Maid* (1825).

The story of the Willow pattern was an English invention, written after the print had already enjoyed considerable success. It first appears in published form in the *Family Friend* magazine in 1849 – some decades after Esther's story is set, but I could not resist bringing it forward in time to share.

Note on the Author

Laura Purcell is a former bookseller and lives in Colchester with her husband and pet guinea pigs. Her first novel for Bloomsbury, *The Silent Companions*, was a Radio 2 and Zoe Ball ITV Book Club pick and was the winner of the WHSmith Thumping Good Read Award, while Laura's gothic chiller *The Corset* was acclaimed as a masterpiece by readers and reviewers alike.

laurapurcell.com
@spookypurcell

Note on the Type

The text of this book is set in Linotype Stempel Garamond, a version of Garamond adapted and first used by the Stempel foundry in 1924. It is one of several versions of Garamond based on the designs of Claude Garamond. It is thought that Garamond based his font on Bembo, cut in 1495 by Francesco Griffo in collaboration with the Italian printer Aldus Manutius. Garamond types were first used in books printed in Paris around 1532. Many of the present-day versions of this type are based on the *Typi Academiae* of Jean Jannon cut in Sedan in 1615.

Claude Garamond was born in Paris in 1480. He learned how to cut type from his father and by the age of fifteen he was able to fashion steel punches the size of a pica with great precision. At the age of sixty he was commissioned by King Francis I to design a Greek alphabet, and for this he was given the honourable title of royal type founder. He died in 1561.

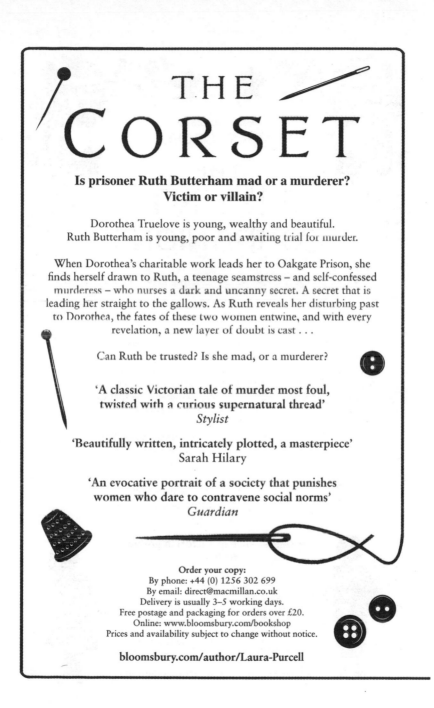

THE CORSET

**Is prisoner Ruth Butterham mad or a murderer?
Victim or villain?**

Dorothea Truelove is young, wealthy and beautiful.
Ruth Butterham is young, poor and awaiting trial for murder.

When Dorothea's charitable work leads her to Oakgate Prison, she
finds herself drawn to Ruth, a teenage seamstress – and self-confessed
murderess – who nurses a dark and uncanny secret. A secret that is
leading her straight to the gallows. As Ruth reveals her disturbing past
to Dorothea, the fates of these two women entwine, and with every
revelation, a new layer of doubt is cast . . .

Can Ruth be trusted? Is she mad, or a murderer?

'A classic Victorian tale of murder most foul,
twisted with a curious supernatural thread'
Stylist

'Beautifully written, intricately plotted, a masterpiece'
Sarah Hilary

'An evocative portrait of a society that punishes
women who dare to contravene social norms'
Guardian

Order your copy:
By phone: +44 (0) 1256 302 699
By email: direct@macmillan.co.uk
Delivery is usually 3–5 working days.
Free postage and packaging for orders over £20.
Online: www.bloomsbury.com/bookshop
Prices and availability subject to change without notice.

bloomsbury.com/author/Laura-Purcell